13.5.2021

The K... S... Matter

KU-005-607

Jean Plaidy, one of the pre-eminent authors of historical fiction for most of the twentieth century, is the pen name of the prolific English author Eleanor Hibbert, also known as Victoria Holt. Jean Plaidy's novels had sold more than 14 million copies worldwide by the time of her death in 1993.

Praise for Jean Plaidy

'One of the country's most widely read novelists' *Sunday Times*

'It is hard to better Jean Plaidy . . . both elegant and exciting'
Daily Mirror

'Outstanding' *Vanity Fair*

'Plaidy has brought the past to life' *Times Literary Supplement*

'One of our best historical novelists' *News Chronicle*

'An excellent story' *Irish Press*

'Spirited . . . Plaidy paints the truth as she sees it'
Birmingham Post

The King's
Secret Matter

JEAN PLAIDY

arrow books

Published by Arrow Books in 2006

5 7 9 10 8 6 4

Copyright © Jean Plaidy, 1962

Initial lettering copyright © Stephen Raw, 2005

The Estate of Eleanor Hibbert has asserted its right to have Jean Plaidy
identified as the author of this work.

First published in the United Kingdom in 1962 by Robert Hale Ltd

Arrow Books
The Random House Group Limited
20 Vauxhall Bridge Road, London SW1V 2SA

Random House Australia (Pty) Limited
20 Alfred Street, Milsons Point, Sydney,
New South Wales 2061, Australia

Random House New Zealand Limited
18 Poland Road, Glenfield,
Auckland 10, New Zealand

Random House (Pty) Limited
Isle of Houghton, Corner of Boundary Road & Carse O'Gowrie,
Houghton 2198, South Africa

Random House Publishers India Private Limited
301 World Trade Tower, Hotel Intercontinental Grand Complex,
Barakhamba Lane, New Delhi 110 001, India

Random House Group Limited Reg. No. 954009
www.randomhouse.co.uk

A CIP catalogue record for this book is available from the British Library

The Random House Group Limited supports The Forest Stewardship
Council® (FSC®), the leading international forest-certification organisation.
Our books carrying the FSC label are printed on FSC®-certified paper.
FSC is the only forest-certification scheme supported by the leading
environmental organisations, including Greenpeace. Our
paper procurement policy can be found at
www.randomhouse.co.uk/environment

ISBN 9780099549864

Typeset by SX Composing DTP, Rayleigh, Essex

Printed and bound in Great Britain by Clays Ltd, St Ives plc

🏵 Contents 🏵

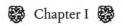 Chapter I

THE CARDINAL'S REVENGE

Katharine, Queen of England, sat at her window looking down on the Palace gardens; her hands lay idly in her lap, her tapestry momentarily neglected. She was now approaching her thirty-fifth birthday, and her once graceful figure had grown somewhat heavy during the years of disappointing pregnancies; yet she had lost none of her dignity; the humiliation she was forced to suffer could not rob her of that serene assurance which reminded all who came into her presence that she was not only the Queen of England but the daughter of Isabella of Castile and Ferdinand of Aragon.

She wore the fashionable five-cornered hood which glittered with jewels, and from it hung a black mantilla, for although it was nineteen years since she had left her own country she still clung to certain customs and fashions of her native land; her gown was of blue velvet trimmed with sable; and as she sat, her feet gracefully crossed, her petticoat of gold-coloured satin was visible; at her throat were rubies, and similar jewels decorated the *cordelière* belt which encircled her thick waist and fell to her feet.

Now as she gazed out of the window the expression on her regular, though heavy, features was serious in the extreme; and the high forehead was wrinkled in a frown. The woman who was watching her felt compassion welling up within her, for she knew that the Queen was uneasy.

And the reason was obvious, thought Lady Willoughby who, as Maria de Salinas, had come with Katharine to England nineteen years before, and until her marriage to Lord Willoughby had never left her mistress's service; and even now returned to her whenever she found it possible to do so.

Katharine the Queen had anxieties enough.

If there could only be a male child, thought Maria. *One* male child. Is that too much to ask? Why is it denied her?

They had been so close to each other for so many years that there were occasions when they read each other's thoughts, and the Queen, glancing away from the gardens, caught Maria's pitying look and answered that unspoken thought.

'I have a feeling that it will never be, Maria,' she said. 'There have been so many attempts.'

Maria flushed, angry with herself because she had betrayed thoughts which could only bring further pain to her beloved mistress.

'Your Grace has a charming, healthy daughter.'

Katharine's face became young and almost beautiful as it invariably did when her daughter, the five-year-old Princess Mary, was mentioned.

'She grows more beautiful as the months pass,' murmured the Queen, smiling to herself. 'She is so gay, so merry, that she has won her father's heart so certainly that I do believe that when he is with her he forgives her for not being a boy.'

2

'No one could wish the Princess Mary to be other than she is,' murmured Maria.

'No. I would not change her. Is that not strange, Maria? If it were possible to turn her into a boy I would not do so. I would not have her different in any way.' The smile disappeared and she went on: 'How I wish I could have her more often with me here at Greenwich.'

'It is because the King is so eager that she shall enjoy the state which is due to her that he insists on her maintaining a separate household.'

The Queen nodded and turned to her tapestry.

'We shall be leaving for Windsor shortly,' she said; 'then I shall have her ferried over from Ditton Park. I long to hear how she is progressing with the virginals. Did you ever know a child of five who showed such musical talent?'

'Never,' answered Maria, thinking: I must keep her mind on Mary, for that will give her a respite from less pleasant matters.

But as she was reminding Katharine of that occasion when the King had carried his daughter down to the state apartments and insisted on the ambassadors of France and Spain paying homage to the little girl's rank and accomplishments, a shout from the grounds diverted the Queen's attention to other matters, and Maria noticed the momentary closing of the eyes which denoted that disgust she felt for what was happening down there.

It was a mistake, Maria told herself, for the Queen to hold aloof from the King's pastimes; and while she sympathised with Katharine and understood her mistress's revulsion, she felt that it was unwise of her to show such feeling. The King was a man who looked for adulation and, because it was almost always unstintingly given, he was quick to perceive when it

3

was not; and merely by declining to accompany him to the arena, the Queen had doubtless offended him. True, she had pleaded indisposition; but the King, who was himself so rarely indisposed, was apt to regard the illness of others with scepticism and derision.

No, it was unfortunate that while the King, surrounded by his courtiers, was watching a bear being torn to pieces by his ban dogs, which had been kept hungry for hours in order to increase their ferocity, the Queen should be sitting over her tapestry with one faithful friend at her side.

More shouts followed, and the sound of trumpets came through the open window.

Katharine said: 'The game will have ended. How thankful I am that I was not there to witness the death agony of some poor creature.'

'We shall never grow accustomed to English sports, I fear,' answered Maria. 'After all these years we remain Spanish.'

'Yet we are English now, Maria, by reason of our marriages. We both have English husbands, and Spain seems so very far away; yet I shall never forget the Alhambra and my mother.'

'You would like to return to Spain, Your Grace?'

Katharine shook her head. 'I did not want to after she had died. For me she *was* Spain. I do not think I could have endured life there after she had gone. There would have been too much to remind me. It is so many years since she died . . . yet for me she never died. She lives on in my heart and brings me comfort still. I say to myself, when I think of my own sweet daughter: Katharine of Aragon will be such a mother to the Princess Mary as Isabella of Castile was to Katharine of Aragon.'

'She was both great and wise.'

'There are times,' went on Katharine, 'when I wish with all

4

my heart that she were here, that she had her apartments in this Palace and that I could go to her, tell her what perplexes me, so that out of her great wisdom she might tell me what to do.'

What could even great Isabella tell her daughter? wondered Maria. How could she advise her to please that wayward husband of hers? She could only say, as so many at Court could say: Give him a son. Then you will be safe.

Katharine looked at the woman who for so long had been her dearest friend. She knows of my troubles, thought the Queen. It would be impossible for her not to know. Who in this Court does not know that the King is persistently unfaithful to his wife, that he is beginning to find her five years seniority distasteful, that he is dissatisfied because, although she has proved herself capable of becoming pregnant, she has also shown herself unable to bear him a healthy male child? Twelve years of marriage had resulted in several miscarriages and only one healthy child – a daughter.

She was not one to ask for sympathy; she knew it was dangerous to confide in others. Yet Maria de Salinas was her very dear friend and she believed there was no one in her life who loved her more. It was a sad admission. Her husband no longer loved her; she was fully conscious of that sad fact. Her mother who had loved her dearly – even as she herself loved Mary – was long since dead. Recently her father, the ambitious, parsimonious Ferdinand, had died; but of course Ferdinand had never had much love to spare for any one person, his possessions taking all the affection he had to give; and to him she had merely been an important counter in the game of politics which was his life. Mary loved her; but Mary was a child.

God grant she never has to suffer as I have, thought the Queen hastily.

5

But all would be well for Mary who was now heir to the throne, because there was no Salic law in England. If there were no male children born to her parents, and one day she ascended the throne, she would be Queen in her own right, which was a very different matter from being a King's Consort.

Katharine's mother had been a Queen in her own right and, much as she had loved her husband, she had never forgotten it; for although Ferdinand had often been unfaithful – there were several illegitimate children to prove it – although she had accepted this as inevitable, forgiven him and remained his loving and submissive wife, in state matters she had held rigorously to her supremacy.

'Oh, Maria!' she sighed. 'I am passing through troublous times, and I feel . . . alone.'

Maria went to Katharine and kneeling, buried her face in the blue velvet. 'Your Grace, while I live to serve you, you are never alone.'

'I know it, Maria . . . my very good friend. I love you dearly, as you love me, and to no other would I speak of these matters. But to you I will say this: I despair of getting a male child. There is so little opportunity. The King rarely visits my bed. And since the birth of a son to Elizabeth Blount his manner towards me grows colder.'

'That sly creature!' Maria said angrily.

'Nay, do not blame her. She was a shy girl, and he is her King. He said, 'Come hither' and the girl has no more power to resist than a rabbit facing a stoat. And she has given him this son.'

'I hear that she no longer pleases him.'

The Queen shrugged her shoulders. 'He has taken the boy away to be brought up.'

6

'In seclusion, Your Grace,' said Maria quickly.

'But royally. If another woman should give him a son . . .'

Maria knew that the Queen was thinking of that catastrophe which she feared so much that she would not even speak of it. It was summed up in one dangerous word which was whispered throughout the Court: Divorce.

Impossible! Maria assured herself. Even Henry would never dare. How could he when the nephew of the Queen was not only King of Spain but Emperor of Austria, the greatest monarch of them all. No, it was all so much talk. Had the Queen been some humble princess, there might have been cause for fear; but the aunt of the Emperor was surely safe from all such indignities.

The Queen went on: 'There is this new girl.'

Maria waited.

'She was in France; he found her during that extravagant frolic. She is of a bad reputation and is known in the court of France as a wanton. I cannot understand him. But I have decided to send for the girl.'

Maria trembled. She wanted to say: Oh . . . no . . . no. It is folly. Let the King have his women, and look the other way.

'She is the daughter of Thomas Boleyn. I believe he has two girls and a boy. The other girl is in France now and much younger, and is said to be more intelligent than her sister. It is to be hoped this is so. But I shall have something to say to this Boleyn girl.'

'And His Grace . . .'

'His Grace was amused by her wantonness . . . as it appears many have been before.'

'Your Grace, this affair has gone . . .'

'As far as it is possible to go. It would not surprise me if Mary Boleyn is not already with child . . . perhaps twins. Boys, I'll dare swear.'

It was unlike the Queen to show such feeling, and Maria trembled afresh. Characteristically the Queen noticed the expression in Maria's face and was sobered by it – not because she feared for herself, but because she had troubled her friend.

'Have no fear, Maria,' she said. 'I shall dismiss this girl from the Court. I shall know how to deal with such a one. The King has amused himself with her, but she is no Elizabeth Blount. He will do nothing to detain her at Court. He will merely look about him and . . . find another.'

'But if he will find another . . .'

'I understand your meaning, Maria. Why dismiss this girl? Simply because her reputation is so light. No, if the King must have a mistress it should be one who has not shared the beds of quite so many. I hear that she even included the King of France among her lovers, briefly, oh very briefly. Elizabeth Blount at least behaved decorously and she was connected with the Mountjoys. These Boleyns, I have heard, have descended from trade.'

'Is that so, Your Grace? When one considers Thomas Boleyn that is surprising.'

'Thomas Boleyn gives himself airs, indeed. A very ambitious man, Maria. I wonder he does not take this girl of his and put her into a convent. But I do assure you that I have not been misinformed as to his origins, for when I heard of the King's . . . connection . . . with this girl I had enquiries made. One Geoffrey Boleyn was apprentice to a mercer in London . . . oh, it is a long time ago, I grant you, and he became rich; but he was a tradesman, no more, no less. Becoming Lord Mayor of

8

London and buying Blickling Hall from Sir John Falstaff, and Hever Castle from the Cobbhams, does not alter that. So this family rose through trade and advantageous marriages. They are connected with the Ormonds, and Thomas's wife is Norfolk's daughter. But this girl . . . this Mary . . . is doubtless a throw-back to the days of trade.'

How bitter she is, thought Maria; and how unlike herself. My poor Queen Katharine, are you becoming a frightened woman?

'It is a deplorable state of affairs when such people are allowed to come to Court,' went on Katharine.

There was a brief silence and Maria took advantage of it to say that she had heard the Emperor might again visit England, and how she hoped this was true.

'I hope so too,' said Katharine. 'I think the King has changed the opinion he once held of my nephew.'

'All who saw him on his visit to England were impressed by his serious ways and his fondness for Your Grace.'

Katharine smiled tenderly. 'I could not look on him without sadness, although it gave me so much pleasure to see him. He is indeed worthy of his destiny, but I could not help thinking of my sister.'

Maria winced and wished she had not turned the conversation in this direction. There was so much tragedy in the life of the Queen that it seemed impossible to avoid it. Now in reviving her memories of her nephew's visit she had reminded her of her poor sister Juana, Charles's mother, who was insane and living out her sad life in the castle of Tordesillas and who would have been the ruler of Spain had she not lost her reason.

'Poor Juana,' went on Katharine, 'she was always wild, but

we never thought it would come to this. There are times when I can feel almost happy because my mother is dead. I always thought that the deaths of my brother and eldest sister shocked her so deeply that she went earlier to her tomb than she would otherwise have done. But if she were alive now, if she could see her daughters – one mad, the other tormented . . .'

Maria interrupted, forgetting that it was a breach of etiquette to do so. 'Your Grace's troubles will be over one day. You have a healthy daughter; there will surely one day be a son.'

And so they had arrived back at the matter of the moment; this was the subject which occupied the minds of all at Court. A son. Will there be a son born to the King and Queen? There must be . . . for, if there is not, the position of Queen Katharine in England will be uncertain.

The Queen had turned back to the window.

'They are coming now,' she said, and picked up her tapestry.

The two women worked in silence for some moments while the sounds from without increased. Those of voices accompanied by laughter floated up to them, but they kept their eyes on the tapestry.

The King's voice was immediately recognisable; loud and resonant, it was that of a man who knew he only has to speak to achieve the result he wished. If he wanted laughter his courtiers gave it in full measure, with the required implication that his jokes were more witty than any other's; his frown was also more terrifying.

Katharine was thinking: Yet at heart he is only a boy. He plays at kingship. It is those about him who hold the power; men such as Thomas Wolsey on whom he depends more and more. An able man, this Thomas Wolsey, but an ambitious one, and the daughter of Ferdinand must know that ambition could warp a man's nature. But so far Wolsey's ambition was – like the King's strength – in check, and it seemed that Wolsey acted for the good of the state. Katharine had thought him her friend until recent months, when there were signs of a French alliance. Then she had not been so sure.

But it was not such as Thomas Wolsey whose company she most enjoyed. There were even now occasions when she could be at peace in the King's company; this was when he invited men such as Dr Linacre or Thomas More to his private apartments for an intimate supper. In particular was Katharine drawn to Thomas More; there was a man whose gentle charm and astringent wit had made an instant appeal to her, but perhaps what she had admired most of all was that integrity which she sensed in the man. It was so rare a quality that all seemed to change when they came into contact with it; even Henry ceased to be the licentious young man and was a serious monarch, determined to increase his intellectual stature and work for the good of his people. It was small wonder that she looked forward with pleasure to those days when the King said: 'Come, Master More, you shall sup with us tonight, and you may talk to us of astronomy, geometry or divinity; but willy-nilly we shall be merry with you.'

And strangely enough they would be for, with Thomas More leading the conversation, however serious its nature, it must be merry.

But on this day such as Thomas More and Dr Linacre would not be the King's companions.

She glanced out of the window. The King was leading his

courtiers towards the Palace, and with him were his brother-in-law the Duke of Suffolk, William Compton and Thomas Boleyn.

Katharine's mouth tightened at the sight of the last.

Thomas Boleyn was the kind of man who would be delighted to offer his daughter to the King in exchange for honours. The honours were evidently being granted, and the man had been at the King's side during his meeting with the King of France – that ostentatious and vulgar display of the 'Field of the Cloth of Gold' – and he remained there.

But not for long, vowed Katharine – unless he can hold his place by his own qualities and not through the lewdness of his daughter.

Wherever the King went there was ceremony. Now the heralds stationed at the doors were playing a fanfare – a warning to all those who had been within the Palace while the King was at sport to leap to attention. He would stroll through the Palace smiling graciously, if his mood was a good one; and it would seem that it was so now from the sound of his voice, and the laughter which followed his remarks.

She wondered whether he would go to his own apartments or come to hers. What did he wish now? Sweet music? Would he call for his lute and entertain the company with one of his own musical compositions? Would he perhaps summon Mary Boleyn and dismiss his courtiers? He was a young healthy animal and his whims and moods could change in a moment.

'He is coming here,' she said, and she saw the faint flush begin in Maria's cheeks as the door was flung open.

The King stood on the threshold looking at his Queen and her attendant bent over their tapestry.

Maria rose immediately, as did Katharine, and they both

made a deep curtsey as Henry came into the room chuckling, his fair face flushed, his blue eyes as bright as chips of glazed china with the sun on them; his golden beard jutting out inviting admiration; he had recently grown it because King François had one, and he believed that a golden beard was more becoming than a black one.

Beside him most other men looked meagre, and it was not merely the aura of kingship which made them so. It was true they fell away from him, giving him always the centre of the stage, for every word, every gesture which was made in his presence must remind him that he was the King whom they all idolised.

He was glittering with jewels. How he loved colour and display! And since he had returned from France he had worn brighter colours, more dazzling jewels. It was true that he did so with a hint of defiance; and Katharine knew that it would be a long time before he forgot the sly looks of the King of France, the caustic wit which, it had to be confessed, had set the King of England at a loss; that long nose, those brilliant dark eyes, had frequently seemed to hold a touch of mockery. The King of France was the only man who in recent years had dared snap his fingers at Henry and make sly jokes at his expense. Oh, the extravagant folly of that Field of the Cloth of Gold! All sham, thought Katharine, with two monarchs swearing friendship while hatred filled their hearts.

But Henry was not thinking of François now as he stood at the threshold of his wife's apartment. He was in a favourite position, legs apart – perhaps to display that fine plump calf; his jerkin was of purple velvet, the sleeves slashed and puffed; his doublet of cloth of gold decorated with pearls; on his head was a blue velvet cap in which a white feather curled and diamonds scintillated; about his neck was a gold chain on which hung a large pearl and ruby; the plump white fingers were heavily loaded with rings, mostly of rubies and diamonds.

It was small wonder that wherever he went the people shouted for him; unlike his father he was a King who looked like a King.

'How now, Kate?' he said; and she straightened herself to look into his face, to read the expression there – his was the most expressive face at Court – and Katharine saw that for this moment his mood was a benign one. 'You've missed a goodly sight.' He slapped his thigh, which set the jewels flashing in the sunlight.

'Then 'twas good sport, Your Grace?' answered Katharine, smiling.

''Twas so indeed. Was it not?' He turned his head slightly and there was an immediate chorus of assent. 'The dogs were game,' he went on, 'and the bear was determined to stay alive. They won in the end, but I've lost two of my dogs.'

'Your Grace will replace them.'

'Doubt it not,' he said. 'We missed you. You should have been at our side.' His expression had changed and was faintly peevish. She understood. He had been with Mary Boleyn last night and was making excuses to himself for conduct which shocked him a little, even though it was his own. She knew that he was tormented periodically by his conscience; a strange burden for such a man to carry. Yet she rejoiced in the King's conscience; she believed that if he ever contemplated some dastardly act, it would be there to deter him.

'It was my regret that I was not,' answered Katharine.

He growled and his eyes narrowed so that the bright blue was scarcely visible. He seemed to make a sudden decision, for he snapped his fingers and said: 'Leave us with the Queen.'

There was immediate obedience from those who had accompanied him into the apartment; and Maria de Salinas hurried to where the King stood, dropped a curtsey, and followed the others out. Henry did not glance at her; his lower lip was protruding slightly as the plump fingers of his right hand played with the great ruby on his left.

Katharine experienced a twinge of that apprehension which was troubling her more and more frequently nowadays. He had felt contented when he was watching his animals; when he had crossed the gardens and come into the Palace he had been happy. It was the sight of her sitting at her tapestry which had aroused his anger.

When they were alone he grumbled: 'Here is a pleasant state of affairs. The King must sit alone and watch good sport because his Queen prefers not to sit beside him that people may see their King and Queen together.'

'I believed I did not displease Your Grace in remaining in my apartment.'

'You knew full well that I wished you to be beside me.'

'But Henry, when I explained my indisposition, you seemed contented enough that I should remain in the Palace.'

It was true; he had shrugged his shoulders when she had pleaded a headache; would she never learn that what he accepted at one time with indifference could arouse his anger at another?

'I liked it not,' he growled. 'And if this headache of yours was so distressing, do you improve it with the needle? Nay, 'twas our rough English sports that disgusted you. Come, admit it. Our English games are too rough for Spanish ladies, who faint at the sight of blood. 'Tis so, is it not?'

'It is true that I find the torturing of animals distasteful.'

''Tis odd in one who comes from Spain where they make a religious spectacle out of torturing people.'

She shuddered; the thought of cruelty was distasteful to her; she knew that during the reign of her revered mother the Spanish Inquisition had tortured heretics and handed them over to the Secular authorities to be burned to death. This she had often told herself was a matter of faith; those who suffered at the *autos-de-fé* in her native land did so because they had sinned against the Church. In her eyes this was a necessary chastisement, blessed by Holy Church.

She said quietly: 'I do not care to witness the shedding of blood.'

'Bah!' cried the King. ''Tis good sport. And 'twould be well that the people see us together. Like as not we shall be hearing that all is not well between us. Rumours grow from such carelessness, and such rumours would not please me.'

'There are rumours already. I'll warrant the secret of your mistresses is not kept to the Court.'

The King's ruddy face grew a shade darker and there was a hint of purple in it. She knew she was being foolish, knew that he was like an ostrich, that he fondly imagined that no one was aware of his infidelities or, if they were, looked upon them as a kingly game no more degrading than the hounding of animals to death.

'And is it meet that you should reproach me for seeking elsewhere what I cannot find in your bed?' he demanded.

'I have always done my best to please you there.'

The eyes narrowed still more; the face was an even darker shade, the chin jutted out in a more bellicose manner; and only the beard prevented his looking like a boy in a tantrum.

'Then,' he shouted, 'let me tell you this, Madam. You have not pleased me there!'

She closed her eyes waiting for the onslaught of cruel words. He would not spare her because, with the guilt of his adultery heavy upon him, he had to find excuses for his conscience. He was talking to that now – not to her.

The tirade ended; a slightly pious expression crossed the scarlet face; the blue eyes opened wider and were turned upwards. His voice was hushed as he spoke.

'There are times, Kate, when I think that in some way you and I have offended God. All these years we have prayed for a boy and again and again our hopes have been disappointed.'

And those words smote her ears like a funeral knell; the more so because they were spoken quietly in a calculating manner; he had momentarily forgotten the need to appease his conscience; he was planning for the future.

He had expressed that thought before, and always in that portentous manner, so that it sounded like the opening chorus, the prelude to a drama on which the curtain was about to rise.

So now she waited for what would follow. It must come one day. If not this day, the next. Perhaps a week might elapse, a month, a year . . . but come it would.

He was eyeing her craftily, distastefully, the woman who no longer had the power to arouse any desire in him, the woman who after twelve years of marriage had failed to give what he most desired: a son born in wedlock.

There was nevertheless still to be respite; for suddenly he turned on his heel and strode from the room.

But Katharine knew that the curtain was soon to rise.

❁ ❁ ❁

As the courtiers left the King and Queen together, many an understanding glance was exchanged. It was common knowledge that all was not well between the royal pair. Who could blame the King, said the gay young men, married to a woman five years older than himself – a woman who was over-pious and a solemn Spaniard – when he was surrounded by gay young English girls all eager for a frolic! It would have been different of course had there been a son.

There was one among the company whose smile was complacent. This did not go unnoticed. Edward Stafford, third Duke of Buckingham, had good reason to be delighted by this lack of royal fertility. Secretly Buckingham believed himself to be more royal than the Tudors, and there were many who, had they dared to express such an opinion, would have agreed with him.

Buckingham was a proud man; he could not forget that through his father he was descended from Thomas of Woodstock, son of Edward III, and that his mother had been Catherine Woodville, sister of Elizabeth Woodville who had married Edward IV. And who were the Tudors but a bastard sprig from the royal tree!

Never could Buckingham look on the King without this thought crossing his mind: There but for the chances of fate might stand Edward Stafford.

Such thoughts were only safe when locked in the secret places of the mind; and it was unwise to betray, even by a look, that they existed. Buckingham was a rash man and therefore, since he lived under Henry VIII, an unwise one.

The old Duke of Norfolk who was at his side, guessing his thoughts, whispered: 'Caution, Edward.'

As Buckingham turned to look at his friend a faint frown of exasperation appeared on his brow. Further resentment flared up in his mind against the King. Why should he have to be cautious lest the stupid young King should realise that he fancied himself in his place? If Henry had a spark of imagination, he would guess this was so.

Norfolk and Buckingham were intimate friends and there was a connection between the families because Buckingham's daughter had married Norfolk's son.

Buckingham smiled wryly. The old man would want no trouble to befall his friend and connection by marriage, and would be thinking that such trouble often embraced the whole of a family.

'Your looks betray your thoughts,' whispered Norfolk. 'There are those who are ready to carry tales. Let us go to your apartments where we shall be able to talk in peace.'

Buckingham nodded and they disengaged themselves from the crowd.

'You should be watchful,' murmured Norfolk as they mounted the staircase on their way to Buckingham's apartment.

Buckingham shrugged elegant shoulders. 'Oh come,' he said, 'Henry knows that I'm as royal as he is. He doesn't need my careless looks to remind him.'

'All the more reason for caution. I should have thought you would have been warned by the case of Bulmer.'

Buckingham smiled reminiscently. It had been worth it, he decided; even though at the time he had suffered some uneasy moments.

But he was glad that he had shown his daring to the Court; there was no doubt of that when he had approached Sir William

Bulmer, who was in the service of the King, and bribed him with an offer of better service in his own retinue. He had done this out of bravado, out of that ever persistent desire to show the King that he was of equal standing. Buckingham had never forgotten how Henry had sought to seduce his, Buckingham's, sister, as though she were some serving girl at the Court. Perhaps Henry also had not forgotten Buckingham's action in having the girl whirled out of his orbit by her enraged husband just at that moment when successful seduction seemed imminent. Buckingham had scored then. It was a glorious victory for a Duke to win over a King. And he had tried again with Bulmer. Not so successfully, for the King, no longer an uncertain boy, had summoned Bulmer to the Star Chamber and accused him of having deserted the royal service. Bulmer had cowered before the onslaught of the King's anger and had been kept on his knees until he despaired of ever being allowed to rise.

But at length Henry had relented, forgiven Bulmer and taken him back into his service. The affair, however, was meant to be a warning – chiefly to an arrogant Duke. Yet the Duke still thought his dangerous thoughts; and it was possible to read them in almost every gesture that he made.

'Ah, Bulmer,' he mused now. 'That man was a coward. He should have returned to me.'

'It might have cost him his head,' suggested Norfolk.

'I would rather lose my head than be known as a coward.'

'Take care that you are not called upon to prove those words, Edward.'

'Henry does not possess a surfeit of bravery,' retorted Buckingham. 'Look how he let my sister go.'

'It would be a different state of affairs if that had happened today. Henry was a boy when he decided on your sister. I do believe that up to that time he had never been unfaithful to the Queen. Those days are over.'

'He realised that we Staffords would not accept the insult.'

'You deceive yourself. If he fancied your wife or mine he'd care not a jot for our families. The King is no longer a boy to be led. He is a man who will have what he wants and thrust aside all those who stand in his way.'

'If he respects royalty he must include those who are as royal as he is.'

'Henry sees only one point of view, his own. He is the King. The rest of us, be we Dukes or lords, are so far beneath him that he would have our heads, ay, and feel it was but his due, should the fancy take him. That is why I bid you to be cautious. Ha, here comes Wolsey, on his way to the royal apartments, I'll swear.'

'The butcher's dog is for ever sniffing at the heels of his master,' said Buckingham, without taking the precaution of lowering his voice.

Thomas Wolsey was making his way towards them, an impressive figure in his scarlet Cardinal's robes. He was a man of about forty-five, his expression alert, his face mildly disfigured by smallpox, and the lid of one eye hanging lower than the other, which gave an added expression of wisdom to his clever face.

Buckingham did not pause as he approached; his gaze became cold and he looked beyond the Cardinal as though he could not see the red-clad figure.

'A merry good day to you, gentlemen,' said the Cardinal.

'Good day to you,' answered Norfolk.

'I trust, my lords, you enjoyed good sport and that His Grace is happy because of it.'

'The sport was fair enough,' murmured Norfolk; but Buckingham, who had not spoken, was walking on.

Wolsey did not appear to have noticed; he inclined his head slightly and Norfolk did likewise, as Wolsey went on towards the King's apartments, the two Dukes on to Buckingham's.

''Tis my belief he heard your words,' said Norfolk.

''Tis my hope that he did.'

'Curb your pride, Edward. Will you never understand that he is forever at the King's side, ready to pour his poison in the royal ear?'

'Let him pour – if the King listens to the butcher's boy he is unworthy to be King.'

'Edward . . . you fool! When will you learn? You already have an enemy in the Cardinal; if you love your life do not seek one in the King.'

But Buckingham strode on ahead of Norfolk, so that the old man had to hurry to keep up with him; and thus they came to his apartments.

As they entered three men of his retinue who were conversing together bowed to him and his companion. These were Delacourt his confessor, Robert Gilbert his chancellor, and Charles Knyvet who was not only his steward but his cousin.

The Dukes acknowledged their greetings and when they had passed into Buckingham's private apartment he said: 'My servants are aware of it. They know full well that their master might, by good chance, ascend the throne.'

'I trust,' put in Norfolk nervously, 'that you have never spoken of such matters in their presence.'

'Often,' laughed Buckingham. 'Why, only the other day Delacourt said to me: 'If the Princess Mary died, Your Grace would be heir to the throne.' Why, my friend, you tremble. Norfolk, I'm surprised at you.'

'I never heard such folly.'

'Listen to me,' murmured Buckingham soothingly. 'The King is not such a fool as to attack the nobility. He has too much respect for royalty to harm me. So set aside your fears. This much I tell you: I will be treated with the respect due to me. Now, what do you think the King is saying to his Queen at this moment? He is upbraiding her for not accompanying him to watch the sport; but what he really means is that she is of no use to him since she cannot give him a son. I do believe he has begun to despair of ever getting a boy by her.'

'But the boys he gets by others will not provide the heir to the throne.'

Buckingham chuckled. 'No. There'll be no heir – and is the Princess Mary really a healthy child? But the King would do well to forget his anxieties. He has good heirs in me and mine.'

It was useless, Norfolk saw, to turn Buckingham from the subject which obsessed him; nevertheless he tried; and they talked awhile of the Field of the Cloth of Gold and the treaties which had been made with François Premier and the Emperor Charles.

Norfolk, who had not accompanied the royal party to France on that occasion, grumbled about the cost to which England had been put, and Buckingham agreed with him. The nobility would be on short commons for the next few months in order to pay for all the finery they had had to provide.

'And for what?' demanded Buckingham. 'That our Henry might show François what a fine fellow he is! As if François could not match pageant with pageant!'

Norfolk sourly agreed. He had not stood in high favour with

the King since Thomas Wolsey had risen to such eminence; he hated the Cardinal as much as Buckingham did, but he had had an opportunity of realising the venom and power of the man, and he was too shrewd to take unnecessary risks.

Buckingham was in a rebellious mood that day and, being conscious that members of his retinue were hovering, and fearing some indiscretion might be uttered in their presence, in which he might be involved, Norfolk took his leave as soon as he could politely do so.

When he was alone Buckingham brooded on that favourite subject of his, which aroused such bitterness within him and which, try as he might, he could never succeed in dismissing from his mind. He could work himself to a fury over what he construed as an insult from anyone of lowlier birth than his own, and the very presence of Wolsey at Court seemed an affront.

Norfolk's warnings had only succeeded in intensifying his recklessness, and when Knyvet came to his apartment to ask his advice about some matter of his stewardship, the Duke said: 'His Grace of Norfolk has been talking to me of the affair of William Bulmer.'

'Ah, Your Grace,' said Knyvet, 'that man is now back in the King's service. Some say he had a lucky escape.'

'Oh yes, he went back like a whipped cur. He would have done better to have remained with me. I shall not forget that he deserted me . . . when the time comes.'

Knyvet looked startled. 'It is not easy to disobey the King's command.'

Buckingham lifted his shoulders. 'At one time I believed the King was preparing to have *me* sent to the Tower for my part in that affair.'

'Your Grace to the Tower!'

Buckingham nodded. 'Kings do not last for ever,' he mused. 'My father learned that. He was in conflict with Richard III. But my father was no coward. He planned that when he was brought to the King he would have his dagger ready and plunge it into that false heart. I do assure you, cousin, that had an indignity been forced upon me, I should have been as ready to avenge the honour of my family as my father was.'

Knyvet murmured: 'Your Grace cannot mean . . .'

'And,' interrupted Buckingham fiercely, 'if the King were to die and the Princess were to die, I should take over the crown of this Kingdom, and none should say me nay.'

Knyvet recoiled, which amused Buckingham. How terrified everyone was of being drawn into a conspiracy! Such fear in others spurred the Duke on to further recklessness. He said: 'Is Hopkins, the monk, in the Palace today?'

'Yes, Your Grace.'

'Then send him to me. I have heard that he can see into the future. I want him to look into mine.'

'I will have him brought to Your Grace.'

'With all speed,' cried Buckingham.

He paced excitedly up and down his apartment while waiting for the monk; and when the man was brought to him he shouted so that several of his servants could not fail to hear him: 'So, Hopkins, you are here. I want you to tell me what the future holds for me. I want you to tell me what chance I have of attaining the throne.'

The monk shut the door and put his fingers to his lips. The face which peered out of his hood was shrewd. He took in the details of the apartment; the love of luxury was apparent. Here

25

was a noble Duke who could do him much good in exchange for the prophecy he wanted. Hopkins knew that if he told the Duke that he would be more likely to end his days on a scaffold than on a throne (and one did not have to be a soothsayer to suspect that) he would be dismissed without reward. But such as this Duke would be ready to pay well for what he wanted to hear.

Hopkins looked long into that arrogant face, half closed his eyes and murmured: 'I see greatness ahead for Your Grace.'

'What sort of greatness?'

'All that you desire will be yours. I see a crown . . .'

A slow, satisfied smile spread across the Duke's face. This fellow has great and unusual powers, he told himself. It *shall* come to pass. Has he not prophesied that it shall?

So he presented the monk with a heavy purse; and from that moment his manner grew a shade more arrogant.

In one of the privy gardens of the Palace a young man and woman sat on a wicker seat, their arms about each other. In the distance the shouts from the arena could be heard but both were oblivious of everything but the ardour of their passion.

The woman was plump and dark-haired; her body voluptuously curved; and the expression of her face, soft and sensuous, betrayed her nature. One glance was enough to see that she was one who had been endowed by nature with a deep appreciation and knowledge of fleshly pleasures; and her generous nature was one which wanted to share these. It was the secret of her great appeal to almost every man who saw her. And if they tired of her quickly it was because she could hold nothing back, but must give all that was demanded; so that in a short time there was little to learn of Mary Boleyn.

Since her early teens Mary had been in and out of more beds than she could remember. The Kings of England and France had been her lovers; so had the humblest officers of the Court. Mary was overflowing with desire which demanded appeasement and, being on such terms with pleasure and of a generous nature which never sought material gain, her favours had until this time been bestowed on most of those who asked for them.

Now she was in love and discovering that the emotions this young man aroused in her were of a different nature from those she had ever felt for any other person. She was still Mary, as uninhibited as a young animal in forest or jungle; lust was strong in her but it was tempered by affection, and when she thought of her future with her lover it was not only sharing his bed that filled her mind, but sharing his table, his fortune, and being a mother to the children they would have. This was a new and exciting experience for Mary Boleyn.

'And so,' he was saying now, as his hands caressed the bare plump bosom, 'we shall marry.'

'Yes, Will,' she answered, her lips slightly parted, her eyes glazed, while she wondered whether they dared here in full daylight. If they were discovered and tales carried to the King . . . ! It was only a few nights ago that His Grace had summoned her to his bed. He might be somewhat angry if he knew of her love for Will Carey.

'And when shall I speak to your father?'

Mary was alarmed. She caught his hand and pressed it against her breast. It was so easy to lose oneself in a sensuous dream and forget reality. In truth she was more afraid of her father than of the King. The King might decide that it was a good idea that she married. It was often the case in relationships such as theirs. He had found a husband for Elizabeth Blount and there was always a possibility that a mistress might become pregnant, when the necessary hasty marriage could be a little undignified. No, she did not think the King would object to the marriage; though he might insist that husbandly activities were confined only to giving his wife his name. Mary would not be greatly perturbed. Could she imagine herself living in a house with Will, and not . . . The thought made her want to laugh.

But her father – approaching him was another matter.

Thomas Boleyn had never thought much of his daughter Mary until she had caught the King's eye. Now he was inclined to regard her with greater respect than he had even for his son George; and all knew how clever George was.

Strange that Mary should have been the one . . . with her wantonness which had earned her many a beating in the past . . . to have brought honours to the family. But if Will Carey went to her father and asked for his daughter's hand there would be trouble.

'He'll never give his consent,' she said sadly.

'Why should he not?'

'You do not know my father, Will. He is the most ambitious of men, and of late he has risen high in the King's service.'

'Does he not wish to see his daughter married?'

'Mayhap, but alas, Will, you have no money and are only a younger son of your father. To us such matters are of no moment because we love, and that is all we ask. But my father does not believe in love. He will never give his consent.'

'Then what can we do?' Will asked in despair.

Mary took his face in her hands and kissed his lips. The kiss was full of invitation and promise. She was telling him that, even if they had to wait awhile for marriage, they had much to give each other in the meantime.

'I want to take you away from Court, Mary.'

'And I want to go.' She frowned. If the King sent for her, she must go to him. But it would really be Will with whom she wished to make love.

'What *can* we do about it? We must do something. I cannot wait for ever.'

'Something will happen, Will, never fear. We will be patient . . . about marriage . . . and something will happen; you see.'

Will fell upon her in a storm of passion. She was the ideal mistress, never withholding, always ready to give. But he wanted to take her away that he might keep her all to himself and that no others might share the pleasures which she gave so wholeheartedly. He knew about the King, of course. He could never be sure, when she was not with him, whether she was with the King.

She soothed him as she well knew how and after a while she said: 'I will speak to my father of your offer.'

'And if he forbids us to meet?'

'No one could prevent our meeting, Will.'

But Will was unconvinced.

'They are returning from their sport now,' went on Mary. 'My father will surely have been with the King. It may well be that his mood is a good one. Will, what if I spoke to him now?'

'But it is surely I who should speak to him, Mary.'

She shook her head, imagining her father intimidating her lover. Will was a man who might easily be intimidated, and her father, who had always been formidable, had become more so during the years of success.

She withdrew herself from him, sighing regretfully. 'Nay, Will,' she said, 'I will find him, and if the moment is a good one, speak to him. I know him better than you and if he shows signs of anger I shall know how to withdraw and pretend that our matter is of no importance.'

'You will not let him dissuade you?'

'No one shall persuade me to give you up, Will.'

He believed her, because he knew that she could be strong where her passions were concerned.

Thomas Boleyn, taking a moment's respite in his private apartments of the Palace whither he had retired when the King dismissed the courtiers that he might be alone with the Queen, was confronted by his daughter, who asked to speak with him in private.

Graciously he granted this permission, for Mary had become an important member of the household since the King had elevated her to the position of mistress.

Even so Thomas regarded her with faint distaste. Her dress was crumpled and her hair escaping from her headdress. Though, Thomas thought fleetingly, it may be the slut in her which appeals to the King. Yet although he was pleased with her, he was often anxious because he must constantly ask himself how long she would continue to hold the King's attention.

It was difficult to reconcile himself to the fact that Mary had sprung to such importance. She had always been the fool of the family. The other two were such a precocious pair. He had high hopes of George and it was his plan to bring him into prominence at Court at the earliest opportunity; he was sure that when that young man was a little older he would prove an amusing companion for the King. As for Anne, she was too young yet to make plans for. At the present time she was at the Court of France whence he heard news of her from time to time, and how her cleverness and charm pleased the King and Queen and members of their Court. But that the little slut Mary should have found favour with the King . . . was incredible.

'Well, my daughter?'

'Father, I have been thinking that it is time I married.'

Thomas was alert. Had the King put this into her head? If so he would be following the normal procedure. The King would feel happier with a mistress who had a husband; it forestalled an undignified shuffling into marriage if the need to do so should arise. No doubt Henry had found some worthy husband for his favourite; and Thomas, even if he wanted to, would not be such a fool as to refuse his consent to a marriage suggested by the King.

'Perhaps you are right, Mary,' he said. 'Whom have you in mind?'

Mary smiled in what seemed to the practical Thomas a vacuous manner as she murmured: 'It is William Carey, Father.'

'William Carey! You cannot mean . . . No, you could not. I was thinking of Carey's son . . . a younger brother . . .'

'It is that Will, Father.'

Thomas was astounded and horrified. Surely the King would never suggest such a lowly match for a woman in whom he had been interested. It was an insult. The blood rushed to Thomas's face and showed even in the whites of his eyes. 'The King . . .' he stammered.

'The King might not object to this marriage,' Mary began.

'He has suggested it to you?'

'Oh . . . no! It is because Will and I have fallen in love.'

31

Thomas stared at his daughter. 'You must be mad, girl. You . . . have fallen in love with this Will Carey? A younger son of a family that can scarcely be called distinguished!'

'One does not think of family honours or wealth when one falls in love,' said Mary simply.

'You have lost your wits, girl.'

'I believe it is called losing one's heart,' replied Mary with some spirit.

'The same thing, doubtless. Well, you may put this young man out of your mind. I want to hear no more of such nonsense. It may well be that, if you are patient, the King will suggest a good marriage for you. Indeed, it might be a good plan for you to make some light suggestions. Carefully, mind. Hint perhaps that marriage might be necessary . . .'

Mary bowed her head that he might not see the defiance which had sprung into her eyes. Hitherto she had been as easily swayed as a willow wand, but the thought of Will had stiffened her resistance. Strangely enough she was ready to put up a fight, to displease her father and the King, if need be, for the sake of Will Carey.

Thomas laid his hand on her shoulder; he had no doubt of her obedience. He was confident of his power when he looked back and saw how far he had come in the last years. He was forty-three years old, in good health, and his ambition was limitless. The King's pleasure in him was stressed by the fact that he had designated Sir Thomas Boleyn to play such a large part in making the arrangements for the Field of the Cloth of Gold; and now that Henry had favoured his daughter he was more grateful to Thomas than ever, because he had produced such a willing and comely girl. Mary had always been pliable, lacking the arrogance and temper of George and Anne.

Had he looked a little closer at Mary on that occasion he might have noticed that when her jaw was purposefully set, as it was at this moment, she bore a striking resemblance to her headstrong brother and sister.

But Thomas was too sure of his daughter, too sure of his ability to subdue her, to be alarmed.

He patted her shoulder.

'Now, my daughter, no more of this foolishness. There'll be a grand marriage for you, and now is the time to ask for it. I see no reason why you should not become a Duchess. That would please you, His Grace, and your family.'

Still she kept her head lowered, and giving her a playful push he dismissed her.

She was glad to escape because of the overwhelming desire to tell him that she was no longer his puppet, nor the King's; Mary Boleyn in love, fighting for the future she desired, was as formidable as any young woman of spirit.

The great Cardinal was alone in his audience chamber, where he stood at the window looking out over the parkland of that most magnificent of his residences, Hampton Court. He could always find delight in this place which he regarded as essentially his own; for how different it had become in those years since he had taken over the lease from the Knights of St John of Jerusalem and raised this impressive edifice to what it was at this time, built around five courts and containing 1500 rooms.

Here was opulence of a kind not seen even in the King's own palaces; the walls were hung with the finest tapestry which the Cardinal caused to be changed once a week; throughout the palace were exquisite pieces of furniture and treasures which proclaimed the wealth of their owner. The Cardinal was a man who liked to be constantly reminded of his possessions, for he had attained them through his own brilliance, and because he remembered humbler days he found the greater pleasure in them. He did not care that the people murmured and said that his court was more magnificent than that of the King; that was how he wished it to be. He often said to himself: 'All that is Henry's is his because he is his father's son. All that is mine, is mine because I am Thomas Wolsey.'

He encouraged ostentation. Let noblemen such as Norfolk and Buckingham sneer. They would sneer once too often. Let them make sly references to the butcher's shop in which they swore he had been born. What did he care? These men were fools; and Wolsey believed that one day he would triumph over all his enemies. He was determined to do so, for he was not the man to forget a slight.

He smoothed the crimson satin of his robes and caressed his tippet of fine sable.

Oh, it was good to be rich. It was good to have power and to feel that power growing. There was very little he wished for and did not possess, for he was not a man to seek the impossible. The greatest power in England, the Papal Crown . . . these were not impossibilities. And if he longed to install his family here in Hampton Court, to boast to the King of his son – his fine sturdy Thomas, named after himself, but known as Wynter – he accepted the impossibility of doing so. As a prelate he could not allow the fact of that uncanonical marriage of his to be known; he was therefore reconciled to keeping his family in the background while he could bestow honours on his son.

He was smiling to himself now because he knew of the activities which would be going on in the great kitchens. There was a special banquet this day; the King would be present in some disguise. Wolsey had not been specifically told that Henry would come; he had merely heard that a party of gentlemen from a far country planned to test the hospitality of Hampton Court, for they had heard that it vied with that to be enjoyed at the King's Court.

Wolsey laughed aloud. Such childish games! One among them would be the King, and the company must express its surprise when he discarded the disguise, and then the great delight and pleasure all felt in the honour of having their King with them.

'A game,' mused Wolsey, 'that we have played countless times and will doubtless play countless times again, for it seems that His Grace never tires of it.'

But was His Grace tiring? Had there been an indication recently of a change in the King's attitude to life? Was he taking more interest in matters of state, a little less in masking?

The longer the King remained a pleasure-loving boy the greater pleased would the Cardinal be. Those workmanlike hands of his were the hands to hold the helm. He wanted no interference.

Let the golden boy frolic with his women. Wolsey frowned a little. Boleyn was growing somewhat presumptuous on account of that brazen girl of his; and the man was becoming a little too important. But the Cardinal could deal with such; it was the King's interference that he most feared; and while the King was concerned with a girl he could be expected to leave matters of state to his trusted Chancellor.

The guests were already arriving. He would not join them

until the coming of the party of gentlemen in disguise, for that was beneath his dignity. His guests must wait for him to come among them, as at Greenwich or Westminster they waited for the King.

He knew that they would whisper together of the magnificence they saw about them, of the manner in which he dressed his servants, so that many of them were more richly clad than his guests. In the kitchens now his master cook, attired in scarlet satin with a gold chain about his neck, would be directing his many servants as though he himself was the lord of this manor; and that was how Wolsey would have it: that each man – from his steward who was a dean, and his treasurer who was a knight, to his grooms and yeomen of the pastry and his very scullery boys – should know, and tell the world by his demeanour, that it was better to be a page of the pantry in the household of Cardinal Wolsey than a gentleman steward in the house of any nobleman under the King.

As he brooded, his man Cavendish came to the door of the apartment and craved his master's indulgence for disturbing him, but a certain Charles Knyvet, late of the household of the Duke of Buckingham, was begging an audience with him.

Wolsey did not speak for a second. He felt a surge of hatred rise within him at the mention of the hated Buckingham. There was a man who had been born to wealth and nobility and who never failed to remind the Cardinal of it. It was in every look, every gesture and, often when he passed, Wolsey would hear the words: butcher's dog.

One day Buckingham was going to regret that he dared scorn Thomas Wolsey, for the Cardinal was not the sort to forget a grudge; all insults were remembered in order to be repaid tenfold; for that dignity which he had had to nurture, having cost him so much to come by, was doubly dear to him.

This was interesting. Knyvet to see him! He knew that the fellow was related to Buckingham – a poor relation – who had been in the Duke's employ until recently. There had been some difference of opinion between Master Knyvet and his rich relation, with the result that Knyvet had been dismissed from the ducal household.

So he came to see the Cardinal.

Wolsey regarded his hands thoughtfully. 'You discovered his business?'

'He said it was for the ears of Your Eminence alone.'

The Cardinal nodded; but he would not see the man – not at the first request. That would be beneath the dignity of the great Cardinal.

'Tell him he may present himself again,' he said.

Cavendish bowed. The man was favoured. At least the Cardinal had not refused his request for an interview.

So Cavendish went back through the eight rooms, which had to be traversed before the Cardinal's private chamber was reached, and in which none who sought an audience might wait.

Now Wolsey could hear shouts on the river, the sound of music, and he decided it was time for him to leave his apartment and cross the park to the water's edge, there to receive the party, for it would contain one before whom even a great Cardinal must bow.

He made his way down his private staircase and out into the sunshine; standing at the river's edge he watched the boat approach the privy stairs. In it was a party of men dressed in dazzling colours, all heavily masked and wearing beards, some of gold wire, some of black. The Cardinal saw with some dismay that the masks, the false beards, and caps of gold and scarlet which covered their heads were all-concealing, and this was going to be one of those occasions when it was not easy to pick out the King.

Usually his great height betrayed him; but there were several who appeared to be as tall. A faint irritation came to the Cardinal, although he hastened to suppress it; one of the first steps to disfavour was taken when one betrayed a lack of interest in the King's pastimes. That was one of the lesser ways in which the Queen was failing.

'Welcome, gentlemen,' he cried, 'welcome to Hampton Court.'

One of the masked men said in a deliberately disguised voice which Wolsey could not recognise: 'We come from a strange land, and news of the hospitality of the great Cardinal has been brought to us, so we would test it.'

'Gentlemen, it is my pleasure to entertain you. Come into the palace. The banquet is about to be served, and there are many guests at my table who will delight you as you will delight them.'

'Are there fair ladies?' asked one.

'In plenty,' answered the Cardinal.

One tall man with a black beard came to the Cardinal's side. 'Fair ladies at the table of a Cardinal?' he murmured.

Wolsey spread his hands, believing he heard mockery in the voice. This disturbed him faintly for he fancied it might well be the King who walked beside him.

'My lord,' he answered, 'I give all I have to my guests. If I believe the company of fair ladies will enliven the occasion for them, then I invite fair ladies to my table.'

' 'Tis true you are a perfect host.'

They had come to the gates of the palace beside which stood two tall yeomen and two grooms, so still that they looked like statues, so gorgeously apparelled that they looked like members of the nobility.

'Methinks,' said the black-bearded man in an aside to one of his companions, 'that we come not to the Cardinal's court but to the King's Court.'

'It pleases me that you should think so, my lord,' said Wolsey, 'for you come from a strange land and now that you are in the King's realm you will know that a Chancellor could possess such a manor only if his master were as far above him as you, my lord, are above my grooms whom you so recently have passed.'

'Then is the King's Court of even greater brilliance?'

'If it were but a hut by the river it would be of greater brilliance because our lord the King was therein. When you have seen him you will understand.'

He was feeling a little uneasy. It was disconcerting to be unsure of the King's identity. The game was indeed changing when that golden figure could not be immediately discovered.

'It would seem that you are not only a great Cardinal but a loyal subject.'

'There is none more loyal in the kingdom,' replied Wolsey vehemently; 'and none with more reason to be. All that I am, I am because of the King's grace; all that I possess comes from his mercy.'

'Well spoken,' said the black-bearded man. 'Let us to your banquet table; for the news of its excellence has travelled far.'

In the banqueting hall the guests were already assembled, and the sight was magnificent, for the great hall was hung with finest tapestry, and many tables were set side by side. In the place of honour was a canopy under which it was the Cardinal's custom to sit, and here he would be served separately by two of his chief servants. The brilliance of the gathering was dazzling, and the members of the Cardinal's retinue in their colourful livery contributed in no small way to the opulence of the occasion.

Wolsey's eyes were on the black-bearded man. 'You shall be seated in the place of honour,' he said.

'Nay, my lord Cardinal, it pleases us that you should take your place under the cloth of state and behave as though we were the humblest of your guests.'

But as he took his place under the canopy the Cardinal's apprehension increased. Previously during such masquerades he had discovered the King immediately and acted accordingly. Irritated as he was, he forced himself to appear gracious and to behave as though this really was a party of foreign travellers who had come unexpectedly to his table.

But it was difficult. Who were behind those masks? Buckingham doubtless. Boleyn? Compton? Suffolk? All Henry's cronies and therefore casting wary eyes at a man of the people who had risen so far above them.

He signed to his servants to serve the banquet but his eyes ranged about the table. The napery was exquisite; the food as plentiful as that supplied at the King's table. Everything was of the best. Capons, pheasants, snipe, venison, chickens and monumental pies. Who but the Cardinal's cooks could produce such light pastry with the golden look? Peacocks, oysters, stags, bucks, partridges, beef and mutton. There were fish of many descriptions; sauces made from cloves and raisins, sugar cinnamon and ginger; and gallons of French wines with Malmsey, and muscadell – all to be drunk from fine Venetian glasses which were the wonder of all who saw them.

But while the company gave themselves to the appreciation of this banquet Wolsey continued uneasy, and suddenly he raised his voice and said:

'My friends, there is one among us who is so noble that I know it to be my duty to surrender my place to him. I cannot sit under this canopy in good spirit while he, who is so much more worthy than I, takes his place unrecognised at my table.'

There was silence, and then one of the masked men spoke; and a great hatred seized Wolsey when he recognised the disguised voice as that of Buckingham. 'My Lord Cardinal, there are many members of the nobility present.'

'I speak of one,' said Wolsey.

Then one of the masked men said in a muffled voice: 'Since Your Eminence believes there is such a noble personage among us, you should remove the mask of that man that all may see him.'

It was the invitation to unmask, always the great climax of these childish games.

The Cardinal stood up. 'It shall be so,' he said. And he walked along the tables to that man with the black beard, and stood before him.

'Take off his mask if you believe it to be he,' commanded a voice which was husky with suppressed laughter.

And Wolsey stretched up and removed the false beard and the mask, to disclose the features of Charles Brandon, Duke of Suffolk.

While he stared with dismay there was a shout of laughter and a tall figure rose and confronted Wolsey.

'So my lord Cardinal,' he cried, removing his mask, 'you would deny your King!'

41

Wolsey knelt and took Henry's hand.

'May God forgive me,' he murmured.

Henry, his face scarlet with pleasure, his blue eyes sparkling, flung his gold wire beard from him. He began to laugh in that deep rumbling way which appeared to be infectious for the whole company laughed with him.

Thomas stood up and raised his eyes to the jovial giant.

'So Thomas, my friend, you did not know me.'

'Your Grace, I have never seen you so perfectly disguised.'

Henry slapped his satin thigh. ' 'Twas a good mask. And I'll applaud Suffolk. He led you astray, did he not. Yet I thought you would have seen he lacked that inch or so.'

'But surely Your Grace stooped to deceive me?'

'Ha! Stoop I did. And 'twas effective.'

'And I had thought I could find Your Grace anywhere . . . in any circumstances.'

'So, friend Thomas, you offer me your seat of honour, eh?'

'Everything I have belongs to Your Grace. And now I would crave your indulgence and ask you to wait awhile before you sit to table. That which was served for a band of travellers is not what I would put before my King.'

'How so, Thomas?'

'If Your Grace will excuse me I will send for my master cooks. When the King comes to Hampton Court that which is served must not only be fit for a King but fit for the King of England.'

Henry's eyes gleamed with pleasure. There was never such a one as Thomas Wolsey. He could be trusted to rise to any occasion. Whether it was matching the wits of his great enemy, François Premier, or talking of treaties with the Emperor Charles, Wolsey was the man he wanted to have beside him.

And in a mask such as this he could be as effective as at the Council table.

'Go to, Thomas,' he said; and when Thomas gave a quiet order to his stewards the King's merry eyes watched the ceremonial arrival of Thomas's cooks in their scarlet velvet livery and golden chains.

'The fellows look as royal as myself,' he said in an aside to Suffolk. But he enjoyed it. He admired Wolsey for living in this manner; it was a credit to his country and his King.

'We are honoured by the presence of the King,' said Wolsey to his cooks. 'Have this food removed; bring in new and scented napery; set new dishes on the tables. I wish for a banquet – not worthy to set before His Grace, for that would be impossible – but the best we can offer.'

The cooks bowed and with ceremony left the hall followed by their clerks of the kitchens, surveyors of the dresser, clerks of the hall-kitchens and clerk of the spicery who followed the master cooks as Wolsey's gentlemen of the household followed him on his ceremonial journeys from Hampton to Westminster Hall.

Then the guests left the tables and Wolsey led the King to another apartment; the banquet was postponed for an hour that it might be made worthy of the King.

Nothing could have pleased Henry more, for the climax of his game was that he should receive the homage due to him as King. Buckingham might grumble to Norfolk that the butcher's cur was vulgar in the extreme; but there was not a man present who did not know that it was the red-clad figure which led the way and that which was clad in jewelled cloth of gold followed, because it was pleasant and easy to do so.

So it was with Wolsey that Henry walked in the hall of Hampton Court, his arm laid heavily on the shoulder of the

Chancellor so that all could see – if they had ever doubted it – that he looked upon Thomas Wolsey as his friend, that he rejoiced in the Cardinal's possessions because they were a symbol of how high a humble man could rise in his service, that he saw Thomas's glory as a reflection of his own power. Nothing the jealous near-royals could do would alter that.

And when the food was prepared and the company re-assembled in the great banqueting hall, Henry took his place under the canopy of state and all were merry as it pleased the King to be; but Henry would have, seated on his right hand, his host and friend, Thomas Wolsey.

He wanted all to know that he had great love for that man.

The next morning when Knyvet again asked for an audience with the Cardinal, Wolsey received him.

The Cardinal, in crimson damask on this morning, sat at his table, his hands – very white in contrast to the crimson – spread out before him.

'You have something to tell me?' he asked.

'My lord Cardinal, I have wrestled with my conscience . . .'

How they always wrestled with their consciences! As though it was not the desire for revenge which so often brought them to him!

'I am listening,' said Wolsey.

'It concerns my Lord Buckingham.'

'In whose service you are.'

'In whose service I was, Your Eminence.'

'So you are with him no longer?'

Wolsey's face was impassive but he was chuckling inwardly. So the fool Buckingham had dismissed a man from his service after having been indiscreet before him. The trouble with Buckingham was that he felt himself too important to need caution. It might be that the time was near when he would learn that he misjudged that importance.

'A little difference between us, Your Eminence. The Duke has a hasty temper.'

'I am sorry.'

'Your Eminence, it is a matter of relief to me to be free of him. Although he is my cousin I must say that.'

There was venom there. It might be usefully employed.

'And why have you come to see me?'

'Because I felt it my duty to do so.'

'You wish to tell me something about the Duke?'

'Yes, Your Eminence.'

'I am listening.'

'I would have Your Eminence know that it is my duty to King and State which impels me to lay these matters before you.'

'I accept that.'

'Then I would say that my lord and cousin has uttered remarks against the King's Grace which seem to me treasonable.'

'And what were these remarks?'

'Before the Princess Mary was born he claimed to be heir to the throne. Since Her Highness's birth he has said that should she die he would be the heir.'

'Is that so?'

'Your Eminence, he has referred constantly to his noble birth and has made slighting remarks concerning the bastardy of a certain family.'

Wolsey nodded encouragingly.

'Your Eminence, he has consulted a soothsayer who has told him that the crown will one day be his.'

'It would seem that your cousin is a rash man, Master Knyvet.'

''Twould seem so, Eminence. You will remember that he lured Sir William Bulmer from the King's service into his.'

'I remember the occasion well. The King was angry and declared he would have no servant of his hanging on another man's sleeve.'

'Yes, Eminence, and my Lord Buckingham told me that had the King reprimanded *him* and sent him to the Tower, he would have asked for an audience with His Grace, and when it was granted would have stabbed the King and taken over the rule of this kingdom.'

'His recklessness is greater than I believed it to be. Why was he such a fool as to dismiss a man to whom he had uttered such treasonable words?'

Knyvet flushed uncomfortably. 'He accused me of oppressing the tenantry.'

'And he dismissed you? And it was only when you were dismissed that you recognised these remarks of his as those of a traitor?'

Knyvet shivered and began to wish that he had not come to the Cardinal, but Wolsey had begun to smile as he laid a hand on the ex-steward's shoulder.

'My lord, I came to you because I felt it to be my duty . . .'

'It was indeed your duty. But what will be said of a man who only recognises his duty when his master dismisses him from his service?'

'You would not find it difficult to prove the truth. I was not the only one who heard these remarks. There were Hopkins the monk, and my lord's confessor, Delacourt, and Gilbert his chancellor. My lord lacks caution and speaks his mind before his servants.'

The Chancellor waved a hand, which was enough to tell Knyvet that he was dismissed.

Knyvet looked at him in amazement; he had often heard Buckingham sneer at Wolsey; surely, he reasoned, Wolsey should reward one who brought such evidence to him.

But the Cardinal's white hand was now at his lips suppressing a yawn; and there was nothing Knyvet could do but bow and retire with as much dignity as possible.

When he was alone the Cardinal took a tablet from a drawer and set it before him; then he began to write: 'Hopkins the monk, Delacourt the confessor, Gilbert the chancellor.'

It might be that he could use these men if and when a certain occasion arose.

The Queen had dismissed all her women with the exception of Maria de Salinas.

'I think, Maria,' she said thoughtfully, 'that when the woman comes in, you should go.'

Maria bowed her head. She was sorry that the Queen had made up her mind to see this woman. It would have been better, she was sure, to ignore her. Moreover, if the woman went to the King and complained to him, what an undignified position the Queen would be in!

'You are thinking that I am being unwise?' Katharine demanded.

'Your Grace, who am I to think such thoughts?'

'I am not the King, Maria, in constant need of flattery. I like to hear the truth from my friends.'

'I think, Your Grace, that the interview may be distasteful to you.'

'There is so much that is distasteful to me,' Katharine answered sadly.

'Your Grace, I hear voices without.'

'She is come. When she enters, Maria my dear, leave at once.'

A page entered and told the Queen that Mistress Boleyn was without and saying that she had come at the Queen's command.

'It is true. Bring her to me. Now Maria, you will go.'

Maria curtseyed and went out as Mary Boleyn entered.

Mary came to stand before the Queen; she made a deep curtsey, raising her big, dark eyes fearfully to the Queen's face as she did so.

Mary shivered inwardly. How frozen she looked! No wonder Henry went elsewhere for his comforts. She would be a cold bedfellow.

So this is the girl for whom he has neglected me! thought Katharine. She has the look of a slut. Why does he not choose someone more in keeping with his rank?

'Mistress Mary Boleyn, pray rise,' said the Queen.

The girl straightened herself and stood forlornly waiting for what the Queen had to say.

'You are the centre of a most distressing scandal,' began Katharine, and, watching the slow flush mount to the girl's forehead, thought that it was some small comfort that she felt some shame. 'It is unbecoming of you and . . . in those who share your misdemeanours.'

Mary looked at her helplessly. She wanted to explain: It was at Ardres or Guisnes – she was not quite sure. She had noticed his eyes upon her; and she had known the meaning of the looks he gave her. Then he had caught her alone one day and when his hands had strayed over her body there was nothing she could do but say Yes. She would have said Yes to anyone who was as handsome and had such need of her. With the King, of course, there could be no thought of refusal. Did not the Queen understand this? Poor lady. Mary believed she really did not. She did not know the King very well then. She did not know the way of the Court.

But how explain? She hung her head for she was ashamed; and she was deeply sorry that she had caused the good and pious Queen distress. Strangely enough she had never thought of the Queen; she could never think of anything at such times but the need for gratification, and when it was over it was too late. Mary was not the sort to waste regrets on things which it was too late to change.

What was the Queen asking of her now? To refuse the King! Did anyone ever refuse the King?

Then an idea occurred to her. The Queen still had some power, even with the King. Although she was so old and the King was clearly tired of her, she was still a Princess of Spain and her nephew was the most important monarch in Europe.

Mary had wanted to tell the Queen that she was sorry, that she would willingly end her liaison with the King tomorrow if she could. But it was so difficult to explain. So Mary did the only thing possible; she burst into tears.

Katharine was quite unprepared for such a loss of control, and for a few moments did not know what to say to the girl.

'Your Grace,' sobbed Mary. 'I wish I were a good woman . . . but I'm afraid I'm not. I was made this way. And now that I want to marry Will . . . Oh dear, it is all so difficult, but I wish . . . oh how I wish . . .'

'You should control yourself,' said the Queen coldly.

'Yes, Your Grace,' said Mary, dabbing at her eyes.

'What is this talk of marriage?'

'I am in love, Your Grace, with Will Carey. He is a younger son, and my father does not find him a good enough match for me. He has . . . forbidden us . . .'

'I see. So this young man is willing to marry you in spite of the scandal you have brought on yourself.'

'There would be no more scandal, Your Grace, if only I could marry Will. I want none but Will, and he wants none but me. If Your Grace would speak for us . . .'

A strange state of affairs, pondered the Queen. I send for her to reprimand her for her lewd conduct with the King, and she asks me to help her to marry with a young man whom she says she loves.

Yet there was something lovable about the girl. Katharine had never thought that she could feel a slight degree of tenderness towards any of her husband's mistresses, but she was finding that this could be so. Mary with her plump bosom that seemed to resent being restrained within that laced bodice, her tiny waist and her flaring hips, had the air of a wanton even when she was distressed as she was at this moment; and there was also a look of the slattern about her; and yet that gentleness, that desire to please, that certain helplessness was appealing.

How could he deceive me with such a one? Katharine asked herself. Elizabeth Blount had been different – a young and beautiful virgin when he had first seen her; and their *affaire* had been conducted with decorum. But Katharine was certain that the King had not been this girl's first lover.

And for many nights he had not visited his wife because the creature had claimed his attention. This slut had been preferred to a princess of Spain; the daughter of Thomas Boleyn – who for all his airs had his roots in trade – had been preferred to the daughter of Isabella and Ferdinand!

There were so many questions she wanted to ask. She was jealous of this girl, because she knew that there would be such passion between her and the King as there never had been between the King and his wife. How did you manage to attract him? she wanted to ask. How did you manage to keep him? He went to you in spite of his conscience, in spite of the scandal which he hates. Yet he cannot bring himself to come to me when it is right and proper that he should, and it is his duty to give me the chance of bearing a son.

She ought to hate the girl, but it was impossible to hate her when she stood there, an occasional sob still shaking her body.

The Queen said: 'So you have spoken to your father of this marriage?'

'Yes, Your Grace. He is against it.'

'Why so?'

'Because Will is only a younger son.'

'And do *you* not think that you might look higher?'

'I could not look higher, Your Grace, than the man I love.'

Katharine was shaken. She had expected to find a calculating mind beneath that voluptuous exterior; but the girl's looks did not lie. She was indeed soft and loving.

'That is a worthy sentiment,' murmured the Queen. 'When I sent for you I had thought of dismissing you from the Court, of sending you back to your father's castle at Hever.' The Queen half closed her eyes, visualising the scene with Henry if she had dared to do this. 'But,' she went on, 'since you speak to me of your love for this young man, and speak of it with sincerity, I feel that I should like to help you.'

'Your Grace!' The babyish mouth was slightly open; the dark tearful eyes wide.

'Yes,' said the Queen. 'I can see that you need to be married. Your husband will then keep you out of mischief.'

'And Your Grace will . . .'

'I will arrange for your marriage to Will Carey. The ceremony shall be here at Court and I myself will attend.'

'Your Grace!'

There was no mistaking the joy in the girl's face.

Katharine held out her hand, Mary took it and pressed a damp hot face against it.

'You may go now,' said the Queen graciously, and watched the girl depart.

A slut, she thought. And no virgin when he found her. Yet he desired her as he never did his wife.

Why should this be? Katharine asked herself passionately. Is there no hope left to me? What is the use of praying for a son when the King has given up all hope of begetting one? How can there be a son when he never comes to me, when he spends his manhood on girls such as Mary Boleyn?

There were isolated moments in life, thought Katharine, which were sheer happiness; and what had happened in the past and what the future held could not touch them. As she sat watching her daughter Mary leaning against her father's knee while he instructed her in playing the lute, she assured herself that this was one of them.

The King's face was flushed and he was smiling; there was rare tenderness about his mouth; he dearly loved children, and he would have been a contented man if, instead of one small girl in the nursery, there were half a dozen – and more than one lusty boy among them.

But in this happy moment he was well pleased with his little daughter.

How enchanting she is! thought Katharine. How dainty! How healthy with that flush in her cheeks and her long hair falling about her shoulders! Why am I ever sad while I have my Mary?

'Ha!' boomed the King, 'you are going to be a musician, my daughter. There is no doubt of that.' He turned, smiling to Katharine. 'Did you hear that? She shall have the best teacher in the land.'

'She already has that,' said Katharine meaningfully, and she went to the pair and laid her hand lightly on the King's shoulder. He patted that hand affectionately.

Holy Mother of God, the Queen prayed silently, if we had only one son, all would be well between us. Who would believe, witnessing this scene of domestic felicity, that he continually betrays me and that . . .

But she would not allow herself to say it even to herself. It was impossible. Only her enemies had whispered it because they hated her. They must have forgotten that she was of the House of Spain and that the Emperor was her own sister's son.

'Henry,' went on Katharine, 'I want to discuss her general education with you. I wish her to receive tuition in languages, history and all subjects which will be of use to her in later life.'

'It shall be so,' agreed Henry.

'I have been talking to Thomas More on this subject.'

'A good fellow, Thomas More,' murmured the King, 'and none could give you better advice.'

'His daughters, I have heard, are the best educated in England. He firmly believes that there should be no difference between the education of girls and boys.'

The King's look of contentment faded; his lower lip protruded in an expression of discontent.

I should not have said that, thought Katharine. I have reminded him that while Thomas More has a son, he, the King, has none – at least not a legitimate son.

These pitfalls appeared on every occasion. Was there no escaping them?

The King was staring at Mary's brown curls, and she knew that he was thinking to himself: Why was this girl not a boy?

The little girl was extremely sensitive and this was not the first time that she had been aware of the discontent she aroused in her father. She lowered her eyes and stared at the lute in his hands. He frightened her, this big and glittering father, who would sometimes pick her up in his arms and expect her to shout with glee because he noticed her. She did shout, because Mary always tried to do what was expected of her, but the glee was assumed, and in her father's presence the child was never completely free from apprehension.

She longed to please him and applied an almost feverish concentration on her lessons, and in particular her music; and because she knew that he liked to boast of her abilities, she was terrified that she would fall short of his expectation.

Those occasions when he smothered her with his exuberant affection were almost as alarming as when he showed his displeasure in her sex.

She had begun to ask herself: 'Where did I fail? What could I have done to have made myself be born a boy?'

She took a swift glance at her mother. How glad she was

that the Queen was present, for in the company of her mother she felt safer. If she could have had her wish they would have been together always; she would have liked to sleep in her mother's chamber, and stay with her the whole day long. Whenever she was afraid, she thought of her mother; and when they were alone together she was completely happy.

Now she raised her eyes and found her mother's gaze upon her. The Queen smiled reassuringly because she immediately sensed her little daughter's disquiet.

We must never show our differences in the child's presence, thought Katharine. But how long can I protect her from rumour? She already knows that her father constantly rages against the fate which made her a girl and not a boy.

The Queen said quickly: 'Now that you have the lute in your hands, Henry, play us one of your songs, and sing to us.'

The frown lifted from the King's brow. He was still boyish enough to be drawn from discontent by a treat. It was like offering a child a sweetmeat, and compliments were the sweet-meats Henry most desired.

'Since you ask me, Katharine, I will sing for you. And what of my daughter? Does she wish to hear her father sing?'

The little girl was alert. She said in a shy voice: 'Yes, Your Grace.'

'You do not sound quite certain,' he growled.

The Queen put in hastily: 'Mary is all eagerness, but a little shy of showing her pleasure.' She held out her hand to the Princess who immediately ran to her.

Oh the comfort of those velvet skirts, the joy of hiding her face momentarily in them, of feeling that gentle, protective hand on her head! The Princess Mary looked up at her mother with adoration shining in her eyes.

The Queen smiled and held that head against her skirts once more. It would not be wise for her father to see that the love she had for her mother was greater than that which she had for him. Mary did not understand that he demanded always to be the most admired, the best loved.

'I do not look for shyness in my daughter,' murmured the King. But his fingers were already plucking at the lute and he was singing his favourite song in a pleasant tenor voice.

The Queen settled herself in her chair and kept her arm about her daughter.

Snuggling up to her Mary prayed: 'Please, Holy Mother of God, let me stay with my mother . . . always.'

The song came to an end and the King stared before him, his eyes glazed with the pleasure he found in his own creation, while the Queen clapped her hands and signed to her daughter to do the same. Thus the King was appeased.

When their daughter had been returned to her governess, Katharine said to the King: 'Mary Boleyn has been to see me to plead for permission to marry.'

The King did not speak for a moment. Then he said: 'Is that so?'

'Yes. It seems that she wishes to marry a certain William Carey, who is a younger son and I fancy not to her father's liking.'

'Thomas Boleyn wants a better match for the girl, I'll warrant.'

'Thomas Boleyn is an ambitious man. I have promised to help the girl.'

The King shrugged his shoulders. 'The matter is in your hands.'

'I had thought in the circumstances . . .'

He swung round on her, his eyes narrowed. What was she hinting? Was she reproaching him because he had found the girl attractive?

'In what circumstances?' he demanded.

She saw that she had strayed into one of those pitfalls which it was always so necessary to avoid. She should have murmured that, as the girl was of the Court and her father stood high in the King's favour, she had believed that she should first ask for the King's approval before consenting to her marriage.

But her natural dignity revolted. Was she not, after all, a daughter of the House of Spain? Should she allow herself to be treated as a woman of no importance? The recent interview with her daughter had reminded her of her own mother, and she believed that little Mary felt for her the same devotion that she herself had felt for Isabella of Castile. Isabella would never have lost her dignity over one of her husband's mistresses.

Katharine said coldly: 'In view of the fact that the girl is – or was – your paramour . . .'

The King's face darkened. In his eyes sins seemed blacker when they were openly referred to. He might placate his conscience to some extent ('I am but a man. The girl was more than willing. My wife is sickly and after each pregnancy she grows more so. Providence sends me these willing girls, who, by God, lose nothing through the affair, that I may save my wife discomfort') but when his wife actually spoke of the matter with that smouldering resentment in her eyes she emphasised the unworthiness of his conduct. Therefore if he had been dissatisfied with her a moment before, as soon as she uttered those words he hated her.

'You forget to whom you speak, Madam,' he said.

'Why should you think that? Is the girl then the mistress of others? I must say it does not surprise me.'

'This girl's marriage is of no interest to me,' cried Henry. 'But your insolent accusations are, Madam, I would have you know. I have suffered much. I have been a loving husband. You forget how I brought you out of poverty . . . exile, one might say. You forget that against the advice of my ministers I married you. And how did you repay me? By denying me that which I longed for above all else. All these years of marriage . . . and no son . . . no son . . .'

'That is our mutual sorrow, Henry. Am I to blame?'

His eyes narrowed cruelly. 'It is strange that you cannot bear a son.'

'When Elizabeth Blount has done so for you?' she demanded.

'I have a son,' He raised his eyes to the ceiling and his attitude had become pious. 'As King of the realm and one whose task it is to provide his country with heirs I thought it my duty to see wherein the fault lay.'

How could one reason with such a man? He was telling her now that when he had first seen that beautiful young girl and had seduced her, it was not because he had lusted after her, but only to prove to his people that, although his Queen could not give him a son, another could.

No, it was impossible to reason with him because when he made these preposterous statements he really believed them. He had to believe in the virtuous picture he envisaged. It was the only way in which he could appease his conscience.

He was going on: 'I have prayed each day and night; I have heard Mass five times a day. I cannot understand why this should be denied me, when I have served God so well. But there is a reason.'

Cunning lights were in his eyes; they suggested that he had his own beliefs as to why his greatest wish should have been denied him. For a moment she thought he was going to tell her; but he changed his mind, and turning, strode to the door.

There he paused, and she saw that he had made an effort to control his features. He said coldly: 'If you wish to arrange the marriage of any of the Court women, you should consult me. This you have done and in this case I say I pass the matter into your hands.'

With that he left her. But she was scarcely listening.

What plans was he making? What did he say of his marriage, behind locked doors in the presence of that man Wolsey?

A cold fear touched her heart. She went to her window and looked out on the river. Then she remembered the visit of the Emperor and that he would come again.

Henry wanted the friendship of the Emperor, for England, even as she did.

He would not be so foolish as to dare harm, by word or deed, the aunt of the most powerful monarch in Europe.

On a bleak January day Mary Boleyn was married to William Carey. The Queen honoured the bride and bridegroom with her presence, and the ceremony was well attended because Mary, on account of her relationship with the King, was a person of interest.

When Mary took the hand of her husband, there were whispers among those present. What now? they asked each other. Surely if the King were still interested in the girl he would have made a grander match for her than this. It could only mean that he had finished with her, and Mary – silly little Mary – had not had the wits to ask for a grand title and wealth as a reward for services rendered.

But Mary, as she passed among the guests, looked so dazzlingly happy that it appeared she had gained all she sought; and the same could have been said for Will Carey.

The Queen received the young couple's homage with something like affection – which seemed strange, considering how proud the Queen was and that the girl had lately been her rival.

The general opinion was that the King's affair with Mary Boleyn was over. The fact that Thomas Boleyn did not attend the ceremony confirmed this.

'I hear he has renounced her,' said one of the ladies to the nearest gentleman.

'Small wonder!' was the reply. 'Thomas was climbing high, doing his duty as complaisant father. He's furious with the girl and would have prevented the marriage if Mary had not won the Queen's consent.'

'And the Queen readily gave it – naturally.'

'Well, it is a strange affair, I grant you. This is very different from the Blount affair.'

'What of that child?'

'Doubtless we shall hear news of him some day, unless of course the Queen surprises us all and produces that elusive male heir.'

'Stranger things have been known to happen.'

Many furtive glances were sent in the Queen's direction and the whispered gossip went on, but Katharine gave no sign that she was aware of this.

She felt sure that there would be other mistresses. That had become inevitable since she no longer appealed to the King as a woman; and because she could not safely suffer more pregnancies he was not interested in her.

She had her daughter Mary, and Mary would one day be Queen because it was impossible for the King to have a legitimate son. It was sad, but it was something they must accept.

This at least, she told herself, is the end of the Boleyn affair.

The King and Queen sat at the banquet table; about them were assembled all the great personalities of their Court, for this was a ceremonial occasion. On the King's right hand sat the Cardinal, and every now and then they would put their heads together to whisper something which was for their ears alone. The complacent expression on the Cardinal's face was apparent; there was little he liked more than these grand occasions when the King selected him from all others and showed his preference.

This was particularly delightful when the noblemen of the Court could look on and see the King's reliance on him; and on this occasion the Duke of Buckingham was present, and he made no secret of his distaste for the King's preference.

The musicians played as the sucking pig was brought in and ceased as it was placed on the table by the steward; homage to the dish was expressed by a respectful silence.

The King looked on the table with drowsy eyes; he had already partaken of many dishes and his face was flushed with wine. His bright blue eyes were slightly glazed as they rested on the group of young girls who sat together at some distance from him.

It seemed that he was no longer enamoured of Mary Boleyn and that others might hope to take her place.

The Cardinal was aware of the King's glances and rejoiced.

He liked the King to have his pleasures. He had no desire for him to discover that statecraft could be more absorbing than the pursuit of women; when he did, that could mean a slowing down in Wolsey's rapid journey to the heights of power.

Wolsey wished his King to remain the healthy, active boy – the young man who could tire out five horses a day at the hunt, who could be an easy victor at the joust, who could beat all his opponents at a game of tennis; and whose thoughts ran on the pursuit of women.

Thomas More had said once: 'If the lion knew his strength, it would be hard for any man to rule him.'

No one knew the truth of this better than Wolsey. Therefore he planned to keep the lion unaware of his strength. At the moment he was so. Not through any lack of conceit but because it was so pleasant to be a figure of glory in the tiltyard, at the masques and balls, and to leave state matters to the efficient Cardinal. Why should he tire his eyes by studying state papers? Wolsey was the man for that. The King had often said with a rumbling laugh that a state document could bring a brighter shine to Wolsey's eyes than any wench could.

It pleased Henry that the shrewd Cardinal should be the perfect complement to the dazzling King. But the lion must not know his strength.

Wolsey looked about the company and his eyes came to rest on the Queen. There was one of whom he must be wary. Relations between them had been less cordial since the friendship of England with France, for, like the good Spaniard that she was, Katharine hated the French. She looked at Europe and saw the only two rulers of consequence there – François Premier and the Emperor Charles – and she knew that they must inevitably be the most bitter of enemies. Each fought for power and there would be continual strife between them. It was Katharine's great desire that England should be the ally of her nephew Charles; and she had blamed Wolsey for the *rapprochement* with François which had led to that fantastic spectacle at Guisnes and Ardres. She had been cool with him, a little arrogant, and would have to learn in time that none was allowed to show arrogance towards the great Cardinal – not even the Queen.

Rarely had the Cardinal felt so contented as he did at this banquet. He was climbing high and would go higher, never forgetting that the ultimate goal was the Papal chair, for once he had attained it he would be free from the whims of the King of England. Until then he must feign to submit to them.

He shall be kept in ignorance, thought Wolsey. Such blissful ignorance. Those bright blue eyes must be kept shining for conquest in the tiltyard and the ladies' chambers; they must not discover the delights of statecraft until the Cardinal had become the Pope.

The King's plump white hands were greasy with sucking pig; he called for music, and the minstrels began to play one of his songs, which could not fail to increase his good humour.

How easy to handle! thought Wolsey, and his eyes met those of Buckingham who gave him a haughty stare.

Buckingham turned towards Norfolk who was sitting beside him and made a comment which Wolsey knew was derogatory to himself. But Buckingham was a fool. He had spoken during the playing of the King's music.

'You do not like the song?' demanded Henry, his eyes suddenly narrowed.

'Your Grace,' answered Buckingham suavely, 'I was but commenting on its charm.'

'It spoils the pleasure of others when you drown the music with your chatter,' grumbled the King.

'Then,' answered Buckingham, 'would Your Grace allow the musicians to play it again that all may hear it in silence?'

Henry waved a hand and the tune was repeated.

Fool Buckingham! thought Wolsey. He was heading straight for trouble.

The Cardinal excelled at collecting information about those he wished to destroy. His spy ring was notorious throughout the Court. Did Buckingham think that because he was a noble duke – as royal as the King, as he loved to stress – he was immune from it?

The music over, the King rose from the banqueting table. On such an occasion it was the duty of one of his gentlemen to bring a silver ewer in which he might wash his hands. The duty was performed by noblemen of the highest rank, and on this occasion the task fell to the Duke of Buckingham.

The ewer was handed to Buckingham by one of his ushers; he took it and bowed before Henry who washed his hands as was the custom.

When the King had finished, the Cardinal, who had been standing beside Henry, put his hands into the bowl and proceeded to wash them.

For a few seconds Buckingham was too astonished to do anything but stand still holding the bowl. Then a slow flush spread from his neck to his forehead. He, the great Duke of Buckingham, who believed himself more royal than Henry Tudor, to hold the ewer for a man who had been born in a butcher's shop!

In an access of rage he threw the greasy water over the Cardinal's shoes, drenching his red satin robe as he did so.

There was silence. Even the King looked on astonished.

The Cardinal was the first to recover. He turned to Henry and murmured: 'A display of temper, Your Grace, by one who thinks himself privileged to show such in your presence.'

Henry had walked away and the Cardinal followed him.

Buckingham stood staring after them.

''Tis a sad day for England,' he muttered, 'when a noble duke is expected to hold the ewer for a butcher's cur.'

❀ ❀ ❀

In the King's private chamber, Henry was laughing.

''Twas a merry sight, Thomas, to see you there with the water drenching your robes.'

'I am delighted to have provided Your Grace with some amusement,' murmured Wolsey.

'I have rarely seen you so astonished. As for Buckingham, he was in a rage.'

'And in your presence!'

Henry clapped a hand on Wolsey's shoulder. 'I know Buckingham. He was never one to hold in his temper. And when you . . . Thomas Wolsey . . . not a member of the nobility, dipped your hands into the bowl . . .'

'As Your Grace's Chancellor . . .'

'Buckingham pays more respects to a man's family tree than to his attainments, Thomas.'

'Well I know it, for the man's a fool, and I thank the saints nightly that this realm has been blessed with a ruler who is of such wisdom.'

The King smiled almost roguishly. 'As for me, Thomas, I care not whether men come from butchers' shops or country mansions. I am the King, and all my subjects are born beneath me. I look down on one and all.'

'Even on Buckingham!'

'Why do you say that, Thomas?'

'Because the Duke has strange notions about his birth. He fancies himself to be as royal as Your Grace.'

The roguishness disappeared and a look of cruelty played about the tight little mouth. 'You said Buckingham was a fool, Thomas. We are once again in agreement.'

Now it was Thomas's turn to smile.

He believed the time had come to make an end of his enemy.

The Cardinal allowed a few weeks to pass; then one day he came to the King in pretended consternation.

'What ails you, Thomas?' asked Henry.

'I have made discoveries, Your Grace, which I hesitate to lay before you, of such a shocking nature are they.'

'Come, come,' said the King testily; he was in a white silk shirt and purple satin breeches, puffed and slashed, ready for a game of tennis.

'They concern my Lord Buckingham. I must regretfully advise your Grace that I believe him to be guilty of treason.'

'Treason!'

'Of a most heinous nature.'

'How so?'

'He lays claim to the throne and declares he will have it one day.'

'What!' roared the King, tennis forgotten. There was one subject which filled him, as a Tudor, with alarm. That was the suggestion that anyone in the realm had a greater right to the throne than he had. His father had had to fight for the crown; he had won it and brought prosperity to England, uniting the houses of York and Lancaster by his marriage; but the hideous Wars of the Roses were not so far behind that they could be forgotten; and the very mention of a pretender to the throne was enough to rouse Henry to fury.

'I have long suspected him,' the Cardinal soothed. 'Hence his hatred of me and the enmity between us. This I should feel towards any who sought to harm Your Grace. I have made it my duty to test his servants, and I now have the results of these labours to lay before Your Grace.'

'What are these results?'

'In the first place Buckingham feels himself to be as royal as your Grace.'

'The rogue!' cried Henry.

'He has said that there is no bar sinister on his escutcheon.'

Wolsey had the pleasure of seeing the red colour flame into the plump cheeks. 'He has told his confessor, Delacourt, that if you were to die and the Princess Mary were to die, he would have the throne.'

'By God!' cried the King. 'He shall lose his head – for it is his just deserts.'

'That is not all,' went on the Cardinal. 'I have learned that he consults a soothsayer, and that he has been told that one day he will mount the throne.'

'And how can he do this? Tell me that. Does he think to go to war . . . with *me*!'

'He's a fool, Your Grace, but not such a fool as that. He knows the people love you and that you have your friends. Soothsayers often practise another trade. I have heard they are often well versed in the art of poison.'

Henry was speechless for a few seconds. Then he burst out: 'We'll have him in the Tower. We'll have him on the rack. We'll have the truth from him. By God, his head shall be forfeit for what he has done.'

'Your Grace,' murmured the Cardinal, 'we must build up a case against him. This I believe we can do.'

'You mean we can send him to the scaffold?'

'Why should we not, if we can prove him guilty of treason?'

'He would have to be tried before his peers. Forget not, Thomas, that this is Buckingham; 'tis true that there is royal blood in his veins. You think his peers would judge him worthy of the traitors' death?'

'If the case were strong enough against him.'

'Norfolk would be one of his judges. You know the bonds between them. He and his fellows would be loth to condemn one of such nobility. Had he raised an army against the Crown, that would be another matter. But it would seem that he has done nothing but prate.'

'Against Your Grace!'

'Thomas, I understand you well. You serve me with all your heart. I brought you up, and you have had little but insults from these men. But they are the nobility; they make a shield around the throne. They have certain privileges.'

'Your Grace, I concern myself only with the safety of my master.' The Cardinal snapped his fingers. 'I care not that for this shield. Your Grace, I crave pardon but I say this: You know not your strength. All men about the throne should tremble at your displeasure . . . be they scullions or noble dukes. This could be so. This must be so. You are our lord and our King.'

For a few seconds the two men regarded each other. The

Cardinal knew that this was one of the most significant moments of his career.

He was showing the young lion that the golden walls of his cage were only silken strands to be pushed aside whenever he wished. Yet looking at this man of turbulent passions, even then the Cardinal wondered what he had done. But he was vindictive by nature; and from the moment he had seen the greasy water splash his satin robes he had determined at all costs to have his revenge.

The news spread round the Court.

'This cannot be,' it was whispered. 'What has he done, but talk? Who can prove that this and that was said? Who are the witnesses against him? A pack of disgruntled servants! This trial is a warning. Do not forget this is the noble Duke of Buckingham. He will be freed with a pardon and a warning.'

But the King's anger against Buckingham was intense when he examined the evidence which his Chancellor had put before him.

His face was scarlet as he read the report of Buckingham's carelessly spoken words. It was infuriating that anyone should dare *think* such thoughts, let alone express them. And in the hearing of servants, so that those words could be repeated in the streets, in taverns, wherever men congregated! This was treason.

And what care I, thought Henry, if this be a noble duke! Am I not the King?

For the first time he had realised the extent of his power. He was going to show all those about him that none could speak treason against the King with impunity. He was greedy for blood – the blood of any man who dared oppose him. He could shed that blood when and where he wished; he was the supreme ruler.

Norfolk came to him in some distress. Henry had never felt any great affection for Norfolk. The Duke seemed so ancient, being almost fifty years older than the King; his ideas were set in the past, and Henry thought that the old man would have liked to censure him if he dared. He had been young and daring in the days of Henry's maternal grandfather, Edward IV, but those days of glory were far behind him.

'Well, well?' Henry greeted him testily.

'Your Grace, I am deeply disturbed by the imprisonment of my kinsman, Buckingham.'

'We have all been deeply disturbed by the treason he has sought to spread,' growled the King.

'Your Grace, he has been foolish. He has been careless.'

'Methinks that he has too often repeated his treason to offer the excuse that he spoke in an unguarded moment. This is a plot . . . a scheme to overthrow the Crown, and there is one word for such conduct; that is treason. And I tell you this, my lord Duke, there is but one sentence which right-minded judges can pronounce on such a man.'

Norfolk was startled. He knew the King was subject to sudden anger, but he had not believed that he could be so vehemently determined on the destruction of one who had been in his intimate circle and known as his friend. And for what reason? Merely a carelessly spoken word repeated by a dissatisfied servant!

Norfolk had never been noted for his tact; he went on: 'Your Grace, Buckingham is of the high nobility.'

'I care not how high he be. He shall have justice.'

'Your Grace, he has erred and will learn his lesson. I'll warrant that after the trial he will be a wiser man.'

'It is a pity that there will be so little time left to him to practise his new-found wisdom,' said the King venomously.

Then Norfolk knew. Henry was determined on the death of Buckingham.

But even so, he could not let the matter end there. He and Buckingham were not only friends but connected by the marriage of his son and Buckingham's daughter. He thought of the grief in his family if Buckingham should die; moreover he must stand by the rights of the nobility. This was not rebellion against the King; Buckingham had not set out to overthrow the Crown. The King must be made to understand that, powerful as he was, he was not entitled to send the nobility to death because of a careless word.

'Your Grace cannot mean that you demand his *life*!'

The King's eyes narrowed. 'My lord Norfolk,' he said significantly, 'do you also seek to rule this realm?' Norfolk flinched and Henry began to shout: 'Get from here . . . lest you find yourself sharing the fate of your kinsman. By God and all His saints, I will show you, who believe yourselves to be royal, that there is only one King of this country; and when treason stalks, blood shall flow.'

Norfolk bowed low and was glad to escape from the King's presence. He felt sick at heart. He had received his orders. Buckingham was to be judged guilty by his peers; he was to pay the supreme penalty.

The pleasure-loving boy King was no more; he had been replaced by the vengeful man.

He stood at the bar, the reckless Buckingham, facing the seventeen peers, headed by Norfolk, who were his judges. His arms folded, his head held high, he was ready to throw away his life rather than beg for mercy.

Old Norfolk could not restrain his tears. He wanted to shout: This is madness. Are we going to condemn one of ourselves to the scaffold on the evidence of his servants?

But Norfolk had received his orders; he had looked into those little blue eyes and had seen the blood-lust there. Insults to the King, though carelessly uttered, must be paid for in blood; for the King was all-powerful and the old nobility must realise that.

Calmly Buckingham heard the charges brought against him. He had listened to prophecies of the King's death and his own ascension to the throne; he had said that he would kill the King; he had many times mentioned the fact that only the King and the Princess Mary stood between him and the throne.

He defended himself against these charges. He pointed out that none but his unworthy servants had been able to speak against him. Was the court going to take the word of disgruntled servants before that of the Duke of Buckingham?

But Wolsey had prepared the case against him skilfully; and moreover all seventeen of his judges knew that the King was demanding a verdict of guilty; and if any of them refused to give the King what he wanted, it would be remembered against them; and it was likely that ere long they would be standing where Buckingham now stood.

The old Duke of Norfolk might weep, but nevertheless when his fellow judges agreed that the prisoner was guilty he read the terrible sentence.

'Edward Stafford, third Duke of Buckingham, you are

found guilty of treason.' His voice faltered as he went on: 'You shall be drawn on a hurdle to the place of execution, there to be hanged, cut down alive, your members to be cut off and cast into the fire, your bowels burned before your eyes, your head smitten off, your body to be quartered and divided at the King's will. May God have mercy on your soul.'

Buckingham seemed less disturbed than Norfolk.

When he was asked if he had anything to say, he replied in a clear, steady voice: 'My lord, you have said to me as a traitor should be said unto, but I was never a traitor. Still, my lords, I shall not malign you as you have done unto me. May the eternal God forgive you my death, as I do!' He drew himself to his full height and a scornful expression came into his eyes. 'I shall never sue the King for my life,' he went on. 'Howbeit, he is a gracious Prince, and more grace may come from him than I desire. I ask you to pray for me.'

They took him thence back to his prison of the Tower, and those who had gathered to watch his progress knew that he was condemned when they saw that the edge of the axe was turned towards him.

Maria de Salinas, Countess of Willoughby, was with the Queen when she heard that the Duke of Norfolk was begging an audience.

Katharine had him brought to her at once, and the old man's grief distressed her because she guessed at once what it meant.

'I pray you be seated, my lord,' she said. 'I fear you bring bad news.'

He gazed at her, and he seemed to be in a state of bewildered misery.

'Your Grace, I have come from the court where I have pronounced the death sentence, for treason, on the Duke of Buckingham.'

'But this is impossible.'

The old Duke shook his head. 'Nay, Your Grace. 'Twas so.'

'But to find him guilty of treason . . .'

'It was the King's wish.'

'But his peers?'

The Duke lifted a trembling hand in resignation.

Katharine was indignant. She had known Buckingham to be arrogant, to have offended the Cardinal, to have been over-proud of his royal connections, but these were venial sins; a noble duke was not condemned to the barbaric traitors' death for that.

'It is known what influence Your Grace has with the King,' went on Norfolk. 'I have come to plead with you to beg him to spare Buckingham's life. I am certain that this sentence will not be carried out. I am sure that the King means only to warn him. But if Your Grace would but speak to the King . . .'

'I promise you I shall do so,' said Katharine.

The Duke fell to his knees and taking her hand kissed it.

'Maria,' said Katharine, 'send for my lord Surrey that he may look after his father.'

The Duke shook his head. 'My son is in Ireland, Your Grace. Despatched thither on the orders of the Cardinal.' His lips curved ironically.

'The Cardinal doubtless thought to spare him the anxiety of his father-in-law's trial,' the Queen suggested.

'He sent him away because he thought he might have spoken in his father-in-law's favour,' Norfolk replied roughly.

Poor old man! thought Katharine. Buckingham is very dear

to him and if this terrible sentence is carried out there will be mourning, not only among the Staffords, but the Howards also.

She shivered, contemplating the hideous ceremony of pain and humiliation. They could not do that to a noble duke!

She laid her hand lightly on Norfolk's shoulder. 'Rise, my lord,' she said. 'I will speak to the King and implore him to show mercy.'

'Your Grace is good to us,' murmured Norfolk.

When he had gone, Maria looked sorrowfully at her mistress.

'Your Grace . . .' she began.

Katharine smiled sadly at her dear friend. 'I know what you want to say, Maria. This is a dangerous matter. You want to advise me not to meddle.'

Maria said quickly: ''Tis so.'

'No harm can come to me if I plead for Buckingham. I am at least the King's wife, Maria.'

Maria did not answer. She was afraid of the new trend of events, afraid of what effect it would have on her mistress.

'I shall go to the King at once,' said Katharine. 'I want to put those poor people out of their misery as quickly as possible.'

There was nothing Maria could do; so, as Katharine left her apartment for the King's, she went to the window and stood looking broodingly out over the gardens.

The Cardinal was with the King.

'What now, Kate?' asked Henry, mildly testy.

'I would have a word with Your Grace if you will grant me a few minutes.'

'Say on,' said Henry.

Katharine looked at the Cardinal who bowed and went with reluctance towards the door.

'Henry,' said Katharine, catching her husband's sleeve, 'I want you to show mercy to the Duke of Buckingham.'

'Why so?' he demanded coldly.

'Because I believe that a warning will suffice to make him your very good friend in the future.'

'So we are to allow traitors to live?'

'It was not treason in the accepted form.'

'And what, I pray you, is the accepted form?'

'There was no rebellion. He did not take up arms against you.'

'How can you know what methods he used against me? I believe he was planning to poison me.'

'Henry, he would never do that. He was rash and foolish . . . but I do not think he would ever commit a crime like that.'

'And what can you know of the schemes of such a rogue?'

'I knew him well. He it was who met me when I first came to England.'

'I tell you this, Madam,' roared the King. 'Any who acts treason against me shall pay with his life – be he your dearest friend on Earth.'

'But Henry, he is a noble duke . . . the highest in the land.'

'So he believed. 'Twas his opinion of himself which brought him to where he is this day.'

'His relations are the most powerful in the land,' persisted Katharine. 'His wife, the daughter of Northumberland; the Percys will not forget. His son married to Salisbury's daughter. This will alienate the Poles. His daughter is married to Norfolk's son. The Howards will grieve deeply. Then there are the Staffords themselves. Four of our noblest families . . .'

Henry moved a step nearer to his wife. 'I forget none of this,' he said. 'And were my own brother – and I had one – guilty of treason, he should suffer a like fate.'

Katharine covered her face with her hands. 'Henry, shall a noble duke be taken out and barbarously killed before the eyes of the people!'

'The fate of traitors is no concern of mine. He was judged by his peers and found guilty.'

Meanwhile the Cardinal waited anxiously in the ante-chamber. He knew that the Queen had come to plead for Buckingham. She must not succeed.

Moreover it was necessary that the Queen herself should learn her lesson from the fate of this man. Once she and the Cardinal had been good friends; but now, since the friendship with France, she had looked on him with suspicion. He had heard himself referred to as a butcher's boy in her hearing, and she had offered no reprimand to the speaker.

It was not only noble dukes who must be taught that it was unwise to lose the friendship of the Cardinal.

He picked up a sheaf of papers and looked at them. Then with determination he passed through the ante-room into the King's chamber.

'Your Grace,' he said, 'I crave your pardon for the intrusion. An important matter of state requires your attention . . .'

The Queen looked angry, but that was of small importance as the King was not displeased.

He was saying: 'He shall die. But we will show mercy unto him. It shall be the executioner's axe in place of the sentence which you feel to be an insult to his nobility.'

The Cardinal was not ruffled.

The method mattered little to him, as long as Buckingham died.

❀ ❀ ❀

On a bright May day the Duke was brought out from his lodging in the Tower to meet his death on the Hill.

There were many to watch this nobleman's last hour on Earth. There were many to sigh for him and weep for him. He had been arrogant and reckless; he had been harsh to some of his tenants, causing them great hardship with his enclosure laws; but it seemed cruel that this man, who was in his early forties, should have to walk out of his prison to face death on such a bright May morning. His good characteristics were remembered; he was a very religious man and had founded colleges. And now he was to die because he had offended the King and the Cardinal.

He met his death bravely, as all expected he would; and while his body was being taken to its burial place in Austin Friars, among those who thought of him were the King, the Queen and the Cardinal . . . the Queen with sorrow, the King with righteous indignation, and the Cardinal with deep pleasure which was however pricked by apprehension.

Buckingham would insult him no more, but the Cardinal was too shrewd a man not to know that he had paid a high price for his vengeance.

A subtle change had crept into the King's demeanour. The lion was no longer couchant. He had risen; he was testing his strength.

And, when he had assessed the full measure of that power, who would be safe? A Queen? A Cardinal?

Chapter II

THE QUEEN'S ENEMY

In her apartments at Greenwich Palace the Princess Mary was being prepared by her women for a ceremonial occasion. They were all very excited and kept telling the little girl that she would be the target of all eyes on this occasion.

She wriggled beneath her headdress which seemed too tight.

'Be careful, my precious one,' said her governess. 'Remember, you must walk very slowly and as I have taught you.'

'Yes,' said Mary, 'I will remember.'

The women looked at her fondly. She was such a good child, rather too serious perhaps, but always eager to learn her lessons and please those about her.

Six-year-old Mary felt uncomfortable in the stiff gown, but she liked the dazzling jewels which decorated it; she pulled at the gold chain about her neck because it seemed so heavy.

'Careful, my lady. Hands down. That's right. Let me see the sort of curtsey you will make to your bridegroom when you meet him.'

Mary obediently made a deep curtsey, which was not easy in

the heavy gown, and several of the women clapped their hands.

'Does she not look beautiful!' asked one of another.

'She's the most beautiful and the luckiest Princess in all the world.'

Mary did not believe them, and knew that they were bribing her to behave in such a way that she would be a credit to them.

'What is the Emperor Charles like?' she asked.

'What is he like! He is tall and handsome and the greatest ruler in the world – save only your royal father, of course. And he loves you dearly.'

'How is it possible to love people whom one does not know?'

The child was too clever for them.

'Do you not love the saints?' her governess asked. 'And do you know *them*? Have you seen them and talked with them? Thus it is with the Emperor Charles. He has come all across the seas to hold your hand and promise to marry you.'

The little girl was silent, but there was nothing to fear, because her mother had told her that she was not to go away from her. Being affianced to the Emperor would make no difference at all; they would be together as before, she and her beloved mother.

Mary wished they could be together now, the two of them alone, in the royal nursery, bent over the books while she learned her Latin, and perhaps if her progress pleased her mother, to shut up the books and be allowed to sit at her feet while she told stories of those days when she was a little girl herself in far away Spain. There she had learned lessons in her nursery, but she had had sisters and a brother. How Mary wished that she had sisters and a brother. Perhaps only a brother would suffice. Then her father would not frown so when he remembered she was his only child and a girl.

No, there was no need to feel anxious about this coming ceremony. She had been affianced before. Strangely enough, although last time it had been to a French Prince, the ceremony had taken place in this very Palace; and she was not sure whether she remembered the occasion or her mother had told her about it and she thought she remembered; in any case it was vivid in her mind: Herself a little girl of two in a dress made of cloth of gold, and a cap of black velvet which was covered in dazzling jewels. There had been a man who had taken the place of her bridegroom-to-be because her bridegroom could not be present. He had only just been born, but he was very important because he was the son of the King of France, and her father had wanted to show his friendship for the King of France at that time. A diamond ring had been put on her finger; she was sure she remembered the difficulty she had had in trying to keep it on.

But that was four years ago, and now her father was no longer the friend of the King of France. She often wondered about that baby and whether he had been told that while he was in his cradle he was affianced to her; she wondered what he thought about it.

Now, of course, it might never have taken place; it was of no importance whatsoever.

What she did remember though, was her mother coming into her apartment and taking her in her arms and laughing with her, and weeping a little. 'Only because I am so happy, my darling daughter,' she had said.

The reason for the Queen's happiness was that there would be no French marriage. Instead there was to be a Spanish one.

'And this makes me happy,' said the Queen, 'because Spain is my country; and you will go there one day and rule that country as the wife of the Emperor. My mother, your grandmother, was once the Queen of Spain.'

So Mary had been happy because her mother was happy; and she shivered with horror to think that she might have been married to the little French boy; then she smiled with pleasure because instead she was to marry the Emperor who was also the King of Spain.

A page came into the apartment with the message for which Mary had been waiting.

'The Queen is ready to receive the Princess.'

Mary was eager, as always, to go to her mother.

The Queen was waiting for her in her own private apartments and when the little girl came in she dismissed everyone so that they could be alone; and this was how Mary longed for it to be. She wished though that she was not wearing these ceremonial clothes, so that she could cling to her mother; she wished that she could sit in her lap and ask for stories of Spain.

The Queen knelt so that her face was on a level with her daughter's. 'Why, you are a little woman today,' she said tenderly.

'And does it not please Your Grace?'

'Call me Mother, sweeting, when we are alone.'

Mary put her hands about her mother's neck and looked gravely into her eyes. 'I wish we could stay together for hours and hours – the two of us and none other.'

'Well, that will be so later.'

'Then I shall think of later all the time the ceremony goes on.'

'Oh no, my darling, you must not do that. This is a great occasion. Soon I shall take you by the hand and lead you down to the hall, and there will be your father and with him the Emperor.'

'But I shall not go away with him yet,' said Mary earnestly.

'Not yet, my darling, not for six long years.'

Mary smiled. Six years was as long as her life had been and therefore seemed for ever.

'You love the Emperor, Mother, do you not?'

'There is no one I would rather see the husband of my dearest daughter than the Emperor.'

'Yet you have seen him but little, Mother. How can you love someone whom you do not know?'

'Well, my darling, I love his mother dearly. She is my own sister; and when we were little she and I were brought up together in the same nursery. She married and went into Flanders, and I came to England and married. But once she came to England with her husband to see me . . .'

Mary wanted to ask why, if her mother loved her sister so much, she always seemed so sad when she spoke of her; but she was afraid of the answer, for she did not want any sadness on this occasion.

But into the Queen's eyes there had come a glazed look, and at that moment she did not see the room in Greenwich Palace and her little daughter, but another room in the Alcazar in Madrid in which children played: herself the youngest and the gravest; and Juana, in a tantrum, kicking their governess because she had attempted to curb her. In those days Juana had been the wild one; her sister had not known then that later she would be Juana the Mad. Only their mother, watching and brooding, had suffered cruel doubts because she remembered

83

the madness of her own mother and feared that the taint had been passed on to Juana.

But what thoughts were these? Juana was safe in her asylum at Tordesillas, living like an animal, some said, in tattered rags, eating her food from the floor, refusing to have women round her because she was still jealous of them although her husband, on whose account she had been so jealous, was long since dead. And because Juana was mad, her eldest son Charles was the Emperor of Austria and King of Spain and, since the discoveries of Columbus, ruler of new rich lands across the ocean. He was the most powerful monarch in the world – and to this young man Mary was to be affianced.

'*I* wasn't here when Charles's mother came.'

'Oh no, my darling, that was long, long ago, before you were born, before I was married to your father.'

'Yet you had left your mother.'

Katharine took the little face in her hands and kissed it. She hesitated, wondering whether to put aside the question; but, she reasoned, she has to know my history some day, and it is better that she should learn it from me than any other.

'I left my mother to come here and marry your uncle Arthur. He was the King's elder brother and, had he lived, he would have been the King, and your father the Archbishop of Canterbury. So I married Arthur, and when Arthur died I married your father.'

'What was my uncle Arthur like, Mother?'

'He was kind and gentle and rather delicate.'

'Not like my father,' said the girl. 'Did he want sons?'

Those words made the Queen feel that she could have wept. She took her daughter in her arms, not only because she was overcome by tenderness for her, but because she did not want her to see the tears in her eyes.

'He was too young,' she said in a muffled voice. 'He was but a boy and he died before he grew to manhood.'

'How old is Charles, Mother?'

'He is twenty-two years old.'

'So old?'

'It is not really very old, Mary.'

'How many years older than I?'

'Now you should be able to tell me that.'

Mary was thoughtful for a few moments; then she said: 'Is it sixteen?'

'That is so.'

'Oh Mother, it seems so many.'

'Nonsense, darling; I am more than ten years older than Charles, yet you can be happy with me, can you not?'

'I can be so happy with you, Mother, that I believe I am never really happy when I am away from you.'

The Queen laid her cheek against her daughter's. 'Oh my darling,' she said, 'do not love me too much.'

'How *can* I love you too much?'

'You are right, Mary. It can never be too much. I loved my mother so much that when I left her and when she left this Earth it seemed to me that she was still with me. I loved her so much that I was never alone.'

The child looked bewildered and the Queen reproached herself for this outburst of emotion. She, who to everyone else was so calm and restrained, was on occasions forced to let her emotions flow over this beloved daughter who meant more to her than any other living person.

I frighten the child with my confidences, she thought, and

stood up, taking Mary's hands in hers and smiling down at her.

'There, my love, are you ready?'

'Will you stand beside me all the time?'

'Perhaps not all the time, but I shall be there watching. And when you greet him I shall be beside you. Listen. I can hear the trumpets. That means they are close. We should be waiting to greet them. Come. Give me your hand. Now, darling, smile. You are very happy.'

'Are you happy too, Mother?'

'Indeed, yes. One of the dearest wishes of my heart is about to be fulfilled. Now we are ready to greet my nephew, who will be my son when he is the husband of my beloved daughter.'

She held the little hand firmly in hers; and together they descended to the hall for the ceremonial greeting.

As the royal cavalcade came from Windsor to Greenwich the people massed in their thousands to watch their King pass by. Loudly they cheered him, for he was a magnificent sight on horseback, and beside him the Emperor appeared a somewhat poor figure. The King of England was over six feet tall, his skin was pink and smooth as a boy's, his blue eyes were bright and clear, and he glowed with good health, so that in comparison the Emperor looked pallid and unhealthy. His teeth were prominent and none too white, and he breathed through his mouth which was perpetually ajar; his aquiline nose had a pinched look and the only colour in his face was the blue of his eyes. He was serious, whereas the King of England was gay; he smiled faintly while Henry roared forth his good humour.

But he seemed happy to be in England, and Henry was clearly pleased with him because of the contrast they made and the attention which was therefore called to his own many physical perfections.

As they rode along Henry was thinking of the masques and pageants with which he would impress this young man; but Charles was thinking of the loan he must try to wring from the English. As his father had been, he was perpetually in need of funds to maintain his vast Empire, and in his struggle with the King of France he needed money to pay his mercenaries.

He knew that he would have to pay a price for English gold and English support, and had at last decided that he would accept betrothal to the Princess Mary. He had come to this decision with some reluctance – not because he was against an English match, not that he did not believe the child to be un-usually accomplished; but it was distressing to contemplate her age and that he could not hope for an heir until at least eight years had passed. However, there was nothing to be done but accept the inevitable as graciously as he could, for he was fully aware that alliance with England was not only desirable but a necessity.

So as they rode along he listened to the King's conversation, laughed at his jokes and gave an impression to all who saw them that they were the best of friends.

In the cavalcade rode the Cardinal and, as always, his retinue was as magnificent as that of the King. He was wearing his red robes of taffety this day – the finest obtainable – and about his neck hung a tippet of sables; borne before him was the great seal, and one of the noblemen, whom he had deigned to take into his household, carried his Cardinal's hat on a cushion and was bareheaded to indicate the respect he had for it; behind him rode other gentlemen of his household and his higher servants in their red and gold livery.

Wolsey was uneasy during that ride. He felt that since the death of Buckingham the King had taken too great an interest in state affairs. He was inclined to meddle and he did not always want to follow in that direction in which Wolsey would have led him.

The Cardinal was no more sure of this quiet young man than he was of the flamboyant François. In fact he felt that it would be necessary to be even more wary of the Emperor. François was dashing, bold, reckless and lecherous; and a shrewd statesman could often guess which turning he would take. But this pale, serious young man, who was somewhat hesitant in speech and had an air of humility – which Wolsey knew to be entirely false – might be unpredictable and by far the shrewdest ruler of the three who were now so important in Europe.

Charles had had the foresight to recognise that, if he were to consolidate the alliance he wished for, he must first placate Wolsey, and for that reason he had promised the Cardinal a considerable 'pension'. The thought of vast sums being paid to him from the Imperial coffers was sweet, but some promises were made to be broken; and Wolsey was not certain whether Charles was to be relied on. He had also promised what was more important still: to use his influence at the Papal election, for the great goal of the Cardinal was the Papal crown since, possessing that, he would stand apart from kings, a ruler in his own right. He yearned for that crown.

There had been a disappointment early that year when Pope Leo X had died and a Papal election had taken place. Wolsey had felt that his chances of election were slender, but the promise of Imperial favour had sent his hopes soaring. He received only seven votes, and Adrian VI was elected.

This was not such a bitter disappointment as it might have

been, for the Cardinal did not believe Adrian would live long and it seemed certain that another election would be held before many months had passed. If by that time Wolsey could show himself to be the true friend of the Emperor it might be that the promise of help would this time be fulfilled.

Perhaps he had no reason to feel disappointed; he was rising higher and higher in his own country and only last year Henry had presented him with the Abbey of St Albans, doubtless to repay him for the money from his own pocket which he had spent on the recent embassy to Calais, whither he had gone to help settle differences between François and the Emperor.

And now the friendship with Charles was being strengthened and a treaty had been signed at Windsor in which Henry and Charles agreed on an invasion of France before the May of 1524.

This was where the King had shown himself inclined to meddle. Wolsey himself was not eager to go to war. War to him meant expense, for even with victory the spoils were often scarcely worth the effort made to obtain them. But war to Henry meant the glory of conquest, and it was as irresistible to him as one of the games he played with such *élan* at a pageant.

Still, a goodly pension from the Emperor, the promise of Imperial support at the next Papal election, and the need to fall in with the King's wishes – they were very acceptable, thought Thomas Wolsey as he rode on to Greenwich.

At the door of the Palace stood the Queen holding the hand of her daughter.

The Emperor dismounted and went towards them. He knelt before his aunt and, taking her hand, kissed it fervently.

Mary looked on, and she thought she loved the Emperor – firstly because he was so delighted to see her mother and looked at her so fondly; secondly because her mother was so pleased with him; and thirdly because there was nothing in that pale face to alarm a six-year-old girl.

Now he had turned to greet Mary. He took her hand and stooped low to kiss it; and as he did so there was a cheer from all those watching.

The King could not allow them to keep the centre of the stage too long and was very quickly beside them, taking his daughter in his arms to the great delight of all who watched, particularly the common people. They might admire the grace of Charles, but they liked better the King's homely manners. Henry knew it, and he was delighted because he was now the centre of attention and admiration.

So they went into the Palace, Mary walking between her father and mother while the Emperor was at the Queen's side.

Katharine felt happy to have with her one who was of her own family, although Charles did not resemble his mother in the least, nor was he, with his pallid looks, like his father who had been known as Philip the Handsome.

A momentary anxiety came to Katharine as she wondered whether Charles resembled his father in any other way. Philip had found women irresistible, and with his Flemish mistresses had submitted the passionate Juana to many an indignity, which conduct it was believed had aggravated her madness.

But surely there was no need to fear that her daughter would be submitted to similar treatment by this serious young man.

'I am so happy to have you with us,' she told her nephew.

'You cannot be more delighted than I am,' replied Charles

in his somewhat hesitant way; but Katharine felt that the slight stammer accentuated his sincerity.

Henry said: 'After the banquet our daughter shall show Your Imperial Highness how skilful she is at the virginals.'

'It would seem I have a most accomplished bride,' replied Charles and when, glancing up at him, Mary saw he was smiling at her with kindliness, she knew he was telling her not to be afraid.

So into the banqueting hall they went and sat down with ceremony, when good English food was served.

The King looked on in high good humour. He was pleased because he and the Emperor were going to make war on François, and he had sworn vengeance on the King of France ever since he, Henry, had challenged him to a wrestling match only to be ignobly thrown to the ground by that lean, smiling giant.

He was even pleased with Katharine on this occasion. She had played her part in bringing about the Spanish alliance; for there was no doubt that the Emperor was more ready to enter into alliance with an England whose Queen was his aunt than he would otherwise have been.

Henry caught the brooding eye of his Cardinal fixed on the pale young man.

Ha! he thought, Wolsey is uncertain. He is not enamoured of our nephew. He looks for treachery in all who are not English. 'Tis not a bad trait in a Chancellor.

He thought of how Wolsey had bargained when they had made the treaty. A good servant, he mused, and one devoted to the interests of his King and country.

Enough of solemnity, he decided, and clapped his hands. 'Music!' he cried. 'Let there be music.'

So the minstrels played, and later Mary sat at the virginals and showed her fiancé how skilful she was.

'Is it possible that she is but six years old!' cried Charles.

And the King roared his delight.

'I think,' said the Emperor, 'that with one so advanced it should not be necessary for me to wait six years for her. Let me take her with me. I promise you she shall have all the care at my court that you could give her at yours.'

Katharine cried in alarm: 'No, no. She is too young to leave her home. Six years is not so long, nephew. You must wait six years.'

Charles gave her his slow, kindly smile. 'I am in your hands,' he said.

Mary who had been listening to this conversation had grown numb with terror. Six years was a life-time, but he wanted to take her now. This young man no longer seemed so kindly; he represented a danger. For the first time in her life she became aware that she might be taken from her mother's side.

Katharine, who was watching her, noticed her alarm and knew the cause. She said: 'It is past the Princess's bed time. The excitement of Your Excellency's visit has exhausted her. I ask your leave for her to retire to her apartments.'

Charles bowed his head and Henry murmured: 'Let her women take her to bed, and we will show our nephew some of our English dances.'

So Mary was taken away while the royal party went into the ballroom; and soon the King was dancing and leaping to the admiration of all.

Katharine slipped away when the revelry was at its height and went to her daughter's apartment, where she found Mary lying in her bed, her cheeks still flushed, her eyes wide open.

'Still awake, my darling?' Katharine gently reproved.

'Oh, Mother, I knew you would come.'

Katharine laid a hand on the flushed forehead. 'You are afraid you will be sent away.'

Mary did not answer but her small body had begun to tremble.

'It shall not be, my little one,' went on the Queen.

'The Emperor said . . .'

'He meant it not. It was to compliment you that he spoke those words. It is what is called diplomacy. Have no fear, you shall not leave me for a long, long time . . . not until you are old enough to want to go.'

'Mother, how could I ever want to go from you?'

Katharine lifted the little hand and kissed it.

'When you grow up you will love others better than your Mother.'

'I never shall. I swear I never shall.'

'You are too young to swear eternal love, my darling. But I am here now. I slipped away from the ball because I knew you would be fretting.'

Katharine lay on the bed and held the child in her arms.

'Oh Mother, you love me, do you not?'

'With all my heart, sweeting.'

'And I love you with all of mine. I never want to go away from England, Mother . . . unless you come with me.'

'Hush, my sweetheart. All will be well. You will see.'

'And you will not let the Emperor take me away?'

'No . . . not for years and years . . .'

The child was reassured; and the Queen lay still holding her daughter fondly in her arms, thinking of a young girl in Spain who had been afraid and had told her mother that she wished to stay with her for ever.

This is the fate of royal children, she told herself.

The comfort of her mother's arms soothed Mary and soon she slept. Then Katharine gently disengaged herself; the Queen must not stay too long from the ball.

The King was momentarily contented. He was at war with France and he dreamed of being one day crowned in Rheims. His temper was good. He spent more time than he ever had engaged on matters of state, and the Cardinal, seated beside him, explaining when the need arose to do so, was feeling certain twinges of uneasiness.

He had been forced to support the war somewhat against his wishes; yet he was too wily to let anyone know that he was against it. The King wished it and Wolsey had no intention of arousing Henry's anger by seeming lukewarm about a project which so pleased the King.

Henry had inherited the wealth which his miserly father had so carefully accumulated; but he had spent lavishly and already the treasury was alarmingly depleted.

'Nothing,' said the Cardinal, 'absorbs wealth as quickly as war. We shall need money if we are to succeed in France.'

The King waved a plump hand. 'Then I am sure there is no one who can raise it more ably than my good Chancellor.'

So be it, thought Wolsey. But the levying of taxes was a delicate matter and he suspected that the people who were obliged to pay them would blame, not their glittering charming King, but his apparently mean and grasping Chancellor.

There was talk of the King's going to France with his army,

but although Henry declared his eagerness to do this, nothing came of it. His adventures abroad with his armies in the earlier years of his reign had not been distinguished although he had thought they had at the time. Much as Henry would have enjoyed riding through the streets of Paris, a conqueror, and even more so returning home to England as the King who had brought France to the English dominions, he was now wise enough to realise that even hardened campaigners did not always succeed in battle, and that he was a novice at the game of war. Failure was something he could not bear to contemplate. Therefore he felt it was safer to wage war on the enemy with a strip of channel between himself and the armies.

François Premier was a King who rode into battle recklessly; but then François was a reckless fellow. He might win his successes, but he also had to face his defeats.

So Henry put aside the plans for a personal visit to the battlefields. But war was an exciting game played from a distance, and Wolsey must find the money to continue it.

These were happy days for the Queen. Her husband and her nephew were allies and they stood together against the King of France whom she believed to be more of a menace to Christianity than the Turk. François, already notorious for his lecherous way of life, must surely come to disaster; and since her serious-minded nephew had the power of England beside him she was certain that Charles was invincible.

She had her daughter under the same roof with her and she herself supervised her lessons.

Mary was docile and happy as long as her mother was with

her. The King left Katharine alone, it was true, but she believed that even he had ceased to fret for a son, and accepted the fact that their daughter Mary was heir to the throne; and one day when she married Charles she would be the Empress of Austria and the Queen of Spain as well as the Queen of England. That matter was happily settled.

She was constantly seeking the best method of teaching her daughter, and one day she summoned Thomas More to her that she might discuss with him the manner in which his own daughters were educated.

As usual she found great pleasure in his company. She talked a little about the war but she saw that the subject was distressing to him – which was to be expected, for he was a man to whom violence was abhorrent – so she turned the conversation to his family, which she knew could not fail to please him.

She told him of her desire that the Princess Mary should receive the best education in all subjects which would be of use to her, and Thomas said: 'Has your Grace thought of consulting Juan Luis Vives?'

'I had not until this moment,' she said, 'but now that you mention him I believe he is the man who could help me in the education of the Princess. I pray you, bring him with you and come to see me at this hour tomorrow.' When Thomas had left her she wondered why she had not thought of Vives before. He had so much to recommend him. In the first place he was one of her own countrymen and she felt that, as her daughter was after all half Spanish and would be the wife of the King of Spain, there must be a Spanish angle to her education.

Both Erasmus and Sir Thomas More had called her attention to Juan Luis Vives, and those two were men whose intellectual abilities had won the admiration of the world. Vives was a man, said Thomas, forced by poverty to hide his light under a bushel. He was living at Bruges in obscurity; he had published very little of his writings and few people had ever heard of him. Erasmus would bear him out, for Vives had studied Greek with him at Louvain. It was Thomas's opinion that Vives should be brought to England and encouraged by the Court, for there was little his native Valencia or the city of Bruges could offer him.

Katharine, out of her great admiration for Thomas, had immediately sent money to Vives with a letter in which she explained her interest in his work. It had not been difficult to persuade Henry – with the help of Thomas More – that Vives would be an ornament to the English Court; and Henry, who, when he was not masking or engaged in sport, liked occasionally to have conversation with men of intellect (François Premier boasted that his Court was the most intellectual in Europe and Henry was eager to rival it) very willingly agreed that Vives should be given a yearly pension.

Thus in gratitude Vives dedicated his book, *Commentaries on Saint Augustine* to Henry, which so delighted the King that he called him to England to lecture at the college which Wolsey had recently founded at Oxford.

This had happened some years before, but Vives made a point of spending a certain part of each year in England with his friends and patrons; and it so happened that he was in London at this time. So the very next day he arrived in the company of Thomas More for an interview with the Queen regarding her daughter's education.

Katharine received them in her private apartment and they sat together at the window overlooking the Palace gardens as they talked.

'You know, Master Vives, why I have commanded you to come to me?' asked Katharine.

'My friend has given me some idea of what Your Grace desires,' Vives answered.

'My daughter's education is a matter which is of the utmost importance to me. Tell me how you think this should be arranged.'

'Sir Thomas and I are of one opinion on the education of young people,' said Vives.

'It is true,' added Thomas. 'We both believe that it is folly to presume that a girl's education is of less importance than that of a boy.'

'It is but natural,' went on Vives, 'that an intelligent girl may come to a better understanding of Latin and Greek than a boy who is not possessed of the same intelligence.'

'I would have my daughter educated in scholarly subjects, but at the same time I wish her to learn the feminine arts,' answered Katharine.

'In that I am in full agreement with Your Grace,' said Vives.

'What more charming sight,' mused Thomas, 'than a girl at her embroidery?'

'Or even at the spinning wheel working on wool and flax,' added Vives. 'These are excellent accomplishments, but Your Grace has not summoned me to discuss them.'

'I am going to appoint you my daughter's tutor,' the Queen told Vives, 'and I wish you immediately to draw up a list of books for her to read.'

Vives bowed his head. 'I will go to my task with the utmost pleasure, and I can immediately say that I think the Princess should read the New Testament both night and morning, and also certain selected portions of the Old Testament. She must become fully conversant with the gospels. She should, I believe, also study Plutarch's *Enchiridion*, Seneca's *Maxims*, and of course Plato and Cicero.' He glanced at his friend. 'I suggest that Sir Thomas More's *Utopia* would provide good reading.'

The Queen smiled to see the look of pride on Thomas's face, thinking that his few vanities made him human, and therein lay the secret of his lovable nature.

'And what of the *Paraphrase* of Erasmus?' asked Thomas quickly.

'That also,' agreed Vives. 'And I think the Princess should not waste her time on books of chivalry and romance. Any stories she might wish to read for her entertainment should either be sacred or historical, so that her time is not wasted in idleness. The only exception I would make is the story of Griselda, which contains such an excellent example of patience that the Princess might profit from it.'

Katharine said: 'I can see that you will be an excellent tutor, but we must remember that she is but a child. Her life must not be all study. There must be some pleasure.'

Vives looked surprised; to him the greatest pleasure was in study, and he believed the Princess to be the most fortunate of children, having such a plan of study made for her.

Thomas laughed. 'I'll swear the Lady Mary, who so loves her music, will find time to escape to it from her books now and then. I know my own daughters . . .' (Katharine noticed the look of pride when he spoke of his daughters, which was even more marked than when he spoke of his books) '. . . are proficient in Greek and Latin but they find time to be merry.'

'Yours is a merry household,' answered the Queen.

And she found that she was comparing the King and Thomas More – two fathers who could not be more unlike. She had seen Thomas in company with his eldest daughter, Margaret, had seen them walk, their arms entwined, had heard the girl's unrepressed laughter ringing out as she scolded her father in an affectionate way. It was impossible to imagine Mary and Henry thus.

What a fortunate man, this Thomas More; what a fortunate family!

'There is much merriment at Court,' answered Thomas gravely.

But he understood of course – he was a man who would always understand – and a great tenderness touched his face; the Queen knew that it expressed the compassion he felt for her little daughter, who would study alone – not as Thomas's family did – and would be taught by the somewhat stern though excellent Vives instead of merry Thomas.

Somewhere from the grounds she heard the sound of laughter, and glancing down saw a group of young people. They made a charming picture on the grass in their brightly coloured clothes, and there was one girl among them who appeared to be the centre of attraction. She was dark-haired, dark-eyed, somewhat sallow of complexion and, although not a beauty, certainly striking. She seemed to have more vitality than any other member of the group and was quite clearly taking the attention of the young men from the other girls who were present.

'A high-spirited party,' said the Queen; and Vives and Thomas More glanced out of the window. 'That girl seems familiar but I do not recall who she is. Surely that is Thomas Wyatt with her – and Henry Percy.'

'The girl is Thomas Boleyn's daughter, Your Grace,' Thomas told her.

Then Katharine knew of whom the girl reminded her. It was Mary Boleyn. The resemblance was slight, otherwise she would have realised immediately. This girl had an air of dignity and assurance, and pride too – all qualities in which Mary had been dismally lacking.

'This is the second girl, I believe,' said the Queen.

'Recently home from France on account of the war,' explained Thomas.

'Doubtless her father is looking for a place at Court for her,' said the Queen.

'He will find it,' replied Thomas, 'not only for Anne but for his George also.'

'I trust,' said the Queen, 'that this Anne is not like her sister in her morals, and that George does not bear too strong a resemblance to his father.'

'From what I have seen of them,' Thomas answered, 'I should say they are a dazzling pair.'

'Well then, I suppose we must resign ourselves,' said the Queen with a smile, 'for it seems the Boleyns have come to Court.'

The Cardinal had shut himself in his private apartments at Hampton Court; seated at the window from which he could see the river, he was waiting for a message which was all-important to him, for it would tell him whether his greatest ambition was realised or not.

The pale November sun shone wanly on the river. He thought: I shall miss Hampton Court; I shall miss England.

He would miss his family too; but he would find means of seeing them. He would have young Thomas in Rome with him, because he would very quickly overcome all difficulties. He thought of Rodrigo Borgia, Alexander VI, who, while living in the Vatican, had yet arranged to have his children with him; for a Pope was as powerful as a King; and once he was supreme in the Vatican, the frowns of unpredictable Henry would be of little moment to him.

Yet, he mused, I shall not forget my own country, and it will be a good day for England when an Englishman takes the Papal Crown.

How long the waiting seemed! He would see nobody. He had told his secretaries that he was to be disturbed only by messengers from abroad because he was working on important matters of state.

But soon the messenger must come.

He began to pace the apartment because he could no longer bear to stare at the river.

His chances were good. On the death of Leo X when Adrian VI had been elected, his hopes had been slender. Why should the Cardinals have elected a comparative newcomer to their ranks, an Englishman who had not previously worked closely with the Vatican? That election had taken place at the beginning of the year, and Adrian's tenure of the Papacy had indeed been a short one for in September news had come to England of his death, and for the next two months the Cardinal had given less thought to affairs in England; his mind was on what would happen at the next conclave.

Since the election of Adrian and his death the Emperor Charles had visited England, and he had become more aware than he had been before of the important part played by the Cardinal in the foreign policy of England. To win Wolsey's approval of the alliance he had offered large sums of money, a pension no less; but Wolsey had begun to grow uneasy because none of these sums of money had yet been paid; and he could get no satisfaction as to when they would be from Louis de Praet, who was now Charles's Ambassador in England.

Money was needed to prosecute the war, was the excuse, and Wolsey was angry to contemplate the riches which were being squandered on useless battlefields in Europe, riches which could have been used not only to make the country prosperous but would have enabled him to increase his personal treasures.

But there was one concession which Charles could make and would cost him little in money; and this was what the Cardinal needed more than anything else in the world: His influence at the Conclave. The powerful Emperor, of whom every Cardinal would stand in awe, had but to make it known that he wished to see an English Pope in the Vatican and that those who depended on his bounty were to give their vote to Cardinal Wolsey, and the Papal crown would be won.

This the Emperor could do. He would do it, He must . . . since he had failed to supply the pension.

'If he does not . . .' said Wolsey aloud, but he did not continue.

He would not face the possibility of failure. The Emperor could and would.

The Cardinal's unpopularity throughout the country was growing, and people looked on sullenly when he paraded the streets on his way to Westminster. He went in all his splendid pomp, but that did nothing to appease the people's anger, but rather increased it. They were openly murmuring against him.

He had always known, during his brilliant career, when it was time to move on, so now he was aware that he had reached the pinnacle of power in England, and that it was time to take the final step to Rome. It must be now, for there might not be another opportunity.

This war will end in failure, he thought. And when there are failures, scapegoats are sought. Who would make a better scapegoat, in the eyes of the people, than the opulent Cardinal?

He was alert because he had seen a boat pulling up at the privy stairs, and he guessed it could be his messenger.

He tried to curb his impatience; he was so eager to go down to meet the man, but, as much as he longed to, he must remember his position and his dignity.

How long it seemed to take for him to cross the park! Now he had entered the palace. Soon the usher would come to his door.

I must be calm, he told himself. I must show no excitement, no eagerness.

Cavendish was at the door.

'A messenger is without, Your Eminence. He asks that he may be brought at once to your presence.'

'A messenger?' He was sure the beating of his heart disturbed the red satin of his robe. 'Let him wait . . . no, on second thoughts I will see him now.'

Cavendish bowed low. Now he would be traversing the eight rooms to that one in which the messenger waited . . . the all-important messenger. It seemed an hour before he was standing on the threshold of the room.

'You have a message for me?' he said.

'Your Eminence,' said the man and held out a roll of parchment.

As Wolsey took it it seemed to burn his fingers, but still he restrained himself.

'You may go now to the kitchens. Tell them I sent you and you are to be refreshed.'

The man bowed and was gone; so at last he was alone.

He tore at the parchment, his trembling fingers impeding him; he felt dizzy and it was some seconds before he read the words which danced like black demons on the parchment scroll.

He stared at them and tried to force them by his dominant will to reform themselves into what he wished to read.

But of what use was that? The result was there for him to see and there was nothing he could do to alter it.

'Cardinal de' Medici has been elected the new Pope of Rome, Clement VII.'

Never since the days of his obscurity had he known a defeat like this. Disappointed he had been when Adrian was elected; but then he had been sure that there would shortly be another conclave, and he had needed the time to consolidate his forces.

But when would he have another chance? Perhaps never.

This was the darkest moment of his life so far. He had come such a long way; he could not believe in failure. Was he to fail with the very peak of achievement in sight? It seemed so.

Then a burning rage took possession of him. It was directed against one man – a sly pallid youth who had promised so much and done so little, who had seemed perhaps a little simple in his humility. But there was no real humility behind those mild blue eyes. A wily statesman lurked there, a statesman who believed he could best outwit his rivals by deceiving them with their belief in his own incompetence.

Wolsey spoke softly to himself: 'The Emperor has done this. He has refused me the Papal crown as he has the pensions he promised me. He shall regret it, as all those shall who become the enemies of Thomas Wolsey.'

All through the winter Wolsey successfully hid his rancour against the Emperor while he was waiting for his opportunity. Determined to break the friendship between Henry and Charles, he kept a sharp watch on Katharine for, since her nephew was his enemy, she must be also.

He asked the King's permission to introduce a new woman to the Queen's intimate circle, and Henry, delighted to do his Chancellor a favour, agreed that the woman should become one of the Queen's maids of honour.

Katharine did not like the woman, but she was enjoying her new peaceful existence too much to protest. She need not see much of her; and in any case she was so completely wrapped up in her daughter that she had little time for anything or anyone else. Vives's curriculum was certainly a strenuous one and sometimes she thought Mary spent too much time in study; however the little girl was a willing pupil and, to help her, Katharine herself studied with her and commanded some of the ladies of the Court to do likewise.

Being so pleasantly engaged she scarcely noticed the woman and thus gave her excellent opportunities for hiding herself when the Spanish Ambassador called and had conversations with the Queen; nor was it difficult to find a means of conveying those letters, which the Queen wrote to her nephew, to Wolsey before they were sent to Spain.

As for the Cardinal, he had always been able to wait for revenge and, as he had never favoured the Spanish policy and had always thought that alliance with the French would be a better alternative, he began to plan to this end.

The winter passed; there were good reports of the progress

of the war, but no material gains came the way of the English; and the King preferred to forget what was happening on the Continent in the Christmas and New Year Revels.

During these Katharine was aware on several occasions of Thomas Boleyn's daughter Anne who always seemed to be in the centre of a merry and admiring group, with either Wyatt or Henry Percy at her side. Katharine had noticed the King, glowering at these young people as though their high spirits annoyed him. Could it be that he was angry because he was no longer quite so young; was he tiring of pageants and masques?

All through the spring and summer there was news of the war, but none of it good. Wolsey was trying to raise money; the Emperor was still making promises to pay, not only what he had borrowed, but Wolsey's pension.

That is money we shall likely never see, thought Wolsey; but he did not tell the King this because Henry was at the moment eager to maintain his alliance with Charles, and his hatred of François was as strong as ever.

One summer's day Dr Linacre, the King's physician, begged an audience of the Queen, and when he came into her presence he brought a bouquet of beautiful roses.

Katharine congratulated him warmly because she knew that he had recently brought this rose to England, and had succeeded in making it grow in English soil.

The doctor was delighted and as he bowed low before her Katharine smiled at his enthusiasm and held out a hand to take the roses.

'They are beautiful,' she cried.

'I knew Your Grace would think so. I have come to ask permission of you and the King to present you with trees I have grown.'

'I am sure His Grace will be delighted.'

'I had doubts that they would grow in our soil. Our climate is so different from that of Damascus.'

'And you have succeeded magnificently. I know the King will be as pleased as I am to accept these trees.'

'I have called it the Damask Rose,' said the doctor.

'An excellent name, and so explicit.'

She was still admiring the roses when the King entered the apartment. The peaceful atmosphere was immediately disturbed for the King's face was of that faintly purplish tinge which nowadays indicated anger, and his eyes ice-blue, his mouth tight.

'Your Grace,' began the doctor, who could think of nothing but the pleasure his roses gave him and, he believed, must give all those who looked at them, 'I have been showing the Queen the new Damask Rose.'

'Very pleasant,' said the King shortly.

'Dr Linacre wishes to present us with trees too,' said the Queen.

'They will be some of the first to be planted in this country, Your Grace,' went on the doctor. 'I shall count it an honour ...'

'We thank you,' said the King. He took one of the roses in his hand and studied it, but Katharine knew that he gave it little attention. 'It is indeed beautiful. We accept the trees. They shall be tended with care, and I am sure give us pleasure for many years to come.'

The doctor bowed and asked the Queen's permission to take some of the roses to the Princess Mary. Katharine gave that permission willingly and the doctor took his leave.

When he had gone, Henry walked to the window and stood glowering out.

Katharine knew that it was on occasions like this when his dogs and all wise men and women kept their distance from him, but she was his wife and must know what disturbed him, so she asked: 'Does aught ail you, Henry?'

He turned and she noticed how his lower lip jutted out.

'Oh, 'tis naught but the folly of young Percy.'

'Northumberland's son?'

'Yes, Henry Percy. The young fool has been presumptuous enough to promise marriage to one of the girls of the Court.'

'And you cannot grant permission for this marriage?'

'Northumberland's is one of the most noble families in the land,' growled Henry.

'Is the girl whom he has chosen so lowly?'

'She is not of his rank.'

'So far below him then?'

'It is Thomas Boleyn's girl.'

'Oh?' The Queen thought of the girl as she had seen her about the Court – a flamboyant personality, one made to attract attention to herself, decidedly French in manners and style of dressing. Indeed since the beginning of the French wars, when the girl had come to England, fashions had been changing and becoming more French, which was strange when it was considered that the English were at war with that country. 'I have noticed her often,' went on the Queen. 'She seems to be one who attracts attention to herself. I have seen Percy with her and Wyatt also.'

'Wyatt is married so he could not make a fool of himself,' muttered the King.

'Thomas Boleyn has risen in your favour in the last years, Henry. Is the girl so very much below Percy?'

'Come, come, he is the eldest son of Northumberland. His father will never consent to the match.'

'But the girl's mother is a Howard and . . .'

Henry made an irritable gesture, wriggling his shoulders like a petulant boy. 'Northumberland is coming to Court to forbid his son to have anything to do with the girl. Indeed she is pledged already to marry the son of Piers Butler. As to Percy, he is to marry Shrewsbury's girl – Mary Talbot . . . a suitable match.'

Katharine stared sadly before her. She was sorry for the lovers.

'I thought the Boleyn girl to be well educated, and she has a certain dignity.'

The King turned on her angrily. ''Tis a most unsuitable match. The Cardinal has already reprimanded that young fool Percy and made him see his folly. 'Tis a pity he ever took service with the Cardinal, since it has brought him into close contact with the girl.'

'Percy will be docile,' said the Queen. She remembered him as she had last seen him at the side of that vital, glowing girl, and she had seen what a contrast they made – she so full of life, he so gentle, weak almost. She was certain there would be no rebellion from Percy.

'He had better be,' said the King. 'In any case he's banished from Court and has been ordered not to see the girl again. His duty now is to marry Mary Talbot as soon as possible, and we shall see that that is done.'

'Ah well, Henry, then the matter will be settled. But I am surprised that you should feel so strongly about it.'

'You are surprised!' The King's eyes were fierce. 'Let me tell you that the welfare of the young people at my Court is my greatest concern.'

'I know it well.'

The King strode from her apartment; and she continued to wonder why he should have been so incensed by such a trivial matter.

She saw Anne Boleyn a few days later, and all the sparkle seemed to have gone out of her. She was dejected and sullen.

Poor girl! pondered the Queen. She is heartbroken at the loss of her lover.

She wondered whether to send for her and offer her comfort; but decided that would be unwise, and tantamount to acting against the wishes of the King.

A week passed and she remembered that she had not seen the girl; so she asked one of her women if Anne Boleyn was still at Court.

'No, Your Grace,' was the answer, 'she has returned to Hever Castle on the King's command.'

Banished from Court! And simply because she accepted Percy's offer of marriage.

The King's anger was unaccountable.

As the Cardinal bent over the documents on his table his usher entered and told him that a merchant of Genoa was craving an audience with His Eminence.

'What is his business?' asked the Cardinal.

'He would tell me nothing, Eminence, except that he had merchandise to show you which he would show no other, and that he felt sure you would be willing to grant him an interview if you would but look at the nature of the articles he has to lay before you.'

Wolsey was thoughtful. Was he right when he fancied there was a hint of subtlety in the merchant's words? What was the nature of the merchandise he wished to show? Could it be information – secret information?

A year ago he would have had the merchant told that he might call again; since his defeat at the Papal election he had added that to his caution which he had subtracted from his dignity.

'Bring the man to me,' he said.

Cavendish retired and returned in a few moments with a dark-skinned man who carried a bag in a manner to suggest that what it contained was very precious indeed.

'You may leave,' Wolsey told Cavendish; and as soon as he was alone with the Genoese, the man set down his bag and said: 'My lord Cardinal, I am not merely a merchant. I come on behalf of one who is eager to negotiate with you.'

'And who is that?'

'The Duchesse of Savoy.'

The Cardinal was silent. He knew that in truth this man was a messenger from François Premier, because, in everything François did, his mother, Louise of Savoy, was firmly behind him. Therefore if this man did indeed come from the Duchesse, it was tantamount to coming from the King of France.

At last Wolsey spoke. 'For what purpose are you here?'

'My lady Duchesse knows full well the perfidy of the Emperor, which Your Eminence has so recently had reason to deplore. She believes that England would be happier in friendship with the King of France than with this perfidious Emperor. She knows that the King of England is deeply involved with the Emperor, that the Princess Mary is the Emperor's betrothed; but she feels that a greater understanding could be possible between France and England if Your Eminence and she were friends. She sends you letters which I bring to you; and if it should please Your Eminence to answer these letters, your reply can be safely trusted to my care.'

'Your credentials?' asked the Cardinal.

The merchant opened his bag and produced papers which Wolsey studied.

These told him that he was in the presence of Giovanni Joachino Passano, a man whom he could trust; Passano was in England as a merchant and would carry on that trade. If the Cardinal could find lodgings for him it would make their meetings easier to arrange and he would be always at his disposal as the go-between for correspondence between France and England.

The Cardinal was thoughtful.

He was determined to end the war, the cessation of which was necessary for England's solvency; he was equally determined to show the Emperor that he could not neglect his promise to Thomas Wolsey with impunity. Secret communications with France would be useful at this moment.

'I shall lodge you in London with a servant of mine in whom I have the utmost trust,' he said. 'As a merchant of Genoa it will be understood that you are constantly travelling between London and the Continent. I shall study these papers you have brought to me and it may be that I shall wish you to carry my answers to the Duchesse.'

'If that is so, Your Eminence, I shall be at your service.'

'Let me see the articles you have brought with you to sell.'

For the next ten minutes the Cardinal examined the

exquisite cloth which the merchant showed him; then he summoned one of his pages and told him to send in a certain servant, one who did not live in the Cardinal's intimate entourage but had his lodgings in London.

When this man arrived he said to him: 'Here is Giovanni Joachino Passano, a merchant from Genoa, who has brought me rich cloth. I wish him to return to Genoa in due course to bring me more, but for the time being he needs lodgings in London. Take him into your house, that he may be near at hand when I wish to give him my orders.'

The servant was delighted to be so selected and assured the Cardinal that the Genoese merchant should have the best room in his house, and all the respect deserved by one whose merchandise pleased the Cardinal.

Wolsey nodded his approval in a manner which implied good services would not be forgotten.

And so the agent of Louise of Savoy – who was naturally the servant of François Premier – had his lodgings in London; and the Cardinal often called him to Hampton Court, where they would remain together and alone, sometimes for hours at a time.

The King came riding to Greenwich from Hever Castle where he had been spending a night as the guest of Sir Thomas Boleyn. As soon as he reached the Palace he summoned the Cardinal to his presence.

He greeted Wolsey with the pleasure he habitually bestowed upon his favourite minister, but there was a change in his manner which baffled the Cardinal.

He seemed almost subdued, which was rare in Henry; he

looked more like a boy than ever and there was a certain gentleness about him which the Cardinal had never seen before.

''Twas pleasant in the country,' he said. 'I declare Boleyn's castle of Hever is a restful place in which to spend a night.'

That was strange also. When had Henry ever asked for restfulness?

'Your Grace took but a small party with you?'

''Twas enough. I declare, Thomas, I am weary of ceremony on every occasion.'

''Tis pleasant for Your Grace to escape now and then; and may I say that it is doubly pleasant for your servant to see you again.'

'Good Thomas,' murmured the King, but the Cardinal felt that his attention was elsewhere.

Was this a good time to let him know that it might not be difficult to make peace with France, to whisper in the royal ear those first drops of poison regarding the Emperor? It seemed likely while he was in this gentle mood.

'Boleyn entertained me royally at his castle,' went on Henry musingly. 'I thought I would show my gratitude by granting him certain land. You might see what we could do for him.'

'It shall be so, Your Grace.'

'I had thought of elevating him to the peerage . . . as Viscount Rochford.'

'This would take time, Your Grace.'

'Yes, yes,' said Henry testily. 'But it is in my mind to do so.'

'He is a fortunate man to have found such favour in Your Grace's eyes, particularly as his daughter so recently offended you.'

'Ah . . . the girl.' The King began to smile. 'A haughty wench, Thomas. I saw little of her during my stay at Hever.'

'She was absent from her home?'

'Indisposed.'

'Your Grace was doubtless glad not to be bothered by the presence of the girl, preferring the company of her father.'

'Bold,' mused Henry, 'and haughty.'

'Your Grace believes this indisposition to have been sulks on account of banishment from Court. The saucy wench should be clapped into prison for behaving so.'

'Nay nay,' said the King. 'I do not disturb myself with the vagaries of girls. I believe her to have declared she will be revenged on you, Thomas.'

Thomas laughed. 'Should I tremble, Your Grace?'

'I notice she has flashing black eyes and the look of a witch. She blames you for sending Percy back to his father.'

'She should blame Percy for being so easily persuaded, or herself for choosing such a lover.'

'As usual, Thomas, you speak good sense.'

Wolsey bowed his head in appreciation of the compliment and went on: 'Your Grace, I confess I am disturbed about the war.'

'Ah yes.' The King seemed reluctant to end the discussion of his trip to Hever.

'I do not trust the Emperor.'

'I begin to agree with you, Thomas.'

'We have been pouring our resources into war and have so far not gained a foot of French soil. If Your Grace considers our expenditure . . .'

'I am considering it, Thomas, considering it with great sadness.'

'Look at the progress the Emperor has made. He has driven the French from Italy. But what gain to us is that? He has strengthened his frontiers in the Netherlands and Spain. That is good . . . for the Emperor. I would say, Your Grace, that in Charles we have another such as Maximilian.'

Henry nodded and his face darkened, as he remembered how he had been duped by Charles's grandfathers – the Emperor Maximilian and Ferdinand of Aragon.

'I had hoped much from the rising of the Duke of Bourbon against François,' said Henry.

'And we hoped in vain, Your Grace.'

'Well, Thomas, what can we do?'

'I should be ready to forget all that we have spent on this enterprise and put out feelers for a separate peace with France.'

The King's frown sent a shiver of alarm through the Cardinal. Fleetingly he wondered what Henry's reaction would be if he discovered that Giovanni Joachino Passano paid regular visits to him, not to sell him cloth but to carry letters back and forth between the chief of the King's ministers and the mother of François. One thing was certain; he was playing a dangerous game.

The King was like a child who had set his heart on a certain glittering bauble; in this case the conquest of France. Such a project was an impossibility – Wolsey knew.

'Despatches from the Emperor have been increasingly gloomy, Your Grace.'

Henry stuck out his lower lip like a petulant child.

'I have poured money into this project,' he began.

'And the Emperor asks for more, Your Grace. He says that unless we provide it the entire enterprise may be fruitless. It would appear now that even the Pope . . . .' Wolsey's voice was faintly bitter . . . 'whom he helped to elect, is uncertain of him!'

'Ah, the Pope!' said Henry, and an alert expression had

crept into his face. He knew it had been a bitter disappointment to Wolsey that he was not elected, and he wondered how he himself would have fared, robbed of the services of his Chancellor. It seemed to him in that moment that there was a tinge of disloyalty in the Cardinal's disappointment. 'You were over-eager to leave us, Thomas,' he said with a trace of petulance.

'Solely that I could have worked for England from the Vatican.'

Henry was sorry for his suspicions. 'I believe that to be so,' he said. 'Well, it did not happen as we wished it, Thomas. But Clement is a good friend to you and to me.'

'He could not be the friend of one and not the other,' said Wolsey.

''Tis true,' answered the King. 'And I rejoiced when he confirmed your Legateship for life, and gave you the Bishopric of Durham.'

'Your Grace is good to me.'

'Well, you have a King and a Pope as your good friends, Thomas; I wonder which you value the more.'

'Your Grace does not need me to answer that question.'

Henry smiled well pleased, and the Cardinal knew that no rumours had reached him concerning the French spy in their midst.

'Then Your Grace would not be prepared to think of peace?'

'Thomas, there is one reason why I stand firmly with the Emperor and, no matter what our losses, there I shall remain. Do not forget that he is betrothed to the Princess Mary. While he adheres to that promise we must forgive him if he breaks some others.'

The Cardinal then understood that he must continue to work in secret.

The Queen and her daughter sat with some of the women of the Court busily working with their needles. As they bent over their work one of their number read to them from Thomas More's *Utopia*; this was a custom which Katharine remembered from the days of her childhood, when her mother had sought to have the hands usefully employed while the mind was exercised.

Katharine's life was becoming increasingly busy. She spent a great deal of time with her daughter, whose education was, she believed, in constant need of her supervision. Her daughter was her greatest joy, and while she had her with her she could not be unhappy. Mary was now nine years old and it was distressing to remember that in three more years she would be expected to leave her home and go to the Court of the Emperor. Three years was such a short time. But I must not be selfish, thought the Queen. My daughter will be a great Queen, and it is not for me to regret that which is necessary to make her so.

Nevertheless, she wished to have her with her at every moment of the day, so that none of the time which they could spend together would be lost.

Now they were working on small garments which would be given to the poor women who had babies and no means of clothing them. Katharine was alarmed by the growing poverty among some classes in England; she knew that many people were wandering from town to town, village to village, homeless, sleeping in barns and under hedges, working when they could, eating when they could; and, as was inevitable in these circumstances, now and then stealing or starving to death.

Thomas More, when he came to her intimate suppers, had on several occasions spoken of his growing anxiety about the new conditions in England. He had pointed out that the prosperity of the upper classes was in some measure responsible for the poverty of the lower. There was a great demand for fine cloth which meant that many of the land-owners, deciding to keep more sheep, took small-holdings from the men who had hitherto farmed them, and turned them into grazing land. The land which had been rented to them lost, turned out of their cottages, hundreds of these small farmers had become vagabonds.

Thomas More had said that the enclosing of land had so far affected no more than about five per cent of the entire population but he felt that to be a great deal.

Katharine was therefore doing all she could to right this evil, and she had appointed her Almoner to distribute funds from her own purse to the poor. She set aside a regular portion of her income for charity and took a great pleasure in providing the needy with clothes and food. Thus, temporarily, she abandoned the tapestry which she delighted to work and set herself and her women making garments for the poor.

Thus they were sitting together when a page entered to tell the Queen that the Seigneur de Praet, the Emperor's ambassador in England, was without and begging an audience.

As it was rarely that she had an opportunity of seeing her nephew's ambassador, she said that she would receive him at once; and this meant the dismissal of all present.

Seeing the look of disappointment in Mary's face she took the child's hand in hers and kissed it. 'Go along now for your practice on the virginals,' she said. 'When the Seigneur has left I will come and hear how you are getting on.'

Mary smiled and curtseyed; and the Queen's eyes remained on her until she had disappeared. Almost before the ladies had all left the apartment the Seigneur de Praet was being ushered in.

Katharine received him with graciousness although she did not feel the same confidence in him as she could have had in an ambassador of her own nationality. But the Seigneur, as a Flemish nobleman, was preferable, in Charles's eyes, to a Spaniard. Katharine had to remember that Charles was more Fleming than Spaniard because he had spent very little time in Spain and had been brought up in Flanders, so it was natural, of course, that he should choose Flemings rather than Spaniards to represent him.

The Seigneur was a very grand gentleman and he had already been unwise enough to show his lack of respect for Cardinal Wolsey on account of the latter's humble birth. It seemed incredible to him that he should be expected to treat with one who, so rumour had it, had spent his infancy in a butcher's shop.

As for the Queen, he found her so Spanish in some ways, so English in others, that he had never felt on very easy terms with her. Moreover whenever he had sought an interview he had always found it difficult to reach her; and he suspected the reason. The Cardinal contrived this – and for what cause? Because, for all his outward protestations, he was no friend of the Emperor.

Now de Praet was excited because he had made an important discovery and was determined at all costs to lay it before the Queen. Strangely enough on this occasion he had found no difficulty in reaching her.

As Katharine welcomed him and he bent over her hand, one of the women who had been in the sewing party slipped away unnoticed from the group of women who had just left and went swiftly into the ante-room adjoining the Queen's apartment. There she took up her stand near the door and very quietly lifted the latch so that it was slightly ajar without seeming to be so.

'Your Grace,' said de Praet, 'it is a great pleasure to find myself at last in your presence.'

'You have news for me from the Emperor?'

'No, but I have discovered treachery which I must immediately lay before you. Our enemy is working against us. Your Grace knows whom I mean.'

'The French?'

'*They* work continually against us. I was referring to one nearer at home who, while he pretends to be our friend and supports the King's war, is in fact working against us.' He lowered his voice and whispered: 'The Cardinal.'

'Ah!' said Katharine.

'It does not surprise you.'

'Nothing the Cardinal did would surprise me.'

'What can be expected . . . He was not born to this.'

'Do not let us underestimate his skill,' said the Queen. 'He is a brilliant man. It is for this reason that we must be very wary of him.'

'Your Grace will be surprised when I tell you that I have discovered he is in secret negotiations with the French.'

'Without the King's knowledge!'

'That I cannot say, Your Grace, but he is a traitor to my master and your nephew. There is a certain merchant from Genoa, now lodging with one of his servants, and this man is a regular go-between for François and Wolsey.'

'It is impossible!'

'Not with such a one. I can tell you we should never have trusted him.'

'The King knows nothing of this, I am sure.'

De Praet lifted his shoulders. 'It is impossible to know what the King knows, how far Wolsey works in conjunction with His Grace, how far on his own account.'

'Should not the King be told of Wolsey's action?'

'If the King is already aware of these negotiations with France – and we must not lose sight of this – we should be playing into their hands by telling them of our discovery.'

Katharine was horrified. It seemed to her that Charles's ambassador was drawing her towards a controversy in which she might well, by supporting her nephew, be obliged to work against her husband. This was reminiscent of those days of humility before her marriage to Henry when her father, Ferdinand, had used her in his negotiations with Henry's father.

She said quickly: 'I fear my nephew has made promises which he has not kept.'

'The Emperor is engaged in bitter war and needs all the money he can find to prosecute that war; he has little to spare for bribes.'

'He has accepted loans and has not repaid them,' Katharine reminded him.

'He will . . . in due course. Your Grace knows that he is a man of honour.'

'I am sure of that.'

'Then Your Grace will write to the Emperor and tell him of these discoveries? He should be warned.'

'I could not work against the King.'

'This would not be so. You would merely be telling him of the Cardinal's perfidy. Your Grace, it is imperative that he should be aware of this. I myself shall write and tell him, and to stress the urgency of the situation I beg of you to do the same.'

'I will write to him,' said the Queen.

De Praet bowed. 'If you would do so with all speed I believe you would be doing your nephew a great service.'

'I will do so without delay.'

'Then I shall take leave of you that you may lose no time. I do assure Your Grace that the matter is urgent.'

As soon as he had left her she went to her table and took up writing materials, carefully considering what she would say to her nephew. She began by imploring him to be frank with her husband, to let him know exactly how the war was progressing, and above all not to make promises unless he was sure he could keep them. She added that the Cardinal was aggrieved because he believed that with the Emperor's help he might have achieved the Papacy. She implored Charles to be aware of Wolsey who was as vindictive as he was ambitious. There were rumours that he was already pondering the desirability of a *rapprochement* with the enemy. Charles must not make the mistake of so many who believed that because of Wolsey's humble origins he lacked ability; rather should he believe that the Cardinal possessed a shrewd and brilliant brain; for the more lowly his beginnings, the greater must be his brilliance, since he had come so far.

Carefully she sealed the letter and summoned a page.

One of her women was coming towards her, having slipped unseen from the ante-room wherein she had overheard the conversation between Katharine and de Praet.

'I want a page to take this to the courier,' said Katharine.

'If Your Grace will allow me I will take it to him.'

Katharine handed the letter to the woman, who took it not to the courier, but to another of the Cardinal's spies. It was not difficult to find one as the Cardinal had them placed in the most strategic positions in the Court, and one of these was undoubtedly the Queen's household.

'Take this with all speed to the Cardinal,' she instructed.

Then she joined the ladies who were stitching together and listening to *Utopia*.

The Cardinal read the Queen's letter which she had addressed to her nephew. So it was known that he was in negotiation with the French! He did not relish the Queen's comments about himself; but they did not surprise him for he had long suspected that she regarded him as an enemy.

It would be unfortunate if his negotiations with Louise of Savoy through Passano were made known to the King by Charles's ambassador. He did not think this was likely, because his spies were thick about the ambassador and all his correspondence came to Wolsey before it went overseas. It was not difficult to reconstruct the ambassadorial seal; and the Cardinal had felt it was a matter of common sense that he should ascertain what de Praet was writing to his master at such a time.

If the letters contained news which Wolsey did not wish Charles to receive they were destroyed; only those which were innocuous went through. De Praet was scarcely a subtle ambassador; Charles must realise this. He would have been wiser to have chosen a Spaniard rather than a Fleming. The Cardinal had always had more respect for the solemn subtleties of the Spaniards than for the brash *bonhomie* of the Flemish.

De Praet concerned him but little for if he became dangerous some means could be found to remove him; it was the Queen with whom his thoughts were occupied. She would be an enemy of some consequence. He would never lose sight of the fact that she was not only the King's wife and mother of the heir to the throne, but also the aunt of the Emperor. Relations between the King and the Queen were not of the best; but still she was the Queen and as such wielded a certain influence.

She was therefore a potential enemy to be watched with the utmost diligence; and as the Cardinal had always believed in crippling the power of those who he feared might harm him, he began to think frequently about the Queen.

In the meantime he burned the letter which she believed was on its way to the Emperor, and decided to be ready for the first opportunity which came his way.

It came soon, as he expected it would.

He had been going over the cost of the war with Henry, a subject which never failed to make the King angry. Wolsey could see that it would not be difficult to wean him from the Emperor, and that it was only the hope of marrying Mary to Charles that caused him to remain Charles's ally.

'This marriage is of such importance,' murmured Wolsey. 'And it should be taking place within three years. The Queen already mourns because her daughter will have to go away. Alas, daughters must leave their royal homes; which is always so sad for those who love them. With sons . . .'

The King was startled. Few people were bold enough to mention the subject of sons in his presence. He looked at the Cardinal who was staring idly before him.

Wolsey went on as though to himself: 'I do not altogether despair.'

'What's this?' growled Henry.

Wolsey made a show of appearing startled. 'Your Grace, I crave your pardon. My thoughts ran on. It is unforgivable in your presence, but I forgot . . .'

'Of what do you not despair?'

Wolsey pretended to hesitate. Then as the King frowned he went on: 'It is a matter which occupies my thoughts day and night.'

'What is?'

'Your Grace's happiness; Your Grace's contentment.'

The King looked slightly mollified but he said sullenly: 'You speak in riddles.'

'Louis XII did it satisfactorily. Your Grace's sister Margaret did it in Scotland . . .'

Light dawned in the King's face; the little eyes were suddenly ablaze with interest. There was no need to ask what his Chancellor meant, because the people he had mentioned had rid themselves of unwanted spouses.

'Well,' said Henry as Wolsey did not go on, 'what have you in mind?'

'I have spoken too soon,' murmured Wolsey. 'I am certain there must be a way . . . I am certain that we can find it. But so far I cannot see it clearly.'

'Thomas,' said the King almost tenderly, 'I have known you but once fail to reach your objective and that was when you did not get the Papal Crown.'

'I relied on false friends then, Your Grace. It is a good lesson to have learned. Henceforth let us rely on none but ourselves.'

Henry nodded.

'And you say there is a way out for me?'

'I shall not rest,' said the Cardinal, 'until I see Your Grace the sire of a healthy boy . . . nay, not one, but several.'

'How is this possible?'

'As it has been possible for others.'

'Divorce!' whispered Henry.

'Your Grace, let us make this our secret matter. Let us keep it constantly in our minds. That is what I do when a problem baffles me. Leave it there . . . maturing, one might say. It so often happens that after a while the answer presents itself.'

The King grasped his Chancellor's hand.

'You bring me that which I had almost lost, Thomas. You bring me hope.'

The Cardinal returned that affectionate smile. 'It shall come to pass because Your Grace can only know contentment when he gives his country what it most needs.'

'How well you know me, Thomas.'

'It may be necessary for Your Grace to harden his heart. You will remember how nobly you married your brother's widow. Your brother's widow . . .' he repeated emphatically.

'I know full well,' replied Henry. 'But I tell you this, Thomas, though I am a man with feelings most tender, I am a King also.' The little mouth was prudish suddenly. 'And I would not consider the fine feelings of Henry Tudor if my duty to my kingdom dictated that I should overcome them.'

'Then, Your Grace, let us bring our minds to bear on it . . . and for a time . . . this shall be our secret matter.'

The King was excited and well pleased.

So the battle had begun, the Cardinal told himself. Let those who set themselves against Thomas Wolsey beware – even though they be queens.

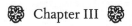

Chapter III

THE JILTING OF MARY

The King glanced at his confessor, John Longland the Bishop of Lincoln, and shook his head gloomily. He had confessed his sins and received absolution; but he did not dismiss the Bishop who waited, believing that the King had not confessed all that was on his conscience.

'Your Grace has something else to tell me?'

'A certain matter hangs heavily upon my conscience,' began the King.

'It appears so, Your Grace.'

'Then I will tell you, for it may well be that you can find some comfort to offer me. I would have you turn to the twentieth chapter of Leviticus, and you will see what disturbs me.'

The Bishop took his bible and turned to that chapter.

'I pray you read verse twenty-one,' said the King.

The Bishop read: ' "And if a man shall take his brother's wife, it is an unclean thing; he hath uncovered his brother's nakedness; they shall be childless." ' He stopped reading and was silent, not daring to make comment.

Then Henry said: 'You see! You have read that. Does it not

state clearly God's will? They shall be childless . . . and in all these years . . .'

Seeking to comfort the King, the Bishop said quickly: 'God cannot be displeased with Your Grace. He has given you the Princess Mary.'

'A girl!' snarled the King. 'I think of those sons which were born to us. Born dead. Again and again God gave us signs of His displeasure . . . and we heeded them not. We went on living . . . in sin.'

'Your Grace distresses himself unduly. There may yet be a son.'

'There will be no son,' Henry shouted.

'Your Grace, there was a dispensation. There is no need for Your Grace to feel anxious.'

The King's eyes narrowed. He snapped: 'There is every need. This burden of sin lies heavy on my conscience. I, who have lived as near to God as a man can live . . . I who have heard Mass five times a day . . . have confessed my sins regularly and have always obtained absolution . . . I, the King, have offended against the laws of God. I have lived for all these years with a woman who is not my wife in the eyes of God. So He tells me this . . . He denies me my son. Do you not see that while I live thus there will never be a son!'

'Your Grace, let us pray for God's help.'

Henry could have cuffed the Bishop. He was no Thomas Wolsey. He was anxious to please the King but he lacked the Chancellor's wits. He thought to please him by assuring him that he had nothing to fear, that his marriage was legal.

Fool! Fool! he thought. Then he remembered the Chancellor's injunctions: As yet it is our secret matter.

He went on to his knees, and while the Bishop prayed he

thought: Thomas is right. Good Thomas. 'Tis a delicate matter. There is the Emperor to be thought of. He will never stand aside and see his aunt repudiated. We have to go carefully. So . . . caution for a while.

When they rose from their knees, the Bishop said: 'Your Grace is unduly concerned; I shall redouble my prayers that you may be blessed with a son.'

And the King's feelings were under such control that instead of roaring 'Fool' at the man, he merely murmured: 'I thank you, Bishop. I too shall pray.'

In his private chamber at Hampton Court the Cardinal was reading the letters which de Praet had written to the Emperor. There was matter therein which if laid before the King could bring about the man's downfall.

Had the time come to expose the ambassador to the King?

Wolsey was for prompt action. François and Louise were restive, and they were anxious for an immediate secret alliance with the English against the Emperor. An end, thought Wolsey, to this senseless war. What could be more desirable?

Although his spies worked well for him, there must be occasions when it was impossible to learn all that passed between the Queen and her nephew's ambassador.

The case against the Queen must necessarily move slowly. But, thought Wolsey, you are doomed, Madam. You have yet to discover that. But I shall find a French Princess for Henry, and then the bonds with your perfidious nephew will be cut for ever.

What of Mary? Well, that marriage was three years away and more royal marriages were proposed than celebrated.

He wished that he could take de Praet's letters to Henry and say: You see how your ally's ambassador works against you. You see what an opinion he has of your Chancellor who cares more for your welfare than his own.

He was sure Henry would be furious; and then would be the time to bring forward those French ambassadors, whom he had waiting in hiding, that they might treat with Henry.

Yet how could he go to the King and say, My spies bring me the ambassador's letters; I have a method of breaking the seals and resealing them so expertly that none could guess they have been tampered with. Might not the King question the honour of his Chancellor? Of course he could explain that what he had done had been in the interest of the State; but it was never wise to expose one's methods too freely.

Wolsey had an idea. The city gates were closed each evening, and if any foreigner tried to pass through them he would be arrested by the watch and brought before a royal officer. If the Cardinal gave orders that any letters found on suspected persons were to be brought to him personally, and if he could delay de Praet's courier until the gates of the city had been closed, it was certain that the letters found on that courier would find their way to his table. It was almost certain too that those letters would contain words which would not please the King. And what more reasonable than that the Cardinal, so assiduous in the protection of the King's realm, should read those letters in person, and lay them before his master?

It was the way to deal with the matter and not difficult, with so many spies surrounding the ambassador, to waylay his courier and prevent his attempting to leave the city until after the gates were closed; and as the man did not know the city's laws the plot worked as smoothly as Wolsey could have hoped.

In a very short time the courier had been arrested by the watch as he attempted to leave the city, searched, and the letters found. They now lay on Wolsey's table.

Luck was with him. Both the King and Wolsey were referred to in these documents in a manner which was slighting, and Wolsey could scarcely wait to reach the King's apartments.

'A matter of some importance, Your Grace.'

The King waved a hand and those men who had been with him immediately departed leaving Henry alone with his Chancellor.

Wolsey quickly told Henry what had happened and as he laid the documents before him, was delighted to see the rich colour flood the plump cheeks and the eyes blaze with anger.

'I had long suspected him,' said Wolsey; 'and now Providence has enabled me to lay evidence of this man's perfidy before Your Grace.'

'He shall go to the Tower!'

'A foreign ambassador, Your Grace?'

'By God, this is treason.'

'As he is an ambassador of the Emperor, might I suggest that we place guards at the door of his house and forbid him to leave?'

'Let it be done!' commanded the King.

The Seigneur de Praet stood before the Cardinal in the latter's private chamber at Hampton Court. The Flemish nobleman looked with something like scorn at the red satin garments of the Chancellor; he had felt incensed, as he disembarked at the privy stairs and walked across the grass, at the sight of that magnificent edifice; but when he had entered the place and seen the gloriously apparelled servants, the valuable treasures in every room, he had said to himself: Is it possible that a man of the people could own so much? He was resentful, believing possessions and honours to be the prerogative of the nobility.

It was easy when he was not in the presence of Cardinal Wolsey to sneer at his origins; when he stood before him he could not help being conscious of the man's intellectual power; the rather protruding brown eyes of the man of the people seemed to look into his mind, discovering his secret thoughts, to suggest that the reason he clung to the importance of his noble birth was because, knowing himself at a mental disadvantage, he sought to flaunt every little asset he possessed.

Archbishop of York, Cardinal, Papal Legate and Chancellor. So many great titles for one man to hold – and he a man who had risen from the people. In spite of one's prejudices, one must feel in awe of such achievements.

He was received almost haughtily by the Cardinal's stewards. They would make His Eminence aware of the Seigneur's arrival. Had His Eminence summoned him to Hampton Court? Because if this was not so, they doubted whether they could disturb His Eminence at such an hour.

This was an insult. It did not occur to him that it might be intended. He presumed the servants to be ignorant of his standing.

'Tell the Cardinal,' he said in his haughtiest manner, 'that the Ambassador of His Imperial Highness, The Emperor of Austria and the King of Spain, calls upon him at his own wish.'

He was kept waiting for fifteen minutes and then, fuming

with rage, was led through the eight splendid rooms to the Cardinal's private apartment. Wolsey was seated at his table and did not rise when the ambassador entered.

What can one expect of a butcher's son? de Praet asked himself.

Wolsey continued to study the paper before him for a few seconds until de Praet said angrily: 'I have come as you asked me to, my Lord Cardinal.'

'Oh, yes,' said Wolsey, laying aside the paper with what appeared to be reluctance. 'I have bad news for you, Mr Ambassador.'

There was insult in the title and de Praet felt the blood rushing to his face. Was he, the Emperor's ambassador, to be kept standing while the Cardinal remained sitting at his desk! He might be a servant come to receive a reprimand.

'Bad news!' he cried. 'What bad news is this?'

'Your courier was arrested last night and certain documents were taken from him.'

'My courier! This is an insult to the Emperor.'

'It happened quite naturally,' explained the Cardinal. 'He delayed his departure until the gates of the city were closed. As you may know, the law says that all foreigners, attempting to enter or leave the city after the gates are closed, are arrested and searched.'

'But he should have left before that. What delayed him?'

The Cardinal lifted his shoulders and smiled. 'It is useless to ask me to keep an eye on your servants, Seigneur. This is what has happened. The letters you have written to the Emperor were brought before me. I had no recourse but to read them. We have to be very careful when dealing with those whom we believe to be spies. As it so happened I considered the contents of those letters treasonable, and I saw that it was my duty to lay them before the King.'

De Praet was startled. He remembered the frankness with which he discussed the King and Cardinal in his letters to his master; he remembered the slighting comments he had made about them both – particularly this man who was now smiling blandly at him.

'His Grace,' went on Wolsey, 'was much displeased. It seemed to him that we have been harbouring an enemy in our midst.'

De Praet shouted: 'You have done this. You had the man arrested. It is a plot.'

'And the letters? Shall you say that I wrote those treasonable documents?' Wolsey demanded with a smile.

'They were intended for the Emperor.'

'I did not expect for a moment that they were intended for the King and myself.'

'I shall go to the King,' said de Praet. 'I have evidence against you, Master Wolsey. I know that you have been receiving a spy from France. I know that you are working to destroy the alliance between the King and the Emperor. The King does not know the Cardinal whom he trusts. If he did he would not trust him. But he shall know. I have the evidence. I shall go back to my house; and when I have collected this evidence, which shall bear out my word, I will lose no time in going to the King and laying before him all I have discovered.'

Wolsey continued to smile, and the ambassador turned and walked quickly out of the apartments. The Cardinal went to the window and watched him hurrying across the grass to his boat.

'Helpful of him to explain his intentions in such detail,' he murmured to himself, and then called his stewards to him and began to give orders.

De Praet cursed the slowness of his boat as he was rowed back to London. His indignation increased as he rehearsed what he would say to the King.

When he reached his house he went in and collected certain documents which he had kept in a safe place, and made a careful list of all the people he would call as witnesses against the Cardinal.

Then he was ready to set out for Greenwich. But as he attempted to leave his house two guards barred his way. He saw then that many of them were stationed about his house.

'What is the meaning of this?' he demanded fiercely, but his fierceness had no effect on the guards.

'Begging Your Excellency's pardon,' said one of them, 'you are not to leave this house.'

'Who dares to restrict the Imperial ambassador?'

'The King, Your Excellency.'

De Praet was so angry that for a moment he could find no words to express his indignation; but as he grew a little calmer he realised that he was defeated. They called him the King's prisoner, but he was in truth that of the Cardinal.

Yet, he reflected, in this country that was one and the same thing.

With satisfaction Wolsey presented himself to the King.

'The spy is a prisoner in his lodging,' he said. 'He can do little harm now.'

'Let him remain so,' said Henry, who was still smarting from the references to himself in the ambassador's correspondence;

accustomed to flattery he was always surprised when he did not receive it, and on those rare occasions when he discovered disparaging comments had been made about him he never failed to be deeply shocked.

This was the moment to drive home the advantage, and Wolsey murmured: 'It may be that Your Grace will see fit to acquaint our own ambassador with your horror. It is for the Emperor to send us an ambassador, not a spy.'

'I shall write to Dr Sampson and command him to express my displeasure to the Emperor.'

'Your Grace is wise. It is as well that he should be acquainted with your displeasure. In this campaign he has had all the advantages.'

Henry scowled but he believed that what Wolsey said was true.

'Your Grace,' went on the Chancellor, 'as you know, I am ever watchful and I have discovered that there are in England at this moment emissaries from France.'

The King's face flamed, and Wolsey with great temerity continued before he could speak: 'If Your Grace would but see these men there would be no necessity to commit yourself in any way. But in view of the manner in which the Emperor has behaved towards us, I personally see little harm in listening to these men. It may be that Your Grace, in his greater wisdom, has some reason for not wishing to see them. If that is so, then I shall see that they are sent back to France without delay.'

'Were it not for the betrothal to our daughter, Thomas, I should be seeking a way out of this alliance.'

'We must remember the importance of this match,' agreed Wolsey. 'But could we not say that this is a matter apart? If we listened to the French we could then perhaps use their desire for friendship to extract some advantage from the Emperor. Your Grace knows full well that we have had little so far.'

'I know it well.' The King hesitated. 'I see no harm in listening to what these men have to say.'

Wolsey consolidated his gains before the King had time to withdraw.

'I beg of Your Grace to come to Hampton Court; I shall send for the men, and if you see them there it will make less talk than if they came to Greenwich.'

The King was agreeable. He was beginning to take a deep interest in Hampton Court, and the Cardinal had thought somewhat uneasily that occasionally he saw an acquisitive gleam in the blue eyes. 'I will come to your fair manor, Thomas,' he said. 'I confess to a fondness for the place.' His eyes narrowed slightly. 'And there's something else, I confess. My own palaces look a little less grand, less like the residences of a King, after my visits to Hampton Court.'

'I have furnished the place that it might be a refuge for Your Grace at any time it is your pleasure and my delight that you visit it.'

'Then let us see these men from France at Hampton, Thomas.'

Victory! thought the Cardinal. But in a measure uneasy victory. The King had changed since Buckingham's execution. Often one had the feeling that he was eager to prove the power he had over all men – including his dear friend and counsellor, Thomas Wolsey.

The King paced up and down his bedchamber. He was alone, which was rare for him; but he had wished it so. He was not at ease. He did not want to see these messengers from France; what he wanted was news of the Emperor's victory, to hear that the fair land of France was conquered and that the King of England was invited to go to Rheims to receive the crown he longed for.

But to make peace would mean an end of that dream.

He hated the King of France as, he believed, he could never hate Charles. François was bold and witty; handsome and clever; he was a rival as Charles – pallid, without good looks, serious – could never be. So while Henry hated François he could only distrust Charles. Not that he did not distrust François also. But the Emperor was young, his wife's nephew and therefore his own. Charles had called Henry Uncle when he was in England and deferred to his advice. Not that he had taken it. He was sly, full of pretence; but he was young and when they were together Henry could patronise him. When he was with François he had to summon all his wits and then be outwitted.

It seemed to him that he had reached a stage of his life when all that he longed for most was denied him. He wanted the crown of France and cynical François stood between him and it; he wanted a son and Katharine stood between him and that goal; he wanted a young girl who had caught his imagination, and she flouted him, telling him that he, being married, was in no position to make advances to her.

So he, the King, was frustrated of his three greatest desires. It was a state of affairs which he had not thought possible.

He knew the position in Europe was so bad that it could not continue; and if he did not win France this year, perhaps he would win it some other year. He would never give up hope. The matter of getting a son was more urgent. He was not old by any means, but being thirty-four years of age he was no longer a boy. He was impatient for sons. Yet he remained married to Katharine – if it was a marriage. His conscience was telling him that it was not, and that the sooner he made this known to his people the more pleased God would be with him. But Thomas Wolsey was to be trusted and he had said: Wait.

And then the girl. He had seen her at the Court, and had been maddened at the thought of her marrying Percy – maddened with the foolish young man for thinking to take what the King desired, and with the girl herself for agreeing to the marriage; then he had seen her in her father's garden at Hever, where she had treated him not as the King but as a would-be lover who did not please her. He should have been angry; he should have had the girl sent to the Tower; but a strange softness, which he had never felt before, had come to him. He had merely allowed himself to be so treated, which was wonderfully mysterious.

He had ridden away from Hever, still thinking of her and – although he was surprised at himself for doing so – had visited the place again and again . . . not as a King honouring a subject but as a humble suitor cap in hand.

Yet she continued to resist him. So here again he was frustrated.

A king must not consider his own personal desires, he told himself. I must not think of her but of these men who come from François.

He stood at the window looking out on the river, but he did not see it because instead he saw a garden at Hever and in it the most fascinating young woman he had ever known.

There was a bustle below, and as he turned from the

window, roughly jolted from his dream of Hever, the Cardinal came into the room.

The King was surprised by his unceremonious entry, and by the fact that his cap was somewhat askew. The pockmarked face was as pale as ever but the brown eyes gleamed so that Henry knew the Cardinal came to announce some matter of importance.

'Your Grace . . . news . . .'

Wolsey was breathless and the King saw that behind him stood a man who was obviously travel-stained and looked as though he had ridden far.

'What news?' demanded the King who, in spite of the excitement, was still faintly bemused by memories of the bold and haughty girl who had dared repulse him.

'From the battlefield, Your Grace. The Imperial troops have routed the French at Pavia. The French army is destroyed and François himself is the Emperor's prisoner.'

Henry clapped his hands together and his great joy showed in his face.

At last the vision of Hever was replaced by one of a handsome, golden-haired, golden-bearded King receiving the crown at Rheims.

'This is news which gives me the greatest pleasure. It is certain . . . ? There has been no mistake?'

The Cardinal turned to the travel-stained man behind him, who came forward and bowed low before the King.

'Your Grace, this is true. The King of France has been taken prisoner at Pavia and is now the Emperor's captive.'

Henry laid his hand on the man's shoulder. 'You are as welcome as the Angel Gabriel was to the Virgin Mary!' he declared. 'Why, Thomas,' he went on, turning to the

Cardinal, 'this is the best news we have had for many a long day.'

Wolsey bowed his head as though in assent; and while the King fired questions at the messenger he slipped away to send his own messenger to meet the French emissaries. He wished them to be told that the King could not see them as he had hoped to on this day.

'Now,' Henry wrote to the Emperor Charles, 'is the time for us to invade France jointly. Let us meet in Paris. Let France be handed to me that it may come under the domination of England. I shall then have the greatest pleasure in accompanying Your Imperial Highness to Rome where I shall see you crowned.'

He was so delighted that he went about the Court in high good humour. He was jubilant with Katharine, for was it not her nephew who had captured the King of France? Had not she helped to strengthen the bonds between the two countries? Their daughter was the affianced bride of the Emperor who was now more powerful than ever. When she married him and had her first son, that son should be proclaimed the future King of England, lord of Ireland and Wales, and now . . . France. This boy would be the greatest monarch in the world, for he would also inherit Spain, Austria, the Netherlands, Naples, Sicily and the recently discovered dominions of the New World. This would be a boy with Tudor blood in his veins. Perhaps it was not so important that *he* had no son when his grandson would be a monarch such as the world had never seen before.

He was gay and jovial with his Queen – although he could

not bring himself to share her bed. The memories of a laughing girl, who would not be put out of his mind, prevented that.

As for the girl herself, who had more respect for her own virtue than the King's royalty, she should be dismissed from his mind. There would be other girls at his Court only too eager to comfort him for her loss.

Those were good days, spent chiefly in making plans for his coronation in France.

Katharine was delighted; at last she could share the King's pleasure. He liked to walk with her in the gardens of the Palace, his arm in hers while he made plans for his journey to France.

But Henry could not forgive Charles's ambassador for the manner in which he had written of himself and the Chancellor, and de Praet was still kept a prisoner in his house. In vain did Katharine plead for him; in vain did she ask permission for the man to come and see her. Henry became sullen when she mentioned these matters, and replied shortly that he would not tolerate spies in England, even Spanish spies. And finally, when the dispirited de Praet asked for leave to return to his own country and Henry gave it, Katharine was not allowed to see him before he left; she consoled herself however that never had Henry's friendship for Charles been so firm as it was at this time, so that the fact that Charles had no ambassador in England did not seem so important as it would have been a short time ago.

When the Emperor read Henry's letter he raised his eyebrows in dismay.

Henry crowned in Rheims King of France! Himself

crowned in Rome! The English King had no idea of the situation.

Charles had taken the French King prisoner, it was true, and that was a success; the army which had served with François was disbanded, but that did not constitute all the men at arms in France. Charles himself had suffered enormous losses; his army was only in slightly better condition than that of the French; moreover he had no money to pay his mercenaries.

Charles was a realist. He knew that the Italian princes, who had had to submit to him, did so with great unwillingness, that the Pope was watching his movements with anxiety. His mercenaries had demanded the spoils of battle as he could not pay them, and as a result the countryside had been ravaged as the troops passed through; and as the sullen people were ready to revolt against the conqueror, this was no time to talk of crowning ceremonies. Henry seemed to think that war was a game and that the winner received all the spoils of victory. Had he not learned yet that in wars such as this there were often very little spoils?

The Emperor was weary of battle. He had the upper hand now; François was in prison in Madrid, and while he was there it would be possible to make him agree to humiliating terms. It was a matter of taking what he could; but it was totally unrealistic to imagine that he could take France and hand it to his ally as though it were a particularly fine horse or even a castle.

'When will my uncle grow up?' he sighed.

There was another matter which was disturbing him. He was twenty-four years of age and affianced to Mary who was nine. He was tired of waiting, and his ministers had implied that the people of Spain were eager for an alliance with Portugal.

His cousin, Isabella of Portugal, was of a marriageable age at this present time, and her dowry was nine hundred thousand golden ducats. How useful such a sum would be! And Mary's dowry? He had had it already in loans from her father, and he knew that to take Mary would merely be to wipe off the debts he had incurred in the war.

He wanted a wife now . . . not in three years' time. In three years' time he might have a lusty son. When he went to war he would have a Queen to leave in Spain as his regent. Moreover Portugal had always been closely allied with Spain. The people wanted one of their own as their Queen, not a strange little girl who, although half Spanish, would seem to them wholly English.

True, he had given his promise, but his grandfathers had made promises when it was expedient to do so; and when state policy demanded that those promises should be broken, they broke them. Charles was sorry because his aunt would be hurt and the King of England would be angry. But he did not greatly care for the King of England. A strip of Channel divided them and they had always been uneasy allies.

Wolsey had turned against him he knew from the few letters he had received from de Praet; and he was certain that he had not received all that de Praet had written. Wolsey was a wily fellow and it was unfortunate that they should be enemies, but that must be accepted.

He could not simply jilt Mary, but he could make a condition that her parents would find it impossible to fulfil. Suppose he demanded that she be sent at once to Spain? He knew his aunt would never agree to part with her daughter at this stage. He would demand half as much again as Henry had already paid towards the cost of the war, knowing that this would be refused. But these would be the terms he

146

would insist on if he were to carry out his part of the bargain.

The Portuguese ambassador was waiting to see him; he would have to have something to tell him when he came. He must decide whether there should be discussions between the two countries regarding the betrothal of himself and Isabella.

He therefore sent for a gentleman of his entourage, and while he was waiting for him he wrote a letter which, on account of the news it contained, he put into code.

When the Knight Commander Peñalosa was shown into his presence, he signed to him to be seated.

'I have a letter here which you are to take to England. It is in code, so you must go at once to de Praet who will decode it for you. Then you will read the contents and discuss with de Praet and the Queen the best manner of putting the proposals it contains to the King of England. De Praet will then inform me of the King's reception of this news. This is of the utmost importance. You must leave at once.'

Peñalosa left with the letter and prepared to set out for England, while Charles received the Portuguese ambassador.

By the time Peñalosa reached England, de Praet had left and there was no one who could decode the letter. Peñalosa sought an audience with the Queen, but the Cardinal, who was more watchful of her than ever, had so surrounded her with his spies that Peñalosa was never allowed to see her except in public. If Katharine's eyes alighted on him by chance she had no notion that he was an important messenger from her nephew.

Katharine was with her women engaged in that occupation which so frequently occupied her – the making of clothes for the poor – when the storm broke.

The King strutted into her apartment and one wave of his hands sent her women curtseying and scuttling away like so many frightened mice.

'Henry,' Katharine asked, 'what ails you?'

He stood, legs apart, that alarming frown between his brows, so that she felt her spirits sink. She knew that he had come to tell her of some great disaster.

In his hand he carried a document, and her heart began to beat rapidly as she recognised her nephew's seal.

'You may well ask,' said the King ominously.

'It is news from the Emperor?'

'It is, Madam. News from the biggest scoundrel that ever trod the soil of Europe.'

'Oh no . . . Henry.'

'Oh yes, Madam. Yes, yes, yes. This nephew of yours has insulted us . . . myself, you and our daughter.'

'The marriage . . .'

'There will be no marriage. Our daughter has been tossed aside as though she were of no importance . . . tossed aside for what he believes to be a better match.'

'It is impossible.'

'So you would doubt my word.'

'No, Henry, but I am sure there is some explanation.'

'There is explanation enough. This treacherous scoundrel believes that he can serve himself better by marriage with his cousin of Portugal. He has already possessed himself of Mary's dowry in loans . . . which will never be repaid. Now his greedy hands are reaching out for his cousin's ducats.'

'But he is promised to Mary.'

Henry came close to her and his eyes looked cruel. 'When have your family ever respected their promises? I should have understood. I should have suspected. I do not forget how your father deceived me again and again. And Maximilian . . . this Charles's grandfather . . . he deceived me in like manner. I am deceived every way I turn. Spain! I would to God I had never heard of that country. What have I ever had from Spain? Broken promises . . . my treasury rifled . . . lies . . . lies . . . lies and a barren wife!'

'Henry . . . I implore you . . .'

'You would implore me? What would you implore, Madam? That I say thank you to this nephew of yours? Thank you for deceiving me. Thank you for jilting my daughter. I'd as lief thank you, Madam, for all the sons you have not given me!'

'That was no fault of mine,' she said with spirit. 'I have done my best.'

'No fault of yours? Then whose fault, Madam? You know I have a healthy son. It is more than you have. All those years and one daughter . . . and that daughter, jilted . . . by *your* nephew.'

For the moment tears came to his eyes – tears of self pity. All that he desired was denied him. The crown of France; the sons; the marriage of his daughter to the greatest monarch in Christendom; the favours of a sprightly young girl who persistently avoided him. Why was the King so frustrated?

His conscience gave him the answer. Because you have offended God. You have lived with a woman who is not your wife because she was first the wife of your brother. You will never know good fortune while you live in sin, for God will continue to turn his face from you.

He hated her then – this woman with her sagging shapeless body. How different from that other! This woman who could no longer arouse the slightest desire within him. The woman whose nephew had betrayed him and their daughter.

It was difficult to hold in the words, to remember that as yet it was the secret matter.

But how he hated her!

She flinched before the cruelty in his eyes; she saw the brutal curve of his mouth. Thus had he looked when he had determined to send Buckingham to the scaffold.

He was controlling himself; she knew that. He was holding in the words he longed to utter. She almost wished that he would speak so that she might know what thoughts were in the secret places of his mind.

He forced himself to leave her; he went straight to his apartments and summoned Wolsey.

He would be revenged on Charles. He could not reach the Emperor, but the aunt should suffer for the nephew. None should treat him so scurvily and escape. Charles should learn that he, Henry, cared nothing for the House of Spain and Austria. Had Charles forgotten that there was one member of that House who was completely in his power?

'Come, Wolsey,' he growled, while he waited for his Chancellor. 'We'll make peace with France; we'll have a French Prince for Mary. We'll form an alliance to make His Imperial Highness tremble. We shall show you, Master Charles, that we care naught for you and yours! A plague on the House of Spain and Austria – and all those who belong to it!'

That June day a ceremony took place in Bridewell Palace and the King had commanded all the high officials of the Court to attend: he was particularly anxious that Peñalosa, who was the only ambassador Charles had in England at the time, should be present at the ceremony and send an account of it to his master.

The hero of this occasion was a small boy, six years old. He was handsome, and his pink and gold Tudor beauty both delighted and exasperated Henry.

Every time he looked at the boy he said to himself: Why could he not have been my legitimate son!

Henry had ceased to think of the boy's mother; she had been handsomely rewarded for giving the King a proof of his ability to beget sons. Manors in Lincolnshire and Yorkshire had been bestowed on her, so she would have no cause to regret those days when she had been the King's mistress.

Henry had watched with smouldering eyes while this handsome boy was created a Knight of the Garter; and now this even more significant ceremony was taking place.

He came to stand before the King; on either side of him were the leading Dukes of England – Norfolk and Suffolk.

But this boy, thought Henry, shall take precedence over all. For I would have all understand that he is my son and living proof of the fact that I can get sons with other women – though not with my wife.

Holy Mother of God, he prayed as he watched; I see my fault. I live in sin with my brother's wife and for that reason my union is not blessed with sons. How could it be when in the eyes of God it is a sinful union!

Now proud Norfolk and Suffolk had taken a step backwards that the newly created Duke might stand alone as one whose titles would henceforth set him above them; he would now be known as the first peer of the land, and his titles were impressive: Henry Fitzroy, Duke of Richmond and Somerset, Lord High Admiral of England, Wales, Ireland, Normandy, Gascony and Aquitaine, Knight of the Garter, and first peer of England.

There was a buzz of excitement throughout Court circles which extended to the streets of the city.

Even in the taverns the importance of the ceremony was understood.

'This means one thing: The King, despairing of sons by his wife, honoured Elizabeth Blount's boy.'

'Note the significance of that title – Richmond,' it was whispered. 'The King's father was Duke of Richmond before he became King. Depend upon it, the King has decided that that boy shall one day wear the crown.'

'It is not possible while Mary lives.'

'If the King decrees, it will be possible. None will dare gain-say him. And this ceremony is to prepare his people for what he intends to bring about.'

'The people would not accept the boy while Mary lives.'

'The people will accept what the King wishes. It is better not to argue against the King. Remember Buckingham.'

The name of Buckingham could still send shivers through most bodies.

And so it was generally agreed that the ceremony at Bridewell was a first step in the direction the King intended to go as regards his illegitimate son.

Katharine who could often suffer in silence on her own account could not do so on her daughter's.

She faced the King boldly on the first opportunity when they were alone and declared her horror and fear at the recognition given to Henry Fitzroy.

'You forget,' Henry told her coldly, 'that the Duke of Richmond is my son.'

'Should you be so proud to call him so?'

'Yes, Madam. Proud I am and always shall be. For his birth gave me the answer I sought. It is no fault of mine that I have no legitimate son.'

'And so you had this one merely to prove this?' she asked with a trace of sarcasm rare in her.

'I did,' said Henry who had told himself this was the case, so frequently that he believed it.

'This is an insult to our daughter. Has she not been insulted enough?'

'By your nephew . . . yes. This is no insult to Mary. I still accept her as my daughter.' A cunning look came into his eyes. 'She is a girl and her position may not be so different from that of the little Duke.'

This was going too far; it was betraying the secret matter. He must be cautious. Katharine did not construe his words as he had meant them. She thought only that he planned to set this illegitimate son before his daughter because of his sex.

'You cannot mean you would set aside our daughter for a . . . bastard!'

His eyes narrowed. He wanted to speak of what was in his mind. He was never one for secrets. He wanted her to know that although she was a daughter of the hated House of Spain, because she had previously married his brother it might well be that she had no legitimate hold on him.

'Mary is a girl,' he said sullenly.

'There is no reason why she should not make as good a monarch as a man. My own mother . . .'

The King snapped his fingers. 'I have no wish to hear of your sainted mother. And know this, if I decide that any man, woman or child in this kingdom shall be elevated . . .' His eyes were even more cruel suddenly . . . 'or set down, this shall be done and none shall be allowed to stand in my way.'

'I wonder,' said the Queen, 'that you allowed our daughter to keep the title, Princess of Wales. Why did you not take that away from her and bestow it on your bastard? Then there could have been no doubt of your intentions.'

He looked at her in silent hatred for a few seconds; then fearing that he would be unable to keep from her all the plans which were fermenting in his mind, he left her.

Wolsey was waiting for him in his apartment. The Chancellor saw the flushed face and angry looks and guessed that Henry had been listening to Katharine's reproaches.

'Your Grace looks displeased,' he murmured.

''Tis the Queen. I have never known her so bold . . . so careless of my feelings.'

'The Queen is afraid, Your Grace. She has her qualms about the marriage, even as you do. Perhaps more so.'

'She could not be more uneasy.'

Wolsey lowered his voice. 'She knows, Your Grace, whether or not the marriage with your brother was consummated.'

'You think this is a sign of her guilt?'

'The guilty are often those who feel most fear, Your Grace.'

'You are right, Thomas. And her boldness astonished me.'

'She is surrounded by women who urge her to behave thus. The Queen herself should be . . . malleable.'

Henry's lower lip jutted out. 'There's strength beneath that gentleness, Thomas.'

'Your Grace is right as usual, but that strength is, shall we say, given support by some of those women about her.'

The King looked questioningly at Wolsey.

'There is the Countess of Salisbury for one. She has ever been close to the Queen. Lady Willoughby is another. Women like that chat in secret, talking of wrongs, urging resistance.'

'They shall be banished from Court.'

'May I suggest, Your Grace, that we move with care? We do not want to rouse too much sympathy in . . . the wrong quarters.'

'You mean that there would be those to take her side against *me*!'

'Among the people, Your Grace. And some men of the Court, in secret. Let Lady Willoughby be sent away from Court. As for Lady Salisbury . . . If Your Grace will trust this matter to me, and commission me to deal with the Queen's household, I will see that those women likely to influence her are removed from her side.'

'Do that, Thomas. By God, she must understand that I'll not stand by and accept her reproaches. She had the temerity to suggest that I might soon take Mary's title of Wales that I might give it to young Henry.'

'The Queen may well wean the Princess's affection from Your Grace.'

The King looked at his Chancellor; and for a few moments they both remained thoughtful.

This was the most cruel blow of all. Katharine had been so stunned when she heard the news that she could not believe it was true.

All the humiliations, all the uneasiness of the past years had been forgotten when she was in the presence of her daughter; her only joy in life had been wrapped up in the child. The love between them was intense, as deep and abiding as that which Katharine had shared with her own mother.

In all her troubles she had been able to tell herself: 'I have my daughter.'

And now Mary was to be taken away from her.

She did not weep. This was too great a sorrow to be assuaged by tears. She sat limply staring before her while her dearest friend, Maria de Salinas, Countess of Willoughby, sat beside her, desperately seeking for words which would comfort her.

But there was no comfort. Maria herself would not long be at the Queen's side. She was to leave Court, and she believed she knew why.

One of the Queen's women had recently been dismissed from the Court and she had confessed to Maria that the reason was because she had declined to act as the Cardinal's spy. His idea was clearly to remove from the Queen's side all those who would not work for him against her.

What did it all mean? Maria asked herself. Should I try to warn her? If only I could stay with her to comfort her.

But now Katharine could think of nothing but her daughter.

'Why should she be taken from me?' she demanded passionately. 'When she marries it may be necessary for her to leave me. There cannot be many years left to us. Why must I lose her now?'

'I think, Your Grace,' said Maria, desperately seeking a reason that might soothe the Queen, 'that the King wishes her to go to Wales so that the country may know she is still Princess of the Principality and heir to the throne.'

The Queen brightened at that suggestion. 'It may be so,' she said. 'The people did not like his elevating the bastard.'

'That is the answer, Your Grace. You can depend upon it, she will not stay long. It is merely a gesture. I feel certain that is the reason.'

'I shall miss her so much,' said the Queen.

'Yes, Your Grace, but perhaps it is well that she should go.'

Katharine said: 'There is one consolation; Lady Salisbury is going with her as her governess. I cannot tell you how that cheers me.'

One more friend, thought Maria, to be taken from the Queen's side.

Katharine rose suddenly and said: 'I shall go to my daughter now. I would like to break this news to her myself. I trust that she has not already heard it. Stay here, Maria. I would be alone with her.'

In the Princess's apartments the little girl was seated at the virginals; one or two of her attendants were with her. When the Queen entered they curtseyed and moved away from the Princess who leaped from her chair and threw herself into her mother's arms.

'That was well played,' said the Queen, trying to control her emotion.

She smiled at the attendants and nodded. They understood; the Queen often wished to be alone with her daughter.

'I was hoping you would come, Mother,' said the Princess. 'I have learned a new piece and wanted to play it to you.'

'We will hear it later,' answered Katharine. 'I have come to talk to you.'

She sat on a stool near the virginals, and Mary came to stand beside her while the Queen put her arm about her daughter.

'You have heard no rumours about Wales?' asked the Queen.

'Wales, Mother? What sort of rumours?'

The Queen was relieved. 'Well, you know you are Princess of Wales and it is the custom for the Prince or Princess to visit the Principality at some time.'

'We are going to Wales then, Mother?'

'You are going, my darling.'

Mary drew away from her mother and looked at her in startled dismay.

'Oh, it will not be for long,' said the Queen.

'But why do you not come with me?'

'It is the wish of your father that you go alone. You see, *you* are the Princess of Wales. *You* are the one the people want to see.'

'You must come too, Mother.'

'My darling, if only I could!'

'I will not go without you.' For a moment Mary looked like her father.

'My darling, your father has commanded you to go.'

Mary threw herself against her mother and clung to her. 'But it is so far away.'

'Not so very far, and you will come back soon. We shall write to each other and there will be the letters to look forward to.'

'I don't want to go away from you, Mother . . . ever.'

The Queen felt the tears, which she had so far managed to keep in check, rising to her eyes.

'My love, these partings are the fate of royal people.'

'I wish I were not royal then.'

'Hush, my darling. You must never say that. We have a duty to our people which is something we must never forget.'

Mary pulled at the rings on her mother's fingers but

Katharine knew she was not thinking of them. 'Mother,' she said, 'if I were to plead with my father . . .'

The Queen shook her head. 'He has decided. You must go. But do not let us spoil what time is left to us in grieving. Time will pass, my darling, more quickly than you realise. I shall hear of you from your governess and tutors, and you will write to me yourself. You see I shall have all that to live for.'

Mary nodded slowly. Poor child! thought the Queen. She has learned to keep her feelings in check. She has learned that the fate of Princesses can often be cruel and that one thing is certain, they must be accepted.

'You will go to Ludlow Castle,' said the Queen trying to speak brightly. 'It is a beautiful place.'

'Tell me about when you were there, Mother.'

'It was long . . . long ago. I went there with my first husband.'

'My father's brother,' murmured Mary.

'It was so long ago,' said the Queen, and she thought of those days when she had been married to the gentle Arthur who was so different from Henry; Arthur who had been her husband for scarcely six months.

'Tell me about the castle,' said Mary.

'It rises from the point of a headland,' the Queen told her, 'and is guarded by a wide, deep fosse. It is grand and imposing with its battlemented towers; and the surrounding country is superb . . . indeed some of the best I have ever seen.'

The Princess nodded sadly.

'You will be happy there,' murmured Katharine, putting her lips to Mary's forehead. 'We shall not be very far away from each other, and soon you will come back to me.'

'How soon?' asked Mary.

'You will be surprised how soon.'

'I would rather know. It is always so much easier to bear if you know how long. Then I could count the days.'

'My darling, you will be happy there. When I left my mother, the ocean separated us. This is not the same at all.'

'No,' said Mary slowly. 'It is not the same at all.'

'And now, my love, go to the virginals. Play the piece which you wished me to hear.'

Mary hesitated and for a moment Katharine feared that the child would lose her hold on that rigid control. But obediently she rose, went to the virginals, sat down and began to play; and as she did so, the tears, which would no longer be kept back, rolled silently down her cheeks.

Chapter IV

THE PRINCESS AT LUDLOW CASTLE

The Princess Mary was melancholy in the Castle of Ludlow and the Countess of Salisbury was alarmed on her account. The only thing which could bring the child out of that languid indifference as to what went on around her was a letter from her mother.

Each day she told the Countess how long they had been at Ludlow; and she would ask wistfully if there were any news of their returning to her father's Court.

'All in good time,' the Countess would say. 'With the passing of each day we are a little nearer to our return.'

The Princess rode often in the beautiful woods close to the castle; she had to admit that the country was some of the fairest she had ever seen; but it was clear that when she was separated from her mother she could not be happy, and the Countess feared that her health would be affected by her melancholy.

Great plans were afoot for the celebrations of Christmas, The New Year and Twelfth Night.

'There will be plays, masques and a banquet . . . just as at your father's Court,' the Countess told her.

'I wonder whether my mother will come,' was all the Princess could say.

It was true that she had a certain interest in her lessons; she worked hard at her Latin and her music and sometimes she would chuckle and say: 'My mother will be surprised that I have come so far. I shall write to her in Latin, and when she comes I shall play all my new pieces.'

The Countess was grateful that she had this interest in her Latin and music, and made the most of it. There had been rumours which had come to the Countess's notice before she left Court and, although she could not believe there was much truth in them, they made her very uneasy. The fact that the Queen had married the King's brother could have no effect on the present marriage. The Pope had given the necessary dispensation, and during all the years the King and Queen had been married there had never before been any suggestion that the marriage might not be legal.

She was a wise woman, and in her fifty-two years she had seen much tragedy. None understood, more than she did, the Tudors's fierce determination to fight off all those who threatened to take the crown from them. It was natural that the King wanted to make sure of the Tudor succession. Desperately he needed a son, and Katharine had failed to give it to him.

There were times when Margaret Pole, Countess of Salisbury, wished that she were not a Plantagenet and so near to the throne. She had lived through troublous times. Her maternal grandfather had been that Earl of Warwick who had been known as the Kingmaker; her father had been the Duke of Clarence, brother of Richard III, who had been imprisoned in the Tower and there, it was believed, had been drowned in a butt of malmsey. She had been a young child when that had happened and it had made a deep and terrible impression on her; ever after she had been aware of the insecurity of life and the favour of Kings; and it seemed to her that those who lived nearest the throne had the most to fear. That was why she often thought with deep compassion of the Queen, and now as she sat with her royal charge she could grow quite melancholy wondering what the future held for her. Only recently tragedy had struck at her family through her youngest child, Ursula, wife of Henry Stafford, son of the Duke of Buckingham whose life had recently come to an end on the block.

Henry VIII had occasionally been kind to her family; she had fancied that he wanted to make amends to them for his father's murder of her brother Edward who, as the Earl of Warwick, had been a menace to the throne. But how long would that favour last? She believed now that she was regarded with suspicion by Wolsey because of her close friendship with the Queen.

If Katharine could have been with her in Ludlow she would have been almost happy. It was peaceful here and seemed so far from the world of ambition. And how happy little Mary would have been if the Queen were here! But as the weeks stretched into months the love between the governess and her charge grew deeper and did – so the Countess fervently hoped – compensate in some measure for the child's loss of her mother.

Margaret tried to replace that mother, and it was a great joy to her to know that the times of the day to which Mary looked forward more than any other were those when she and the Countess were alone together; and the little girl, released from her lessons which Margaret often felt were too much for her, would sit at the Countess's feet and demand to hear stories of her life.

And when Mary said: 'My mother used to tell me stories of the days when she was a girl in Spain . . .' Margaret knew that the substitution had taken place in the child's mind; and she wrote to the Queen telling her of these pleasant hours which seemed to give consolation to Mary for her exile.

Through Margaret's description of her family Mary began to know the Pole children so well that they seemed to be her intimate friends. There was Henry, Lord Montague, who had followed the King to France to the Field of the Cloth of Gold. Margaret did not tell the child of the anxiety she had suffered when Henry had been arrested at the time of the trial of the Duke of Buckingham because his father-in-law was a connection of the Duke's; in any case he had been speedily released, and very soon afterwards had been restored to favour, being among those noblemen who had greeted the Emperor Charles on his arrival in England. The Countess would talk of her sons, Arthur, Reginald, Geoffrey and her daughter Ursula, with such loving detail that the Princess knew that these quiet hours were as enjoyable to the Countess as they were to her.

But it was of Reginald that Mary liked best to hear; Reginald was learned and deeply religious, and Mary had always felt that to give lifelong devotion to religion was the best way of living. Therefore Reginald became her hero.

The Countess told how she had always meant him to go into the Church and how eager he had been to follow that calling, although he had not yet taken holy orders.

'There is no better man in the world than my Reginald,' said Margaret proudly, and Mary began to believe her.

'When he was a boy at Oxford he astonished his tutors,' the fond mother declared. 'In truth I think they began to realise that he was more clever than they. He became a Dean at Wimborne though still a layman. He held many posts, and then he decided to go to Padua, and that is where he is now. The King, your father, is pleased with him and there is great hospitality in his house there. Scholars flock to see him. He thinks it is because he is a kinsman of the King.'

'But it is really because of his noble character,' Mary asserted.

'I believe that to be so. Mary, I think he will soon be coming to England.'

Mary clasped her hands in ecstasy. 'And will he come to Ludlow?'

'Come to see his mother! Of a certainty he will. You do not know my Reginald.'

'I do,' declared the Princess.

And after that they often spoke of his coming and when Mary awoke in the mornings she would say to herself: 'Will there be news from my mother today?' And then: 'Is Reginald now on his way to the Castle?'

It was only these hopes which made the separation tolerable. But the months passed and there was no news of Mary's joining her mother; and Reginald continued to stay in Italy.

Henry cut himself off from communication with his Queen, and she rarely saw him. She lived quietly, working on her garments for the poor, reading religious books, going to Mass, praying privately. Her great joy was writing letters to her daughter, but what a difficult task this was when she must suppress her fierce longing, and not convey her fears that the long absence was stifling that deep affection they had for each other!

Henry was growing impatient. He had begun to wonder whether Wolsey was working as wholeheartedly for him as he had once believed. Wolsey was a man who had seen that his own pockets were well lined; and should a king feel such gratitude towards a man who in his service had grown as rich as surely only a king should be?

Wolsey was constantly whispering caution, and Henry was becoming a little uncertain of the game the Chancellor was playing. There was a new faction springing up at Court, and at the centre of this was George Boleyn whom the King found a fascinating young man, largely because he was the brother of Anne.

Anne remained at Hever, but she should not do so for long. Henry had already shown his favour to the family by raising Sir Thomas to the peerage, so that he now bore the title of Viscount Rochford. He had even given poor Will Carey, Mary's husband, a post at Court as gentleman of the Privy Chamber. He was certain that soon the haughty girl would give in to his pleading, and stop talking about her virtue.

But at the same time it was this Boleyn faction which was making him doubt Wolsey. He sent for his Chancellor in order to discuss a matter which was of great concern to them both at this time: the marriage of the Princess Mary.

When Wolsey entered, the King did not greet him with the affectionate look which the Chancellor usually received from him. Wolsey was acutely aware of the King's changing attitude towards him and it was doubly alarming because he was not sure of its origin.

'I have news from France,' said Henry. 'It seems that François is rejecting our offer of my daughter.'

Wolsey nodded gravely. Here was one matter on which they were in agreement; they shared the desire for a marriage between Mary and a member of the royal French family. Nothing would disturb the Emperor more; at the same time if Mary were to marry into France she would very soon be sent to that country; and if the King were about to rid himself of the Queen, Mary's presence in England could prove an embarrassment. There was no need to speak of this matter. Each knew that it was well to the fore in the mind of the other.

The King took a document from his table which had been sent to him from Louise of Savoy who was her son's Regent while he, François, remained the Emperor's prisoner in Madrid.

'Read it,' commanded the King; and Wolsey read that the Duchesse of Savoy could not express sufficient regret that the marriage between her son and the Princess Mary was not possible. She knew that the Princess of England excelled all other Princesses; she had heard nothing but good of her character, her attainments and her beauty. Alas, a tragic fate had befallen her son; he was in the hands of the Emperor and harsh terms were being imposed on him. Not the least harsh of these – in view of the offer of the Princess's hand from England – was that he should marry the Emperor's sister Eleanora whom Emanuel of Portugal had recently left a widow. It seemed likely that the King of France would have to comply with this unless Eleanora refused to marry him.

The Duchesse however hoped that this might not make an end of their desire for a French-English alliance. She had grandsons. She was certain that François would welcome the Princess Mary as the wife of his son Henri, Duc d'Orléans.

'Well,' the King demanded, 'what do you think of this proposition?'

'A fair one. Marriage to young Henri would, in truth, be more suitable than marriage with François.'

'A second son,' murmured the King.

'Eldest sons sometimes die,' Wolsey reminded him.

'That's so,' replied the King, himself a second son. He was thoughtful for a while. 'The child is young . . . not yet ten years of age. There is time. But it shall be a French match for her.'

'I am in full agreement with Your Grace.'

'I rejoice to hear it.' Was it his imagination, wondered Wolsey, or was there a trace of sarcasm in the King's voice. The little blue eyes swept over the rich satin robes. 'We shall be having French ambassadors here soon, I doubt not. When they come it would be well for them to be entertained at Hampton Court.'

'Hampton Court is, as always, at Your Grace's command.'

'These foreigners . . .' mused Henry. 'They do not think they are at Court until they are received at Hampton. Is it meet a subject should possess such a palace?'

Wolsey quickly saw the meaning behind the words. He had always gambled. He gambled now.

'There is only one reason why a subject could possess such a palace,' he answered quickly, 'and that is that he can put it into the hands of his King.'

Suddenly the peevish animosity died in the King's face and the old affection was back there. The blue eyes were so bright that Wolsey was not sure whether it was tears of friendship or covetousness which he saw there.

The Chancellor felt a catch of fear at his heart; it was as though he were running towards danger; and that only by throwing his most valued possessions to his pursuers could he stave off the evil moment of disaster. He was playing for time. He believed that he could regain his power over the King . . . given time. If he could arrange a divorce for Henry, get him married to a French Princess, put an end to unprofitable wars – then he would be able to rout all his enemies. But he needed time.

The King put his own construction on those words.

'A goodly gift,' he said, 'from a loyal subject to his affectionate master. I would not offend you, Thomas, by refusing your handsome gift. But you shall live on there . . . you shall entertain these foreigners there . . . in my name, eh? Then they will no longer sing in the streets: "The King's Court or Hampton Court . . ." for from now on Hampton Court *is* the King's Court.'

Wolsey bowed his head and taking the King's hand kissed it. He was glad to hide his face for a few seconds; the loss of his most cherished possession was a blow, and he found it difficult to hide the sorrow he was feeling.

The days were dreary to Katharine, one so much like another. She had no friend in whom she could confide. Maria de Salinas was no longer at Court; Margaret Pole was in Ludlow with Mary; and, saddest of all, there was no mention of Mary's returning.

The women who surrounded her, she knew, were not her true friends, but had been put there by her enemy, Wolsey, to spy on her. She saw the King frequently but never in private; he was courteous to her but she fancied that he was afraid to meet her eye and always seemed relieved when he parted from her.

On one or two occasions she had mentioned their daughter, to which he invariably replied with prompt finality: 'It pleases me that she now has her own Court in her own Principality. She will learn something of government there in Ludlow.'

She wanted to protest: She is only a child. At least allow me to go and stay with her there.

But she knew that it was impossible to speak of such things in public, and there was never an opportunity of doing so in private.

She guessed that there was a mistress – perhaps several. Light-o'-loves, she thought contemptuously; and as she could not discuss this matter with the women who surrounded her, who would report to their master every word she said, she was silent.

She knew that negotiations were going forward with a view to a French alliance for Mary. She prayed that this might not be carried through. What she dreaded more than anything was alliance with France because she longed to restore friendship between her nephew and her husband. She believed that, if only Charles could explain in person, or if only he had a good and efficient ambassador, Henry would understand that he had been forced to do what he had done. None could be more disappointed at his rejection of Mary than she was. Had it not been the dearest dream of her life that her nephew and daughter should marry? But Charles was no longer very young and it was understandable that he should feel the need to marry without delay. She did not believe that Charles had wantonly deceived her husband; it was pressure of circumstances – and that must at times afflict every head of state – which had made him do so.

She wrote many letters to Charles – cautiously worded – for

she could not be sure that they would reach him. A little spice was added to those dreary days by this game of outwitting the Cardinal, whom she had now begun to regard as her greatest enemy.

And one day in the spring of that long year a letter from her nephew was smuggled to her and she felt a great triumph, as at least one of hers had reached him. That made her feel that she had some friends at the English Court.

Charles wrote that he was sending a new ambassador to England, Don Iñigo de Mendoza, who would be travelling through France and should arrive in England not long after she received this letter. He knew, of course, that Wolsey was doing his utmost to make a French alliance for Mary and that Katharine would agree with him that such an alliance would be fatal to their interests. He believed that she would find Mendoza more to her liking than ambassadors from Flanders, and it was for this reason that he was sending a Spaniard to England.

When Katharine read this letter she felt the tears of joy rushing to her eyes. Mendoza was coming. A Spaniard, one with whom she could converse in her native tongue. She even knew Iñigo. He had been her mother's favourite page, and she had seen him often riding in the entourage when Isabella had gone from town to town visiting her dominions, her family with her, as she had insisted whenever possible. Perhaps they would talk of Granada and Madrid, of the days of Isabella's greatness.

Katharine closed her eyes and thought of her early life in Spain, when she had never been forced to suffer the humiliation she had endured since coming to England, when she had been surrounded by the love of her family and, most of all, that of her mother.

'Oh Holy Mother,' she murmured, 'how sad life becomes when the greatest joy it has to offer is in remembering the past.'

Through the spring and summer Katharine awaited the arrival of Mendoza in vain. A little news did seep through to her and eventually she discovered that the French were determined to delay the arrival of the Spanish ambassador in England until a French embassy had been able to arrange for the marriage of Mary with the Duc d'Orléans.

They had promised Mendoza free passage through France, but shortly after he had set foot on that land he was arrested as a foreign spy and put into prison where he remained for months without trial.

Katharine was in despair because plans for the French marriage were going forward, although she did console herself that the matter could not be viewed with any certainty. François had been released from his prison in Madrid but he had only been allowed to go home if he promised on oath to send his two sons to Madrid as hostages for his good faith in carrying out the terms Charles had imposed on him. Thus the little boy who was betrothed to Mary was now the Emperor's prisoner in his father's stead.

Katharine was reminded now of those days between the death of her first husband, Arthur, and her marriage with Henry, when she lived through the uneventful yet dangerous months. Unable to be lulled by a false feeling of security and with dreadful premonition always in her mind that a storm was soon to break about her, she waited, knowing that when it did come it would contain an element of the unexpected, to face which she would need every scrap of courage she possessed.

It was December of that year when Mendoza arrived in London, but by that time she knew it was too late to stop the negotiations with France.

The first action of Mendoza was to beg an audience of the Queen. This she granted and he came speedily to her apartments.

She received him with emotion because of the memories of early and happier days he brought with him.

'It gives me great pleasure to see you,' she told him.

'I cannot express to Your Grace my pleasure in being here. I have found the delay almost intolerable.'

She looked at him closely and saw what those months in a French prison must have done to him; but, of course, when she had seen him in her mother's entourage he had been nothing but a boy. She was forgetting how many years ago that was.

This was not the time to waste on reminiscences and she said: 'There is much we have to say to each other. I am seriously alarmed about the relations between my nephew and this country.'

'The Emperor greatly desires to put them back on a friendly footing.'

'The King is incensed on account of his treatment of Mary.'

'Your Grace is also displeased.'

'It was of course a bitter disappointment to me.'

'The Emperor was pressed hard by the people of Spain, and he needed money from Portugal.'

'I know . . . I know. But let us talk of what we shall do to put matters right between Spain and England. I must tell you that the Cardinal is my most bitter enemy. I am surrounded by his spies and I know not whom I can trust. You will know that he is the most powerful man in England.'

Mendoza nodded. 'We shall have to make sure that he cannot interfere with our correspondence as he did with de Praet's.'

At that moment a page appeared at the door. Katharine looked at him in surprise, because she had given orders that she was not to be disturbed.

The page's look was apologetic, but before he could speak he was thrust aside and a red-clad figure came into the room.

'My lord Cardinal!' cried the Queen.

'Your Grace . . . Your Excellency . . . I come on the King's orders.'

'What orders are these?' demanded Katharine haughtily.

'He requests the Imperial Ambassador to come to his apartment without delay.'

'His Excellency called to see me . . .' the Queen began.

The Cardinal smiled at her whimsically. 'The King's command,' he murmured.

'His Excellency will call on the King within an hour.'

'The King's orders are that I shall conduct him to his presence with all speed.'

Katharine felt exasperation. She turned to the Ambassador and said rapidly in Spanish: 'You see how it is. I am constantly overlooked.'

But there was nothing to be done and the Ambassador must leave at once for the King's apartment, having achieved nothing by his visit to the Queen.

Katharine, with resignation, watched him go, knowing that future meetings between them would be difficult to arrange, and that when they talked together they would never be sure who overheard them; they must remember that anything they wrote to the Emperor would almost certainly be first censored by the Cardinal.

❀ ❀ ❀

Two wonderful events befell the Princess Mary.

It was strange, she reflected afterwards, that she should have waited for these things to happen and that they should have followed so swiftly on one another.

She was in one of her favourite haunts on a tower looking out over the battlements. The country was so beautiful that she found great peace merely by looking at it. She enjoyed riding in the woods with a party from her suite; during the warm days they had picnicked on the grass, and that was pleasant; but one of the most pleasurable occupations was kneeling up here on a stone seat inside the tower and looking out over the hills. This was her favourite view, for below in all its beauty was the valley of the Teme with the Stretton Hills forming a background.

She had been here so long that she was beginning to believe she would never leave the place; and yet every day she awoke with the thought in her mind: Will it be today?

Sometimes she let her fancy wander, imagining that a party of riders appeared in the valley, that she watched as they came nearer; and seeing the royal standard, knew that her mother had come.

It was nearly eighteen months since they had been parted.

How fortunate that I did not know how long it would be! she thought. If I had, I should never have been able to endure it.

But all through those months hope had been with her, and she often prayed that whatever happened to her she would always be able to hope.

She had grown considerably in the months of separation.

Her mother would see a change. She had learned a great deal; she could write Greek and Latin very well now, and could compose verses in these two languages. As for her music, that had improved even more.

One day, as she knelt in her favourite position, she did see a party of riders in the valley. She stared, believing in those first moments that she was dreaming, so often she had imagined she saw riders.

She kept her eyes on the party and as it came nearer she saw that it was a group of men and that they were making straight for the Castle. She watched until they were within its walls before she turned from the battlements and went to her own apartments, knowing that she would soon be told who the newcomers were.

It was the Countess herself who came into Mary's apartment and, in all the eighteen months during which they had been in Ludlow Castle, Mary had never seen the Countess so radiant.

'Your Highness,' she cried, 'I have wonderful news. There is someone who is most eager to meet you. I want your permission to present him to you at once.'

And there he was, in the room; tall, handsome, obviously of the nobility, austerely dressed though not in clerical robes, he seemed godlike to Mary.

'My son Reginald,' went on Margaret, 'who is also your humble servant.'

He knelt before Mary and she smiled at him as she bade him rise. 'Welcome,' she said. 'I feel I know you already because we have talked of you so often, your mother and I.'

'Yes,' agreed Margaret. 'Her Highness insisted on hearing tales of my family.'

'I found those tales interesting,' said Mary. She turned to

Margaret. 'I trust they are busy in the kitchens preparing a welcoming banquet.'

In that moment she felt grown up, the mistress of the Castle, Margaret noticed, and a wild hope was born in her mind.

She said: 'I will leave my son with you while I go to the kitchens. I want to give orders myself for, as Your Highness says, this is a special occasion and we wish everyone within the Castle to know it.'

Mary scarcely noticed that she had left. She went to the ornate chair which was kept especially for her and sat down, signing for Reginald to be seated too.

'We live somewhat simply here,' she told him, 'when compared with my father's Court. I pray you tell me about your stay on the Continent.'

'It has been a very long one,' he answered. 'It is five years since I left England. A great deal can happen in five years; I have lived in Padua and Rome, and I have now come to complete my studies at Sheen . . . in the Carthusian monastery there.'

'How wonderful! Your life is dedicated to God.'

'All our lives are dedicated to some purpose,' he replied. 'I was fortunate to be able to choose the way I should go. My mother wanted me to go into the Church. I was very happy to do this but I have not yet taken Holy Orders.'

'Have you come straight here from Rome?'

'Oh no, I visited London first and presented myself to Their Graces.'

'You have seen my mother!'

'Yes, I saw her and when I told her that I should visit my mother at Ludlow she begged me to commend her to you and to tell you that she sends her dearest love.'

Mary turned away for a moment, overcome by her emotion. Even the arrival of this man who had played a part in her dreams could not stifle her longing for her mother.

She asked questions about the Court. He did not tell her of the plans for a French marriage, nor of the speculations as to the efforts the Queen and the new Spanish ambassador would make to prevent this. He thought her charming, but a child; and yet during that first interview he was made aware of her serious turn of mind and that she had long ago put away childish things.

When Margaret returned and found them, absorbed in each other, and saw her son's interest in the child and Mary's in him – for Mary was unable to disguise the change his coming had made, and during the whole of her stay at Ludlow she had not looked so joyous – she said to herself: 'Foreign matches seem to come to nothing. Why should not Mary marry my son?'

Oh, but how handsome he was! Twenty-seven years old, yet he looked younger; his gentle, noble nature had left his face unlined. There was in him the nobility of the Plantagenets, and the resemblance to his ancestor, Edward IV, was at times marked. It would strengthen the crown if Tudor and Plantagenet were joined together, thought Margaret. And she was glad that Reginald had not yet taken Holy Orders.

During the next days the two of them were continually together. They rode out of the Castle, surrounded by the Princess's attendants naturally, but they were always side by side, a little apart from the rest of the cavalcade. She played on the virginals for his pleasure; and there were balls and banquets as well as masques in Ludlow Castle.

The Princess Mary was growing pretty, for the sternness and slight strain, which had prevented her being so before, had left her; her pale cheeks were flushed and she was less absorbed in her lessons than she had been.

It was not possible, thought Margaret, for an eleven-year-old child to be in love with a man of twenty-seven, but Mary's feelings were engaged and she was ready to idealise the man who for so long had figured in her reveries.

And as though the tide of Mary's fortune had really turned, a week or so after the arrival of Reginald Pole, Margaret came to her apartment one day holding a letter in her hand.

Mary's heart leaped with excitement because she saw that it bore the royal seal.

'I have news from Court,' she said. 'We are to prepare to leave at once for London.'

'Oh . . . Margaret!'

'Yes, my love. We have waited so long, have we not. But did I not tell you that if we were patient it would come? Well, here it is.'

Mary took the letter and read it. Then she said slowly: 'And Reginald . . . will he come with us?'

'There would be no point in leaving him in Ludlow. He will surely accompany us on the journey.'

Mary looked as though she were about to dance round the room; then she remembered her dignity, and smiling she said in a clear, calm voice: 'I am well pleased.'

🌸 Chapter V 🌸

THE KING'S CONSCIENCE

ach morning when Cardinal Wolsey awoke, he would immediately be conscious of a black cloud of depression. He was not quite certain what it meant, but it was no phantom left over from a nightmare. It was real and it was hanging over him; each day it seemed to take him a little longer to assure himself that he could overcome any difficulties which might present themselves.

On this morning he awoke early and lay listening to the birds singing their songs in the trees of Hampton Court Gardens.

Once he could have said to himself: All this is mine. Those trees, that grass, this magnificent palace and all it contains. But that glory was of the past. He had lost some of his treasures; he must hold firmly to what he had.

Each day, it seemed to him, he was more and more unsure of the King's temper.

Yesterday Henry had looked at him slyly and murmured that he had heard from Mistress Anne Boleyn's lips that she had no love for My Lord Cardinal.

Why should he care for the malicious words of a careless girl? He would know how to deal with Anne Boleyn if she were ever important enough to demand his attention. At the moment she was amusing the King.

'Let be, let be,' murmured Wolsey. 'I like the King to amuse himself with women. While he does so it keeps him from meddling in state affairs.'

And it was true that of late the King was paying less attention to state affairs; although of course, in a manner characteristic of him, he would think the 'secret matter' the biggest state affair of all. To rid himself of Katharine, to take a new French Princess to be his bride . . . a French bride for the King; a French bridegroom for the Princess Mary . . . what heavier blow could be struck at the Emperor?

The King was eager that they should begin working out the details of his separation from Katharine. The difficulty was that, if the King's marriage was no true marriage, what then of the Princess Mary? A bastard? Would François Premier want to betroth his son to a bastard?

The situation was full of dangers. Not that he did not believe he could overcome them; but he wished the attitude of the King had not changed towards him.

He had thrown Hampton Court to his master, and one would have thought that such a gift was something to remember for as long as they both should live; but the King did not seem to think so, for although he now proudly referred to 'my palace at Hampton,' his attitude to the Cardinal had not grown more kindly.

There was no doubt about it; the King must be placated. And what he was demanding was the end of his marriage.

Wolsey rose from his bed and within an hour of his rising he was receiving Richard Wolman, who had been Vicar of Walden in Essex and Canon of St Stevens in Westminster until the King, recently, had made him his chaplain, since when he had lived at Court.

When Richard Wolman stood before the Cardinal, Wolsey said: 'I have sent for you that we may discuss the delicate matter of the King's conscience.'

Wolman bowed his head.

'You know of this matter,' stated Wolsey.

'His Grace has mentioned it to me on several occasions.'

'Then you should go to him and accuse him of living in sin. Tell him that you think that as a sinner of nearly eighteen years' standing he should put himself before his Archbishop and the ecclesiastical Court to answer the charges which you have brought against him.'

Richard Wolman turned pale. 'Cardinal . . . you cannot mean . . . Why, the King would . . .'

Wolsey laughed, and lately his laughter was tinged with bitterness. 'The King will frown at you, stamp his feet and show rage. But he'll not forget those who serve him . . . as he wishes to be served. Go now and be thankful that you have been chosen to serve the King . . . and yourself.'

Wolman bowed his head. 'You can be assured of my obedience,' he said.

'That is well,' answered Wolsey. 'Lose no time. The King grows impatient.'

The King narrowed his eyes and studied his chaplain. 'Speak up!' he barked. 'Speak up!'

'Your Grace, it is in all humility I bring this charge against you.'

'You bring a charge against me!' The voice was fierce but

there was a note of eagerness in it. He was like a tame lion going through his tricks.

'Your Grace, it is after much meditation and prayer . . .'

'Get on! Get on!' said Henry impatiently.

'I have been considering Your Grace's marriage, and I come, with much fear and trembling, as Your Grace's chaplain to . . . to charge you with living in sin for eighteen years with a woman who cannot be your wife.'

'What! This is monstrous!'

Henry stamped his foot and gave such a good imitation of genuine anger, that Wolman began to tremble. 'Your Grace,' he said, 'I crave your pardon. If I have offended you . . .'

'*If* you have offended me! You come here and charge me . . . and who has more earnestly endeavoured to lead a godly life? . . . you charge *me* with . . . immorality.'

Wolman fell to his knees. He was thinking: This is a plan of the Cardinal's to ruin me. What a fool I was to allow myself to be persuaded. This is the end of my career at Court, perhaps on Earth.

'I crave Your Grace's pardon. I spoke carelessly. If Your Grace will overlook . . .'

'Silence!' thundered the King. Then his voice softened suddenly. 'If my chaplain has a criticism of my conduct I am not the man to turn a deaf ear to that criticism.'

'It was presumptuous of me, Your Grace. I pray you forget . . .'

'Alas, I cannot forget. How could I forget a matter which for so long has given me many troublous thoughts?'

Great relief swept over Wolman. This was no trick. In coming here and making the accusation he had served the King and the Cardinal as they wished to be served.

'Get up,' went on Henry. 'Now you have spoken, and right glad I am to have this matter brought into the light of day. I married a woman who was my brother's wife, and in the Book of Leviticus we are told that this is a sin in the eyes of God. I have been shown God's displeasure. I have been denied a male heir. What are you and your ecclesiastics prepared to do in this matter?'

Wolman, completely restored to confidence, began to outline Wolsey's plan. 'Your Grace will know that I have talked of this matter with His Eminence the Cardinal.'

Good Thomas, thought Henry. Acquisitive, avaricious he might be, but he could be relied upon to work out a plan of action which would bring the King his desires.

'The Cardinal feels it will be necessary to summon Your Grace before a Council led by himself and the Archbishop of Canterbury.'

The King nodded. He could rely on Thomas; as for Archbishop Warham, he was a timid fellow and could be trusted to do as his King commanded.

'There,' went on Wolman, 'the matter would be discussed, and if the Council found that Your Grace had never in truth been married . . .'

The King interrupted: 'I should then be free to marry.'

'It would be necessary doubtless to have the matter con-firmed in Rome.'

The King nodded. Clement was a good friend to him and Wolsey. He felt jubilant.

He clapped his hand on Wolman's shoulder. 'You have been bold,' he said, with a twinkle in his eyes, 'thus to accuse me. But we ever like bold men even when they upbraid us for our sins.'

Gabriel de Grammont, Bishop of Tarbes, led his train into the King's apartment, where Henry, with Wolsey, Warham and several of his most eminent ministers, was waiting to receive them.

Wolsey was delighted because he felt that at last the alliance with France was secure. This would mean war with the Emperor. Wolsey visualised a Europe rising in unison against that young man. Henry had recently received an appeal from Clement who implored him to stand against the Emperor; if he did not, declared the Pope, Charles would shortly be the universal monarch. The Italian countryside had been devastated by his troops, and there was only one course of action: England, France, and the Vatican must stand against the conqueror. The letter had come at an opportune moment and Henry had been deeply impressed by it. And when Wolsey had pointed out: 'We must stand by Clement now, for it may be that shortly we shall wish him to stand by us' Henry understood, and was as eager as his Cardinal for the French alliance.

So they had helped the Pope by sending Sir John Russell to Rome with money which would enable Clement to pay his troops and assist in the garrisoning of the City. His Holiness, when he heard English help was on the way, had called a blessing on the English King and Cardinal, and had said that their friendly action had restored him from death to life.

The moment was certainly ripe to apply to him for the Bull which would confirm that the marriage between the King of England and the Emperor's aunt was not valid and that therefore the King of England was free to marry where he wished.

Henry listened to the French Ambassadors outlining the terms of the new alliance which would mean certain war with the Emperor. François was not the man who would sit down under defeat; he would want to regain all that he had lost; he was waiting for his turn to impose harsh terms on Charles.

Henry nodded shrewdly. He knew that his people had always regarded the French as their natural enemies; and that since the coming of Katharine to England they favoured the Spanish alliance. Katharine had contrived to endear herself to the people, because they thought her serious and virtuous and there were many who had profited from her charities. Henry was a little disturbed that she had made such a good impression, but the people must be forced to understand the desirability of getting a male heir. When they realised that the important men of the Church, backed by the Pope himself, considered the King's marriage unlawful, they would be as eager as he was to accept it as no marriage at all. They would look forward to the pageantry a royal marriage would mean.

Henry pictured it: His bride beside him in the Palace of the Tower of London where she would come before her Coronation; he saw the glittering crown on her head; he saw her sitting beside him in the tiltyard, all haughtiness gone, only gratitude and love for him who had lifted her to such eminence. And the face he saw beneath the crown, the eyes that smiled at him with a faint hint of mockery, were not those of some stranger from France but a well-known young lady, a well-loved one, one who had haunted him ever since he had first seen her at Court and who had beguiled him in the gardens of her father's castle of Hever.

'By God!' he whispered to himself. 'Why not?'

He could hear her voice, high-pitched and imperious: 'Your

wife I cannot be, both in respect of mine own unworthiness and because you have a queen already. Your mistress I will not be.'

And, strangely enough, he who had never been humble was so before this girl; he, who had looked upon the gratification of his desires as his Divine right, was content to wait and plead.

He had to rouse himself from his reverie to listen to the Frenchmen; and when he did so the words of Grammont startled him.

'There is one point which I feel compelled to raise at this time,' he was saying. 'Rumours are circulating concerning the King's marriage. My master would wish to know whether it is certain that the Princess Mary is the legitimate daughter of the King.'

Sudden anger flamed in Henry's eyes to be replaced by immediate exultation.

If the legitimacy of the Princess Mary was in question, who could blame him for his determination to have the circumstances of his marriage examined?

He forced a look of intense sadness into his face and glanced towards Wolsey, who said quietly: 'We heed the Bishop's words. Little good can come of discussing that matter further at this stage.'

Katharine watched her daughter riding into the Palace of Richmond and she thought: This is one of the happiest moments of my life.

How radiant the child looked! How she had grown! Was she as happy as her mother was by this reunion?

Mary came forward ceremoniously, her eyes lowered. It is

because she fears her emotions, Katharine decided. What a Queen she will make when her time comes.

With Mary came her governess, Margaret Pole, Countess of Salisbury, and Margaret's son Reginald, both good friends of the Queen. So here was further cause for rejoicing.

Now her daughter knelt before her, and Katharine, who could stand on ceremony no longer, raised her up and embraced her.

'My dearest daughter . . .'

'Oh Mother, it has been so long.'

'Soon we shall be alone, my darling, and able to talk freely to each other.'

'That will be wonderful, Mother.'

She has not changed towards me, thought Katharine exultantly. How foolish of me to fear that she would.

She turned reluctantly from her daughter to greet Margaret. 'I thank you for the good care you have taken of my daughter.'

'To serve Your Grace and Her Highness is my pleasure,' answered Margaret formally, but the gleam in her eyes was certainly not formal.

'And your son is here too.' She smiled at Reginald. 'That gives me great pleasure.'

So they entered the Palace, and as soon as possible Katharine took her daughter to her private apartments that they might be alone.

'I have longed for this,' she told Mary.

'Oh, Mother, if you could only know how much I longed to see you. I used to kneel in the turret watching for a party of riders which would be you and your suite on the way to the Castle.'

'My dear child . . . and I never came!'

'No, but I always hoped. I never knew before how important hope is. One goes on being disappointed and loses it for a while, and then . . . there it is again.'

'You have learned an important lesson, my dearest.'

'And one day, Mother, Reginald came. That was a consolation.'

'Ah, I noticed that there was friendship between you.'

'Is he not wonderful, Mother? He is so clever and yet so kind. I think he is the gentlest man I ever knew.'

Katharine smiled. 'And you liked his gentleness?'

'So much, Mother. With him I felt at peace. And after he had been with us a short time the message came that I was to return to you. We shall not be parted again.'

Katharine did not answer. It was her duty to prepare her daughter to receive the French ambassadors who would carry news of her beauty, accomplishments and deportment to the King of France.

And if this marriage were to take place within a year . . . or very little longer . . . Mary would be sent to France, for there could be no excuse for keeping her at home any longer. Katharine felt she could not endure another separation.

'You are sad, Mother,' said Mary. 'Is it this marriage they are arranging for me which makes you so?'

The Queen nodded. 'But we will not think of unpleasant things. It could not happen for a very long time. I will tell you this: I will do everything in my power to postpone, nay prevent it.'

Mary threw herself into her mother's arms and cried passionately: 'Yes, please do. Do not let them send me away from you again. Why could I not marry in my own country?'

Katharine stroked her daughter's hair.

'Because, my darling, you would have to marry someone who is as royal as yourself.'

'There are people here who are as royal as I am.'

Katharine felt a twinge of alarm. Such words, when applied to one of the King's subjects, could be dangerous. Buckingham had used them too often.

'Edward IV was Reginald's ancestor and mine also. So Reginald is as royal as I am.'

The Queen was silent, thinking: Then has she thought of Reginald as a husband?

The idea excited Katharine. And why not? It was true Reginald Pole had Plantagenet blood in his veins. Surely it was a better policy to arrange marriages rather than executions for those whose royalty could be a threat to the crown.

If Mary married Reginald Pole, she could remain in England. Katharine visualised a happy future with her daughter never far from her side. She pictured herself with Mary's children who would take the place in her heart of those she had never had. If only it could be. If only she could prevent this French alliance!

'Yes,' she said slowly, 'Reginald Pole has royal blood in his veins. I am glad that you feel affection for him because I know him to be a good man, and his mother is one of my dearest friends.'

Mary was astute enough to read the promise in those words. She embraced her mother in sudden ecstasy as though, thought Katharine, she believes me to be all-powerful.

But let her think that, because it makes her happy; and we must be happy in these hours of reunion.

Later Katharine sat with her dear friend Margaret Pole and they were alone together, which gave pleasure to them both.

Katharine was saying: 'This is one of the happiest days of my life. I have dreamed of it ever since Mary went away.'

'As she has too,' added Margaret.

'It pleases me that she and Reginald should be drawn to each other.'

'They have indeed become good friends. The Princess is such a serious child that the difference in their ages is scarcely noticeable. My son considers her to be one of the most highly educated ladies it has been his pleasure to meet.'

'Your son has not taken Holy Orders?'

'No, he has not done so yet.'

'Does he intend to?'

'I think he is eager to study more before he does so. That is why he is going to the Carthusians at Sheen.'

The Queen smiled and a thought came to Margaret which she had had before; then it had seemed a wild dream, but it did not seem so now because she believed she read the Queen's thoughts correctly.

Katharine went on: 'The French marriage does not please me.'

'But the King and the Cardinal . . .'

'Oh yes, the Cardinal leads the King the way he wishes him to go.'

Margaret was surprised that the Queen should speak so frankly; then she realised that Katharine did so because the bond between them was a little closer even than it had been before.

'I shall not allow Mary to receive the French ambassadors tomorrow,' went on the Queen. 'I shall make the excuse that she is too weary after her long journey from Ludlow. Depend upon it, I shall do all in my power to prevent this proposed marriage. Nor do I despair of so doing. Monarchs are fickle, and François more fickle than most. Mary was betrothed to this boy once before, you remember. There was great enthusiasm . . . even a ceremony . . . and then a few years later it was as though that ceremony had never taken place.'

'The Princess is sensitive. One does not care to think of her in a foreign court. And I believe that that of the French is the most licentious in the world.'

The Queen shuddered. 'How I should like to make a match nearer home for her. There are more worthy men in England than across the seas.'

The two women had drawn closer together; they were not Queen and subject merely, not only lifelong friends; they were two mothers discussing the future of the children who meant everything in the world to them.

While the Queen sat with Margaret Pole, Iñigo de Mendoza called at the Palace and asked for an interview with her. It was imperative, he declared, that he see Her Grace without delay.

When the message was brought to the Queen, Margaret, without being bidden to do so, left her presence and Mendoza was ushered in.

Katharine saw from his expression that he was extremely agitated, and his first words told her why.

'The Cardinal is working to separate you and the King; he has called together certain bishops and lawyers that they may secretly declare the marriage to be null.'

Katharine could not speak. She knew that the King no

longer desired her; that his disappointment at the lack of a male child continued to rankle. But to cast her off as a woman who had been living with him all these years outside the sanctity of marriage, was unthinkable. Such a thing could not happen to a Daughter of Spain.

'I fear I have given you a great shock,' said the ambassador. 'But it is a matter which must be faced quickly. This must not be allowed to happen.'

'It is the Cardinal who has done this,' said the Queen. 'He has long been my enemy.'

'He could not have done it without the King's consent,' the ambassador reminded her.

'The King is a careless boy at heart. He is tired of me . . . so he allows Wolsey to persuade him that he should be rid of me.'

'Your Grace, we must act immediately.'

'What can we do if the King has decided to rid himself of me?'

'We can do our best to prevent him.'

'You do not know the King. All that he desires comes to him. He takes it as his Divine right.'

'He may have his will with his own subjects, but Your Grace is of the House of Spain. Have you forgotten that the Emperor is the son of your sister?'

'They care little for the Emperor here now,' said Katharine wearily.

'Your Grace,' the ambassador replied almost sternly, 'they will have to care.'

Katharine covered her eyes with her hand. 'So this is the end,' she said.

'The end! Indeed it is not. Your Grace, if you will not fight for yourself, you must fight for your daughter.'

'Mary! Of course ... she is involved in this.' The Queen had dropped her hand, and the ambassador saw how her eyes flashed. 'Are they saying that Mary is a bastard?'

'If the marriage were declared null, that is what I fear she would be called, Your Grace.'

'That shall never be,' said the Queen firmly.

'I knew Your Grace would say that. I beg of you, be as calm as you can, for it is calmness we need if we are to outwit those who work against us. It would be helpful, I am sure, if you could behave as though you know nothing of this which is being called the King's Secret Matter. The only help we can hope for must be from the Emperor and in view of existing relations our task is made difficult. I beg Your Grace to speak of this matter to no one until we have found a means of conveying the news to my master, your nephew.'

'This we must do without delay.'

'Your Grace is right. But to send a letter might be to act rashly. I feel sure that everything that leaves my hands is in danger of falling into those of the Cardinal's spies. We must find a messenger who will go to the Emperor with nothing written down, who will tell him by word of mouth what is happening here in England. Let us discover such a man, who must be humble enough not to excite suspicion, yet loyal enough to keep his secrets until he arrives in Spain.'

The Queen, knowing that the ambassador spoke wisely, agreed.

'I will call on you tomorrow,' he told her. 'By then I hope to have some plan. In the meantime I trust Your Grace will give no sign that we have wind of the King's Secret Matter.'

When Mendoza left her, Katharine sat for a long time, very

still, an expression of melancholy amplifying the lines on her face.

Such a short while ago she had felt so happy because her daughter was returned to her. Now her happiness had been shattered, for she knew that the greatest calamity which could befall her was threateningly near.

'There are times,' she murmured, 'when I think God has deserted me.'

As Henry prepared to set out for the Cardinal's Palace of York Place, a complacent smile played about his mouth, and his eyes were gleaming with satisfaction in which humour mingled.

It was an amusing situation when a King was summoned to appear before a court, charged with immorality. He believed that those lawyers and men of the Church must be telling themselves that here was the most tolerant King on Earth. He might have had them all clapped into the Tower for their presumption. But what had he done? Meekly accepted the summons to appear before them and hear his case thrown from the prosecuting to the defending counsels like a ball in a game.

He was certain that the outcome of the case would be that he was found guilty, after which there would be nothing to do but his penance for his sins, receive absolution and marry again that he might do his duty to his country and give it a male heir. The Pope would be called in to have the dispensation, which Julius II had given, declared invalid, but he need have no qualms about that; Clement was the friend of England. It had been a clever stroke to answer his appeal for help against the Emperor. Wolsey was to be commended for his far-sightedness.

So the King set out for York Place in high spirits.

As he stepped from his barge he studied the Palace and thought how grand it looked. It was the town residence of the Archbishops of York and thus it had passed into Wolsey's possession; but the Cardinal had added a magnificence to it which it had not possessed before, and although it may have lacked the grandeur of Hampton Court it was a very fine palace. Henry's eyes smouldered a little as he surveyed it. Hampton Court was now his, yet he felt a little resentful that a subject should possess such a residence as that of York Place.

He was slightly mollified when he entered and was received by the Cardinal who exchanged with him a secret look which was meant to imply that the stage was set and in a very short time they would have achieved their desire.

At the end of a hall on a dais Wolsey took his place beside William Warham, Archbishop of Canterbury.

Among those gathered in the hall were John Fisher, the Bishop of Rochester, who was said to be one of the wisest and saintliest men in England, Dr Bell who was to be the King's Counsel, and Dr Wolman who was to state the case against Henry's marriage.

Dr Wolman opened the proceedings against the King.

'Henry, King of England, you are called to this archi-episcopal court to answer a charge of living in sin with your brother's wife . . .'

Henry listened with the shocked appearance of a man who, in his innocence, has been caught up in a sinful intrigue, and when Wolman had stated the case against the King's marriage Dr Bell rose to speak for him.

His Grace had, it was well known, married his brother's widow, but it was said that the marriage of Prince Arthur and the Infanta Katharine had never been consummated. The reigning King, Henry VII, had expressed his desire that this consummation should not take place on account of the bridegroom's youth and delicate state of health. And when he died, six months after the marriage, Katharine had stayed in England and in the year 1509 had married their sovereign lord. A dispensation had been received from Pope Julius II, and it was the defence's case that the King had married in good faith and that it had not occurred to him that his marriage could be anything but legal. Then the Bishop of Tarbes had made a suggestion, and it became clear that this was the result of some pernicious rumour he had heard. It was the King's desire to stand by the finding of this court, but he was going to ask them to say that his marriage to Katharine of Aragon was a legal one.

Henry's eyes narrowed as he studied Dr Bell, but Wolsey had assured him that they could trust Bell. He must put the King's case in such a manner that it would appear to be a case for the defence. But Bell would know how to act when the moment came.

Wolman was on his feet; he did not think the marriage could have remained unconsummated during the six months the married pair lived together. It would be remembered that they travelled to Ludlow with their own Court and there made merry together. If the marriage had been consummated then, Katharine of Aragon had been the wife of the King's brother in actual fact, and Wolman maintained that the marriage was illegal.

When it was Henry's turn to speak he did so with apparent sincerity, for he had convinced himself that it was solely because he wished to stand unsullied in the eyes of God and his subjects that he was glad the matter had been brought to light.

'I can but rejoice that this matter has been brought into the light of day,' he told the court. 'Lately it has much troubled my conscience. I could not understand why our prayers should be unanswered. The Queen's persistent ill health has been a matter of great concern to me, and I trust you learned gentlemen will unravel this delicate matter that I may peacefully return to my wife or – which will cause me much sorrow – declare that our marriage was no marriage and our union must end without delay.'

William Warham listened intently. He lacked the guile of Wolsey and he was coming to the end of an arduous life. He was in his seventies and often it seemed to those about him that he was failing. He was simple enough to believe that the reason for this enquiry was the fact that the Bishop of Tarbes had raised the question of the Princess's legitimacy. He was anxious to give the matter his most careful attention with the hope that he might lead the members of this court to come to the right conclusion.

The details of the King's marriage were discussed at length; Katharine's arrival in England was recalled, followed by her marriage to Arthur which had lasted only six months.

'If that marriage was consummated,' said Warham, 'then the Queen has most certainly been the wife of Prince Arthur, and the King could be said to have taken his brother's wife.'

'Which,' sighed the King, 'according to the Holy Word is an unclean thing. Such unions shall be childless, says the Bible. And behold a son has been denied me.'

'But there was a dispensation from the Pope,' put in the Bishop of Rochester. 'I think Your Grace should not reproach yourself.'

'The Pope would have been under the impression that the marriage had not been consummated, when he granted the dispensation,' said Wolman. 'If it could be proved that the marriage *had* been consummated, then clearly there could be no marriage between the King and Katharine of Aragon.'

'I think,' persisted Rochester gently, 'that the King should suppress his qualms, for there seems little doubt that his marriage is a good one and that the Bull, which legalised it, was sufficient to do so.'

Henry studied John Fisher, Bishop of Rochester, from beneath lowered lids. He found it hard to hide his animosity. A curse on these saintly men who expressed their opinions with freedom even before their rulers. Fisher was the Queen's confessor and clearly her partisan. Wolsey should not have included the man in this court. It was folly to have done so.

Warham was weak and growing simple in his old age. Warham could be handled. But the King was not sure of Fisher.

By God, he thought, I'll have him in the Tower, beloved of the people though he may be, if he dares to stand out against me.

'My lords,' Wolsey was saying, 'I beg of you to come to a quick decision in this case, for the matter is grievous to the King. His Grace is perplexed. If you decide that his union is unlawful, remember it will be necessary for him to part from the Lady Katharine at once, and this will afford him great sorrow for, though he be not in truth her husband, he has a husband's affection for her.'

Warham's gentle grey eyes were sad. He was thinking of the Queen who would be deeply disturbed if she knew what was happening at York Place.

Henry was now on his feet telling the court how devoted he was to his wife, how there was no other motive in his heart but the desire to free himself from a sinful union that he might live in peace with God. Katharine had been his wife for eighteen years, and he had found in her all he had hoped to find in a wife.

'Save in one thing!' His voice thundered. 'And that, gentlemen, is this matter which is of the utmost importance to my kingdom. Our marriage has not been as fruitful as we wished. We have but one daughter. Again and again it seemed that my wife would produce the son for whom we prayed each night and day; but we were disappointed. It is not until now – when the Bishop of Tarbes comes to my kingdom with his revealing enquiry – that I see the divine pattern of these continual misfortunes. Ah, gentlemen, if you decide that my marriage is no marriage, if I must part with her . . . whom I love dearly and have always regarded as my wife . . . then your King will be the most unhappy of men. For the Lady Katharine is of such virtue, such gentleness and humility, possessed of all the qualities pertaining to nobility; and if I were to marry again – and it were not a sin to marry *her* – she is the woman I would choose above all others.'

As he spoke he seemed to see a vital young face laughing at him, mocking him. There was more than a trace of mockery in Anne. It was part of her witchery and it enslaved him.

He found himself answering her in his thoughts: Well, 'tis for our future. Were I to tell these Bishops of my need for you, they would never understand. Poor old fellows, what could they know of what is between us two!

But the mood passed quickly, and in a few moments he was believing all he said. The little mouth, which had grown slack as he thought of Anne, tightened and became prim. I should never have thought of casting off Katharine but for the continued gnawing of my conscience, he told himself; and he immediately believed it. Katharine was the woman he had insisted on marrying eighteen years ago; it was not because her body had grown shapeless, her hair lacked lustre, and that she provoked no physical desire in him that he would be rid of her. It had nothing to do with the most fascinating woman he had ever known, who still kept aloof and would not submit to him, yet maddened him with her promises of what would be his if she were his wife. No, he told himself sternly, Anne was apart from this. He loved Anne with every pulse of his body; his unsatisfied desire was becoming more than he could endure; and since he had discovered that no other woman would suffice in her place, he was making secret plans now to give Anne what she wanted. (By God, she asks a high price for herself, a crown no less. But worth it, my beauty!) Yet, he assured himself, but for the demands of conscience he would never have questioned his marriage to Katharine. It was solely because he feared he was living in sin, and must quickly cease to do so, that he was here before his bishops and lawyers this day.

'This matter cannot be settled in any haste,' said Warham. 'The findings of the court must be examined.'

Henry fidgeted. He was almost on his feet. He wanted to shout at them: You idle fellows Time to examine your findings! What do you want with that? I tell you I want a divorce, and, by God, a divorce I shall have or clap every man of you into the Tower.

But in time he saw the horror which was dawning in the Cardinal's eyes and restrained himself with difficulty.

So the court was adjourned.

The King was with the Cardinal when the messengers arrived; these were messengers with no ordinary tidings; they demanded that they be taken with all speed to the King's presence, assuring those who tried to detain them that it would go ill with them if the news they carried were kept from the King an instant longer than it need be.

When this message was brought to Henry he said: 'Let them come to me at once.'

They came in, travel-stained and breathless from their haste, their eyes alight with the excitement of those who have news which is such as is heard once in a lifetime.

'Your Grace . . . Your Eminence . . .' The words then began to tumble out. 'Bourbon's troops have attacked Rome. The city is in the hands of savage soldiery. The Pope has escaped with his life by shutting himself up in the Castle of St Angelo. The carnage, Your Grace, Your Eminence, is indescribable.'

Henry was horrified. The Pope a prisoner! Rome in the hands of lewd and savage soldiers! Never had such a disaster befallen Christendom.

The Constable of Bourbon, the declared enemy of the King of France, was siding with the Emperor, and his army it was which had launched this attack on Rome. Bourbon himself was dead; indeed, he had had no desire to attack Rome; but his army was reduced to famine; there was no money with which to pay them; they demanded conquest and would have killed him if he had stood in their way.

So on that fateful May day this ragged, starving, desperate army had marched on Rome.

Bourbon had been killed in the attack but his men did not need him. On they had rushed, into Rome.

Never had men and women seen such wanton destruction;

the fact that this was the city of Rome seemed to raise greater determination to destroy and desecrate than men had ever felt before.

The invaders stormed into the streets, killing men, women and children who were in their way; they battered their way into the palaces and great houses; they crammed food into their starving mouths; they poured wine down their scorching throats. But they had not come merely to eat and drink.

They invaded the churches, seizing the rich ornaments, images, vases, chalices which were brought into the streets and piled high into any means of conveyance the marauders were able to snatch. Every man was determined to have his pile of treasures, to reward himself for the months of bitter privation.

During those five terrible days when the soldiers were in possession of Rome, they determined that every woman should be raped and not a single virgin left in the city. The greatest amusement was afforded them by the nuns who had believed that their cloth would protect them. Into the convents burst the soldiers. They caught the nuns at prayer and stripped them of those robes which the innocent women had thought would protect them. Horror had pervaded the convents of Rome.

In the streets wine ran from the broken casks, and satiated soldiers lay in the gutters exhausted by their excesses. Priceless tapestry and gleaming utensils which had been stolen from altars and palaces and thrown from windows were lying in the street. The soldiers were mercenaries from Spain, Germany and Naples; and to the desecration of Rome each brought the worst of his national characteristics. The Germans destroyed with brutal efficiency; the Neapolitans were responsible for the greatest sexual outrages; and the Spaniards took a great delight in inflicting subtle cruelty.

It was not enough to commit rape and murder; others must join in their fun. So they brought monks and nuns together, stripped them of their robes and forced the monks to rape the nuns, while these vile soldiers stood by applauding and mocking.

Never had such sights been seen in Rome, and the people who had managed to escape with their lives cried out in great lamentation, declaring that if God did not punish such wickedness it must be believed that He did not trouble Himself about the affairs of this world.

This was the story the messengers brought to the King on that May day, and to which he listened in increasing anger and horror.

He sent the messengers away to be refreshed, and when they had gone he turned to the Cardinal.

'This is the most terrible tale I ever heard.'

'And doubly so,' answered Wolsey, 'coming at this time.'

Henry was startled. While he was listening to the tale of horror he had forgotten his own predicament.

Wolsey went on: 'The Pope a prisoner in the Castel Sant' Angelo! Although Bourbon led the attack on Rome, the Pope is now the Emperor's prisoner. Your Grace will see that, being the prisoner of the Emperor, he will not be in a position to declare invalid the dispensation regarding the Emperor's aunt.'

'By God, I see what you mean,' said Henry. 'But he will not long be a prisoner. It is monstrous that the Holy Father should be treated so.'

'I am in agreement with Your Grace. But I fear this will mean delay.'

The King's mouth was petulant. 'I weary of delay,' he murmured.

'We must act quickly, Your Grace, and there are two tasks which lie ahead of us. We must send an embassy to France without delay in order that we may, with the help of our ally, liberate the Pope from this humiliating situation.'

'Who will go on such an embassy?'

'It is a delicate matter, in view of what is involved,' said Wolsey.

'You must go, Thomas. None could succeed as you will. You know all that is in my heart at this time; and you will bring about that which we need.'

Wolsey bowed his head. 'I will begin my preparations at once, Your Grace.'

'You spoke of another task.'

'Yes, Your Grace. The Queen will have heard rumours of our court of enquiry. I think she should be told of Your Grace's conflict with your conscience.'

'And who should tell her this?' demanded Henry.

Wolsey was silent and Henry went on sullenly: 'I see what is in your mind. This should come from no lips but my own.'

The Princess Mary was seated in her favourite position on a stool at her mother's feet, leaning her head against the velvet of Katharine's skirt. She was saying how happy she was that they could be together again, and that the long sojourn at Ludlow seemed like a nightmare.

'Oh Mother,' cried the Princess, 'is there any more news of my marriage?'

'None, my darling.'

'You would tell me, would you not. You would not try to shield me . . . because, Mother, I would rather know the truth.'

'My dearest, if I knew of anything concerning your marriage I should tell you, because I believe with you that it is well to be prepared.'

Mary took her mother's hand and played with the rings as she used to when she was a baby.

'I fancied you seemed distraught of late. I wondered if there had been some evil news . . .'

Katharine laid her hand on her daughter's head and held it firmly against her. She was glad Mary could not see her face. Evil news! she thought. The most evil news that could be brought to me! Your father is trying to cast me off.

But she would not tell Mary this, for who could say how the girl would act? She might be foolhardy enough, affectionate enough, to face her father, to upbraid him for his treatment of her mother. She must not do that. Henry could never endure criticism, more especially when he was doing something of which he might be ashamed. He could harm Mary as certainly as he could harm Katharine. Indeed, thought the Queen, my daughter's destiny is so entwined with mine that the evil which befalls me must touch her also. Better for her not to know of this terrible shadow which hangs over us. Let her be kept in ignorance for as long as possible.

'There is no further news of your marriage,' said the Queen firmly. 'Nor do I think there will be. These friendships with foreign countries are flimsy. They come and go.'

'It would be so much better if I were married to someone at home here,' said Mary.

'Perhaps that may happen,' replied the Queen soothingly. 'Who shall say?'

Mary turned and lifted a radiant face to her mother. 'You see Mother, not only should I marry someone who was of my own country . . . speaking my own language, understanding our ways . . . but I should be with you. Imagine, for evermore we should be together! Perhaps I should not always live at Court. Perhaps I should have a house in the country; but you would come and visit me there . . . and often I should be at Court. When my children are born you would be beside me. Would that not be so much happier than our being separated and your hearing the news through messengers?'

'It would be the happiest state which could befall us both.'

'Then you will tell my father so?'

'My darling, do you think I have any influence with your father?'

'Oh . . . but you are my mother.'

The Queen's brows were drawn together in consternation and, realising that she had let a certain bitterness creep into her voice, she said quickly: 'Kings are eager to make marriages of state for their sons and daughters. But depend upon it, Mary, that if I have any influence it shall be used to bring you your heart's desire.'

They were silent for a while and the Queen wondered whether Mary was really thinking of Reginald Pole when she talked of marriage, and whether it was possible for one so young to be in love with a man.

While they sat thus the King came into the apartment. He was alone, which was unusual, for he rarely moved about the Palace without a little cluster of attendants. He was more sombrely clad than usual and he looked like a man with a private sorrow.

The Queen and Princess rose, and both curtseyed as he approached.

'Ha!' he said. 'So our daughter is with you. It is pleasant to see you back at Court, daughter.'

'I thank Your Grace,' murmured Mary.

'And you play the virginals as well as ever, I believe. You must prove this to us.'

'Yes, Your Grace. Do you wish me to now?'

'No . . . no. I have a matter of some importance to discuss with your mother, and I am going to send you away. Go and practise on the virginals so that you will not disappoint me when you next show me your progress.'

As Mary curtseyed again and went away, Katharine was thinking: What can I say to him now, knowing what I do? How can anything ever be the same between us again?

As soon as Mary had left them, Henry turned to her, his hands clasped behind his back, on his face an expression of melancholy, his mouth tight and prim, the general effect being that before Katharine stood a man who had forced himself to a painful duty.

He began: 'Katharine, I have a grievous matter to discuss with you.'

'I am eager to discuss that matter with you,' she answered.

'Ah,' he went on, 'I would give half my kingdom if by so doing I could have prevented this from happening.'

'I pray you tell me what is in your mind.'

'Katharine, you were poor and desolate when I married you; you were a stranger in a strange land; you were the widow of my brother, and it seemed that there was no home for you in the country of your birth nor here in the country of your adoption.'

'I shall never forget those days,' she answered.

'And I determined to change all that. I was young and idealistic, and you were young too, then, and beautiful.'

'Both qualities which I no longer possess.'

The King turned his eyes to the ceiling. 'That could be of no importance in this matter. But it seems that learned men . . . men of the Church . . . have examined our marriage . . . or what we believed to be our marriage . . . and they have found that it is no true marriage.'

'Then they deceive you,' she said fiercely.

'As I told them. But they are learned men and they quote the law to me. They read the Bible to me and tell me that I have sinned against God's laws. We have both sinned, Katharine.'

'This makes no sense,' retorted Katharine. 'How could we have sinned by marrying?'

'It is so clear to me now. It is in the Bible. Read it, Katharine. Read the twenty-first verse of the twentieth chapter of Leviticus. Then you will see that ours was no true marriage and that for all these years we have been living in sin.'

Katharine stared at him blankly. This was no surprise to her, but to hear it from his own lips, to see that stubborn determination which she knew so well, light up his eyes, shocked her more deeply than she had ever been shocked before.

'I know,' went on the King, 'that this is a matter which distresses you, even as it distresses me. I will admit to a temptation to turn my back on this, to scoff at my critics, to say, let us forget that I married my brother's wife. But I can hear the voice of God speaking to me through my conscience . . .'

'When did your conscience first begin to trouble you?' she asked.

'It was when I heard the suggestion made by the Bishop of Tarbes; when he questioned Mary's legitimacy.'

At the mention of her daughter, Katharine's bravado crumpled; she looked older suddenly and a very frightened woman.

'You see,' went on the King, 'much as this distresses me, and indeed it breaks my heart to consider that we can no longer live together . . .'

'Which we have not done for some time,' she reminded him. 'We had ceased to be bedfellows before your conscience was troubled.'

'Your poor state of health . . . my consideration for you . . . my fears that another pregnancy would be beyond your strength . . .'

'And your interest in others . . .' murmured Katharine.

But Henry went on as though he had not heard her: 'What a tragedy when a King and Queen, so long married, so devoted to each other, should suddenly understand that their marriage is no marriage, and that they must separate. I have given this matter much thought. I have said to myself, What will become of her? For myself, I have not cared. But for you, Katharine . . . you whom I always, until this time, thought of as my wife . . .' He paused, pretending to be overcome by his emotions.

She wanted to shout at him that she despised him, that she knew it was not his conscience that was behind this dastardly plot but his desire for a new wife. She wanted to say: How dare you cast insults at a Princess of Spain? And what of our daughter? Will you, merely that you may satisfy your lust in the sanctity of a marriage bed, cast me off and proclaim our daughter a bastard!

It was the thought of Mary which was unnerving her. Her

usual calm had deserted her; she could feel her mouth trembling so that it would not form the words she wanted to utter; her limbs were threatening to collapse.

Henry went on: 'Knowing your serious nature, your love of the Church and all it stands for, it seemed to me that you would wish to enter a convent and there pass the rest of your days in peace. It should be a convent of your choosing and you should be its abbess. You need have no fear that you would lose any of the dignity of your rank . . .'

A voice within her cried: Do you think you could strip me of that? You have insulted me by telling me that I lived with you for all these years when I was not your legal wife; and now you dare tell me — the daughter of Isabella and Ferdinand — that you will not rob me of my rank!

But the words would not come and the hot tears were spilling over and running down her cheeks.

Henry stared at her. He had never seen her thus. That she, who had always been so conscious of her dignity and rank, should weep, was something he had not considered.

It horrified him.

'Now, Kate,' he said, 'you must not weep. You must be brave . . . as I would fain be. Think not that I cease to love you. Love you I always shall. The Bishops may say what they will; you may not be my wife in the eyes of God but always I shall love you as I did in those days when you were so poor and lonely and I lifted you up to share my throne. Do not grieve. Who knows . . . they may find that there is naught wrong with our marriage after all. Kate, Kate, dry your eyes. And remember this: For the time being this is our secret matter. We do not want it bruited abroad. If I could but come to terms with my conscience I would snap my fingers at these

Bishops, Kate. I'd have them clapped into the Tower for daring to hint . . .'

But she was not listening. She did not believe him. She did not see the virtuous, religious man he was trying to show her; she saw only the lustful King who was tired of one wife and wanted another.

Her tears fell faster, and convulsive sobs shook her body.

Henry stood awhile, staring at her in dismay; then he turned abruptly and left her.

Chapter VI

THE QUEEN AND THE CARDINAL
IN DANGER

When the Queen had recovered from her grief she sent for Mendoza.

'All that we feared has come to pass,' she told him. 'The King is determined to rid himself of me. He has told me that his conscience troubles him because learned men have assured him that we are not truly married.'

'So it has gone as far as that!' muttered Mendoza. 'We shall need a strong advocate to defend Your Grace . . .'

'Where should I find one here in England?' she asked.

'Your Grace can trust none of the King's subjects. We must immediately appeal to the Emperor.'

'I will write to him with all speed.'

Mendoza shook his head. 'It is very doubtful that any appeal from you would be allowed to reach him.'

Katharine stared helplessly at the ambassador.

'Or,' he continued, 'any appeal from me either. The Cardinal's spies will be doubly vigilant. We must smuggle a messenger out of the country, and it must be done in such a way that no suspicion is attached to him.'

'What a sad state of affairs when I am denied a lawyer to defend me.'

'Let us be hopeful,' answered Mendoza, 'and say that the King knows that he has such a poor case that he dare not allow a good lawyer to defend you. Is there any member of Your Grace's household whom you trust completely?'

Katharine thought awhile and then said: 'He must be a Spaniard for he will have to travel into Spain to reach the Emperor. I can only think of Francisco Felipez who has been in my service for twenty-seven years. I am sure he is to be trusted.'

'An excellent choice. He should leave for Spain as soon as possible. But he should carry nothing in writing and it should seem that you do not send him but that he wishes to go of his own accord.'

'I will summon him and together we will form some plan.'

'It would be unwise for Your Grace to send for him now while I am here. I am certain that we are being closely watched. Indeed, it may be unwise to send for him at all, because it will doubtless be suspected that you will try to get a message through to the Emperor. If Your Grace could seize an opportunity of speaking to him when he is performing some duty – just whispering a word to him when no one will notice – that would be the best plan. Then if he expresses a desire to see his family, it will not appear that he is on Your Grace's business.'

'How I hate this intrigue! I feel like a prisoner in the Tower rather than a Queen in her Palace.'

The ambassador looked at her sadly. He wondered what might have befallen her, standing in the King's way as she did, had she not been the aunt of the Emperor.

❀ ❀ ❀

Francisco Felipez presented himself to the King and asked if he might speak to him in private.

Henry granted this request, thinking that the man came with some message from the Queen, but as soon as they were alone Felipez said: 'Your Grace, I am in great distress. My mother is dying and wishes to give me her blessing. I have come to ask your permission to go to her.'

'You are a servant of the Queen,' said Henry. 'Have you not asked her for this licence?'

Felipez looked uneasy. 'I have, Your Grace.'

'Well?'

'And she has refused it.'

The King's blue eyes were wide with astonishment.

'Why so?' he demanded.

'She believes that I do not speak the truth.'

'And has she reason to believe this?'

'None, Your Grace.'

'This is unlike the Queen. I have always thought her to be most considerate of her servants.'

'The Queen has changed. She accused me of seeking to leave her, as all her servants would do in time.'

'But why should she say such a thing?'

The man hesitated, but Henry insisted that he should continue. 'Your Grace, the Queen says that, since you are displeased with her, all her servants will find excuses to leave her.'

'I fear the Queen is suffering from delusions,' said Henry. 'It grieves me that she should have so little thought for her servants. You did well to come to me. I will grant your licence;

I will do more. I will give you a safe-conduct through France which will make your journey so much easier.'

Felipez fell to his knees, tears of gratitude in his eyes.

'We see you are pleased,' said Henry gruffly. 'I will give you your licence now.'

'How can I thank Your Grace?' stammered the man.

But Henry waved a hand and went to the table. He wrote for a while, then handed the man a document.

'This will stuffice,' he said. 'You need have no fear that you will be intercepted. I trust that you will reach your mother in time.'

When Felipez had gone, Henry thought: There is a man who, should he return to England, will be my servant, not the Queen's.

It was some days later when Henry remembered the incident and mentioned it in a letter he wrote to the Cardinal who was now in France.

The Cardinal's answer came back promptly.

'This man but feigns to visit his sick mother. Your Highness will realise that it is chiefly for disclosing your secret matter to the Emperor and to devise means and ways of how it may be impeached. I pray Your Grace to ascertain whether this man has left England and, if he has not, to stop him. If he has left, I will, if it be in my power, have him intercepted in his journey across France, for if this matter should come to the Emperor's ears, it should be no little hindrance to Your Grace.'

When Henry read that letter he was furious. He had been foolish not to see through the ruse. What a cunning woman the Queen had become! He should have seen through her deception. And because the Cardinal had seen at once, and because had the Cardinal been in England the licence would

216

never have been granted, Henry, perversely, felt irritated with the Cardinal.

There was another reason which made him uneasy when he thought of the Cardinal. There were certain matters which he had withheld from his minister. Anne hated Wolsey and she was gradually persuading Henry to hate him.

Anne had said: 'If the Cardinal knew of our desires he would work against us. Never have I forgotten the time when he treated me as though I were the lowest serving wench – and all because Henry Percy had spoken for me.'

'But, sweetheart, if any man can get me my divorce, that man is the Cardinal,' Henry had insisted.

Anne had agreed with that. They should use the Cardinal, for he was a wily man; she did not deny that. But he believed that the purpose of the divorce he was trying to arrange was that Henry might marry Renée, daughter of Louis XII, not Anne Boleyn.

So there were secrets which the King had kept from the Cardinal, and during recent months it had often been necessary to deceive him. Once there had been complete accord between them, but this was no longer so, and now Henry was irritated to think of those secrets; he might have despised himself for his duplicity, but as he could not do that, he gave vent to his feelings in his dislike of Wolsey.

He brushed the man out of his thoughts and had the Court searched for Francisco Felipez. He could not be found. It seemed that he had left England several days before.

The King sent for one of his secretaries, Dr William Knight. This was a man whom he trusted and who had already shown himself a worthy ambassador, for Henry had often sent him abroad on state business.

William Knight was a man of some fifty years and Henry had chosen him for his wisdom and experience.

'Ah, my good William,' said the King as soon as Dr Knight entered his apartment, 'you have been in my service many years, and I have great faith in you; that is why I now assign to you the most important task of your life.'

William Knight was surprised. He stammered: 'Your Grace knows that whatever task is assigned to me I will perform with all my wits.'

'We know it, William. That is why we are entrusting you with this matter. You are to leave at once for Rome, travelling through France of course.'

'Yes, Your Grace.'

'And when you reach Rome you must find some means of seeing the Pope. I wish this matter of the divorce to be hastened. I chafe with the delay. I wish you to ask the Pope to give Cardinal Wolsey the power to try our case here in England. And there is one other matter. As soon as the divorce is settled I shall marry – immediately. I consider it my duty to marry and I have chosen the Lady Anne Boleyn to be my wife.'

William Knight did not answer. He had heard rumours of course. He knew that the Boleyn faction had great influence with the King, but had not realised that the matter had gone so far and that the King could possibly contemplate marriage with Thomas Boleyn's daughter while Wolsey was in France – not exactly negotiating for a marriage with the Princess Renée, but surely with this in mind.

'There is one matter,' went on the King, 'which gives me great concern. I fear there may be an obstacle to my union with the Lady Anne, owing to a relationship I once had with her sister, Mary. Because of the existing canon law a close relationship has been established between the Lady Anne and myself, and in order that this be removed there would have to be a dispensation from the Pope. Your mission in Rome is that you request the Pope, beside giving Wolsey permission to try the case, to give you the dispensation which would enable me to marry the Lady Anne with a free conscience.'

William Knight bowed. 'I will set out for Rome at once,' he told the King, 'and serve Your Grace with all my heart and power.'

Henry slapped his secretary's shoulder.

'Begone, good William. I look to see you back ere long. Bring me what I wish and I'll not forget the service you have rendered. But, by God, make haste. I chafe against delay.'

Wolsey had set out for France, travelling to the coast with even more than his usual pomp. His red satin robes, his tippet of sables, made him a dazzling figure in the midst of his brilliant cavalcade; he held himself erect and glanced neither to right nor left, because he knew that the looks of those who had gathered to see him pass would be hostile. At one time he would have scorned them; he did so no longer; he, the proud Cardinal, would have eagerly welcomed one kindly smile, would have been delighted with one friendly word.

He thought as he rode along that he was like a man climbing a mountain. He had come far over the grassy slopes which had been easy to scale; but now the top was in sight and he had to traverse the glacial surface to reach it. He had come so far that there was no going back; and he was on the treacherous ground where one false step could send him hurtling into the valley of degradation.

All about him were his servants in their red and gold livery. Where the crowd was thick his gentlemen ushers cried out: 'On, my lords and masters, on before. Make way for my Lord's Grace.'

Even he who had been wont to pass each day from York Place or Hampton to Westminster Hall in the greatest pomp had never travelled quite so magnificently as he did at this time. Now he rode as the King's vicar-general, and as he went through the City and over London bridge, through Kent on his way to the sea, he could not help wondering how many more such glorious journeys there would be for him; and what the next journey would be, and whether the people would come from their houses to watch Wolsey pass by.

Yet even though his heart was heavy with foreboding, he could enjoy this ostentatious display. Here he was the central figure among nine hundred horsemen, seated on his mule with its trappings of crimson velvet and stirrups of copper and gilt. In his hand he held an orange, the inside of which had been removed and replaced with unguents and vinegar which would be proof against the pestilential air. Delicately he sniffed it when he passed through the poor villages and from the corner of his eye saw the ragged men and women who had come out to stare at him. Before him were carried two enormous crosses of silver and two pillars, also of silver, the great seal of England and his Cardinal's hat, that all might realise that he was not merely the great Cardinal, as his red robes proclaimed him, but the Chancellor and the richest man in England – under the King.

He proposed to make two calls on his way to Dover. One

should be at Rochester and the other at Canterbury, that he might confer with the Archbishops, Fisher and Warham. The King had commanded him to do this for Henry was unsure of those two. It was Warham who had wanted time to consider the findings of the court. If this had not been so, it might have been declared, before the news of the Sack of Rome reached London, that the marriage was invalid. As for Fisher, since he was the Queen's confessor, Henry suspected him of being the Queen's friend.

So the Cardinal halted at Rochester and there was received in the Bishop's palace.

When they were alone together Wolsey said tentatively that he believed the Bishop was not fully informed of the King's Secret Matter and that the King was eager that this should be remedied. He then went over the old ground to stress the suggestion made by the Bishop of Tarbes and the King's consequent misgivings.

Fisher listened gravely, and his compassion for the Queen was intensified by all he heard.

'I fear,' said Wolsey, 'that when His Grace broached the matter to the Queen she became hysterical, much to the King's displeasure.'

'I am sorry to hear it,' answered Fisher.

'As her confessor,' Wolsey replied, 'you might bring her to a mood of submission. His Grace feels that you have much influence with her and that you might remind her of the comfort to be found in a life of seclusion.'

The Bishop nodded and, when the Cardinal had left him, he was on his knees for a long time praying for the Queen.

Then on to Canterbury to see Warham and to hint to him that Henry would expect no opposition to the divorce; and, sure that he was bringing Warham to the right state of mind, he continued on his way.

And so to France, there to pass through the countryside, to be gaped at and watched in silence as he proceeded along the road to Paris.

There was nothing lacking in the welcome given him by François and Louise. Pageants and balls were arranged for his pleasure; plays were enacted before him; and all of a greater wit and subtlety than those he was accustomed to witness at the Court of England. François insisted on showing him some of the fine building he was carrying out; building was one of the French King's passions and almost as important to him as the pursuit of women. Wolsey was enchanted by the superb architecture he saw in France, and dreamed of rebuilding some of his own residences in England. This made him think of Hampton Court which was no longer his and, because when he had been obliged to throw that mansion to the King it had been a gesture which marked the change in their relationship, he was depressed; and it occurred to him then that he would never be able to plan new additions to his palaces.

But his skill was still with him. He completed the treaty with France and gave a pledge that Mary should marry the Duc d'Orléans. As yet he could do little but hint of the King's marriage with the Princess Renée, because it was scarcely diplomatic to discuss the proposed marriage of a man who was not yet recognised as a bachelor in the eyes of the world. But François could understand a hint better than most; and naturally he was fully aware of the King's Secret Matter, and he gave hint for hint; he would welcome a marriage between the Princess Renée and the King of England, once the latter was free to take a wife.

Wolsey was resting at Compiègne when Dr Knight caught up with him. The Cardinal was surprised to see his fellow countryman and received him warmly, eager to know on what business he had come to France.

Dr Knight had received no instructions not to inform Wolsey of his mission; he believed that the Cardinal was perfecting the more difficult negotiations with François while he, Knight, had the simpler task – for it would be simple once he could reach the Pope – of requesting the required dispensation and asking permission for Wolsey to conduct the enquiry into the divorce.

When the two men were alone together, Knight explained: 'The King decided, soon after you had left, that he would send me to Rome. I am now on my way there.'

Wolsey was startled and depressed. If the King was not keeping him informed of all the measures he was taking, it was a bad sign.

'What is your mission in Rome?' he asked, hoping to sound casual.

'In the first place to get the permission of His Holiness for you to try the case.'

Wolsey gave a great sigh of relief. It was reasonable that such a request should not come from him personally, and he immediately saw the point of the King's engaging Knight for this commission.

'And in the second place?' he asked.

'Oh . . . a simple matter. The King's conscience worries him regarding a previous connection with Mary Boleyn.'

'With Mary Boleyn!'

'It seems the girl was his mistress at one time.'

'And his conscience worries him . . .'

'I confess I was a little surprised. It is true that family has been giving itself airs of late but I did not know the King was infatuated so much as to consider marriage.'

'Please explain,' said Wolsey calmly.

'Since the King proposes to marry Anne Boleyn he requires a dispensation on account of his sexual conduct with her sister.'

Wolsey was speechless for a few seconds. Somewhere close by a bell began to toll, and it seemed to him that the bell tolled for Cardinal Wolsey.

He soon recovered his poise. He was eager that Knight should not guess how deep the rift was between him and the King.

'The King's conscience is ever active,' he said lightly.

'He is cautious now – eager that when he marries again it shall be a true marriage and that he runs no risk of offending the Deity and thus be deprived of a male heir.'

Wolsey nodded, eager to be alone with his thoughts.

When Knight had left him he sat for a long time staring before him. He had come to France, and one of his missions was to hint at a French marriage for the King. The King knew this. And yet . . . all the time they had discussed this matter together he had been contemplating marriage with Anne Boleyn.

'That black-eyed witch!' muttered Wolsey; and suddenly so much was clear to him. He knew why the King had slowly but certainly turned his back on him. Mistress Anne had commanded him to do so. Mistress Anne hated the Cardinal who had upbraided her as though she were a humble serving wench at the time when Percy had tried to marry her. Vengeance had blazed from those proud eyes and he had laughed, because he could not believe that he – the great Cardinal – had anything to fear from a foolish girl.

Now this girl was constantly at the King's side; she had bewitched him so completely that, unsuitable as the marriage was (and to think he had declared her not good enough for Percy!) he was determined to marry her. It was desire for this black-eyed girl, not his miserable conscience, that had set this matter in motion. And the most powerful person at Court was now Anne Boleyn, the declared enemy of the Cardinal.

It had happened under his very eyes and he had not seen it. He had been blind – he who had come so far because he had always seen a move ahead of all others. But he was old and tired now and he was afraid.

What now? he asked himself; and once more he heard the tolling of the bell.

He wanted to pray then, for help, for guidance.

I shall overcome this, as I have all other obstacles. I shall make this woman sorry that she proclaimed herself my enemy.

He seemed to hear mocking laughter, and he thought it sounded like Buckingham's laughter. Buckingham had lost his head; it had not been difficult to teach him a lesson, and he was one of the foremost noblemen in the land. Should he fear a woman – and one whose claims to nobility were slight?

No, he was not afraid.

Yet he wanted to pray and suddenly realised that he could not do so. All he could do was sink to his knees and talk of his fear, ask for the power to triumph over his enemies. But that did not seem like a prayer.

He rose. He would return to England and there he would see the King; and now there would be no secrets between them. He was no longer deceived by the King's attitude to the Lady which he had believed to be similar to that which he had felt towards many another.

This was different. This was something the King had never felt before, and it explained the change in their relationship.

Wolsey must tread very warily. Always before he had triumphed; why should he not triumph again?

Tomorrow he would leave for England, his mission completed. He would retire and after a good night's rest he would be refreshed.

He went to the window to look out on the peaceful scene below, and as he stood there he saw that someone had drawn a sketch on the woodwork with a piece of charcoal.

It was not pretty. There was a gallows and there was something lifelike about the figure which hung from it. The Cardinal's robes had been roughly but effectively sketched.

Who had done that? Someone in his suite? Someone who hated him and took a vicious delight in making such a sketch where, more likely than not, his eyes would alight on it.

The Cardinal took his kerchief and was about to rub it away. Then he hesitated. No. It would be a sign of weakness. Let it remain; let others see it. He was accustomed to abuse. It had always been his from the start of the climb, yet it had had little effect on his success. If it had not then, why should it now?

So he went to bed; but he slept ill that night. He dreamed of a black-eyed woman who, for the King's delight, was drawing charcoal sketches of a Cardinal swinging on the gallows.

The Queen's barge sailed from Greenwich to Richmond, and all along the banks the people stood cheering her as she passed. The Princess Mary was with Katharine; she could scarcely bear the girl to be out of her sight, and her greatest fear was that they would be separated.

'God bless the Queen!' shouted the people. 'God bless the Princess Mary!'

Katharine acknowledged their greetings and the Princess did the same. It was comforting to go among these people, for everywhere they showed their pleasure in her. Henry might talk in hushed tones of his Secret Matter, but he was the only one who believed it was a secret, and the King's desire for a divorce was discussed in every tavern along the river. Almost without exception the people were on the side of the Queen. The women were fierce in championing her cause.

'A pretty state of affairs,' they grumbled, 'when a man tires of his wife and says she is not his wife that he may be free to choose a younger woman. If this is marriage, then save us from it!'

Since Queen Katharine had come to England, the English had felt the Spaniards to be their friends, and their natural enemies the French; some believed the latter to be a species of monkey and that many of them had tails which their fine clothes hid.

And the villain behind it all was the Cardinal. They had always hated the Cardinal. 'Who was the Cardinal?' they had often asked each other. 'No better than you or I. Did you know his father was a butcher?'

Who imposed taxes to fight wars which no one wanted? The Cardinal.

Who lived like a king although he was the son of a butcher? Who made treaties with France because France paid him well to do so? Who was responsible for all the poverty in the country? Who chopped off the head of the noble Duke of Buckingham because he had thrown dirty water over his shoes? The answer to all these questions was Wolsey.

They thought of him as they had seen him so many times, riding through the streets on his mule which was caparisoned in scarlet and gold, sniffing his orange as though he disdained them and feared contamination with them.

The King has been led astray by him. The King was jovial, fond of sport; the King was young and easily led. Wolsey had wanted to make an alliance with the French, so he had made the King doubt the validity of his marriage to Katharine of Aragon; and the Princess Mary – the dear little Princess Mary – was proclaimed a bastard!

'Long live Queen Katharine!' cried the people. 'Queen Katharine for ever!'

To the barge came the sound of singing and Katharine took heart as she heard it, for it proclaimed the love of the people for the Princess Mary whom they regarded as the heir to the throne.

> *'Yea, a Princess whom to describe*
> *It were hard for an orator.*
> *She is but a child in age,*
> *And yet she is both wise and sage –*
> *And beautiful in flavour.*
>
> *Perfectly doth she represent*
> *The singular graces excellent*
> *Both of her father and mother.*
> *Howbeit, this disregarding,*
> *The carter of York is meddling*
> *For to divorce them asunder.'*

In that song was not only their love of their Princess and their determination to support Katharine's cause but their hatred of Wolsey, Archbishop of York, whom they sometimes referred to as a carter, sometimes a butcher.

'Long live the Princess Mary!' cried the people; and Mary lifted a hand in acknowledgment of the greeting and smiled in her eager but dignified way which never failed to please them.

And so they came to the oddly shaped turrets of Richmond which glowed in the sunshine like inverted pears.

In the quiet of her apartments Bishop Fisher was waiting for Katharine who had summoned him thither.

'My lord,' she said, when they were alone, 'it pleases me that you have come. I have need of your counsel.'

'I pray Your Grace to calm yourself. Wolsey visited me on his way to the coast. He told me how distressed you were after your interview with the King.'

'I fear I lost control.'

'We must pray for greater control.'

'Sometimes I could hope that death would come to me.'

'When we die, Your Grace, is a matter for God to decide.'

'I know it is wrong of me, but there are times when I feel that life is too bitter to be borne.'

'And you pray that this cup might pass from you,' murmured the Bishop. 'There is one, Your Grace, who needs you now. You must not forget that this matter concerns your daughter.'

'It is that which breaks my heart.'

'We are not defeated yet.'

'My lord, you say *we*. Does that mean that you will stand beside me?'

'I will pray with you and for you.'

She looked at him searchingly. 'I have always felt you to be my friend as well as my confessor. I know you to be a good man. But I am well acquainted with the King's nature. He is a boy at heart, but boys can be selfish, my lord Bishop. They stretch out greedy hands for that which they want, and because they are boys, lacking the experience of suffering, they do not think what pain may be caused to those who stand in their way.'

The Bishop looked at her sadly. He believed she did not understand her husband if she thought of him merely as a boy who had been led into temptation. The Bishop had looked at the King and seen the cruelty behind the jovial mask. He prayed that this gentle woman would never be forced to see her husband in a different light from the one in which she saw him now.

'You will need courage,' said the Bishop. 'Let us pray for courage.'

They prayed and when they rose from their knees the Queen said: 'I shall not go into a convent. That is what they are trying to force me to do.'

'It is what they hope you will do.'

'I know. But I shall never do it. There is my daughter to fight for; and let me tell you this, my lord Bishop: I shall never agree to be put aside, and the reason is that, if I did so, they would brand my daughter with bastardy. That is something I shall never allow to happen.'

John Fisher bowed his head. He believed that the Queen's decision was the right one and a brave one. He had seen the vicious determination in the King's face; he had seen the shrewd cunning in Wolsey's. Could this gentle woman defend herself against them; and what would be the result to herself . . . and to those who supported her?

She had made her choice and he knew that she would not

diverge from it. John Fisher too made his choice.

She would not have many friends when the King abandoned her; but he, John Fisher, Bishop of Rochester, would be one of them.

The Queen was delighted when Mendoza brought her the news.

'Felipez did his work well,' he said. 'I have heard from the Emperor, and he sends notes for you and for the King. I know that His Grace was not pleased with his, as it reproved him for his treatment of you and expressed shock and indignation.'

The Queen clasped her hands together. 'I knew I could trust Charles,' she cried. 'He is immersed in his wars, but when a matter of vital importance arises, such as this, he would always stand by his family. His support will make all the difference in the world.'

'I am in agreement with Your Grace,' said Mendoza. 'And we should not forget that the Pope, without whom the marriage cannot be declared invalid, is at your nephew's mercy. Here is the letter he sends to you.'

Katharine took it eagerly and as she read it a smile of triumph touched her lips.

Charles was horrified; he was shocked beyond measure. It would seem that the King of England had forgotten, so long had his wife been in England, that she was a daughter of the House of Spain. He was sending Cardinal Quiñones, the General of the Franciscans, to Rome with all speed; he would look after her affairs there; and she could trust her nephew to watch over her cause and help her. Clement VII, still in Castel Sant' Angelo, was too wise a man to flout the wishes of the Emperor.

Katharine put her lips to the letter. 'God bless you, Charles,' she murmured. 'Families should stand together always.'

She felt the tears touch her eyes, for she was reminded suddenly of Charles's mother, running wildly round the nursery in the days when they were children, trying to quarrel with her sisters and brother; and their mother drawing the rebellious child to her and explaining that sisters and brothers should never quarrel; they must always stand together against the rest of the world if need be.

Oh to be a child again! thought Katharine. Oh to be back there in Madrid, in Granada, in Valladolid . . . under the loving wing of that best and wisest of mothers . . . never to grow up, never to leave the nest!

Then she thought of her own daughter. Had she remained a child herself she would never have had Mary.

She laughed at her folly. She should feel exultant because Charles had answered her cry for help.

The Cardinal had returned to England, and, hearing that the King was in residence at Greenwich, he sent his messenger to the Palace to tell Henry of his arrival and ask where His Grace would wish to receive him.

Henry was in good spirits when the messenger arrived; a pageant was being enacted before him and it had been the work of Anne Boleyn, her brother George and some of the bright young poets who were members of their set. Henry was finding these young people far more to his taste than the older men and women. Moreover Anne was the leader of the group, and where Anne was, there Henry wished to be.

Anne, imperious in her beauty and fully aware of the hold

she had over the King, bold, flamboyant and arrogant, had already taken upon herself the role of Queen which she expected shortly to be hers in fact. She seemed to delight in shocking those about her by taking such liberties that the King would never have tolerated from anyone else and yet meekly accepted when coming from her.

So when the messenger asked where and when His Grace would wish to receive the newly returned Cardinal, it was Anne who answered in her sprightly way: 'Where should the Cardinal come except where the King is?'

There was a breathless silence. Would the King endure such boldness even from her? Was she suggesting that the Cardinal – still the greatest of the King's ministers – should come into the ballroom, travel-stained as he must be? Was she ordering him to come in as though he were some lackey?

Apparently in the King's eyes she could do no wrong, for he laughed aloud and said: 'That's true enough!' and repeated: 'Where should the Cardinal come except where the King is?'

'Your Grace will receive him here!' said Wolsey's messenger, aghast.

'You heard His Grace's command,' answered Anne sharply.

So the messenger bowed himself from their presence and went to Wolsey who, with the stains of travel on his red satin robes and sweat on his brow, a little breathless from the journey, very weary, hoping for a little time in which to bathe himself, change his linen and rest awhile that he might collect his thoughts and frame his conversation with the King, listened in astonishment.

'To go straight to his presence! You have not heard aright,' he insisted.

'Your Eminence, it is the King's command, given through the Lady Anne, that you should go to him at once.'

The Lady Anne! So she was with him. She was already the Queen of England in all but name. And that would come, for the King demanded it. And he, poor fool, had helped to sow the seeds of that desire for divorce in the fickle mind; he, who had had dreams of a French alliance, a permanent bulwark against the Emperor, had helped to bring the Lady Anne – his most bitter enemy – to where she now stood.

He could do nothing but obey; so, weary, conscious of his unkempt appearance, he went into the ballroom and made his way to the King.

It was as he had feared. There stood the King, and beside him the Lady Anne. The others had moved away leaving the three of them together.

'Your Grace . . . my lady . . .'

The King's eyes were not unkind; but they showed he was absentminded; their blue was shining with pleasure in his companion, desire for her; even as they stood, his hand caressed her shoulder.

And she smiled at Wolsey – the enemy's smile, the smile of one who inflicts humiliation and rejoices. It was as if she were saying to him: Do you remember Anne Boleyn who was not good enough for Percy? Do you remember how you berated her as though she were some slut from the kitchens? This is the same Anne Boleyn who now stands beside the King, who says, You shall come to us now! and whom you dare not disobey.

'I trust you have good news for us, Thomas,' said the King.

'The mission went well, Your Grace.'

But Henry scarcely saw his minister. Good news meant for

him one thing. When could he go to bed with this woman, accompanied by a good conscience?

This was a more dangerous moment than any the Cardinal had yet passed through; he felt now as he had felt when he had heard the bell's tolling at Compiègne, when he had seen the charcoal drawing of a Cardinal hanging on the gallows. No, his apprehension went deeper than that.

He knew that this day there were two people in England who were in acute danger. And if one of these was Katharine the Queen, the other was Cardinal Wolsey.

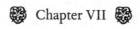

Chapter VII

THE KING PENITENT

Through the winter which followed, Katharine tried to ignore her fears. She continued to live much as she had lived before; her days were made up of sewing, reading, prayers, listening to music and playing an occasional game of cards with her maids.

There was one of these maids of honour who commanded her attention; she could no longer be blind to the position of Anne Boleyn in the Court. At the centre of all the tourneys and masques was this woman, and her constant companions were her brother, Thomas Wyatt and some of the other bright men of the younger artistic set. They wrote plays and pageants which they acted for the King's pleasure; and it was, during those fateful winter days, as though there were two groups – one which revolved round the Queen and the other round Anne; it was in Anne's that the King was to be found.

Often Katharine would absent herself from some entertainment because her dignity would not allow her to see the King treating Anne Boleyn as though she were already the Queen.

She herself did not show by her demeanour that she regarded this woman as different from any other of her maids of honour; she made herself seem blind to the fact that the King was chafing against his marriage to her and made no secret of his desire for Anne.

As for Anne, imperious as she might be to all others, including the King, she was subdued by the dignity of the Queen; and because of Katharine's restraint there were no difficult scenes between them. Henry avoided his wife as much as possible; they shared no part of their private life. He had said that he regarded himself as a bachelor and that while he deplored the necessity of waiting until he was publicly announced to be that, nothing could prevent him from regarding himself as one.

Only once did Katharine show that she knew Anne was trying to usurp her position; that was during a game of cards. Anne had dealt, and Katharine said: 'My Lady Anne, you have good hap to stop at a king; but you are not like others, you will have all or none.'

Anne had seemed a little shaken by this comment and had played her hand badly, but Katharine remained serene, and those who watched said: 'She believes that the King will come to his senses, that he will realise it is impossible for him to cast her off.'

Yet that evening when she was alone she thought of the imperious young beauty, with her flashing dark eyes and her exotic clothes, her grace, her manner of holding herself as though she already wore a crown on her head, and she dared not look too far into the future.

Sometimes she felt so alone. There was her daughter who meant everything to her, but she did not care to speak to Mary of this trouble. She hoped that Mary knew nothing of it; the child was too sensitive.

As long as we are together, she told herself, I suppose I can endure anything. But I shall stand out firmly against a convent, for Mary's sake.

She considered those who might help her. Mendoza would stand beside her but he was only an ambassador and no theologian. His word would carry little weight in this country. Warham was an honest man, but he was old and very much in awe of Wolsey and the King. The women who had been her friends had been sent away from her. How comforting it would have been to have talked with Maria de Salinas! Luis Vives had left England after having been told sharply by Wolsey that he would be wise not to meddle in the King's affairs. Vives was a scholar who was eager to avoid conflict, so perhaps he had thought it as well to leave while he could do so.

Thomas More came to see her. He did not speak of what was known as the King's Secret Matter, but managed to convey to her the assurance that he was her friend.

John Fisher, to whom she confessed her sins, also came and brought comfort.

'I have been warned,' he told her, 'not to meddle in the King's matter, but if I can be of use to Your Grace I shall continue to disobey those orders.'

'I thank God for your friendship,' Katharine told him.

'Let us pray for courage,' answered the Bishop; and they prayed together.

Often during those winter months when her spirits were at their lowest, she thought of Fisher and More, and felt happier because they were not far away, and although they might not have much influence in this matter with the King, they were her friends.

With the spring came news from Rome. The Pope had

appointed Lorenzo Campeggio, Cardinal of Santa Anastasia, to come to England to decide the case in conjunction with Cardinal Wolsey.

There was consternation at Court. It was June and the heat was oppressive. One day a man walking by the river suddenly fell and lay on the bank and, when certain passers-by paused to see what ailed him, it was clear that he was a victim of the sweating sickness.

The same day several more people died in the streets; the epidemic had come to London.

Periodically this scourge returned, killing people in their thousands, and when it appeared in the big cities such as London it brought panic with it for it was in the hot and fetid streets that the sickness was more quickly passed from one to another.

Henry was disturbed when the news was brought to him. He was at Greenwich and he decided that he would stay there for a few days and not journey to Westminster through the infected city even by barge.

It was his gentleman of the bedchamber, William Carey, who had brought him the news. He had been gracious to Will Carey because Anne expected him to be so to all her relations, and Will was in need of advancement, having very little money of his own. Moreover Henry was not displeased to favour the man, for he still thought affectionately of Will's wife Mary, although he now heartily wished that she had never been his mistress, since there was a possibility that this might make it necessary for him to procure a dispensation on her account.

'The sweat is claiming more victims, Your Grace,' said Will. 'I saw several people lying in the streets as I came through the city.'

The King's eyes narrowed. 'I do not know,' he said gloomily, 'why this pestilence should visit my country every now and then. I do believe that there are some of my subjects who are of the opinion that it is sent to us when we have in some way offended God.'

'Ah, it may be so, Your Grace.'

Will was thinking that the King referred to his living in sin with Katharine and, because Mary had told him that they must always stand by Anne who had stood by them so magnificently, he added: 'It may be that when your Grace's matter is settled the sickness will pass.'

'It may well be, it may well be,' murmured the King.

But he was uneasy. He had ceased to co-habit with Katharine these many months, so he could no longer be said to be living in sin; it was strange that God should have sent the sweat now that he had realised his sinful way of life and was seeking to rectify it.

In common with most he believed that pestilences were a sign of Divine anger. Then, in spite of his desire to break away from Katharine, God had sent a pestilence to his Kingdom.

His expression was sullen, and Will, who by living near to him had learned when to remain silent, said no more. Indeed Will himself was experiencing a strange shivering fit which had nothing to do with being in the presence of the King. When Henry had strolled to the window and stood looking out on the river accompanied by certain of his gentlemen, Will seized the opportunity to leave the royal apartments.

Before he had time to reach his own quarters he felt the dreaded sweat on his body.

❀ ❀ ❀

'Your Grace, the sweat is in the Palace.'

Henry heard the dreaded words and stared at the man who was speaking to him.

'One of Your Grace's gentlemen has succumbed to the sickness. He is dead.'

Henry shouted: 'Who?'

'Will Carey, Your Grace.'

Will Carey! He had been speaking to the man only a few hours before.

Henry was trembling. 'Leave me,' he said.

Will Cary dead! Will was a man whom he had favoured because of his relationship to Anne. And he was the first victim in the Palace, the King's own Palace.

Mary would be left a widow with her two young children, and Anne would be seeking help for her ere long, for she was ever zealous regarding the needs of her family.

But even as he thought of Anne his terror caught up with him. Now he must face the truth. Why was he seeking to rid himself of Katharine? Was it indeed because he feared he had lived in sin all these years, or was it because he was tired of Katharine and wanted a new wife?

He half closed his eyes and set his mouth into the familiar prim lines, but he could not hold that expression because he was thinking of Anne, Anne in black velvet, in scarlet and gold, Anne stretching out her arms to him, no longer holding him off. It was no use; there were times when even he could not deceive himself.

He sent for Wolsey; he believed then that in times of peril he would always send for Wolsey.

The Cardinal came from Hampton in his barge. He made no concessions to the plague, beyond the orange which he carried more as an elegant gesture than out of fear. Wolsey had little concern for the sweat; he had other and more pressing matters with which to occupy himself.

'We are deeply disturbed by this pestilence,' said the King. 'It seems that the Almighty is displeased with us.'

The Cardinal asked: 'For what reason does Your Grace think God is displeased?'

'I will admit,' answered the King, 'that I have thought with much eagerness of my approaching marriage.'

Wolsey looked grim. Let the King's conscience worry him. It was well that it should. If he lusted after Anne Boleyn, let him regard that as a sin.

'That may well be,' said Wolsey.

The King looked startled, but the Cardinal's expression was as gloomy as his own.

'It is true that I am not in actual fact married to Katharine,' went on the King almost defiantly.

Wolsey spread his hands. 'Perhaps, Your Grace, it would be well, until we have proved that the marriage with the Lady Katharine is no true marriage, if Your Grace continued to live the life of a bachelor.'

A hot flush spread itself across Henry's features as he muttered: 'I have heard Mass each day . . . more than once. I have confessed each day . . .'

'None knows Your Grace's piety better than I, but it may be that is not enough.'

'Not . . . enough!'

'It may be that it would be wise at this stage to send the Lady Anne back to her father's castle.'

Henry looked so angry for a few moments that Wolsey felt he had gone too far. But after a while the King nodded. He was clearly very frightened.

'Mayhap you are right,' he said.

An easy victory, thought the Cardinal; and that day the Lady Anne Boleyn was sent to her father's castle at Hever.

As for Henry, he changed his mode of life. He made several wills; he was often in the Queen's company when they conversed like good friends, and he would sit with her watching her at her tapestry; when she went to a religious service in the chapel, he would accompany her and none appeared to be more devout than the King. It would seem that he had dismissed Anne Boleyn and returned to the Queen in all but one respect; he would not share her bed.

How virtuously he lived during those hot summer weeks! Soon after Carey's death he insisted that the Court leave Greenwich, and first they went to Eltham and then farther away from the City. Henry kept his physicians beside him; he was in terror that he might become a victim of the sickness.

He made Dr Butts talk to him of plasters and lotions which might serve, in less severe cases, to save the lives of victims. His greatest pleasure was to concoct these cures with the doctor, and he even made a plaster of his own and gave the recipe to apothecaries that they might make it for their customers. It was said to be efficacious in mild cases and was known as The King's Own Plaster.

Still further news came of death. When his old friend Sir William Compton died, Henry was deeply distressed. He remembered how, on his first illness, after his return from

France, when an ulcer had appeared on his leg, he and Compton had made plasters together, for Compton had also suffered with an ulcer.

And now . . . Compton was a victim of the sweat!

The Cardinal, who was so busy with his affairs at Hampton, was surprised by the King's conscience which insisted that at this time he part with Anne Boleyn by sending her home to Hever while he himself posed as a virtuous husband to Katharine, although not sharing her bed. Wolsey wondered whether Henry admitted to himself that he avoided this because he found her unattractive or whether he told himself that he still believed she was not his wife.

But although he had sent Anne away, Henry wrote loving letters to her, erotic letters, telling her of his need of her, hinting at what the future held for them both. As though God, being so busy watching him at confession and Mass, did not see the sly little notes which were sent behind His back.

At one time the Cardinal might have rejoiced in this characteristic of the King's; now he knew how dangerous it might prove. So Wolsey was one who was too concerned with his own affairs to be worried by the possibility of death through the sweating sickness.

Nor was Katharine afraid. If death came she would be ready to welcome it, for life had little to offer her. Many people were dying, and accounts of deaths came every day, but she had few friends to lose. She thanked God that Maria de Salinas was in the country far from risk of infection, and Margaret Pole was with Mary who had also been sent out of danger.

Meanwhile the King lived his ostentatiously virtuous life and longed for the epidemic to pass.

But one day there came news from Hever which threw the

King into a panic: Anne was a victim of the sweating sickness.

Henry threw aside his penitence and sat down at once to write a letter to her.

Her news had made him desolate. He would willingly share her sufferings. He could not send her his first physician because the man was absent at this time and he feared delay, so he was sending her his good Dr Butts. She must be guided by Dr Butts. He longed for her, and to see her again would be greater comfort to him than all the most precious jewels in the world.

Then he settled himself to wait. It was no use. He could no longer pretend. He could no longer sit with the Queen and listen to her conversation; he had to face the truth. He wanted Anne. He would have Anne.

So his conscience – on which he could almost always rely to do what was required of it – began greatly to trouble him once more concerning his marriage with his brother's widow. If the sickness had been a sign of God's anger, that anger was the result of his living in sin with Katharine, and the sooner he was free of her the better pleased would he – and God – be. Why was that Cardinal Campeggio taking such a long time to arrive? Wolsey was a laggard. Why had he not arranged matters better than this?

He waited for news from Hever. He could think of nothing but his need of her. And when that news came, and it was good news, he was full of joy for many days, taking it that, since his darling's life was spared, this was a sign of heavenly approval for their union.

He no longer sat with Katharine; there was no longer need to confess so regularly, to pray so long.

The sickness was abating; Anne had recovered; soon she would be with him.

But where was Campeggio? And what was the sluggish Wolsey doing to bring him his heart's desire?

🏵 Chapter VIII 🏵

THE MARRIAGE BRIEF

Cardinal Lorenzo Campeggio arrived in London in October. It was three months since he had set out from Rome, and he had been expected long before. Wolsey received him at York Place where he arrived inconspicuously, much to Wolsey's disgust, for even now, anxious as he was, he hated to miss an opportunity of giving the people a display of his magnificence. Wolsey would have preferred to go out with his household about him – his silver crosses, his pillars of silver, his seal and his Cardinal's hat – and to have a ceremonial meeting with his fellow Cardinal in public.

Campeggio had other ideas and had kept his arrival a secret until he came quietly to York Place.

Wolsey embraced him and gave orders for apartments to be made ready for the distinguished visitor. 'The best we have to offer. Your Eminence, we have long awaited this pleasure.'

Campeggio winced as Wolsey took his hands. 'I suffer agonies from the gout,' he told his host; and indeed it was obvious that he spoke the truth. When Wolsey looked into that pale face with the lines of pain strongly marked on it, he assured himself that here was a man who would not be difficult to lead. Surely one who suffered as Campeggio did would be more concerned with resting his weary limbs than fighting Katharine's battle.

'We shall do our utmost to make you comfortable here,' Wolsey told him; 'and we shall put the best physicians at your service.'

'There is little physicians can do for me,' mourned Campeggio. 'My friend, there are days when I am in such pain that I cannot bear the light of day. Then I ask nothing but to lie in a dark room and that no one should come near me.'

'Yours must have been a grievously painful journey.'

Campeggio lifted his shoulders despairingly. 'There were times when it was impossible for me to ride; even travelling in a litter was too much for me. Hence the delay.'

Wolsey was not so foolish as to believe that Campeggio's gout was the only reason for the delay. He guessed that the Pope, in his very delicate position, would not be eager to proclaim the marriage of the Emperor's aunt invalid. Clearly Clement was playing for time. Campeggio's gout had been very useful; and doubtless would be in the future.

'The King,' Wolsey told Campeggio, 'is most eager to have this matter settled.'

'So I believe.' Campeggio shook his head sadly. 'It is not good for the Church,' he went on. 'Whatever the outcome, His Holiness will not feel easy in his mind.'

'But if the King's marriage is no marriage . . .'

'His Holiness is horrified at the thought that the King of England and the Infanta of Spain may have been living in sin for eighteen years.'

'It should not be a difficult matter,' insisted Wolsey, 'to

prove that owing to the Queen's previous marriage, that with the King cannot be legal.'

'I cannot agree,' Campeggio retorted. 'It may well prove a most difficult matter.'

Wolsey understood then that the Pope was not going to grant a divorce, because he was too much in awe of the Emperor; and Wolsey believed that Clement had sent Campeggio, who was as much an expert in vacillation as he was himself, to conduct the case with very definite orders that nothing must be settled in a hurry, and before any decision was reached the Vatican must be informed.

The King would be infuriated by the delay, and if he were disappointed in the manner in which the case was conducted, he would blame Wolsey.

When Campeggio had recovered from the strain of his journey, he went, accompanied by Wolsey, to Greenwich to see the King.

Henry received him with outward cordiality but inward suspicions. He did not like the appearance of Campeggio – the Legate was unhealthy; he looked pale and tired; his limbs were swollen with the gout which had so lengthened his journey across France. Could not Clement have sent a healthy man! the King grumbled to himself. Moreover there was a shrewd look in the fellow's eyes, a certain dignity which Henry believed was meant to remind him that he was a servant of the Pope and served no other.

By God, thought the King, there has been delay enough.

'Welcome, welcome,' he said; and bade Campeggio be seated with Wolsey beside him.

When Henry had offered condolences for the Legate's sufferings he plunged into the real reasons for his being in England.

'There has been much delay,' he said, 'and I wish the proceedings to begin at once.'

'As soon as possible,' murmured Campeggio. 'But I would like to say that if we could settle this matter without much noise it would please His Holiness.'

'I care not how it is settled, provided it *is* settled,' said the King.

'His Holiness begs Your Grace to consider the effect of a divorce on your subjects.'

Wolsey watching closely saw the danger signals leap up in the King's eyes. He said quickly: 'His Holiness has no need to ask His Grace to do that. His Grace's one great concern is the wellbeing of his subjects, and it is for their good that he seeks freedom from this alliance which has proved a barren one.'

Henry threw a grateful glance at his Chancellor.

'Then,' went on Campeggio, 'I am sure I have an acceptable solution. His Holiness will examine the dispensation made by his predecessor, Julius II, and adjust it, making a new dispensation in which there can be no manner of doubt that the marriage between Henry Tudor and Katharine of Aragon is lawful.'

Wolsey dared not look at the King because he knew that Henry would be unable to contain his rage.

'So I have waited three months to hear that!' spluttered Henry. 'It may well be that I know more of this matter than any other person. I have grappled with my conscience, and it tells me this: never . . . never . . . shall I find favour in the sight of God while I continue to live with a woman who is not my wife in His eyes.'

'Your Grace knows more of the matter than any theologian, it seems,' said Campeggio with a faint smile.

'That is so!' thundered Henry. 'And all I want of you is a decision whether or not that marriage is valid.'

Campeggio, who had a wry sense of humour, murmured: 'I gather that what Your Grace wishes is a decision that the marriage is *not* valid.'

'His Grace has suffered much from indecision,' added Wolsey.

'The indecision of others,' retorted Campeggio. 'I see that there is no uncertainty in his mind. Now His Holiness is most eager that there should be an amicable settlement of this grievous matter, and my first duty will be to see the Queen and suggest to her that she retire into a convent. If she would do this and renounce her marriage, His Holiness would then without delay declare the marriage null and void. It would be her choice, and none could complain of that.'

Henry's anger was a little appeased. If Katharine would but be sensible, how simply this matter could end. What was her life outside convent walls that she could not make this small sacrifice? She could live inside a convent in much the same manner as she did outside. It seemed to him a little thing to ask.

'She might be told,' he suggested, 'that if she will retire to a convent, her daughter shall not suffer but shall be next in succession after my legitimate male heirs. There, you see how I am ready to be reasonable. All I ask is that she shall slip quietly away from Court into her convent.'

'I will put this matter to her,' replied Campeggio. 'It is the only solution which would please the Holy Father. If she should refuse . . .'

'Why should she refuse?' demanded Henry. 'What has she

to lose? She shall have every comfort inside convent walls as she does outside.'

'She would have to embrace a life of celibacy.'

'Bah!' cried the King. 'She has embraced that for several months. I tell you this: I have not shared her bed all that time. Nor would I ever do so again.'

'Unless of course,' murmured Campeggio rather slyly, 'His Holiness declared the marriage to be a true one.'

The King's anger caught him off his guard. 'Never! Never! Never!' he cried.

Campeggio smiled faintly. 'I see that an angel descending from Heaven could not persuade you to do what you have made up your mind not to do. My next duty is to see the Queen.'

❀ ❀ ❀

Katharine received the two Cardinals in her apartments where Campeggio opened the interview by telling her that he came to advise her to enter a convent. Wolsey, watching her closely, saw the stubborn line of her mouth and knew that she would not give way without a struggle.

'I have no intention of going into a convent,' she told him.

'Your Grace, this may be a sacrifice which is asked of you, but through it you would settle a matter which gives great distress to many people.'

'Distress?' she said significantly. 'To whom does it bring greater distress than to me?'

'Do you remember what happened in the case of Louis XII? His wife retired to a convent and so made him free to marry again.'

'I do not intend to follow the example of others. Each case is different. For myself I say that I am the King's wife, and none shall say that I am not.'

'Does Your Grace understand that unless you comply with this request there must be a case which will be tried in a court?' Wolsey asked.

She turned to Wolsey. 'Yes, my lord Cardinal, I understand.'

'If you would take our advice . . .' began Wolsey.

'Take your advice, my lord? I have always deplored your voluptuous way of life, and I know full well that when you hate you are as a scorpion. You hate my nephew because he did not make you Pope. And because I am his aunt you have turned your venom on me, and I know that it is your malice which has kindled this fire. Do you think I would take advice from you?'

Wolsey turned to Campeggio and his expression said: You see that we have a hysterical woman with whom to deal.

'Your Grace,' interposed Campeggio, 'I would tell you that, if you allow this case to be tried in the light of day, it may well go against you, in which event your good name would suffer grievous damage.'

'I should rejoice if this case were brought into the light of day,' replied Katharine, 'for I have no fear of the truth.'

Campeggio's hope of an easy settlement of this matter was fast evaporating. The King was determined to separate from the Queen; and the Queen, in her way, was as stubborn as the King.

He still did not abandon hope of forcing her into a convent. If he could get her to admit that her marriage with Arthur had been consummated, he believed he could persuade her to go into a convent. He had summed up her character. She was a pious woman and would never lie in the confessional even though, for her daughter's sake, she might do so outside it.

He said: 'Would Your Grace consider confessing to me?'

She did not hesitate for a moment. 'I should be happy to do so.'

Campeggio turned to Wolsey who said immediately: 'I will take my leave.'

He went back with all haste to the King to tell him what had taken place at the interview; and Campeggio and Katharine went into the Queen's private chamber that she might confess to him.

When she knelt the Legate from Rome asked the fatal question: 'Your Grace was married to Prince Arthur for some six months, from November until April; did you never during that time share a bed with the Prince?'

'Yes,' answered Katharine, 'I did.'

'On how many occasions?'

'We slept together only seven nights during those six months.'

'Ah,' said Campeggio, 'and would you tell me that not once during those seven nights . . .'

Katharine interrupted: 'Always he left me as he found me – a virgin.'

'And this you swear in the name of God the Father, the Son and the Holy Ghost?'

'This I swear,' said Katharine emphatically.

He sighed, knowing that she spoke the truth; the gout was beginning to nag and he longed for the peace of a dark room. He could see that this case was not going to be settled without a great deal of trouble; nothing, he decided, must be settled quickly. The situation in Europe was fluid. It would go ill with him and the Holy Father if they granted Henry his wish and then found that the whole of Christendom was in the hands of the Emperor.

Henry was furious when he learned of Katharine's determination not to go into a convent.

He summoned Wolsey, and the Chancellor came apprehensively, wondering in what mood he would find the King. He was not kept long in doubt. Henry was striding up and down his apartment, his little eyes seeming almost to disappear in the folds of puffy flesh; an unhealthy tinge of purple showed in his cheeks.

'So the Queen will not go into a convent!' he roared. 'She does this out of perversity. What difference could it make to her? As for your gouty companion, I like him not. I think the pair of you put your heads together and plot how best you can cheat me of my rights.'

'Your Grace!'

'Ay!' said the King. 'Cardinals! They fancy they serve the Pope.' His eyes narrowed still further. 'They shall discover that the Pope has no power to protect them from the wrath of a King!'

'Your Grace, I admit to sharing your disappointment in Campeggio. He seems to delight in delay. I have reasoned with him. I have told him of your Grace's wishes. I have reminded him that when the Holy Father was in distress he came to you, and how out of your benevolence . . .'

''Tis so,' interrupted the King. 'I sent him money. And what good did it do? You advised it, Master Wolsey. You said: 'We will help him now and later he will help us. Whom do you serve – your King or your Pope?'

'With all my heart and soul, with all the powers that God has given me, I serve my King.'

The King softened slightly. 'Then what are we to do, Thomas? What are we to do? How much longer must I go on in this sorry state?'

'When the case is heard, Your Grace, we shall have the decision of the court . . .'

'Presided over by that man . . . he has his orders from Clement, and I may not like those orders.'

'Your Grace, you have your own Chancellor to fight for you.'

'Ah, Thomas, if they had but let you try this case as I so wished!'

'Your Grace would have been free of his encumbrances ere now.'

'I know it. I know it. But this waiting galls me. There are times when I think I am surrounded by enemies who plot against me.'

'Clement is uncertain at this time, Your Grace. I hear that he is not enjoying good health. The Sack of Rome and his imprisonment have shocked him deeply. It may be that he will not be long for this world.'

Henry looked at his Chancellor and suddenly he burst out laughing.

'Ha!' he cried. 'If we had an English Pope there would not be all this trouble for the King of England; that's what you're thinking, eh Thomas?'

'An English Pope would never forget that he owed his good fortune to an English King.'

Henry clapped his hand on Wolsey's shoulder.

'Well,' he said, 'we'll pray that Clement may see the light or

. . . fail to see aught else. He's shaking in his shoes, that Holy Father of ours. He fears to offend Charles and he fears to offend me, so he sends his gouty old advocate and says: "Do nothing . . . promise nothing . . . wait!" By God and all His saints, I cannot think how I endure him and his master's policy.'

'We shall win our case, Your Grace. Have no fear of it. Remember that your Chancellor will sit with Campeggio, and while he is there Your Grace has the best advocate he could possibly procure.'

'We shall find means of winning our case,' said Henry darkly. 'But it grieves me that the Queen should have so little regard for the fitness of this matter as to refuse our request. Why should she refuse to go into a convent! What difference could it make to her?' His eyes narrowed. 'There are times when I wonder if she does this to spite me; and if she is so determined to do me harm, how can we know where such plans would stop? I have my enemies. It might be that they work against me in secret. If the Queen were involved with them in some plot against me . . .'

Henry fell silent. He could not continue even before his Chancellor; and to Wolsey his words and the secretive manner in which he said them were like a cold breeze on a hot summer's day. The climate of the King's favour was growing very uncertain.

Wolsey could not have much hope for the Queen's future peace if she did not comply with the King's desires. Perhaps she was unwise. Perhaps life in a convent, however abhorrent it seemed to her, would be preferable to what her life would be were she to arouse the full fury of the King's displeasure.

Since the Queen refused to enter a convent, Campeggio realised that there would have to be a court case; and as this was so it was impossible to deny Katharine the advisers who would be granted to any defendant in such circumstances.

Accordingly William Warham and John Fisher, Archbishops of Canterbury and Rochester respectively, were appointed her leading counsel; the Bishop of London, Cuthbert Tunstall and Henry Standish, Bishop of St Asaph's, joined them with John Clerk, the Bishop of Bath and Wells. It was arranged that as the Queen was a foreigner she should not rely entirely on Englishmen for her defence, and Luis Vives and one of her confessors, Jorge de Athequa, were appointed with two Flemings. The Flemings and Vives were abroad, and it seemed unlikely that they would be of much use to her; and she was shrewd enough to know that, with the exception of John Fisher, those who had been chosen to support her cause would be in great fear of offending the King.

Preparations for the hearing were going forward and Campeggio looked on with some misgivings. His great plan was to postpone the hearing on any pretext whatsoever, as he dreaded being forced to give a judgment while the affairs of Europe were so unsettled. His gout provided him with a good excuse, and there were whole days when he shut himself in a darkened room while the servants assured all callers that he was too ill to see them.

One day when Katharine was with her chaplain, Thomas Abell, the priest said to her: 'Your Grace, the Imperial ambassador desires urgent speech with you, and he wishes to come before you disguised as a priest as he is fearful that, if he comes undisguised, that which he has to say to you will be overheard.'

Katharine was torn between her anger that she could not

receive her nephew's ambassador without fear of being over-heard, and apprehension as to what new schemes were afoot.

She looked at Thomas Abell, and wondered how far she could trust him. He had not been long in her service but she could say that during that time he had served her well. She decided that she had such need of friends that she must accept friendship when it was offered, without looking too suspiciously at it.

'He has asked my assistance in this matter,' went on Thomas Abell, 'and being eager to serve Your Grace I told him I would do what I could.'

'Then bring him to me in my chapel,' she said. 'I will speak to him there.'

So it was that Iñigo de Mendoza came to her robed as a priest, a hood concealing his features, and as, there in the chapel, he knelt beside her, she realised at once that he was deeply excited.

'Your Grace,' he said, 'the best of news! Do you remember a de Puebla who once served your father here in England?'

'I remember him well,' Katharine answered. 'He is long since dead.'

'But his son who is now a chaplain lives, and he has found an important document among his father's papers.'

'What document is this?'

'It is a brief of the same date as the Bull of Dispensation granted by Julius II, but this goes more deeply into the matter, and if we could lay our hands on the original – which is among the archives in Madrid – we could show without doubt that your marriage with the King is legal.'

'You have this?'

'I have the copy of it which de Puebla has given me. I propose to put it into the hands of your defending counsel.'

'Then pray do this,' said the Queen.

'I trust none of them save Fisher and I am afraid that, as this case is being heard in England, there will be scarcely a man here who would stand against the wishes of the King. What we must work for is to have the case tried in Rome. Then we could hope for justice. At least we have this document, which I have brought to you. Your best plan would be to give it to Fisher. Tell him that it is but a copy and that the original is in Spain. I think we shall see some consternation among our enemies.'

Katharine took the document and studied it. She was immediately aware of its importance and her spirits rose as Mendoza took his leave and left her in the chapel.

The King, pacing up and down his apartment, stopped to glare at his Chancellor.

'It seems that everyone conspires against me! When is this hearing to take place? When am I to be granted my divorce? With others, these matters are settled in a matter of weeks. With me they must last for years. And why? Because those who should serve me, bestir themselves not at all.'

The Cardinal's thoughts were miles away . . . in Rome. Heartening news had been brought to him a few days before. Clement had suffered a great shock, his health was declining, and it was believed that he could not recover.

Let this be granted to me, prayed the Cardinal. Here is the way out of danger, the path which will lead me to new power. My day is over in England. I am going down . . . down . . . The King grows tired of his Thomas Wolsey who once so pleased him, since Anne Boleyn pours poison into his ear. My great mistake was when I made an enemy of that woman. She will not believe that it was at the King's command that I berated her, that I told her she was not worthy to marry into the House of Northumberland. But she blames me; and she has determined to destroy me.

Once it might have been said: Thomas Wolsey's will is the King's will. That was no longer so, but it was true to say that that which Anne Boleyn desired, the King desired also, for at this time his one wish was to please her.

The woman was a witch. None other could so completely have bemused the King.

So he *must* become the new Pope. He prayed at every possible moment of the day, and often during sleepless nights, for this mercy. But he was not the man to trust to prayer. He had climbed high, he had often said to himself, through the actions of Thomas Wolsey rather than of God. Now Thomas Wolsey must continue to fight. He had asked François for his help, and François had promised to give it. But would the French King prove as unreliable as the Emperor? Wolsey had sent Gardiner to Rome with a list of Cardinals and bags of gold. No expense was to be spared, no bribe was to be considered too much. He would spend all he had to win at the next Conclave, because this time he knew he was not only fighting for power; he was fighting for his life.

So his thoughts wandered during the King's tirade, and fervently he hoped that soon he would be free of the unpredictable moods of the King of England.

But the King's next words were so startling that Wolsey's thoughts were diverted from his hopes of the next Conclave.

'This brief that is in the Queen's hands. We must get it. Warham tells me that it is worked out in such detail that it gives no shadow of a doubt that the marriage is a true one.'

'This . . . brief?' murmured Wolsey.

The King was too excited to show his impatience. 'Warham has brought this news. He says that through de Puebla's son this document has reached the Queen. It is enough to win the case for her.'

Wolsey was alert. He had to remember that the Papal Crown was not yet his; Clement was not even dead; he must not lose his grip on the power he possessed in England. He must show himself as eager as he ever was to work for the King.

He asked a few searching questions and then he said: 'But, Your Grace, this is not the original document. It is only a copy.'

'But the original document is in Spain.'

'First,' went on the Chancellor, 'we shall declare our belief that the paper which the Queen holds will be considered a forgery unless she produces the original. Therefore she must write immediately to the Emperor imploring him to forward the original to her here.'

'And when it comes . . . if indeed it be as the copy?'

'It will come to her counsel,' said Wolsey with a smile. 'We shall not have any difficulty in laying our hands on it when it is in England.'

Henry smiled slyly.

'And,' went on Wolsey, 'when it is in our possession . . .' He lifted his hands in a significant gesture. 'But, Your Grace will see that we must get that brief, and our first step is to persuade the Queen to write to her nephew, urging him to send the document to her.'

'I shall order her to do this without delay,' said the King.

'Your Grace,' Wolsey began tentatively and hesitated.

'Yes, yes?' said the King impatiently.

'It would be well if the Queen wrote on the advice of her counsel. Allow me to send for Warham and Tunstall. They will not hesitate to obey Your Grace.'

Henry nodded and his eyes were affectionate once more. By God, he thought, this man Wolsey has much skill. Then he frowned. He greatly wished that Anne did not dislike the Chancellor so. He had told her that Wolsey was working for them, but she would not believe it. He was her enemy, she said, whose great desire was to marry the King to a French Princess, and now that he knew the King would have none other than Anne Boleyn he sought to delay the divorce with all the means in his power.

There were times when Henry agreed with Anne; but when he was alone with his Chancellor he was sure she was wrong. He did wish that there was not this hatred between two for whom he had such regard.

'Do that,' he commanded.

'We must watch Fisher,' said Wolsey. 'There is a man whom I do not trust to serve Your Grace.'

'He's one of these saints!' cried the King. 'I know full well his kind, that which declares: 'I would give my head for what I believe to be right.' Master Fisher should take care. He may one day be called on to prove his words. And now . . . send Warham and Tunstall to me. By God, we'll have that document in our hands before many weeks have passed. As for Master Campeggio, you may tell him this: If he delays much longer he will have to answer to me.'

Wolsey bowed his head; he could not hide the smile which touched his lips. Campeggio cared not for the King of England, because he answered to one master only – a man who, in his own kingdom, was more powerful than any king.

It was pleasant to brood on Papal power.

Wolsey's lips were mocking; he was praying for the death of Clement and that the result of the next Conclave might bring him freedom from an exacting master and the utmost power in his own right.

Katharine received her advisers and as they stood in a semicircle about her she looked at each man in turn: Warham, Fisher, Tunstall, Clerk and Standish. They were eagerly explaining to her what she must do and Warham was their spokesman.

'It is clear, Your Grace, that the copy of this document cannot be accepted as of any importance. We must have the original. And we know full well that its contents are of the utmost importance to Your Grace's case.'

'Do you suggest that I should write to the Emperor, asking for it?'

'It is the only discourse open to Your Grace.'

'And you are all in agreement that this is what I should do?'

There was a chorus of assent, only Fisher remaining silent.

She did not comment on this, but she understood. The Bishop of Rochester was warning her that on no account must the document be brought to England.

'The King grows impatient,' went on Warham, 'for until this document is produced the case cannot be opened. He declares that Cardinal Campeggio is delighted by the delay, but His Grace grows weary of it. Your Grace should with all speed write to the Emperor imploring him to send this document to you here in England.'

'Since we have a good copy here,' she asked, 'why should that not suffice?'

'A copy is but a copy which could well be a forgery. We must have the original. For your sake and that of the Princess Mary, Your Grace, I beg of you to write to the Emperor for the original of this document.'

She looked at Fisher and read the warning in his eyes. He was a brave man. He would have spoken out but he knew – and she knew – that if he did so he would shortly be removed from her Council of advisers and no good would come of that. But his looks implied that on no account must she write to Spain for the document and that it was false to say that the copy would have no value in the court. This was a ruse to bring the original document to England and there destroy it, since it would prove an impediment to the King's case.

She answered them boldly: 'Gentlemen, we have here a very fair copy. That will suffice to show the court. It is well, I believe, that the original should remain in the Emperor's keeping. I shall not send to Spain for it.'

The men who were pledged to defend her left her, and she saw from Fisher's looks that she had acted correctly.

But when they had gone she was afraid. Hers was a pitiable position, when she could not trust her own Council.

Katharine stood before the Royal Council which was presided over by the Chancellor. Wolsey studied her shrewdly. Poor, brave woman, he thought, what hope does she think she has when she attempts to stand against the King's wishes?

'Your Grace,' said the Chancellor, 'I have to tell you that I speak for the King and his Council. Are we to understand that you refuse to write to the Emperor asking him to return that brief which is of the utmost importance in this case?'

'You may understand that. There is a good copy of the brief which can be used in the court; and I see no reason why the original should not remain for safe keeping in the hands of the Emperor.'

'Your Grace, you will forgive my temerity but, in refusing to obey the King's command, you lay yourself open to a charge of high treason.'

Katharine was silent and Wolsey saw that he had shocked her. Now she would perhaps begin to realise the folly of pitting her strength against that of the King and his ministers who, more realistic than she was, understood that not to obey meant risking their lives.

'Your Grace,' went on Wolsey soothingly, 'I have prepared here a draft of a letter which the King desires you to copy and send to the Emperor.'

She held out her hand for it and read a plea to her nephew that he despatch the brief with all speed to England as it was most necessary for her defence in the pending action.

She looked at the Chancellor, the man whom she had begun to hate because she considered him to be the instigator of all her troubles. He was ruthless; he had to procure the divorce for the King or suffer his displeasure and he did not care how he achieved that end. She did not doubt that when the brief came to England it would be mislaid and destroyed, for it was the finest evidence she could possibly have.

'So I am certain,' went on the Chancellor, 'that Your Grace will wish to comply with the King's desire in this matter.'

She bowed her head. She could see that she would have to write the letter, but she would write another explaining that she had written under duress. She felt desolate, for it seemed that she depended so much on that pale aloof young man who might so easily consider her troubles unworthy of his attention.

Wolsey read her thoughts and said: 'Your Grace must swear not to write to the Emperor any other letter but this. If you did so, that could only be construed as high treason.'

She saw her predicament. She had to give way, so she bowed before the power of her enemies.

As she knelt in her chapel, a priest came and knelt beside her.

'Your Grace,' whispered Mendoza, 'the brief must not come to England.'

'You know I must write to my nephew,' she replied. 'I am being forced to it, and I gave my word that I would write no other letter to him.'

'Then we must find a means of communicating without letters.'

'A messenger whom we could trust?'

'That is so. Francisco Felipez did good service once.'

'Perhaps he would be suspect if he did so again.'

'Is there anyone else in your suite whom you could trust?'

'There is Montoya. He is a Spaniard, and loyal. But I do not think he would be so resourceful as Felipez.'

'Then let us chance Felipez. This time he should not ask for permission, as the matter is very dangerous. Let him leave at once for Spain, with nothing in writing. When he reaches the Emperor he must explain to him how dangerous it would be to send the brief to England as it would almost surely be destroyed.'

'Felipez shall leave at once,' said the Queen. 'He will then have a good start of the messenger with the letter.'

'Let us pray for the success of his journey,' murmured Mendoza. 'But later. Now there is not a moment to be lost.'

The Cardinal, brooding on his affairs in his private apartments at York Place, was interrupted by the arrival of a man who asked permission to speak with him on a private matter.

Wolsey received the man at once, for he was one of his spies in the Queen's household.

'Your Eminence,' said the man, 'Francisco Felipez disappeared from the Queen's household yesterday. I have made one or two enquiries and it seems he was seen riding hard on the road to the coast.'

Wolsey rose and his eyes glowed with anger.

So the Queen, for all her outward resignation, was putting up a fight. Her man must not reach the Emperor, as the King's hopes of procuring a divorce could well depend on that brief. He would not rest – nor would the King – until it was in their hands.

Felipez must be stopped before he reached Madrid.

The Queen was seated with a few women while she worked with her needle and one of them read aloud. She was anxious that there should be no change in her routine.

Yet she was not listening to the reader; her thoughts were with her nephew. Felipez would have reached him by now; he would be explaining all that was happening to the Emperor's aunt in England, and the urgent need for Charles to hold that brief in safe keeping, so that it could be shown to the Pope if there were any attempt to declare her marriage invalid.

Charles was a man of honour; he had the utmost respect for family ties, and he would see that to treat her as Henry was planning to do was an insult to Spain. He would understand, as soon as Felipez explained to him, that the King's ministers were not to be trusted. She blamed the King's ministers – chief of them Wolsey. She could never for long see Henry as the monster he sometimes appeared to be. He had been led astray, she believed. He was young in heart and spirit; he was lusty and sensual and she had never greatly pleased him physically; she was too religiously minded and the sexual act to her was only tolerable as the necessary prelude to child-bearing. Henry had always seemed to her like a boy; those childish games which he had once played at every masque, when he had disguised himself and expected all to be so surprised when the disguise was removed, were symbolic. He had not grown up; he was easily led astray. He was still the chivalrous knight who had rescued her from humiliation when he was eighteen years old. Never would she forget those early days of their marriage; always she would remember that he it was who had rescued her. At this time he was in the thrall of the wicked minister, Wolsey, and he was bemused by the black-eyed witch named Anne Boleyn.

If she could live through these troublous days, if she could bring Henry to a sense of duty, she was sure that they would settle down happily together. This was what she prayed for.

But in the meantime she must continue the fight against the machinations of those about him and the inclinations of his own youthful desires.

There was a commotion below her window and, setting aside her work, she went to it and looking out, saw a man limping into the Palace; his arm was bandaged and it was clear that he had recently met with an accident.

She stood very still, clenching her hands, for she had recognised the man as Francisco Felipez, who should at this time be in Spain.

She turned to the group of women and said: 'I think that one of my servants has met with an accident. One of you must go below and bring him to me at once. I would hear what has befallen him.'

One of them obeyed and Katharine said to the others: 'Put away the work for today and leave me.'

When Francisco Felipez came to her her first emotion was relief to see that he was not seriously hurt.

'You have been involved in an accident?' she asked. His expression was apologetic. 'I was riding through France, Your Grace, and in the town of Abbeville I was set upon by footpads. They knocked me unconscious and rifled my pockets.' He grinned ruefully. 'They found nothing to interest them there, Your Grace. So they left me with a broken arm which meant that I was unable to ride my horse. A merchant bound it for me and helped me to return to England.'

'My poor Francisco,' said the Queen, 'you are in pain.'

'It is nothing, Your Grace. I can only regret that I had to delay so long before returning to you, and that I was unable to continue my journey because of my inability to ride.'

'I will send you to my physician. Your arm needs attention.'
'And Your Grace has no further commission for me?' Katharine shook her head. She understood that he had been seen to leave England, that the nature of his mission had been guessed, that he had been incapacitated by the Cardinal's men, and that the hope of conveying an understanding of her peril to the Emperor was now slight.

The Cardinal sat with his head buried in his hands. He had been reading despatches from Rome, and had learned that Clement, after seeming near to death, was making a remarkable recovery. The position at the Vatican was more hopeful and it seemed as though the Pope had taken a new grip on life. It followed that the chances of a Conclave in the near future were gradually but certainly fading; and the Cardinal's position in England had worsened.

Each day the King viewed him with more disfavour after listening to the complaints of Anne Boleyn. Continually Henry chafed against the delay. Had there ever, he asked himself, been such procrastination over such a simple matter? Other Kings, when they needed to rid themselves of unwanted wives, procured a dispensation and the matter was done with. But he, Henry Tudor, who had always, until now, taken what he wanted, was balked at every turn.

And what could his faithful servant do to hasten the decision when Campeggio had clearly been advised by the Pope to avoid a trial of the case if possible, and if not to use every means to delay bringing matters to a head! Wolsey was powerless to work without Campeggio; and the Pope and the King were pulling in opposite directions.

One of his most trusted servants entered the apartment, and the Cardinal, startled, withdrew his hands.

'I suffer from a headache,' Wolsey explained.

'A pressure of work, Your Eminence,' was the answer.

'Can it be so? I have suffered from a pressure of work, Cromwell, for as long as I can remember.'

Thomas Cromwell sighed sympathetically and laid some documents before the Cardinal. In a lesser degree Thomas Cromwell shared his master's uneasiness, for people in the

Court and in the City were beginning to show their dislike of him, which was entirely due to the fact that he was the Cardinal's man.

He thought of himself as a parasite feeding on the abundance of the Cardinal; and if Wolsey fell, what would happen to Cromwell?

Could Wolsey stand out against all the powers that fought against him? There could not be a man in England who had more enemies. Norfolk and Suffolk were watching like vultures; so was Lord Darcy; and the Boleyn faction, which was daily growing stronger, was standing by eagerly waiting for the kill.

The King? The King was Wolsey's only hope. Henry still admired the cleverness of his minister and was loth to part with his favourite. That was Wolsey's hope . . . and Thomas Cromwell's.

Now suppose the Lady Anne lost a little of her influence over the King; suppose she gave way to his pleadings and became his mistress; suppose Henry made the natural discovery that Anne was very little different from other women . . . then Wolsey might yet retain his hold on the King. That was if the French alliance provided all that Wolsey and Henry hoped for. But François was an unreliable ally – even as Charles had been.

So many suppositions, thought Thomas Cromwell, for a Cardinal's fate to depend on, and the fate of his lawyer who had risen because he was in his service hung with that of his master.

It was nearly six years before that Thomas Cromwell had set up in Gray's Inn and had been called to work for the Cardinal. He had helped to suppress certain small monasteries in order to promote colleges at Ipswich and Oxford in which the Cardinal was interested, and there had been complaints about the manner in which he, Cromwell, and his colleague, John Allen, had set about this business, but the Cardinal had protected them from trouble.

Wolsey had been pleased with him, and since then all his legal business had gone into Thomas Cromwell's hands. Thus it was that a lawyer could rise from obscurity to greatness; but Thomas Cromwell was too shrewd not to know that a man could as easily fall as rise.

He had come a very long way from his father's blacksmith's shop, although his father was a man of enterprise and had been a fuller and shearer of cloth in addition to his trade as blacksmith. Thomas had intended to go farther, and after a somewhat wild youth, which had resulted in a term of imprisonment and flight from the country, he had, following a period spent abroad, returned sobered, with the intention of making his fortune.

He had every reason to be pleased with what he had done until he suddenly understood that the Cardinal's good fortune was turning sour.

'These are troublous times,' murmured Cromwell.

'You speak truth,' answered the Cardinal grimly.

'Your Eminence,' went on Cromwell, 'what in your opinion will be the King's answer if the Pope refuses to grant his divorce?'

Wolsey's body seemed to stiffen. Then he said slowly: 'The King will have only one course of action. He will accept his fate, and give up all plans for remarriage.'

'Your Eminence has noticed, no doubt, that there are many Lutheran books entering the country.'

'I know it. Since that man Luther set the new doctrines before the world there seems no way of preventing these books from coming here. They are smuggled in; they are read, talked of . . .'

'Is it true, Your Eminence, that the King himself is interested in these ideas?'

Wolsey looked up sharply at the thickset lawyer, with the big head which seemed too close to his shoulders; at the strong jaw and thin lips which made his mouth look like a trap, at the cold expression, the gleaming, intelligent dark eyes.

'How did you know that he was?' demanded Wolsey. 'Has he told you this?'

Cromwell smiled deprecatingly to indicate his humility. That smile said: Would the King confide in Thomas Cromwell? 'No, Your Eminence,' he answered. 'But the Boleyns are interested. I believe the Lady passed a book to the King and told him he must read it. And he, being told he must, obeyed.'

Wolsey was silent.

Cromwell leaned forward slightly and whispered: 'What if the King should so dislike the Pope that he became more than a little interested in heresy?'

'He never would,' declared Wolsey. 'Is he not Defender of the Faith?'

'He was a fierce foe of Luther at the time that title was bestowed on him. But times change, Eminence.'

Once more Wolsey looked up into that cold, clever face. He had a great respect for the lawyer's intelligence.

'What mean you, Cromwell?' he asked.

Cromwell shrugged his shoulders. 'That the Lady and her friends might give their support to Lutheranism, seeing thereby a way to dispense with the services of the Pope.'

'I think not,' said the Cardinal, rising and smoothing the red folds of his robe as though to remind himself and Cromwell of the importance of Rome. 'The King has always been devoted to the Church.'

Cromwell bowed and Wolsey said: 'I must go now to His Grace. I have a matter of some importance to discuss with him.'

The lawyer walked from the apartment at the side of the Cardinal, his manner obsequious. He was thinking that Wolsey was growing old and that old men lost their shrewdness. Then his problem was pressing down upon him: What will Cromwell do when Wolsey has fallen? When would be the time for the parasite to leave his host? And where would he find another?

Cromwell's eyes glinted at the thought. He would leap up, not down. Was it such a long jump from a Cardinal to a King?

The Cardinal had summoned Thomas Abell, the Queen's chaplain, to appear before him and the King.

'He will be here in a few minutes, Your Grace,' Wolsey told Henry.

'And you think he is the man for this mission?'

'I am sure we could not find a better, Your Grace, for since he is the Queen's chaplain, the Emperor will think he acts for the Queen.'

'It seems a marvellous thing,' said Henry peevishly, 'that there should be this delay. When . . . when . . . when shall I be granted what I wish? How much longer must I live in this uncertainty?'

'As soon as we have the brief safely in our hands the case can be opened. But let us not despair of the Queen's entering a convent.'

'She is a stubborn woman,' grumbled the King.

'I know, Your Grace, but she pins hope to this brief. Once it is in *our* hands her case will crumble.'

A page entered to say that Thomas Abell was without.

'Send him in,' commanded Wolsey.

Thomas Abell bowed low before the King.

'Now to our business,' said Henry.

'It is His Grace's wish,' said the Cardinal, 'that you should leave at once for Spain. You are to go to the Emperor and hand him a letter from the Queen. He will give you a certain document, and this you are to bring to His Grace with all speed.'

'Your Grace, Your Eminence,' said Thomas Abell, 'gladly would I serve you, but I must tell you that I have little Spanish and I fear that would be an impediment to me in this mission.'

Henry looked at Wolsey who said quickly: 'You shall take a servant and interpreter with you.'

'Then I shall set out with all speed. There is a man in the Queen's household who would make a good servant and is moreover a Spaniard. I refer to Montoya. If this man could accompany me I should have no qualms in setting out immediately.'

'Let it be so,' said the Cardinal. 'You should leave tomorrow, and in the meantime it is His Grace's wish that you should have no communication with the Queen. You must carry with you, apart from this one, no letters from the Queen to the Emperor. To do this would incur the King's displeasure and, as you know, you could then be accused of high treason.'

Thomas Abell said he understood, and withdrew in order to

make his preparations for the journey, while Wolsey summoned Montoya that the importance of his journey might be impressed upon him.

When he left the King and the Cardinal, Thomas Abell was thoughtful. He was to carry a letter from the Queen to the Emperor, and this letter was to be given him by the Cardinal. He was not to take any other message from the Queen to her nephew. It therefore seemed to him that the letter which he carried, although in the Queen's hand-writing and purporting to express her wishes, had no doubt been written under duress.

Thomas Abell was a deeply religious man. His position at Court had by no means increased his ambitions, which were not for worldly gain. He was a man who cared passionately for causes; and it seemed to him that the Queen's cause was more worthy than the King's.

There had been a moment, as he confronted the King and Cardinal, when he had almost refused to obey their orders. No, he wanted to say, I refuse to work against the Queen in this matter of the divorce.

That would doubtless have been construed as high treason and he might have been hustled to the Tower. Such a possibility would not have deterred him in the least. Indeed, he had a secret longing for a martyr's crown. But it had occurred to him that by accepting this commission he might serve the Queen's cause more effectively than by refusing it.

He obeyed the instructions and did not see the Queen before he left, her letter safely in his scrip; the voluble Montoya riding beside him.

They travelled across France and the journey was tedious; but there was much to talk of as they went, for Montoya was well versed in what was known throughout the Court as the

Secret Matter; he filled in gaps for Abell; so that long before they came into Spain, the chaplain knew that the Queen had been forced to write the letter he carried, that she knew that, once the brief left the Emperor's safe keeping, her case was lost, that she had tried to reach him by means of Franciso Felipez who had been set upon and all but killed by the Cardinal's men.

So Abell made up his mind; and when he reached Spain and was taken into the Emperor's presence, with Montoya to translate, he told the Emperor that the Queen had been forced to write the letter asking for the brief, and that unless the Emperor kept the original in his hands the Queen would have no redress; he had, moreover, worked out a plan that a notarially attested copy, which would be valid in any court, should be made and the original kept in safety in Spain.

The Emperor listened gravely and thanked the chaplain, who he saw was his aunt's very good friend. He assured Abell that the copy should be made and he himself would ensure that the original brief would be kept in the royal archives at Madrid.

Abell was delighted with the success of his mission and, while he waited for the copy of the brief to be made, he started to write a book in which he set out the Queen's case; and the more he worked, the clearer it became to him that the King based his desire for a divorce on false premises.

Abell now had a cause for which he was ready to give his life.

He was eager to return to England, there to hand the copy of the brief to Wolsey, and complete his book which he would eventually publish, no matter what the consequences should be.

🦁 Chapter IX 🦁

'COME INTO THE COURT'

enry was growing more and more disturbed. He had noticed the change towards him in the people's attitude. When he rode in the streets there was no longer the spontaneous outburst of cheering; and the approval of the people had always been very dear to him. Anne was growing restive; she continually complained and accused him of making promises which he was unable – or unwilling – to keep. The knowledge of his impotence in this matter infuriated Henry.

Moreover the popularity of the Queen had increased since the plan for the divorce had become known. If she appeared at a balcony crowds would collect and shout: 'Long live our Queen!' as though to remind all who heard them – including the King – that they would not allow her to be cast aside for the sake of Anne Boleyn. Anne herself had on one or two occasions been in danger from the people. They called her the 'whore' and shouted that they'd 'have no Nan Bullen as their Queen!'

Moreover the copy of the brief had arrived, and that was useless for Henry's purpose while the original was in the

Emperor's keeping. The Pope, weak in health and weak in purpose, vacillated between the King and the Emperor, desperately trying to placate first one, then the other.

But the Emperor was nearer at hand and more formidable, so Clement had declared that, since Campeggio seemed unable to proceed with the trial in England, the whole matter had better be referred to Rome.

'Tried in Rome!' shouted the King. 'A fine state of affairs. What hope should I have of obtaining a divorce if the matter were tried in Rome under the whip of the Emperor!'

No. There must be no more delay. They must go ahead with the trial even though the brief did remain in the Emperor's hands. He must rely on Wolsey who knew full well, the King malevolently reminded himself, that if the case did not go in the King's favour Master Cardinal would have a great deal for which to answer.

In the meantime he could not endure his unpopularity with the people and sought to remedy this by making a public pronouncement of his difficulties. He therefore called together as many of the burgesses of London who could be squeezed into the great hall of Bridewell Palace, led by the Lord Mayor, aldermen and many from the Inns of Court; and on a dull November Sunday afternoon he took his place on a dais and endeavoured to put his case before them.

Henry was always at his best when he played a part, because his belief in the part of the moment was absolute.

He was a glittering figure, standing there on the dais, the light filtering through the windows making his jewels scintillate; he was exceedingly handsome, standing in his characteristic attitude, legs apart – which made him look so broad and sturdy – his glittering hands folded across his blue and gold doublet.

He surveyed the crowd before him with the benevolent eyes of a father-figure, for he had already assured himself that what he wanted was for their good rather than his own.

'My friends,' he cried, 'there is much disquiet throughout the land because up to this time God has denied me my greatest wish – to give you the heir who would naturally follow me. This matter has for some time gravely disturbed my conscience, and I doubt not that there have been many evil rumours in the streets concerning it.'

He went on to remind his audience of the prosperity they had enjoyed under his rule.

'My beloved subjects, it is a matter of great concern to me that one day I must die and be no longer with you. So I wish to leave you one, whom I have trained to take the burden of kingship from my shoulders, one on whose head I could contemplate the placing of my crown and die happy. There are some among you who may remember the horror of civil war. If this country were to be plunged into like horror on my death, my friends, my dear subjects, I believe I should have lived in vain. I wish to live in friendship with France and so I plan to marry my daughter to a French Prince. I wish also to live in friendship with the Emperor Charles, for I know full well that this country's disagreements with him have caused certain hardship to some of our people.'

There was grave nodding among the assembly. The clothiers had cried out again and again that they could not live if they could not sell their cloth in the Flemish markets.

'It was during the negotiations for my daughter's marriage that a point was made which has caused me great perturbation. The French ambassador, the Bishop of Tarbes, has raised the question of my daughter's legitimacy. It was a point which I could not ignore since, my friends, this matter had for some time given me cause for uneasiness. I have since consulted bishops and lawyers, and they have assured me that I have, for all the years that I have believed the Lady Katharine to be my wife, been living in mortal sin.

'Ah,' went on Henry, 'if it might be adjudged that the Lady Katharine is my lawful wife, nothing could be more pleasant or acceptable to me, both for the clearing of my conscience, and for her own good qualities, and conditions which I know her to be in. For I assure you all that beside her noble parentage she is a woman of gentleness, humility and buxomness; yea, and of all good qualities pertaining to nobility she is without comparison. So that if I were to marry again I would choose her above all women. But if it be determined in judgment that our marriage is against God's law, then shall I sorrow, parting from so good a lady and a loving companion. These be the sores that vex my mind. These be the pangs which trouble my conscience, for the declaration of which I have assembled you together. I beg of you now go your ways, and in doing so form no hasty judgments on your Prince's actions.'

The meeting was over. Henry left the hall, and those who had assembled to hear him went into the streets where they stood about in little groups talking; but the theme of their conversation was still sympathy for the Queen.

Iñigo de Mendoza, who had learned of the King's oration at Bridewell, sat down to communicate with his master.

'There is nothing I can do here,' he wrote, 'to further the Queen's cause. The King is determined to have an end of this matter and there will be a trial. The Queen's chances of receiving justice at the hands of the judges are slight. She needs an ambassador who is also a lawyer. I therefore implore Your Excellency to recall me from a post which I have not the ability to fulfil.'

All through the winter Mendoza awaited his recall.

It came at the end of the spring, when it had been decided to open the Court at Blackfriars for the hearing of the King's Matter, which was no longer secret.

There could be no more delay. The summons had been sent both to the King and the Queen, and the Legatine Court was to be set up in Blackfriars on the 16th day of June.

Katharine, who during this most difficult time had not changed her mode of life, was with her daughter when the summons came.

Poor little Mary! She was fully aware of the troubles between her parents and how she herself was affected. She had lost her healthy looks and had grown nervous, starting with dismay when any messengers appeared; she still kept her feelings under control, but there were occasions when she would throw herself into her mother's arms and without a word demand to be comforted.

Now as the scroll was handed to her mother Mary began to tremble.

The Queen dismissed the messenger, but she did not look at the scroll. She laid it aside, telling herself that she would study it when her daughter was no longer with her. But although Mary tried to play the virginals, she was thinking of the scroll and her fingers faltered so that Katharine knew that it was useless to try to keep the secret from her.

'You must not fret, my darling,' she said.

'Mother,' answered the Princess, turning from the instrument, 'if you are in truth not married to the King then I am but a bastard, is that not so?'

A hot flush touched the Queen's pale face. 'It is wrong even to question it,' she answered. 'I will not allow it. You are the legitimate daughter of the King and myself, the only heir to the throne.'

'Yes, I know that to be true, Mother; but there may be some who insist it is not so, and if they should succeed, what would become of us?'

The Queen shrugged her shoulders. 'They cannot succeed . . . if there is justice.'

'There is not always justice, is there, Mother?'

The Queen did not answer and Mary went on: 'I was talking to Reginald of this matter. He said that no matter what the verdict of the court was, he would never call anyone but you the Queen of England, and none heir to the throne but myself.'

'So we have some friends,' said Katharine. 'Why should we not have justice too?'

'Perhaps because our friends will not be in the court? That is what you are afraid of, Mother. Your friends are not allowed to stay with you here, so why should they be allowed to act as judges?'

'I think I have some friends.'

'But, Mother, what is important is that we are not separated. That is why, when I am frightened, I remind myself that if they say you are no true Queen, then I cannot be the true heir. So that if you are sent away I shall go with you.'

'My darling . . . my darling,' said the Queen with a sob in her voice; and Mary ran to her and knelt at her feet.

'Is that all you care about then?' asked Katharine.

'I do not care what they say of me,' came Mary's muffled answer, 'if they will but let me stay with you for ever. If I am a bastard the French Prince will not want me. We shall go away from Court, Mother, you and I, and we shall stay quietly somewhere in the country, and there will be no talk of my going over the sea to marry.' She laughed on a high, hysterical note. 'For who will want to marry a bastard!'

'Hush! Hush!' admonished the Queen.

'Oh, but you are afraid, Mother.'

'No . . . no . . .'

'If you are not afraid, why do you not open the scroll?'

'Because we are together now and I do not see you as often as I wish. So matters of state can wait.'

'We are both thinking of it, Mother. We do not escape it by ignoring it.'

The Queen smiled and, going to where she had laid the scroll, picked it up and read it. Mary ran to her and stood before her, anxiously scanning her mother's face.

'It is a summons to appear at Blackfriars,' she said.

'A summons? Should the Queen be summoned?'

'Yes, Mary. For the King will be summoned also.'

'And at this court they will decide . . .'

Katharine nodded. 'They will decide.'

Mary kissed her mother's hand. 'All will be well,' she said. 'If they decide one way you will be the King's wife and we shall be as we were. If the other, we shall go away together, away from the Court, away from the fear of a royal marriage in a strange country. Oh, Mother, let us be happy.'

'Yes, let us be happy while we are together.'

And she tried to set aside the gloom which hung about her.

She did not believe, as Mary did, that if her marriage were proved invalid she and her daughter would be allowed to slip away quietly into oblivion. But she did not tell Mary this. Why disturb the child's peace of mind, and how could she know how long such peace would be enjoyed?

The Queen came to Campeggio's apartment. She felt desolate; she scarcely knew this man, and yet it was to him she must go.

She had confessed to John Fisher on the previous day and they had taken advantage of their privacy to discuss the coming trial. She had not asked Fisher to come to her for this purpose, because she knew that Wolsey's spies were all about her and, although it was reasonable that she should ask the advice of a man who had been chosen to defend her, she did not want to put John Fisher in any danger, for she knew he was an honest man who would speak his mind even though his views were not those of the King and Cardinal.

It was Fisher who had advised her to see Campeggio in the vain hope that she might be able to persuade the Legate to have the case tried in Rome.

Campeggio, who could feel the beginning of an attack of the gout, was irritated by the arrival of the Queen. If only she had shown good sense she would be in a convent by now and he would be back in Italy where he belonged. He had used his delaying tactics, on Clement's command, for as long as he had been able, but it was impossible to hold out any longer against the King's desire. What he must do now was prevent the case from reaching any conclusion, for he was certain that the King would not allow it to be said that there had never been any impediment to the marriage, and

Clement dared not so offend the Emperor as to grant the divorce.

A delicate situation, especially so since his fellow Legate was Cardinal Wolsey whose own fate depended on giving the King what he wanted – and quickly.

Thus he felt irritated by the Queen who could so easily have solved the problem for them all by giving up her life outside convent walls.

'Your Grace . . .' he murmured, bowing with difficulty.

'I regret that you are in pain,' said the Queen with genuine sympathy.

'I am accustomed to it, Your Grace.'

'I am sorry for all who suffer,' said the Queen. 'I have come to ask you not to hold this court. I have lodged an appeal to His Holiness and have high hopes that the case will be heard outside England – where I might have a greater chance of justice.'

'Your Grace,' Campeggio pointed out, 'His Holiness has already appointed two Legates. This is tantamount to having your case tried in Rome.'

'I am surprised that you should have so small an opinion of my intelligence as to push me aside with such a comment,' Katharine retorted scornfully. 'If this case is tried in England all the advantages will be the King's. Have you forgotten who one of the Legates is?'

'The matter has not slipped my memory, Your Grace.'

'Wolsey!' she cried. 'The man whom I have to thank for all my troubles. I have always abhorred his way of life, which is not that of a priest. He hates my nephew because he did not help him to become a Pope.'

'You should pray to God,' Campeggio told her. 'He would help you to bear your trials.'

'And who,' cried Katharine, 'would dare to pronounce a verdict contrary to the King's wishes?'

'I would, if the findings of the court should show me clearly that the King was wrong.'

'The findings of the court!' snapped Katharine. 'Do you not know that there cannot be more than one or two men who would dare give a decision which the King did not want? So you can rely with certainty on the findings of the court!'

'Let us pray,' said Campeggio.

They did so, but Katharine could only think of the fate which was waiting for her and her daughter.

What will become of us? she asked herself. And then she prayed that whatever disaster should befall her, her daughter should remain unscathed.

There was tension in the great hall at the Blackfriars Palace. The case had begun.

Never had those assembled seen anything quite like this before.

Seated on chairs covered by cloth of gold and placed at a table over which was hung a tapestry cloth sat the Legates, Cardinals Campeggio and Wolsey. On the right of the table was an ornate chair with a canopy over it; this was in readiness for the King who was expected to appear in a few day's time; on the left hand side of the table was a chair as rich but lacking the canopy, which was meant for the Queen.

Henry did not appear in person but sent two proxies. Katharine, however, arrived in the company of four Bishops and several of her women.

As Katharine entered there was a stir in the court, for she

was not expected until that day when the King would be there. She did not go to the chair which was intended for her, but to the table where she stood before the Legates. There was a hushed silence in the court as she began to speak.

'My lords, I come to make a protest against this court and to ask that the case may be transferred to Rome.'

Katharine was conscious of the malevolent gaze of Wolsey and the peevish one of Campeggio. To the first she was an enemy to be ruthlessly removed; to the second she was an irritation, the woman who might, by going into a convent, have saved him so much trouble and allowed him to rest his gouty limbs in a more congenial climate. The sight of those two men filled Katharine with further apprehension and an immense determination to fight for her future and that of her daughter.

'Why does Your Grace object to this court?' Wolsey asked coldly.

'I object because it is hostile to me,' replied the Queen. 'I demand to be tried by unprejudiced judges.'

Campeggio appeared to be shocked; Wolsey looked pained, but Katharine went on boldly: 'This case has been referred to Rome; in due course it could be tried there; the verdict must have the sanction of the Holy Father. I protest against this matter's being tried here.'

Wolsey rose and said: 'Your Grace is misinformed.' And Campeggio added: 'Your Grace can be assured that justice shall be done, and I urgently pray you to take confidence in the members of this court who serve none but justice.'

Katharine turned away and, holding her head high, left the court followed by her train.

It was useless, she was telling herself. There was nothing she could do to prevent the trial.

She could only go back to her apartments and wait until that day when she, with Henry, must appear in person before the Legatine court.

'Henry, King of England, come into the court!' The cry rang out in the great hall of Blackfriars.

Henry was seated under the canopy, and above him on the dais were the two Cardinals, magnificent in their robes of scarlet. At the foot of this dais were the Bishops and officers of the court, with William Warham, Archbishop of Canterbury, at their head. There sat the counsellors of the two opposing parties; Dr Bell and Dr Sampson for the King, and the Bishop of Rochester and the Bishop of St Asaph's for the Queen.

The voice of the crier, calling the King, silenced the whispers. Those who were present could not help but marvel that the King and Queen could be called into court as though they were common people.

This, it was murmured, shows the power of Rome. Only the Pope would dare summon the King of England to appear in court in his own country. Since we were ruled by one of the Pope's cardinals – our butcher's son – England has been but a vassal of Rome.

Henry himself felt a wave of anger to be so summoned. He would have refused to attend this trial; he would have stated that he had no intention of accepting any verdict but the one he wanted; but the people must be placated; they were already murmuring against the injustice done to his Queen. It was part of his policy to say: 'Reluctant I am to part from her whom I believed to be my wife, but I do so on the orders of the Church.' Therefore what could he do but submit himself to the jurisdiction of the Church, making sure, of course, that his Cardinal understood how the verdict must go.

So he answered in a voice devoid of rancour: 'Here I am, my lords.'

'Katharine, Queen of England, come into the court.'

Katharine stood up, crossed herself, and to the astonishment of the Bishops and officers of the court, made her way to the chair in which Henry sat. She knelt before him and began to speak in a ringing voice which could be heard all over the hall.

'Sir, I beseech you, for all the love there has been between us, and for the love of God, let me have right and justice. Take pity on me and have compassion for me, because I am a poor stranger born outside your dominions. I have here in this court no unprejudiced counsellor, and I appeal to you as the head of justice within your realm. Alas! Wherein have I offended you? I take God and all the world to witness that I have been to you a true, humble and obedient wife, ever conformable to your will and pleasure. I have been pleased and contented with all things wherein you had delight and dalliance. I loved all those you loved, only for your sake, whether they were my friends or mine enemies. These twenty years I have been your true wife, and by me you have had divers children, although it has pleased God to call them out of this world, which has been no fault of mine. I put it to your conscience whether I came not to you as a maid. If you have since found any dishonour in my conduct, then I am content to depart, albeit to my great shame and disparagement; but if none there can be, then I beseech you, thus lowlily, to let me remain in my proper state.'

There was a hush in the court as she paused for breath. She had at the beginning of the hearing stated that fact which was the crux of the matter. Her marriage to Prince Arthur had been no true marriage; she had stated before this court that she had been a virgin when she married Henry.

The King flinched a little; his face was stern; he did not look at his kneeling wife, but stared straight before him.

'The King, your father,' went on Katharine, 'was accounted in his day a second Solomon for wisdom, and my father, Ferdinand, was esteemed one of the wisest kings that had ever reigned in Spain; both were excellent princes, full of wisdom and royal behaviour. They had learned and judicious counsellors and they thought our marriage good and lawful. Therefore it is a wonder to me to hear what new inventions are brought up against me, who never meant aught but honestly.'

Again she paused. Campeggio moved in his chair to ease his painful limbs. She makes her own advocate, he thought; where could she have found a better? It will not be easy for them to find against her.

He was pleased with her. It was what he wished, for Clement's orders were that the court should come to no decision.

'You cause me to stand to the judgment of this new court,' continued the Queen, 'wherein you do me much wrong if you intend any kind of cruelty; you may condemn me for lack of sufficient answer, since your subjects cannot be impartial counsellors for me, as they dare not, for fear of you, disobey your will. Therefore most humbly do I require you, in the way of charity and for the love of God, who is the just Judge of all, to spare me the sentence of this new court, until I be advertised in what way my friends in Spain may advise me to take. And if you will not extend to me this favour, your pleasure be fulfilled, and to God do I commit my cause.'

Katharine stood up and all in the court saw that there were

tears on her cheeks. The Bishops looked on grimly, not daring to show their sympathy in the presence of the King, who still sat staring stonily before him; but in the body of the hall many a kerchief was applied to an eye and secret prayers for the Queen were murmured.

She took the arm of her receiver-general and instead of making her way back to her seat she began to move through the crowd towards the door.

The crier was in consternation. He called: 'Katharine, Queen of England, come again into the court.'

But Katharine did not seem to hear and, staring before her, her eyes misted with tears, she continued towards the door.

'Your Grace,' whispered the receiver-general, 'you are being called back to the court!'

'I hear the call,' answered the Queen, in tones which could be heard by those about her, 'but I heed it not. Let us go. This is no court where I may have justice.'

'Katharine, Queen of England, come again into the court!' shouted the distracted crier.

But Katharine passed out of the court into the sunshine.

The Queen had gone, and Henry was fully aware of the impression she had made.

He rose and addressed the assembly. He spoke with conviction and considerable powers of oratory; he was well practised in this speech for he had uttered it many times before. He explained that he had no wish to rid himself of a virtuous woman who had always been a good wife to him. It was his conscience which urged him to take action. It had been put to him by learned men – bishops and lawyers – that he was living in sin with a woman who had been his brother's wife. The twenty-first verse of the twentieth chapter of Leviticus had been brought to his notice, and it was for this reason that he – determined to live at peace with God – had decided to ask learned men whether he was truly married. If the answer was in the affirmative he would rejoice, for there was none who pleased him as did the woman who had been his wife for twenty years; but if on the other hand it were shown to him that he was living in sin with her, then, much as this would grieve him, he would part with her.

After Katharine's speech the King's sounded insincere. It was a fact that the whole court and country knew of his passion for Anne Boleyn, and that it was this woman's desire to share his crown before allowing him to become her lover which was, if not the only motive for bringing the case, an important one.

However, Henry, believing in what he said while he said it, did manage to infuse a certain ring of truth into his words.

When he had finished speaking Wolsey rose to his feet, came to the chair in which Henry was sitting and knelt there.

'Your Grace,' he said, 'I beseech you to tell this assembled court whether or not I have been the first to suggest you should part from the Queen. Much slander has been spoken against me in this respect and there are many who feel that, should this be truth, I am no fit person to sit as Legate in this case.'

The King gave a short laugh and cried: 'Nay, my Lord Cardinal, I cannot say you have been the prime mover in this matter. Rather have you set yourself against me.'

Wolsey rose from his knees and bowed to the King. 'I thank your Grace for telling this court that I am no prejudiced judge.'

Wolsey returned to his seat and Warham, Archbishop of Canterbury, rose to produce a scroll which he told the court contained the names of the Bishops who had agreed that an enquiry into the matter of the King's marriage was necessary. He then began to read out the names on the scroll.

When he came to that of John Fisher, Bishop of Rochester, Fisher rose from the bench and cried: 'That is a forgery, for I have signed no such document.'

Henry, who was growing more and more impatient at the delay and wondering when the judges would declare his marriage null and void – which he had believed they would quickly do – was unable to restrain himself. 'How so?' he cried irritably. 'Here is your name and seal.'

'Your Grace, that is not my hand or seal.'

Henry's brows were lowered over his eyes. Once he had loved that man Fisher. It was such men who, in the days of his youth, he had wished to have about him. Thomas More was another. They had never flattered him as blatantly as other people did and when he did wring a word of praise from them it was doubly sweet. John Fisher had at one time been his tutor – a gentle kindly man with whom it had been a pleasure for an exuberant youth to work with now and then.

But now Fisher was on the Queen's side. He was the Queen's counsel. He did not approve of a divorce. He believed that, having married Katharine and been disappointed in her, his King should yet remain her faithful husband.

What did Fisher know of the needs of a healthy man who was in the prime of life?

As he glowered at his one-time tutor, Henry hated the tall, spare figure. The fellow looks as though he spends his time shut in a cell, fasting, he thought derisively. No matter what love I had for him it shall be forgotten if he dares oppose me in this matter. He will have to learn that those who cross me do so at the peril of their lives.

And now what was this matter of a forgery?

Warham was saying: 'This is your seal.'

Fisher retorted: 'My Lord, you know full well this is not my seal. You know that you approached me in this matter and I said that I would never give my name to such a document.'

Warham could see the King's anger mounting. Warham was all for peace. He did not think that Fisher realised the full force of the King's passion in this matter. Perhaps Fisher was too honest to understand that when the King was being driven by his lust he was like a wild animal in his need to assuage it. Warham tried to end the matter as lightly as possible.

'You were loth to put your seal to this document, it is true,' he murmured. 'But you will remember that in the end we decided that I should do it for you.'

'My lord,' said Fisher, 'this is not true.'

The King shifted angrily in his seat. Warham sighed and put down the document; it was a gesture which meant that no good could come of pursuing that matter further.

'We will proceed with the hearing,' Wolsey announced. Henry sat sullenly wondering what effect Fisher had already had on the court. By God, he thought, that man's no friend of mine if deliberately he flouts me in order to serve the Queen.

But all would be well. Katharine had been right when she had said that few in this court would dare disobey him. They would not; and thus they would give him the verdict he was demanding. What difference would one dissenting voice make?

But he hated the dissenters. He could never endure criticism. And when it came from someone whom he had once admired, it was doubly wounding.

He scarcely heard what was being said about him until it was Fisher's turn to make his speech for the Queen.

'Those whom God hath joined together, let no man put asunder . . .'

As soon as Fisher had finished speaking, Henry rose from his seat.

He had had enough for one day. The session was over.

The days passed with maddening slowness for the King. It was a month since the trial had begun and still no conclusion had been reached. Each day the counsels for the King and those for the Queen argued their cases; and it was clear that Fisher alone was determined to do his utmost to win a victory for the Queen.

Campeggio was in despair, for although he applied his delaying tactics whenever possible he could see that he could not extend the proceedings much longer, and, in view of the evidence he had heard, he knew that if he made a decision it would have to be in favour of the King.

This he could not do, as his strict orders from the Pope were that he should give no definite verdict.

Understanding the motives behind his fellow Legate's methods Wolsey was depressed; he knew that Campeggio's one desire was to prolong the action of the court until he could suitably disband it.

This was the state of affairs when the Cardinal was summoned to the King's presence.

Henry was purple with anger, and striding up and down the apartment waving papers in his hands. He did not speak as Wolsey approached, but merely thrust the papers at the Cardinal.

Wolsey read the news and felt sick with horror. François had suffered defeat in Italy and a peace was to be made between him and the Emperor. Margaret, Regent of the Netherlands, who was the Emperor's aunt, and Louise of Savoy, the mother of François, had arranged this peace which was consequently called The Ladies' Peace. It was natural that Clement should at the same time sign a treaty with the Emperor.

'And,' cried Henry, glowering at his Chancellor, 'these matters are settled and we are told nothing of them until they are completed. It seems to me that our French ally is as treacherous as our Spanish ones. Why is it that we are always betrayed?'

'Your Grace,' stammered Wolsey, who was near exhaustion and whose mind had been concentrated on the King's divorce, 'this will mean that Campeggio will never give us the verdict we want.'

'This trial is nothing but a mockery!' roared the King. 'Is it not marvellous that I should be made to wait so long for that which others have for the asking?'

'Circumstances have moved against us, Your Grace. But for the sack of Rome . . .'

'Do not give me your buts . . .' cried the King. 'Give me freedom to marry, that I may provide my kingdom with an heir.'

'It would seem, Your Grace, that we should make another appeal to the Queen. If she would but retire to a convent, I am certain that Clement would immediately grant the divorce. All we need is her consent to do so, nay her desire to do so. The Emperor himself would not object to that.'

'She must be made to see reason,' insisted the King.

'Your Grace, have I your permission to make one more appeal to her?'

'Do so, without delay.'

Wolsey was relieved to escape from the King, and immediately went to Campeggio's apartments, and there made the suggestion that they should go to the Queen and endeavour to show her what a benefit she would confer, not only on herself, but on all others, if she would retire to a nunnery.

❧ ❧ ❧

The two Cardinals went by barge to Bridewell where the Queen at that time had her lodging. She was sitting with some of her women, working on her embroidery, for, she had said, she was so melancholy at this time that working with bright colours raised her spirits.

When she heard that the Cardinals had called on her, she went to greet them with skeins of red and white silk hanging about her neck.

'Your Grace,' said Wolsey, 'we crave your pardon for disturbing your peace, and pray you to give us a hearing.'

'Gladly will I do so,' she answered, 'but I cannot argue with such as you. I am not clever enough.' She touched the skeins about her neck. 'You see how I pass my time, and my maids are not the ablest counsellors, yet I have no others in England. And Spain, where there are those on whom I could rely, is far away.'

'Take us into your privy chamber,' said Wolsey, 'and there we will show you the cause of our coming.'

'My Lords,' answered the Queen, 'if you have anything to say, speak it openly before these folk, for I fear nothing that can be alleged against me, but I would all the world should see and hear it. Therefore speak your minds openly, I pray you.'

Wolsey was uneasy and had no desire to speak before the women, so he began to explain his mission in Latin, but Katharine interrupted.

'Pray, my good lord, speak to me in English, for I can, thank God, speak and understand English, though I do know some Latin.'

So there was nothing to be done but to speak to her in the presence of her women in English, and Wolsey said: 'Your Grace, if you will consent to the divorce you shall lack nothing you desire in riches and honours. If you should desire to go into a convent, which would be a seemly setting for your devout manner of living, you shall have all that you require there. The King will place the Princess Mary next in order of succession to the issue of his second marriage.'

'My lords,' said Katharine, 'I could not answer you suddenly, for I have no one to advise me.'

Campeggio said: 'Cardinal Wolsey and I would gladly give you the advice you need.'

'Then now come to my private chamber and there we will speak of these matters,' she said.

So the two Cardinals and the Queen retired together, and she told them once more that she had no wish to enter a convent, that the Princess Mary was the true heir to the throne, that she herself was indeed married to the King, for she had never in truth been wife to his brother; and this she would maintain no matter what befell her.

It was clear to the Cardinals that they could not make her change her decision, so they left her, Wolsey in deep melancholy, Campeggio determined to bring a speedy end to the case.

'This matter,' said Wolsey as they stepped into the barge,

'must be settled without delay. We must give our judgment, and, on what we have heard, how can we help but decide in the King's favour?'

Campeggio shook his head. 'I am not satisfied that we have heard all the truth. The Queen is right when she says this is a prejudiced court. Nay, there is one course open to us. We must refer the matter to His Holiness.'

'The King will never stomach further delay.'

'This matter,' answered Campeggio, 'is not in the King's hands.'

Wolsey did not answer. He envied Campeggio his freedom. He would return to Rome where he had only to answer to the Pope and by delaying judgment he had carried out his orders. But Wolsey . . . he had served the King, and each day Henry's displeasure and dissatisfaction increased.

So slowly they sailed along the river – Campeggio would leave the barge for his lodgings and the rest for which his limbs were crying out, but Wolsey must return to the King and once more report failure.

Campeggio arrived at the court. He took his place beside Wolsey, but as the proceedings were about to open, he rose and addressed the company.

'This court is under the jurisdiction of Rome,' he announced, 'and the holidays have begun in Rome. Therefore this court is closed until the holidays are over. We shall reassemble here on October the first.'

There was a gasp of astonishment. Wolsey was as startled as the rest, and his brown eyes looked like great marbles in his pallid face. True, he had been expecting something like this, but not so soon. He knew, of course, that Campeggio would never open the court again; that his one idea was to return to Italy and not come back. He had done his duty. He had opened the court of enquiry and had kept it going for a month; now he sought this excuse to close it; and meanwhile the state of affairs in Europe had steadied themselves, giving Clement some indication of which side he must take.

This was disaster at home and abroad. Wolsey's French foreign policy had failed, for the Emperor and François were now friends, and neither felt much affection for England. So he had failed in that, and the people would be more against him than ever. He had also failed the King. He had promised him divorce, yet he was no nearer getting it than he had been more than a year ago.

Suffolk, Henry's brother-in-law, who had been working zealously in the King's cause, suddenly clenched his fist and hammered it on the table.

'England was never merry,' he declared, 'since we had Cardinals among us.'

And as he spoke he glared at Wolsey who could not resist reminding him of that occasion when Suffolk had married Henry's sister Mary and had appealed for the Cardinal's help to placate the King. 'Had it not been for one Cardinal,' he said, 'you my Lord Suffolk, might have lost your head, and with it the opportunity of reviling Cardinals.'

The court broke up, and Wolsey was smiling as he saw Suffolk's crestfallen face. Norfolk was watching him with hatred too. So was Darcy. But they dared not speak against him. He was still the most powerful man in the land – under the King; and while he had the King's support, his enemies were powerless to touch him.

The King had already heard the news when Wolsey reached him.

Henry was alone and the Cardinal was surprised to see that his face was pale rather than scarlet as might have been expected. The eyes were as cold as ice.

'So,' he said, 'the Pope's man has closed the court.'

Wolsey bowed his head in assent.

'And all these weeks have been wasted. He never meant to settle this matter. Meanwhile I am left uncertain.'

'Your Grace, the Papal Legate has from the beginning practised procrastination to a fine degree.'

'You need not tell me this. And the Queen has refused once more to enter a convent!'

'It is so, Your Grace.'

The little blue eyes were narrowed. 'I'll warrant she wishes me dead,' he said.

Wolsey was startled. 'Your Grace . . .' he began.

Henry was scowling. His Chancellor had not the sharp wits which had once been his.

'It would not surprise me,' went on Henry, 'if there should be a plot afoot to kill both me and you.'

'Is it so, Your Grace?' Wolsey was waiting for orders and the King was satisfied.

'If such a plot should be discovered,' went on the King, 'and it was found that the Queen had a part in it . . .' The little mouth was cruel, the eyes ruthless . . . 'she should not expect to be spared,' he added.

Wolsey was thinking: Queen Katharine, you are a fool. Why did you not take yourself off to a convent? There you would have been safe. This is a man who takes what he wants, no matter who stands in his way. And you, Queen Katharine, now stand most dangerously in his path.

The King went on: 'This is a matter which should be laid before the Council. They will be prepared to act if evidence is brought before them. You will see to this, for I hold it to be of great importance to our safety . . . yours and mine.'

Wolsey bowed his assent.

He was vaguely troubled by his conscience, which over the years of good living he had learned to stifle.

So it has come to this, he thought. Katharine, you are in acute danger . . . and so am I.

🏵 Chapter X 🏵

THE FALL OF WOLSEY

Never in the whole of her life had Katharine felt so desolate and alone.

She lay on her bed, the drawn curtains shutting her in a small world of temporary peace. What will become of me? she asked herself, as she had continued to do since the Council's document bad been brought to her. But she was not really thinking of what would become of herself; for there was one other whose safety was of greater concern to her than that of any other living person. She knew what it meant to be alone and friendless. What if such a fate befell her daughter?

'Holy Mother, help me,' she prayed. 'Guide me through this perilous period of my life.'

The evil suggestion was afoot that she was trying to work some ill on the King and the Cardinal. Did they truly think that she – who never willingly harmed the humblest beggar – would try to poison the King and his chief minister? They had wronged her wilfully – at least the Cardinal had; she believed him to be the prime mover against her, and still saw Henry as an innocent boy who could be led. How could they honestly believe that she, a pious woman, could think for one moment of committing murder?

This was another plot of course to drive her into a convent.

Lying in her bed she thought of the comfort of a bare-walled cell, of the pleasant sound of bells, of escape from a world of intrigue. It attracted her strongly.

She sat up in her bed and once more read the scroll which she had been clutching in her hands as she lay there.

It informed her that she had not shown as much love for the King as she ought; that she appeared too often in the streets, where she sought to work on the affections of the people. She showed no concern for the King's preoccupation with his conscience, and the King could only conclude that she hated him. His Council therefore was advising him to separate from her at bed and board and to take the Princess Mary from her.

To take the Princess Mary from her!

If they had not added that, they might have frightened her into a convent. But while she had her daughter to think of she would never retire into oblivion.

Attached to the document was a note in Wolsey's hand. He had written that the Queen was unwise to resist the King, that the Princess Mary had not received the blessing of Heaven and that the brief which was held by the Emperor was a forgery.

'What will become of me?' she repeated. Whatever the future held, she would never allow them to frighten her into a convent, which would be tantamount to admitting that her marriage with the King was no true marriage. Never would she forget the slur this would cast on Mary.

She threw aside the scroll and lay down again, closing her eyes tightly, and said: 'Let them do with this body what they will. Let them accuse me of attempting to murder the King and the Cardinal. Let them make me a prisoner in the Tower. Let them send me to the scaffold. Never will I allow them to brand Mary a bastard.'

Even greater than the Queen's sufferings were those of the Cardinal, for he lacked Katharine's spiritual resignation and constantly reproached himself for his own blindness which, looking back, he could see had brought him to that precipice on which he now stood; he mourned all that he had lost, and there was none of Katharine's selflessness in his grief.

Henry had left London with the Court without seeing him, and was now at Grafton Manor, that beautiful palace which was situated on the borders of the shires of Buckingham and Northampton, and had once been the home of Elizabeth Woodville. Anne Boleyn was with the King, and Anne was now Queen of England in all but name; moreover she ruled the King as Katharine had never done. It was Anne who had suggested that Henry should leave Greenwich without informing his Chancellor; a procedure which but a few months before would have been unthinkable.

And now there had been no summons for him to go to Grafton; he had to beg leave – he, the mighty Cardinal – to accompany Campeggio who must pay his respects to the King before leaving the country.

What a sad and sorrowful journey it was, through London, where the people came out to see him pass! He travelled with his usual pomp but it seemed an empty show now, for the humblest beggar could not feel more fearful of his future than the great Cardinal of England.

Campeggio rode in silence beside him; his gout, he

believed, had not improved since his sojourn in England and he was glad to be leaving and rid of a tiresome and delicate task; yet he had time to be sorry for his fellow Cardinal.

Poor Wolsey! He had worked hard to bribe his way into the Vatican . . . and failed. The Emperor had failed him; François had failed him; and now, most tragic of all, his own sovereign was being pressed to discard him. What then, when the whole world stood against him?

Optimism had never been far below the surface of Wolsey's nature; it was to this quality that, in a large measure, he owed his success. He believed that when he saw the King, Henry would remember how, over so many years, they had worked together, and he would not leave him unprotected and at the mercy of his enemies who were even now massing against him. Lord Darcy had already drawn up a list of his misdeeds in order that he might be impeached. They would be saying of him that he had incurred a *præmunire* because he had maintained Papal jurisdiction in England. He had failed to give the King the divorce he needed, and his enemies would be only too ready to declare that he had served not the King but the Pope. Norfolk and Suffolk had always hated him; and now they were joined by the powerful Boleyn faction headed by Anne herself, who ever since he had berated her for daring to raise her eyes to Percy, had been his enemy and had sought to destroy him with a vindictiveness only paralleled by Wolsey's own hounding of those who he considered had humiliated him.

It was the case of Buckingham repeating itself; only on this occasion the victim was the Cardinal himself.

And so they came to Grafton. There was revelry in the Manor, for Anne Boleyn and her brother George were in charge of the entertainments; and none knew how to amuse the

King as they did. There would be hunting parties by day – the woods about Grafton had been the hunting ground of kings for many years – and the Lady would accompany the King and show him in a hundred ways how happy he would be if only he could discard the ageing Katharine and take to wife her brilliant, dazzling self.

The arrival of the Cardinals was expected and several of the King's household were assembled to welcome them. Campeggio was helped from his mule and led into the Manor to be shown the apartments which had been made ready for him; but no one approached Wolsey, and he stood uncertain what to do, a feeling of terrible desolation sweeping over him. For one of the rare occasions in his life he felt at a loss; it was no use assuming his usual arrogance because it would be ignored; he stood aloof, looking what he felt: a lonely old man.

He became aware that no preparation had been made for him at the Manor and that he would be forced to find lodgings in the nearby village. Such an insult was so intolerable and unexpected that he could not collect his wits; he could only stand lonely and silent, aware of little but his abject misery.

A voice at his side startled him. 'You are concerned for a lodging, my lord?'

It was a handsome youth whom he recognised as Henry Norris, and because he knew this fellow to be one of those who were deeply involved with the Boleyns and formed part of that admiring court which was always to be found where Anne was, Wolsey believed that he was being mocked.

'What is that to you?' he asked. 'I doubt not that lodgings have been prepared for me.'

'My lord, I have reason to believe that they have not.'

Only when Wolsey looked into that handsome face and saw

compassion there, did he realise how low he had fallen. Here he stood, the great Cardinal and Chancellor, close friend of the King, seeking favours from a young gentleman of the Court who, such a short time before, had been wont to ask favours of him.

'I pray you,' went on Henry Norris, 'allow me to put a lodging at your disposal.'

The great Cardinal hesitated and then said: 'I thank you for your kindness to me in my need.'

So it was Henry Norris who took him to a lodging in Grafton, and but for the compassion of that young man there would have been no place for him at the King's Court.

There was excitement at Grafton. The Cardinal was in the Manor but all knew that no lodging had been prepared for him. That was on the orders of the Lady Anne, who commanded all, since she commanded the King. Now she would command Henry to dismiss his Chancellor, and all those who had hated the Cardinal for so long and had yearned to see his downfall were waiting expectantly.

Henry knew this, and he was disturbed. He had begun to realise that his relationship with the Cardinal had been one based on stronger feelings than he had ever experienced before in regard to one of his ministers; and much as he wished to please Anne, he could not bring himself lightly to cast aside this man with whom he had lived so closely and shared so much.

Anne insisted that Wolsey was no friend to the King because he worked for the Pope rather than Henry. And, she ventured to suggest, had the Cardinal so desired, the divorce would have been granted by now.

'Nay, sweetheart,' replied Henry, 'I know him better than you or any other man. He worked for me. 'Twas no fault of his. He made mistakes but not willingly.'

Anne retorted that if Norfolk or Suffolk, or her own father had done much less than Wolsey they would have lost their heads.

'I perceive you are not a friend of my lord Cardinal, darling,' Henry answered.

'I am no friend of any man who is not the friend of Your Grace!' was the reply, which delighted Henry as far as Anne was concerned but left him perplexed regarding Wolsey.

And now he must go to the presence chamber where Wolsey would be waiting with the other courtiers. He could picture the scene. The proud Cardinal in one corner alone, and the groups of excited people who would be watching for the King's entry and waiting to see the Cardinal approach his master – to be greeted coldly or perhaps not greeted at all.

Henry tried to work up a feeling of resentment. Why should he be denied his divorce? Why had not Wolsey procured it for him? Was it true that when the matter had been first suggested the Cardinal had intended a French marriage? Was it possible that, when he had known that the King's heart was set on Anne, he had worked with the Papal Legate and the Pope against the King?

Scowling, Henry entered the presence chamber and it was as he had believed it would be. He saw the expectant looks on the faces of those assembled there – and Wolsey alone, his head held high, but something in his expression betraying the desolation in his heart.

Their eyes met and Wolsey knelt, but the sight of him, kneeling there, touched Henry deeply. A genuine affection made him forget all his resolutions; he went to his old friend and counsellor and, putting both his hands on his shoulders, lifted him up and, smiling, said: 'Ha, my lord Cardinal, it pleases me to see you here.'

Wolsey seemed bemused as he stood beside the King, and Henry, slipping his arm through that of his minister, drew him to the window seat and there sat, indicating that Wolsey should sit down beside him.

'There has been too much friendship between us two for aught to change it,' said Henry, his voice slurred with sentiment.

And the glance Wolsey gave him contained such gratitude, such adoration, that the King was contented, even though he knew Anne would be displeased when she heard what had happened. But there were certain things which even Anne could not understand and, as he sat there in the window seat with Wolsey beside him, Henry recalled the security and comfort which, in the past, this clever statesman had brought to him.

'Matters have worked against us,' continued Henry, 'but it will not always be so. I feel little sorrow to see your fellow Cardinal depart; he has been no friend to us, Thomas.'

'He obeyed orders from Rome, Your Grace. He served the Pope; it was not enough that one of the Legates worked wholeheartedly for his King.'

Henry patted Wolsey's knee. 'It may be,' he said darkly, 'that we shall win without the Pope's help.'

'His Holiness would give it, but for his fear of the Emperor.'

'He's a weak fellow, this Clement. He sways with the wind.'

'His position is so uncertain since the sack of Rome.'

Henry nodded, and Wolsey went on, his spirits rising: 'If

Your Grace will grant me an audience in the morning, before I must depart with Campeggio, we could discuss the matter further. There are many ears cocked to listen here, many eyes to watch.'

''Tis so,' said Henry nodding, and rising he put his arm once more through that of his Chancellor, and went with him back to the group of his gentlemen who were standing some distance from them.

What comfort to rest his weary limbs in the bed for which he must be grateful to young Norris! How simple to explain the neglect!

It had happened without the King's knowledge. Naturally he would have believed that preparations were made for his Chancellor, for his dear friend the Cardinal. It was his enemies who had sought to degrade him. He was fully aware of the existence of them. When had he ever been without them?

As he stretched out blissfully he told himself that he had been unduly worried. He had suffered misfortunes, but he was as strong now as he had ever been and, while the King was his friend, he was invincible.

How he had misjudged his King! Hot tempered, selfish, hypocritical, capable of extraordinary blindness where his own faults and desires were concerned, yet Henry's heart was warm for those who had been his friends; and while that friendship could be relied on, there was nothing to fear. All that he, Wolsey, had done to serve his King was worth while. He would not regret the loss of Hampton Court; the gift was a symbol of the love between them which was indestructible.

Nothing could change it . . . not even the vindictiveness of Anne Boleyn.

And tomorrow, thought Wolsey, we shall be alone together. Before I ride away with Campeggio on our way to the coast, I shall have had my intimate talk with Henry. All misunderstandings will be cleared away and it will be as it was in the old days when there was perfect accord between us. I will procure the divorce for him, but by that time, Mistress Anne Boleyn, he will have recovered from his infatuation. You have declared yourself my enemy; I declare myself yours. It shall be a French Princess for His Grace.

Tomorrow . . . Tomorrow . . . thought Wolsey, and slept. It was the most peaceful night he had enjoyed for a long time.

'A good bed, Norris,' he murmured, when he awoke and saw that it was daylight. 'I'll not forget you.'

He rose and found that it was later than he had at first thought; but there was plenty of time to see the King before he left with Campeggio. In excellent spirits he dressed and, as he was about to make his way to the King's apartments, he met Henry Norris.

'I thank you for a good night's lodging,' he said.

'Your Eminence looks refreshed,' was the answer.

Wolsey patted the young man's shoulder. 'I shall not forget your goodness to me. Now I go to seek the King.'

Norris looked surprised. 'His Grace left early this morning in the company of the Lady Anne.'

Wolsey could not speak; he felt a lump in his throat which seemed as though it would choke him.

'They have gone off with a party for a day's hunting,' continued Norris. 'They'll not be back till dusk.'

It was like arriving at this place and finding no lodging

prepared for him. She was the cause of that; and she was the cause of this. Doubtless she had heard of the King's display of friendship and determined that there should be no more.

So he must leave with Campeggio, and that interview from which he had hoped so much would never take place. His defeat seemed as certain as it had been on his arrival.

In the palace they would be saying: Perhaps his fall is not as imminent as we hoped . . . but it is coming. Look at the warning shadows.

These were uneasy months. The King stormed through the Court sometimes like a bewildered, angry bull, at others like a peevish boy. Why was a divorce denied him? Why was he so provoked?

He was politician enough to know the answer. It was because the Emperor was more powerful at the Vatican than the King of England, and the woman the King wished to put aside was the Emperor's aunt; it was as simple as that.

'Yet I will have my way!' declared the King.

In the Boleyn circle he had met a man who interested him because, although of somewhat obscure origins, he expounded original ideas. This man was a certain Thomas Cranmer, a scholar who had passed through Cambridge and had there become acquainted with Stephen Gardiner and Richard Fox. This man, Cranmer, had, during the course of conversation, which naturally enough turned on the main topic of the day, expressed original views on the way in which the King might obtain a divorce in spite of the continued vacillation of the Vatican.

'It is clear,' Cranmer had said, 'that the Pope is reluctant to grant the divorce because he fears the Emperor. Is it not time that the King looked for a solution to his Matter outside the Vatican?'

Gardiner and Fox had suggested that he should explain how this could be done; to which Cranmer made answer that he believed the King should first make the universities see the reason behind his desires, and then appeal to enlightened opinion. Was England always going to remain a vassal of the Holy See?

Dr Cranmer had voiced these opinions in other circles, and it was for this reason that the Boleyns had taken him under their protection and were making it known that Dr Cranmer was a man of new, startling and brilliant ideas.

When Gardiner and Fox told the King of Cranmer's suggestion, Henry had listened intently and, as he did so, his expression lightened; he cried out: 'By God, that man hath the right sow by the ear! Who is he? Let him be brought to me. I would talk with such a one.'

So Cranmer had been brought forward and Henry had not been disappointed by their discourse, which had started a new train of thought in his mind.

The Queen's melancholy was lifted a little by the arrival of the new Imperial ambassador. This was Eustache Chapuys, an energetic Spaniard who had not been in England long before Katharine realised that here she had a stronger champion than she had had in Mendoza. Of humble beginnings, he had none of the aristocrat's preoccupation with his own nobility and was not constantly looking for slights. His family had, with some struggle, managed to send him to the University of Turin, and from there he had begun to make his fortune. He was now forty years old and this opportunity to work for the Queen against the divorce seemed to him like the chance of a lifetime; he was determined to succeed.

However, arriving in England he had discovered that it was very difficult to speak in private with the Queen, who very quickly warned him that she was spied on at all times, and implored him to be very wary of Wolsey. He understood at once that this was no exaggeration. As for the King, he met the new ambassador with reproaches, complaining that by withholding the Papal brief the Emperor had done a grave injury, not only to his but to Katharine's cause.

'If,' Henry had said, 'I could have been assured that the brief was genuine, I should, at this time be living with the Queen, for that is what I wish beyond all things, and it is solely because my conscience tells me that to resume marital relations with the Emperor's aunt would be to live in sin, that I refrain from doing so. Yet, since the Emperor will not release the brief I must conclude that he knows it to be a forgery and is afraid to submit it to the light of day.'

'Your Grace,' Chapuys had answered, 'I myself can assure you that the brief is no forgery and that the copy you received in England is exact in every detail. Your conscience need disturb you no more.'

Henry had been angry with the ambassador, and this was not a good beginning to their relationship; but at least he would understand that in the new ambassador he had a worthy adversary, and Katharine a good friend.

So Katharine's hope increased, because she believed that her case would be tried in Rome, and there she would have justice. She was convinced that all that was necessary to make Henry send Anne Boleyn back to Hever and turn to his true wife was an order from Rome.

But how sad she was in the Palace, where Anne ruled as though she were Queen, and Katharine was only at the King's side on the most formal occasions! The humiliation she could have endured; but it was Anne's decree that the Princess Mary should not be present at Court, and because Anne commanded this, Mary was kept away.

She fears the King's affection for my daughter, Katharine decided; and there was a little comfort in that belief. But how she longed for the child's company. On those rare occasions when she was with the King she sought to lead the conversation to their daughter's absence in an endeavour to arouse a desire in him to have her with them.

But he was sullenly pursuing Anne, and Katharine often wondered whether his dogged determination to have his way was as strong as his desire.

One day when he had supped in her apartments she seized an opportunity to whisper to him: 'Henry, would you not like to see our daughter here?'

'She is well enough where she is.'

'I miss her very much.'

'Then there is no reason why you should not go to her.'

'To go to her would be to leave you. Why cannot we all be together?'

He was silent and turned away from her. But she could not control her tongue. 'As for myself,' she went on, 'I see so little of you. I am often alone, neglected and forsaken. Who would believe that *I* was the Queen? I must brood on my wrongs continually.'

'Who forces you to do so?' demanded Henry. 'Why do you not count your blessings?'

'My blessings! My daughter not allowed to come to me! My

husband declaring he has never been my husband and seeking to marry another woman!'

'If you are neglected,' said Henry, his voice rising, 'that, Madam, is your affair. There is no need for you to remain here if you wish to go. Do I keep you a prisoner? I do not. You may go whither you like. As for the way I live . . . it is no concern of yours, for learned men have assured me that I am not your husband.'

'You *know* that you are my husband. You know that I was a virgin when I married you. You choose to forget that now. But, Henry, do not rely on your lawyers and doctors who tell you what they know you want to hear. They are not my judges. It is the Pope who will decide; and I thank God for that.'

Henry's eyes narrowed. He was thinking of recent conversations with Cranmer, Gardiner, Fox and Anne, and he said slowly and deliberately: 'If the Pope does not decide in my favour, I shall know what to do.'

She flashed at him: 'What could you do without the Pope's approval?'

Henry snapped his fingers and his lips scarcely moved as he replied, though the words smote clearly on Katharine's ear: 'This I should do, Madam. I should declare the Pope a heretic and marry when and whom I please.'

The Cardinal was taking a solitary tour through York Place, knowing that it was doubtless the last time he would do so. Here were stored many of his treasures which almost rivalled those which had been in Hampton Court when he had lost that mansion to the King.

He stood at the windows but he did not see the scenes below; he leaned his heated head against the rich velvet hangings, as he glanced round the room, at the tapestries and pictures, at the exquisite furniture which he had so treasured.

In the pocket of his gown was the communication he had received from the King. The Lady Anne, it seemed, had set her heart on York Place. She would have no other house in London. Therefore the King asked the Cardinal to offer this up to her.

Hampton Court . . . and now York Place! One by one his treasures were being stripped from him. Thus it would be until he had nothing left to give but his life. Would they be content to leave him that?

He knew that a Bill of Indictment had been registered against him; he knew the hour could not be long delayed when Norfolk and Suffolk would arrive to demand that he give up the Great Seal.

The days of greatness were over. The fight for survival had begun.

He did not have long to wait. Smug, smiling, like dogs who had at last been thrown the titbits for which they had been begging, Norfolk and Suffolk arrived to demand the delivering up of the Great Seal.

He received them with dignity in the beautiful hall, surrounded by rich treasures which he must soon surrender. His dignity was still with him.

'I would see the King's handwriting on this demand,' said Wolsey, 'for how may I know you come at his command if I do not?'

Norfolk and Suffolk flushed and looked at each other. Neither was noted for his quick wits. Then Suffolk spluttered:

'You know full well that we come on the King's command.'

'How should I know, when there is no written order from him?'

'Then is it a surprise to you that you should be asked to hand back the Seal?'

'This is not a question of my emotions, my lords, but of your authority to take the Seal from me. I shall not give it to you unless you bring me a written order from the King.'

The Dukes were angry but they had never been able to argue successfully with Wolsey.

'Come,' said Suffolk, 'we will return in a very short time with what he demands.'

And they left him. It would be a short time, Wolsey knew. But there was a small hope within him. The King had not wished to put his name to a demand for the Great Seal. He had turned his back on Wolsey, but at least he had not joined the pack who were waiting to tear the old minister to pieces.

The Cardinal was in great terror. It was not the fact that Norfolk and Suffolk had returned to take the Seal from him, with a written command from the King. That, he had known, was inevitable. It was not that he was ordered to leave York Place for Esher, an empty house which belonged to his bishopric of Winchester. It was the knowledge that his physician had been taken to the Tower where he might be put to the question, and betray secrets which could mean disaster to Wolsey if they were ever told to the King.

He had been desperate. He had seen disaster coming and had sought to win back all he had lost in one desperate throw. His enemy was Anne Boleyn and he had determined to be rid of her, knowing that if he could do this, he could quickly win back the King's regard.

As a Cardinal he was in a position to have direct communication with the Pope, and he had made use of his advantages by advising the Pope to insist that the King send Anne from the Court or face excommunication. This had seemed to him to offer a solution of his troubles, because if the King dismissed Anne he, Wolsey, would very quickly return to his old position. If the King did not dismiss Anne but defied the Pope, Wolsey calculated that opinion in the country would be split; the situation would be dangerous for England; and the King would quickly realise that there was only one man strong enough to save the country from disaster; that man was Wolsey.

This had been his plan, and it had been made not for the good of the country, not for the good of the King, but for the salvation of Wolsey.

He had failed in his attempt; yet it was not that failure which disturbed him, but the knowledge that his weak physician may have confessed this secret and that the King might soon be aware of what he had done.

What hope would there be for him then? Banishment to Esher! It would not end there.

The grim shadow of the Tower lay before him; he could see himself walking from his prison with the executioner beside him and the blade of the axe turned towards him.

Now outside York Place and all along the banks of the river the people were assembling; craft of all description crowded the river. It was a holiday for them. They believed they were gathering to watch Wolsey on his way to the Tower.

He would pass out of York Place with all the pomp and

ceremony with which he had been wont to make his journey from Hampton to Westminster. There would no longer be the Great Seal to proclaim him Chancellor. But he still had his Cardinal's hat and his magnificently attired entourage. He would have his fool beside him, his cooks and stewards, his ushers and secretaries, as though the journey from York Place to Esher was no different from many another journey he had taken.

But he felt sick and weary. Thomas Cromwell was with him, and Cromwell's dejection was clear to see. Was he mourning for the downfall of a friend, or asking himself what effect the loss of an influential benefactor would have? Who could say? And what did it matter now?

So out of York Place he came to take a barge for Putney. Soon they would be counting the treasures there, and delightedly laying before the King and the Lady the lists of valuables, the costly booty. York Place was following Hampton Court; and Esher lay before him, an empty house where he would endeavour to keep his state until perhaps he was called to an even less comfortable lodging.

He was making up his mind what he would do. There were two courses open to him. It was no use appealing to Parliament, which was under the influence of Norfolk; but he could take his case to the law courts. There he had a fair chance of winning, because he was still the wiliest statesman in the land. But it would never do to win. The King would never forgive that. There was one object which he must keep in mind; one preoccupation which must be his to the exclusion of all else. He must keep his head upon his shoulders. He knew what he must do. He would admit that he had incurred a *præmunire* and he would ask the King, in payment for his sins, to take all that he possessed.

He smiled wryly, thinking of those bright blue eyes alight with acquisitiveness. While Henry studied the lists of possessions which would fall into his eager hands he might spare a little kindness for his one-time Chancellor and favourite minister. He might say: 'Good Thomas, he always knew what would please me best.'

Disembarking at Putney he continued his journey away from the glories of the past into the frightening unknown future. The people watched him sullenly. This was an occasion for which they had long waited.

'His next journey will be to the Tower!' they cried.

And some raised their voices, because there was now no need to fear: 'To the scaffold with the butcher's cur!'

But as he rode through the muddy streets on his way to Esher he was met by Sir Henry Norris, the young man who had given him a lodging at Grafton.

He was moved by the sight of the young man, and he found that he could be touched more deeply by discovering that there were some in the world who did not hate him than by anything else. He realised that, apart from that little family which he kept shut away from his public life and of whom during the last busy years he had seen very little, he had tender thoughts for no one and had used all who came within his orbit in the manner in which they could serve him best. Therefore a sign of friendship from any of these people seemed a marvellous thing.

Thus with Norris. But it was more than his friendship that Norris had to offer on this day.

'Your Eminence,' he said, 'I come from the King. He sent you this as a token of the friendship which he still feels towards you in memory of the past.'

Norris was holding out a ring which Wolsey had seen many times on the King's finger, and when he recognised it the tears began to fall down the Cardinal's cheeks. There had been some true friendship between them then. He had been more than a wily minister to his King.

If I could but reach him, thought Wolsey. Oh Lord, give me one half hour alone with him and I will make him listen to me and share my opinions. There was never ill-feeling between us that was not engendered by that black night-crow. Give me a chance to talk to him . . .

But it was too late. Or was it? Here was the ring . . . the token of friendship.

He must show his gratitude to this young man, so he dismounted and embraced Norris; then he knelt in the mud to give thanks to God because his King had sent him a token of friendship. He could not remove his hat easily because the ribbon was too tightly tied, so he tore the ribbon and knelt bareheaded while Norris looked on embarrassed, and the crowds watched in bewilderment.

The Cardinal had no thought for them. Henry had sent him a token, and with the token – hope.

He gave Norris an amulet – a gold cross and chain – and, wondering what gift he could send to the King which would convey the depth of his gratitude, he saw his Fool standing by and he called to him.

'Go with Sir Henry Norris to the King,' he said, 'and serve him as you have served me.'

The Fool looked at him with mournful eyes and shook his head.

'What means this?' asked Wolsey. 'It is better to serve a King than a Cardinal; did you not know that, Fool?'

He was expecting some merry retort, but none came. Instead the man said: 'I serve none but my master.'

And as he stood there, his satin robes spattered with the mud of the streets, the ring warm on his finger, the Cardinal was once more astonished to find that he who had cared for nothing but ambition had yet found one or two who would serve him for love.

'You are indeed a fool,' he said.

'The Cardinal's Fool, not the King's Fool,' was the answer.

Wolsey signed to him to go, but the Fool knelt and clung to the red satin robes until it was necessary to call six yeomen to drag him protesting away.

The strangeness of that street scene, thought Wolsey, as he rode on to Esher, will remain with me for as long as I live.

In the manor house at Esher there were neither beds, cups, cooking utensils nor sheets.

Wolsey entered the hall and stared about him in dismay at the emptiness. His servants gathered round him wonderingly. Thomas Cromwell moved towards an embrasure and looked out of the window, his eyes alert, his trap-like mouth tight. What now? he was asking himself. Need the end of Thomas Wolsey be the end of Thomas Cromwell?

The Cardinal asked that all his servants should be brought into the hall, and there he addressed them.

'As you see, we have come to a house which is empty of food and furniture. We must bestir ourselves and borrow for the needs of myself and one or two servants. For the rest of you, I advise you to return to your homes. It may well be that in three or four weeks I shall have cleared myself of the charges which are being brought against me; then I shall return to power and call you back to me. Now you must go for, as you see, you cannot stay here.'

Across that room the eyes of Cromwell met those of Wolsey.

Cromwell took five pounds in gold from his purse and said: 'There are many among us who owe what they have to the Cardinal. There was a time when great blessings flowed from him. Now we see him stripped of his possessions, his home this manor in which there is nowhere to lay his head. It is my hope that many here will follow my example and add to this sum, so that some comfort may be bought for His Eminence during the time which may elapse before he returns to favour.'

And before the Cardinal's astonished eyes certain members of his household came forward and laid what sums of money they could afford beside that set down by Cromwell.

Then his servants busied themselves and went out to borrow beds and cooking utensils from neighbouring houses; and there was activity in the manor of Esher.

So, until a call came for him to go elsewhere, he would live there surrounded only by those lower servants who were necessary to look after his physical comforts.

The others – the ambitious men – rode away from Esher; and among them was Thomas Cromwell, who had made up his mind to try his fortune in the King's Court.

There was time, in the weeks which followed, to review his life, to reproach himself with having strayed far from the road of self-denial, to do penance because his ambition had destroyed him first spiritually and now physically.

He was a sick man. He scarcely slept, and when he did he was constantly awakened by nightmares. During his stay at Esher, in much discomfort, he had suffered from dropsy. The house was damp as well as ill-furnished, and he had appealed to the King to allow him to move nearer to London where the air, suiting him better, might help him to throw off his malaise. Henry was still kind to him, though refusing all requests to receive him in audience. Was there some softness in the King's nature which told him that once he and his ex-chancellor were in each other's company all would be forgotten but the friendship they had once had for each other? Was that why the King so stubbornly refused that much-desired interview?

Well, he was alone, shorn of his power; no longer did men come to him seeking favours. But the King had allowed him to move to the lodge in Richmond Park, had sent him another ring with his portrait and had demanded that Anne Boleyn also send him a token of her esteem. An empty gift from the Lady, but showing that even she dared not disdain the Cardinal too harshly in the King's presence. Henry had also sent Dr Butts, with orders that his good physician's commands were to be obeyed.

But Wolsey had not been allowed to stay in Richmond. Norfolk and Suffolk saw to that. Wolsey smiled wryly to hear how disturbed those two were, and how they had put their ducal heads together to plan how to keep him and the King apart. And so he had returned to his house at Southwell for the summer months and attempted to live there in some state. But Norfolk would not leave him in peace and insisted that he go to York.

How painfully he travelled, a sad and lonely exile! Yet he was enjoying a hitherto unknown popularity with the people, and many came to him to ask his blessing.

And so he came to Cawood which was but twelve miles from the city of York, his destination. There he stayed awhile, confirming and blessing people who asked this service of him, in his obscurity living like a man of the Church, as in the role of statesman he had never done before.

Yet always he waited for a word from the King, a sign that Henry was ready to welcome him back. He was a sick man, and there was but one elixir which could restore him to health; it was what he had fought for and won, and now knew he could never live happily without: The King's favour.

Henry missed his Wolsey.

Often he would shout at those who served him: 'It was never thus in the Cardinal's day.'

His new Chancellor was Thomas More, a man for whom he had a deep affection; but More was no Wolsey. He never considered his own comforts nor those of his King. More, who was a lawyer, was a thousand times more a churchman than the Cardinal had ever been, but saintly men made uneasy companions and More had taken office only on condition that he was not asked to act in the matter of the divorce. Henry was aware that Thomas More was one of those who believed him to be truly married to Katharine. It was small wonder that he yearned for his accommodating Wolsey.

But his enemies were pleading for the Cardinal's blood. It did not please them that he should merely be sent into exile. They wanted to see him lay his head on the block.

There was Anne who would not rest until Wolsey was dead. She was scornful, her black eyes flashing. How often had she cried: 'If my father or my lords Norfolk and Suffolk had done half what he has done they would have lost their heads.'

Henry wanted to explain to Anne: We were more than King and statesman. We were friends. I have sent him from me. Let that suffice.

There was Norfolk for ever whispering in his ear. When the King was a little anxious about an ulcer on his leg, which refused to heal, it was Norfolk who cried:

'Your Grace, the Cardinal suffered from the great pox. Is it to be wondered at? Your Grace knows the life he led. Yet knowing that the pox was with him he came to Your Grace, blowing upon your noble person with his perilous breath.'

'Nay,' said the King. 'This ulcer of mine has naught to do with Wolsey.'

'And, Sire, did you know that he spoke often of "The King and I" as though there was no difference in your rank?'

'We were friends,' said Henry with a smile, 'and when I was a young man and given to pleasure, he taught me much.'

'Did Your Grace know that he had as mistress the daughter of a certain Lark, and by her had two children . . . a son and daughter?'

'A son,' said the King wistfully. 'So even Wolsey had a son.'

'I heard that he married the woman off to give her and her children a name. The boy received great benefits.'

The King nodded. He was not to be shocked or moved to anger against his minister.

But there came a day when news was brought to him by both Norfolk and Suffolk.

'Your Grace, the Cardinal's Italian physician, Dr Augustine Agostini has made an important statement.'

'What statement is this?'

'He tells us that the Cardinal suggested to the Pope that he should command you to put aside the Lady Anne and return to the Lady Katharine and, if you failed to do this, to excommunicate you.'

Henry's face grew purple with anger.

'Then he is indeed guilty,' he said. 'He has indeed incurred a *præmunire*.'

'Worse still, Your Grace. He deserves the traitor's death, for what he has done could be called high treason.'

The King nodded. He was distressed; but before he had time to allow his feelings to soften, the warrant for the Cardinal's arrest was put before him and signed.

Norfolk and Suffolk were delighted. No more need they fear the anger of the Cardinal. His days were numbered.

In the Cardinal's lodgings at Cawood there was peace. Wolsey sat at supper. He felt comforted, contemplating that soon he would arrive in York and there, he promised himself, he would endeavour to spend his last months – he was sure it would not be more – in pious living.

As he supped he became aware of a commotion in the house, and then of footsteps on the stairs, and when the door was thrown open, to his astonishment he saw a man who had once been in his service: young Northumberland. He rose somewhat hastily from the table and went forward to embrace the young man who, he believed, had come on a visit of friendship. In those first seconds he forgot that this was the young man whom once, in the days of his power, he had sternly berated for contemplating marriage with Anne Boleyn.

'My friend,' he cried, 'it gives me great pleasure to see you here . . .'

But as he approached, Northumberland drew himself up and did not take the Cardinal's outstretched hands.

He looked down at the old man and said in a voice so soft that it could scarcely be heard: 'My lord Cardinal, I come to arrest you on a charge of high treason.'

'My dear boy . . .' began Wolsey.

But Northumberland's face was expressionless; he looked down on Wolsey, without emotion, without pity.

And as he stood there, the Cardinal saw others come into the room, and he knew that what he had dreaded for so long was about to happen.

❀ ❀ ❀

The painful journey back to London began.

There was time to brood, and he thought of Anne's arranging that Northumberland should be sent to arrest their enemy. Poor, pallid Northumberland, doubtless he would not have been willing, for he had ever lacked Anne's spirit. It would have been an ill match. She should have thanked the Cardinal for breaking it. But how like her, to send Northumberland, she, who resembled himself, and never forgot a slight, and demanded payment in full – with interest.

So, because of her, he was riding back to London, and his constant prayer now was that he would never reach that city. In his dreams he was passing along the dark river and through the traitor's gate; he was placing his head on the block. Was that to be the end of the journey?

There were many halting places as he could not travel far at one time. His dropsy had grown worse, and he suffered from dysentery and mental discomfort. He was an old, tired man, and he longed to rest his weary limbs; how could he travel quickly towards a cold bed in a dismal cell, there to live a few weeks under the shadow of the axe?

So far have I risen, he mused, that there is a long way to fall.

When he arrived at Sheffield Park the Earl of Shrewsbury welcomed him as though he were still the chief minister. He rested there awhile, for he was exhausted and it was physically impossible to ride on.

It was at Sheffield that messengers came from the King, and to his horror Wolsey saw that at the head of them was Sir William Kingston, the Constable of the Tower. This could mean only one thing: Kingston had come himself to take him straight to the fortress; and in spite of Kingston's assurances that Henry still thought of the Cardinal as his friend, Wolsey was seized with violent illness, and all those about him declared that from that moment he lost his desire to live and began to yearn for death.

In the company of Kingston he travelled down to Leicester, blessing the people as he went. How differently they felt about him now. They no longer called him 'butcher's cur' because they were no longer envious of him. They pitied him. They had learned of the pious life he had led in exile, and they regarded him as the holy man his garments proclaimed him.

The party drew up at the Abbey; it was dusk and servants with torches hurried out to welcome them. The Abbot, knowing who his guest was, came forward to salute the Cardinal and receive his blessing; but as Wolsey tried to dismount, his limbs gave way and he collapsed at the Abbot's feet.

'Your Eminence,' cried the Abbot, trying to raise him,

'welcome to Leicester. Your servants rejoice to have you with us for as long as you can rest here.'

With the help of the Abbot the Cardinal rose to his feet; he was trembling with fatigue and sickness.

'Father Abbot,' he said, 'methinks I shall stay with you for ever, for hither I have come to lay my bones among you.'

Alarmed, the Abbot gave orders that the Cardinal should be helped to his room. His usher, George Cavendish, was at his side; indeed, he had been with him through his triumphs and his trials, and nothing but death could part them.

'Stay near me, George,' murmured the Cardinal. 'You know as I do, that now it will not be long.'

Cavendish discovered that he was weeping silently but the Cardinal was too exhausted to notice his tears.

For a day and a night he lay in his room, unable to move, unaware of time. He slept awhile and awoke hungry and asked for food, which was brought to him.

He partook of the food almost ravenously and then paused to ask Cavendish what it was he ate.

''Tis a cullis of chicken, my lord, which has been made especially for you in order to nourish you.'

'And you say we have been here a day and a night; then this will be St Andrew's Eve.'

''Tis so, Your Eminence.'

'A fast day . . . and you give me chicken to eat!'

'Your waning strength needs it, Eminence.'

'Take it away,' said Wolsey. 'I will eat no more.'

'Your Eminence needs to regain his strength.'

'Why George? That I may be well enough to travel to the block?'

'Your Eminence . . .' began Cavendish in a faltering voice.

'You should not distress yourself, George, for I feel death near, and death coming now is merciful to me. Go now. I believe my time is short and I would see my confessor.'

He made his confession; and afterwards he lay still like a man who is waiting patiently though with longing.

Kingston came to his bedside and Wolsey smiled at him quizzically, remembering how the sight of the man had filled him with fear before.

'Your Eminence will recover,' said Kingston.

'No, my lord. For what purpose should I recover?'

'You are afraid that I come to take you to the Tower. You should cast aside that fear, because you will not recover while it is with you.'

'I would rather die in Leicester Abbey, Kingston, than on Tower Hill.'

'You should cast aside this fear,' repeated Kingston.

'Nay, Master Kingston, you do not deceive me with fair words. I see the matter against me, how it is framed.'

There was silence in the room; then Wolsey spoke quietly and firmly, and Kingston was not sure that he addressed himself to him.

'If I had served God as diligently as I have done the King, He would not have given me over in my grey hairs.'

He closed his eyes, and Kingston rose and left the chamber. At the door he met George Cavendish and shaking his head said: 'Your master is in a sorry state.'

'I fear he will not last long, my lord. He is set on death. He thought to die ere this. He said that he would die this morning and he even prophesied the time. He said to me: "George, you will lose your master. The time is drawing near when I shall depart this Earth." Then he asked what time it was and I told him "Eight of the clock." "Eight of the clock in the morning," he said. "Nay it cannot be, for I am to die at eight of the clock in the morning."'

'He rambled doubtless.'

'Doubtless, my lord, but he seemed so certain.'

'Well, eight of the clock passed, and he lives.'

Kingston went on, and Cavendish entered the Cardinal's chamber to see if he lacked anything. Wolsey was sleeping and seemed at peace.

Cavendish was at his bedside through the night and the next morning – when he died.

As the Cardinal drew his last breath, the faithful usher heard the clock strike eight.

🏵 Chapter XI 🏵

THE LAST FAREWELL

Thomas Cromwell was on his way to an appointment with the King. His eyes were gleaming with excitement; he had proved to himself that it was possible for an astute man to profit by disaster, to make success out of failure, for, incredible as it seemed, out of the decline of Wolsey had come the rise of Thomas Cromwell.

Yet he had remained the friend of Wolsey until the end. He wanted men to know that he was a true friend; and he and the Cardinal had been too closely attached for him to break away when Wolsey was in danger. As Member of Parliament for Taunton he had pleaded Wolsey's case in the Lower House and so earned the Cardinal's gratitude and at the same time the admiration even of his enemies.

He was a shrewd and able man. No one could doubt that; and it was said that if he could work so well for one master, why should he not for another. The son of a blacksmith, he must be possessed of outstanding ability to have come so far, a feat which was only outrivalled by that of Wolsey himself.

Shortly after Wolsey's death Cromwell was made a Privy Councillor, not, naturally, of the same importance as Norfolk or Thomas Boleyn, who was now the Earl of Wiltshire, but a man who had already found his way into that magic circle in which limitless opportunity was offered.

It was not long before Cromwell had attracted the attention of the King. Henry did not like the man personally but the shrewdness, the alert mind, the humble origins, all reminded him of Wolsey, and he was already beginning to regret the loss of the Cardinal and remembered those days when, in any difficulty, he summoned his dear Thomas to his side.

Therefore he was more ready than he might otherwise have been to take notice of Cromwell. Thus came Cromwell's opportunity – a private interview with the King.

When Cromwell was ushered into his presence, the King pondered wistfully: The fellow lacks the polish of Wolsey!

But he remembered that Wolsey had singled out this man and that fact counted in his favour. Cromwell had been a good friend to Wolsey in the days of his decline; so he was capable of loyalty.

The King waved his hand to indicate that Cromwell might dispense with ceremony and come to the point.

'Your Grace, I have long considered this matter of the Divorce . . .'

Henry was startled. The man was brash. Others spoke in hushed tones of this matter; they broached it only with the utmost tact. Cromwell looked bland, smug almost; as though he were playing a game of cards and held a trump in his hand.

'You are not alone in that,' said Henry with a hint of sarcasm which did not appear to be noticed by Cromwell, whose dark eyes burned with enthusiasm as he leaned forward and gazed intently at the King.

'Your Grace is debarred from success in this matter by the

cowardly ways of your advisers. They are afraid of Rome. They are superstitious, Your Grace. They fear the wrath of the Pope.'

'And you do not?'

'Sire, I am a practical man unmoved by symbols. I fear only my King.'

'H'm! Go on, go on,' he urged, slightly mollified.

'It has been a marvel to me that Your Grace's advisers have not seen what must be done, ere this. Thomas Wolsey was a Cardinal; it was natural that he should have been in awe of Rome. But those men who now advise Your Grace are not Cardinals. Why should they so fear the Pope?'

It was strange for Henry to have questions fired at him. He did not care for the man's crude manners, but the matter of his discourse had its interests.

'At this time,' went on Cromwell, 'it would seem that England has two heads – a King and a Pope. Furthermore, since the Pope denies the King that which he desires, it appears that the Pope holds more power in England than the King.'

Henry was beginning to frown, but Cromwell went on quickly: 'As a loyal subject of the King this pleases me not at all.'

'The power of Kings is temporal,' murmured Henry.

'I would wish to see my King holding supreme power, temporal and spiritual.'

Henry was startled, but Cromwell continued blithely: 'I cannot see why our King should not dispense with the Church of Rome. Why should not the Church of England stand alone with the King as its Supreme Head? Would it be necessary then for the King to plead in Rome for what he needs?'

Henry was aghast. He had often said that he would declare

the Pope a heretic, that if the Pope would not grant him a divorce he would find some other means of getting it; but this man was proposing a more daring step than he had ever taken. He was suggesting that the Church should sever its connections with Rome; that the King, not the Pope, should be Supreme Head of the Church.

The King listened and his eyes burned as fiercely as those of Cromwell.

'In a few years,' Cromwell told him, 'I could make Your Grace the richest and most powerful King in Christendom . . . but not while you remain a vassal of the Pope.'

It was astounding. It meant more than the Divorce. The King was shaken. There was so much to consider. If only Wolsey were here . . . but Wolsey would never work for the severance of England from Rome. Wolsey had been a Cardinal, his eyes constantly on the Papal Crown; he had even pleaded guilty to attempting to set up Papal jurisdiction in England. New times needed new ideas. Wolsey's day was gone and a new era was beginning.

When Henry at length dismissed Cromwell he was telling himself that Cromwell, like Cranmer, had the right sow by the ear.

Katharine at Richmond was unaware of the great schemes which were absorbing the King and his new ministers. Mary was with her, and she was determined to enjoy the hours she spent with her daughter. Mary was now fifteen years old, an age when many girls were married; but the question of Mary's marriage had been shelved; how could it be otherwise when there was so much controversy about her birth?

During these days Katharine seemed possessed of a feverish desire to make the most of each hour they spent together; each day when she arose she would wonder whether some command would be given and her daughter taken from her. She knew that Henry was as devoted to Anne as ever; that they had taken over York Place and, like a newly married pair, were exulting in all the treasures they found there.

The palace had ceased to be known as York Place, which had been its name as the town residence of the Archbishops of York; it was now the King's palace and, because of the reconstructions which had been made in white stone, it was called White Hall.

Now Wolsey had gone, Katharine felt that she was rid of her greatest enemy. She could tell herself that in good time the Pope would give the only possible verdict, and when Henry realised that their marriage was accepted as valid, he must, for the sake of reason and his good name, accept her as his wife. So she allowed herself to be lulled into a certain peace which Mary's presence made it possible for her to enjoy.

Reginald Pole was in England and it was delightful when he came to visit them, which he did very frequently. He was their friend and staunch supporter. One day, mused Katharine, why should he not be consort of the Queen? What a brilliant adviser Mary would have! What a tender, gentle husband!

'That is what I want for her,' the Queen told her friend, Maria de Salinas, who, now that she was a widow, had come back into the Queen's service. 'A tender, gentle husband, that she may never be submitted to the trials which I have had to bear.'

Katharine and Mary were sitting together over the Latin exercise when a page entered the apartment to tell them that Reginald was without and begging an audience.

Mary clasped her hands together in delight, and Katharine could not reprove her. Poor child, let her not attempt to curb her pleasure by hiding it. Katharine said with a smile: 'You may bring him to us.'

Reginald came in and the three of them were alone together. Mary took both his hands when he had bowed first to the Queen and then to herself.

'Reginald, it seems so long since we saw you.'

He smiled at her youthful exuberance. 'It is five days, Your Highness.'

'That,' said Mary, 'is a very long time for friends to be apart.'

'We have so few friends now,' Katharine quickly added.

'You have more than you know,' Reginald replied seriously. 'Many of the people are your friends.'

'They greet us warmly when we go among them,' Mary agreed. 'But we have few friends at Court whom we can trust. I believe they are afraid of . . .' Mary's lips tightened and she looked suddenly old, '. . . of . . . that woman,' she finished.

Katharine changed the subject. 'Reginald, something has happened, has it not?'

'Your Grace has a penetrating eye.'

'I can see it in your expression. You look . . . perplexed.'

Reginald took a document from the pocket of his doublet and handed it to the Queen. While she studied it he turned to Mary who laid her hand on his arm. 'Reginald,' she said, almost imploringly, 'you are not going away?'

'I do not know,' he said. 'So much depends on the King.'

'Please do not go away.'

He took her hand and kissed it. 'If I followed my own will I would never go away.'

'Nor if you followed mine,' said Mary.

Katharine lowered the document and looked from one to the other. The sight of them together frightened her while yet it pleased her. If only it *could* be, she thought; yet how can it?

'So the King has offered you the archbishopric of York or Winchester,' she said.

Mary caught her breath in dismay. If he became an Archbishop he would take Holy Orders and marriage would be outside his power. Mary loved him with all the force of her serious young nature. She had dreamed that they would go away from Court, quietly with her mother to where they might forget such hateful matters as divorce, such hateful words as bastard, where they would never even think of the Lady who hated them so much and was determined to keep them apart. In her youthful innocence she dreamed of the three of them leaving Court in secret, going out of the country to Padua or some such place which Reginald knew well.

'These offices became vacant on the death of the Cardinal,' Reginald explained, 'and someone is needed to fill them.'

'It is a great honour,' the Queen said almost listlessly.

'It is one, I have told him, that I cannot accept.'

The relief in the apartment was great. Mary laughed aloud and took Reginald's hand. 'I am glad,' she cried. 'I could not bear to think of your stepping into the Cardinal's shoes.'

'Nor I,' he said. 'But that is not all. In my refusal of this offer I implored the King not to be deluded by his ministers and his passion for a wanton woman. I am summoned to his presence in White Hall.'

Mary was horrified; although her father had shown her affection at times, she had never conquered her fear of him.

Katharine was equally afraid. She knew the climate of the King's temper. He was fond of Reginald, but when the people of whom he was fond ceased to agree with him he could easily hate them. She thought of the tenderness he had once shown to her; and she believed that his hatred of her was the greater because of it.

'Oh, Reginald,' she murmured, 'have a care.'

'You should not have mentioned us,' said Mary imperiously.

'I believed I must say what I felt to be right.'

Katharine turned to her daughter and said gently: 'We must all speak and act according to our consciences.'

'I came to see you before I presented myself to the King,' said Reginald. And both understood that he had come because this might, in view of the seriousness of the occasion, be the last time he could visit them. Neither of them spoke, and he went on: 'I should go now. I dare not keep the King waiting.'

He kissed their hands, and Mary suddenly forgot the dignity due to her rank as, like a child, she flung her arms about him; and Katharine was too moved to prevent her.

When he had gone, Mary began to weep, silently.

'My darling, control yourself,' murmured the Queen, putting an arm about her.

But Mary merely shook her head. 'What cruel times we live in,' she whispered. 'What cruel and perilous times!'

When Reginald left the Queen and the Princess he took a barge to White Hall. He knew full well that the archbishopric had been offered him as a bribe. He was of royal blood and the friend of the Queen and the Princess; the King was hinting: 'Come, work with me, and here is an example of the prizes which shall be yours.'

That was why in refusing the offer he had told the King that he firmly believed in the royal marriage and implored his kinsman not to imperil his soul by attempting to deny it.

The result: A summons to White Hall.

As he entered the palace he thought of the great Cardinal who had once occupied it; and all this splendour had been passed to the King – a mute appeal . . . 'all my possessions in exchange for my life . . .' What an example of the worth of treasures upon Earth!

Reginald uttered a prayer for the Cardinal's soul as he made his way to the gallery whither the King had summoned him.

I enter the Palace of White Hall a free man, he thought; how shall I leave it? It was very possible that he would do so with a halberdier on either side of him and thence take a barge to the Tower.

Before he reached the gallery he met his elder brother, Lord Montague, who, having heard of the summons, was waiting for him.

As soon as Montague saw Reginald, he drew him into an anteroom and cried: 'You are a fool. Do you want us all to lose our heads?'

'News travels fast,' Reginald replied. 'So you know I have refused York and Winchester.'

'And have sought to teach the King his business at the same time.'

'The archbishoprics were offered as a bribe; it was necessary to explain why I could not take either of them.'

'It was enough to refuse and thereby offend the King; but to add criticism of his conduct . . . are you mad, brother?'

'I do not think so,' answered Reginald, 'unless it be madness to speak one's mind.'

'That could be a very good definition of mental disorder,' said Montague; and he turned away from his brother, who went on to the gallery.

Henry was expecting him and he was not kept waiting long. The King stood, massive in his jewelled garments, and for a few seconds while Reginald bowed he glared at him through half closed eyes.

'So, sir,' said Henry at length, 'you think so little of my gifts that you haughtily refuse them!'

'Not haughtily, Your Grace.'

'Do not dare contradict me. How dare you tell me what I should do! Is the King to take orders?'

'No, Sire, but perhaps advice.'

'You young coxcomb, so *you* would presume to advise *me*!'

'Sire, I would plead with you on behalf of the Queen and the Princess Mary.'

'You would be wise to keep your mouth shut.'

'Nay, Your Grace, I hold that a wise man is one who speaks out of his love for the truth and not out of expediency.'

Henry came closer to him, and his scarlet glowing cheeks were close to Reginald's pale ones.

'Is it wise then to gamble with your head?'

'Yes, Sire, for the sake of truth.'

'The sake of truth! You dare to come to my presence in the manner of a father confessor . . . you whom I could send to the block merely by signing my name?'

'I come not as a father confessor, Your Grace, but as a humble kinsman of you and the Princess Mary.'

'Ha,' interrupted Henry, 'so you prate of your royal blood. Take care that you do not think too highly of it. Mayhap you remember what befell a certain Duke of Buckingham?'

The sight of Reginald's calm face incensed the King; this was largely because here was another of those men, like Fisher and More, whose approval meant so much to him. They were men of integrity and he needed their approval and support. They maddened him when they would not give it.

'I remember well, Sire,' Reginald answered.

'And the memory does not help you to change your views?'

'No, Your Grace.'

The King's mood altered suddenly. 'Now listen. I am asking you to come down from the seat of judgment. I am assured by learned men that I am not truly married to the Lady Katharine. I need the help of men such as you. You could write a treatise for me; you could explain the need of my severance from the Lady Katharine and my remarriage. I command you to do this. You are a man whom people respect; your word would carry much weight.' He laid a hand on Reginald's shoulder affectionately. 'Come now, Reginald, my dear cousin. Do this for love of me.'

'Sire, on any other matter I would serve you with all my heart, but . . .'

'But!' Henry shrieked, pushing Reginald from him. 'It would seem you forget to whom you speak.'

'I forget not,' answered Reginald. 'But I crave Your Grace to excuse me in this matter.'

Henry's hand flew to his dagger. 'Do you not know that it is high treason to disobey the King?'

347

Reginald was silent.

'Do you?' cried the King. 'By God, if you do not I shall find means to teach you.' He called for a page, and when the young man appeared he shouted: 'Send Lord Montague to me without delay.'

The page departed and in a few moments Reginald's brother came hurrying into the gallery.

Henry shook his fist at Montague. 'By God,' he cried, 'I'll have every member of your family clapped into the Tower. I'll brook no more insolence from you.'

Montague stammered: 'Your Grace, pray tell me what any member of my family has done to displease you.'

Henry pointed at Reginald. 'This brother of yours should be kept in better order. He dares to come here and meddle in my affairs. I'd have you know, Montague, that I have a way with meddlers.'

'Yes, Your Grace; On behalf of my family I offer my deepest regrets . . .'

'Take him away,' shouted Henry, 'before I lose my patience, before I order him to be sent to the Tower.'

'Yes, Your Grace.'

They bowed and left the irate Henry glaring after them, thinking: By God, 'twere better if Master Reginald had never come back to England.

When they were alone Montague turned indignantly to his brother.

'You . . . *fool*!' he cried.

'I will say to you, brother, what I have said to the King. Is it foolish to adhere to what one believes to be the truth?'

'Indeed you are a fool, having been at Court, to ask such a question. A man is a fool who attempts to wrestle with kings. I thought he would commit you to the Tower without delay.'

'I believe he was contemplating the effect it would have on certain of his subjects if he did.'

'You are calm enough. Do you seek a martyr's crown?'

'I hope never to perjure my soul for the sake of my head.' said Reginald quietly.

He left his brother, who was filled with apprehension. Reginald was thinking of the King's suggestion that he should write a treatise. He would; but it would not put forward the reasons why the King should separate from Katharine; instead it would show why the marriage was a true one.

When he was left alone Henry's anger abated a little. He began to think of the earnest young man whom he had threatened. He liked Reginald. He had always admired him; he knew him to be learned and pious; and now he had proved himself to be no coward.

Why could such men not see the truth about this marriage? Why did all the men he most respected set themselves against him?

He had tried to win the approval of Chancellor More but he could not do so. More was a clever lawyer and knew how to back out of any discourse that grew uncomfortable for him. What Henry most wanted was for Thomas More to work with him in all matters, and especially that of the divorce. He wanted Reginald Pole to do the same.

Brooding on these matters he sent once more for Reginald and his brother Montague, and when they stood before him he smiled at them in a friendly fashion.

'It is not meet,' he said, 'for kinsmen to quarrel.'

'Sire, you are indeed gracious,' said Montague.

Reginald did not speak, and Henry went on: 'I am over-wrought. These are troublous times. It may be that I appeared more angry towards you two than I felt.'

'We rejoice to hear it,' said Montague, and Reginald echoed those words.

'Come,' said Henry, stepping between them and slipping an arm through one of each, 'we are kinsmen and friends. Reginald here has his own ideas as to what is right and what is wrong. I will not say that he is alone in this, although many learned men would not agree with him – nor can I, much as I should long to. Remember this: I have to answer to my conscience. Oh, I respect those who have views and do not hide them and are not afraid to say "This I think," or "With that I disagree." I take all that has been said in good part.'

'Thank you, Your Grace,' said Reginald with real emotion in his voice.

Henry's tones softened and he turned almost pleadingly to Reginald. 'Why, if you could bring yourself to approve of my divorce, no one would be dearer to me than you.'

Montague was looking appealingly at his brother; but Reginald remained silent.

Henry released their arms and patted both brothers in a gesture of dismissal.

'Forget it not,' he said.

During the warm June weather the Court rode from Greenwich to Windsor. The Queen was in the party with her daughter and Maria de Salinas; and the King rode gaily with the Lady Anne. In the party Cranmer and Cromwell also rode.

There was a new confidence about the Lady, as there was about the King. All noticed this except the Queen and her daughter, for the former believed firmly that nothing could be settled without the sanction of the Pope, and the latter fitted her mood to that of her mother.

There were grave rumours everywhere and the whole Court was expecting that the King's patience would not last much longer.

Henry brooded as he rode. Why should I endure this continual frustration? he asked himself. He looked at the glowing face of Anne beside him and he longed to be able to soothe his troublesome conscience by telling the world that she was not his mistress but his wife.

But events were moving fast. Cranmer had now obtained the opinions of the universities of Europe regarding the divorce, and had discovered several who believed it was expedient. Henry had made up his mind that when they reached Windsor he would ask the Queen to allow the matter to be judged in an English court.

Once that took place he would have the desired result in a matter of days. Who in England would dare to go against him? He could count the dissenters on the fingers of one hand. More, Fisher, Reginald Pole. There were others, more obscure men whom he did not consider to be of much importance. It was different in the case of those three. The public looked to them for guidance.

A plague on them! he thought. Why must they put obstacles in my path?

As they came to Windsor, the King looked with pleasure at the forest. There would be good hunting, and there was little he liked better than a day in the open; then to return to good feasting and masking, and later to retire between the sheets with the right bedfellow.

She had succumbed at last and he wondered what he would do were she to become pregnant. Then, by God, he told himself, I would make them act.

Oddly enough she did not. But he would not spoil his pleasure by brooding on that. When they could be free in their love, when she could dispense with her fretful questions as to how much longer he would allow the delay; when he could take her with a good conscience . . . ah, then their union would be blessed with healthy boys.

They entered the castle, and the Queen retired with her little court and the King retired with his.

It would seem there are two queens at this Court, grumbled some of the courtiers; but most of them knew to which Court they should attach themselves . . . if they sought advancement. The Lady's bright black eyes missed little, and any attention to the Queen or the Princess Mary was noted.

The Queen in her apartments was attended by her few ladies. She was not so much afraid of spies as she had been in the days of Wolsey; and she was very happy to have her daughter and Maria with her.

She prayed on her arrival and in her prayers, as always, asked that the King might be turned from his sad and evil scheme and come back to her.

Mary was in her own apartment, her women preparing her for the banquet, when Henry came to see the Queen. Her women went scuttling away at a look from him, and Katharine cried: 'Oh, Henry, how pleased I am that you should come to see me. It is a rare honour.'

'I would come often enough if I could but satisfy myself that you were in truth my wife.'

'Henry, I do not think that deep within your heart you believe that I am not.'

It was wrong, of course. She should not say such things; but there were occasions when the bitterness was too much to be hidden.

He ignored her words as though he had not heard them. He said: 'Dr Cranmer has procured the opinions of the universities. There are many who believe we should be formally divorced.'

'Ah, Henry, you have many friends. I alas have few.'

'I think you too have friends,' he said. 'Now I am going to ask you to give me something.'

'There is little I would deny you.'

'I ask only sweet reasonableness.'

'I try always to be reasonable.'

'Then I am sure you will agree that this matter has continued too long, and it is time it were brought to an end. I want to refer it to the arbitration of four English prelates and four nobles.'

Her expression was stony. 'No,' she said.

'Katharine, you call this reasonableness?'

'I do. A court in this country is unnecessary. It is a waste of time, for any court you set up would decide in your favour.'

'This is nonsense.'

'Henry, have done with hypocrisy. You know it to be truth. May God grant you a quiet conscience.'

'You talk to me of a quiet conscience when you know it to be perpetually disturbed by this matter.'

'Let it speak for itself, Henry. Do not provoke it with your desire, but let it say what it knows to be truth. Abide by it. Come back to me and then I think your conscience need never trouble you again on this matter.'

'Never!' cried the King.

She answered his obstinacy with her own.

'Never will I abide by any decision except that of Rome.'

The King gave her a murderous glance before he strode out of her apartment.

Henry called Norfolk and Suffolk to him and when they were alone said: 'I fear the Queen hates me.'

The Dukes looked alert. They had heard this statement from the King's lips before this, and they knew that it was meant to be the prelude to some action which he was willing himself to take.

Henry went on: 'I believe she delights in my discomfiture, that she seeks to prolong it; that, knowing herself not to be my wife, she is determined to proclaim to the world that she *is*. I believe that she is seeking to lure my subjects from me.'

'That,' said Suffolk, 'would amount to treason.'

'Much as it pains me to admit it, I must agree,' replied Henry. 'Eustache Chapuys is nothing but a spy. I believe that it is the Emperor's desire to bring about a civil war in England, to split the country and to set the Queen and the Princess Mary at the head of the rebels.'

'This is indeed treason,' declared Norfolk.

'I have seen some of the letters which Chapuys has written to his master. In them he states that the English people are against a divorce and it would not surprise him if they rose in protest. They have full sympathy for the Queen, he writes significantly. I believe that the Spanish ambassador, with the help of the Queen, is ready to raise an insurrection.'

'Your Grace, should he not be arrested?' asked Norfolk.

Henry raised a hand. 'This is a delicate matter. Although Katharine is no true wife to me, for many years I believed her to be so.'

Henry was thinking of the discontent among the people who, when Katharine's barge sailed up or down river, lined the banks to cheer her. To put Katharine under arrest would be to turn their sympathy into fury and the desire to protect their Queen. Moreover, he did not believe for one moment that Katharine would ever put herself at the head of an insurrection. How lacking in subtlety were these two! Wolsey would have grasped his meaning immediately.

'Nay,' went on Henry, 'she is no wife to me, but I confess to a certain tenderness. I would be lenient with her.'

'But Your Grace will not continue to be in her company,' said Norfolk, who was a little sharper than Suffolk and had at last begun to follow the King's train of thought.

'I fear the time has come when we must part . . . finally,' Henry replied.

'I am in full agreement,' Suffolk put in. 'Your Grace should separate yourself from the Lady Katharine both at bed and board. It would not be safe for you to do otherwise.'

A look of sadness came into the King's face. 'After so many years . . .' he murmured.

But the Dukes were now aware of the part they were expected to play, and Suffolk said sternly: 'Your Grace would do well not to think of a woman with whom you have for so long been living in sin.'

Henry laid a hand on his brother-in-law's arm. 'You do well to remind me.'

His eyes were vindictive suddenly because he was remembering her obstinacy and how quickly this case could have been settled but for that. He went on: ' 'Tis my belief that she sets my daughter Mary against me.'

Suffolk piped up dutifully: 'Your Grace, should not the Princess Mary be taken from her?'

'That might be wise,' answered the King, looking at Norfolk.

The Duke was well aware of what was expected of him. He spoke vehemently. 'Above all, the Princess Mary should be removed from the Lady Katharine. That I consider to be of the greatest importance.'

'Thank you, my friends,' said the King. 'You echo the thoughts which my tenderness would not let me utter. But since this is your advice, and I know it to be based on sound good sense, I will accept your decision.'

Mary came into the Queen's apartments, her face pale, her eyes frightened.

'Mother,' she cried, even before Katharine had had time to sign to the women to leave them, 'I am to go away from you.'

Katharine took her daughter's hands and found that they were trembling. 'Be calm, my precious.'

'I am to go to Richmond. Those are my father's orders.'

'Well, you will go to Richmond and soon I shall come to you there.'

'Suppose you cannot?'

'But why ... *why*?'

'I do not know . . . except that it is a feeling I have. I was told to prepare to leave at once. Why, Mother? What harm am I doing them here? Do I prevent his . . . his . . . being with that odious woman?'

'Hush, my love. Go to Richmond. I will find means of coming to you there.'

Mary had begun to shiver. 'Mother, I am afraid. Reginald is writing his treatise and it is all for us. I tremble for Reginald. I do not believe he understands what this could mean.'

'He understands, my darling.'

'Then he does not seem to care.'

'Reginald is a good man, a brave man. He could not be so if he trimmed his opinions to the prevailing wind. Do not fear for him, my child; for the only thing we should fear in life is our own wrong-doing. Go to Richmond, as your father commands. Think of me, pray for me . . . as I shall for you. You will be in my thoughts every minute of the day, and rest assured that as soon as I am able I shall be at your side.'

'But Mother, what harm are we doing him . . . by being together? Does he not know that this is the only joy that is left to us?'

'My darling, be brave.'

'There is tension in the Castle. Something is about to happen. Mother, I have a terrible fear that, if I leave you now, I shall never see you again.'

'You are overwrought. This is merely another parting.'

'Why . . . why . . . should there be these partings? What harm are we doing?'

'It is the second time you have spoken of harm. No one thinks we are doing harm, my love.'

'They do, Mother. I see it in their looks. Our love harms him in some way and he is afraid of it. I cannot leave you. Let us go away together.' Mary drew away from her mother. Her eyes were brilliant with sudden hope and speculation. 'I will send for Reginald. I will ask him to take us with him to Italy. There the Pope will give us refuge – or perhaps the Emperor will.'

Katharine laughed gently, and drawing her daughter to her stroked her hair.

'No, my love,' she said. 'That would profit us little. We are in your father's hands, but nothing can harm us if we do our duty. It matters little what becomes of our bodies, as long as our souls are pure. Go to Richmond and remember that there I am with you as I am when we are close like this, for you are never absent from my thoughts.'

'Oh, Mother, if I could but rid myself of this fear . . .'

'Pray, my child. You will find comfort in prayer.'

They embraced and remained together until one of Mary's women came to say that her party was ready to leave for Richmond, and the King's orders were that they were to depart at once.

At the door Mary turned to look at her mother, and so doleful was her expression that it was as though she looked for the last time on the beloved face.

How she missed Mary! It was but a few days since she had left, but it seemed longer. She had had no opportunity of appealing to the King as she had not since been in his company alone.

He treated her with cool detachment, and she noticed that never once did he allow his eyes to meet her own; she was aware of the speculative glances of the courtiers; they knew more than she did and they were alert.

One morning she was awakened early by sounds below; she heard the whisper of voices as she lay in her bed, and afterwards the sound of horses' hoofs. People were arriving at the Castle, she supposed, and because she was weary after a sleepless night, she slept again.

In the early morning when two of her women came to awaken her, they brought her a message from the King, which told her that Henry was leaving Windsor and when he returned he wished her to be gone. Since she was not his wife and had no thought for his comfort he desired never to see her again.

She read the message twice before she grasped the full importance of it. Then she said: 'I wish to see the King without delay.'

'Your Grace,' was the answer, 'the King left Windsor with a hunting party at dawn. He is now on his way to Woodstock.'

She understood. He had slunk away without telling her he was going; he had not even wanted to say goodbye. But soon he would be returning to Windsor, and when he did so he expected to find her gone. More than that, he had expressly commanded that she *should* be gone.

'It matters not where I go,' she murmured, 'I am still his wife. Nothing will alter that.'

Maria came to her, for the news had reached her as soon as it had the Queen. She understood that Katharine was now forsaken.

'Where does Your Grace wish to go now?' she asked.

'What does it matter where I go?' retorted Katharine; and she wondered with increasing pain whether the King had determined, not only to live apart from her, but also to separate her from their child.

She recovered her dignity. She had some friends even in

England; and she was sure that the Pope would give his decision in her favour. Her nephew would support her. The battle was not yet lost.

She said calmly: 'We will go to my manor of the Moor in Hertfordshire; there I shall rest awhile and make plans for my future.'

That day they left Windsor, and Katharine knew that she had reached yet another turning point in her life.

🌸 Chapter XII 🌸

POISON AT THE BISHOP'S TABLE

John Fisher, Bishop of Rochester, faced the gathering of Bishops.

He was deeply disturbed, he said, because of a certain request with which he could not comply. The King was asking the Church and clergy to accept him as Supreme Head of the Church of England, and he, John Fisher, could not understand how that could be. There was and had always been one Head of the Church, and that was His Holiness the Pope. He did not see how, by making the claim to this title, it could be the King's.

The Bishops listened with averted eyes. The King had issued what he called this request, yet it was not in truth a request but a command. So many of them who owed their positions to the King dared not contemplate what might become of them should they not bow to his will.

John Fisher seemed oblivious of his danger. This was an impossible thing, he urged them. They could not, with good consciences, change the law of the Church which had existed through the ages.

Warham, Archbishop of Canterbury, fidgeted uneasily as

he listened. That head would be severed from the gaunt body before long, he was sure, if Fisher did not curb his tongue. Oh, that I should have lived so long! he thought. I am too old and tired now to navigate such dangerous waters. What will become of us all?

Alas, for him, as Archbishop of Canterbury, he could not remain silent.

Supreme Head of the Church! he mused. This is a break with Rome. There has never been anything like it in this country's ecclesiastical history. Nothing will ever be the same again. It is an impossible thing. And yet the King commanded it; and Warham knew well that it would go hard for those, like Fisher, who attempted to oppose it.

Fisher was looking at him now. 'And you, my lord Archbishop . . .?'

Everything that he said would be reported to the King. One word spoken which should have been left unsaid was enough to send a man to the block. I am too old, he thought, too old and tired.

He heard his voice speaking the carefully chosen words. 'It is my belief that we might accept the King as Supreme Head of the Church as far as the law of Christ allows . . .'

Beautifully noncommittal, certain to give offence to none. He was aware of Fisher's scornful eyes. But all men were not made to be martyrs.

One of the Bishops added that His Grace, fearing that the Supreme Head of the Church was a title which might not be acceptable to some of the clergy, had modestly changed it to: Supreme Head . . . after God.

Warham felt his lips curved in a smile of cynicism. So Henry was prepared to accept only the domination of God. He was safe enough, for he could expect no opposition to his desires from that direction. His conscience would always stand a firm bulwark between him and God.

Fisher was on his feet again but Warham silenced him.

'We have heard the views of the Bishop of Rochester,' he said, 'and now I would ask the assembled company if they are prepared to accept the King as Supreme Head of the Church, as I am . . . as far as the law of Christ allows.'

There was silence. Heads were downcast in the rows of benches.

'Your silence I construe as consent,' said Warham. He did not look at Fisher who must understand that one voice raised against the King's command was of little matter when so many were in agreement. Fisher should learn wisdom; there were times when silence was salvation.

The Bishop of Rochester lived humbly in his London residence, but his doors were kept open and there was always a meal to be given to any who called on him when there was food on his table.

Perhaps his guests were not so many since the meeting of the Bishops. Those who wished him well deplored his out-spokenness; some sought to advise him; but there were few who wished it to be said that they were in agreement with him.

It was a few days after the meeting when his cook, Richard Rouse, returning to the kitchens after shopping in the markets, was met by a stranger who asked for a word with him.

Richard Rouse was flattered, for beneath the disguise of a merchant he recognised a person of the quality. The cook was a man of ambition; he had not been long in the service of the

Bishop and he was proud to be employed by a man of such importance; he did not see why he should not rise in his profession; the house of an Archbishop might be his next appointment; and after that – why should he not serve the King?

The stranger took him to a tavern where they sat and drank awhile.

'I have heard that you are an excellent cook,' Rouse was told. 'And that your services are not appreciated in that household in which you serve.'

'My master is a good one.'

'Any cook can call a master good who has a poor palate. The Bishop might be eating stinking fish in place of the excellent dishes you put before him. He would know no difference.'

'His thoughts are on other matters,' sighed Rouse.

'That's a tragedy for a good cook. Such a master would never sing his praises in the right quarters.'

'I fear so.'

'How would you like to work in the royal kitchens?'

There was no need for Rouse to answer, but he did. 'It is the ambition of my life.'

'It need not be so far away.'

'Who are you?' Rouse demanded.

'You will discover, if you are a wise man.'

'How can I convince you of my wisdom?'

'By taking this powder and slipping it into the Bishop's broth.'

Rouse turned pale.

'I thought,' said his companion contemptuously, 'that you were an ambitious man.'

'But this powder . . .'

'It is calculated to improve the flavour of the broth.'

'The Bishop will not notice that the flavour is improved.'

'Others at his table might.'

Rouse was afraid, but he would not look at his fear. He tried to find an explanation of the stranger's conduct which would be acceptable to him. The man wanted to help him to a place in the King's kitchens because he believed his talents were wasted on the Bishop of Rochester; therefore he was giving him a new flavouring which would make people marvel at the broth he put before them. Perhaps at the table would be one of the King's higher servants . . . That was a very pleasant explanation. The only other was one he had no wish to examine.

He was a man who was always hoping for a great opportunity; he would never forgive himself if, when it came, he was not ready to take it.

The Lord Chancellor brought grave news to the King.

Henry studied Thomas More with affectionate impatience. Here was a man who might have done so much in moulding public opinion, because if it could be said 'Sir Thomas More is of the opinion that my marriage is no true marriage,' thousands would say 'This matter is beyond me, but if Sir Thomas More says this is so, then it must be so, for he is not only a learned man, but a good man.'

But Thomas was obstinate. His smile was sunny, his manner bland, and his wit always a joy to listen to. But whenever Henry broached the matter of the divorce Thomas would have some answer for him to which he could not take offence and yet showed clearly that Thomas was not prepared to advance his cause.

Now Thomas was grave. 'The Bishop of Rochester is grievously ill, Your Grace.'

Henry's heart leaped exultantly. Fisher had become a nuisance; he always looked as if he were on the point of death. Henry was sentimental enough to remember his old affection for the man, but his death would be a relief. He was another of those obstinate men who did not seem to care how near they approached danger to themselves as long as they clung to their miserable opinions.

'He has been ailing for some time,' the King answered. 'He is not strong.'

'Nay, Your Grace, he became ill after partaking of the broth served at his table.'

'What's this?' cried Henry, the colour flaming into his face.

'He was seized with convulsions, Your Grace, and so were others at his table. It would seem that there has been an attempt to poison him.'

'Have his servants been questioned?'

'Your Grace, his cook has been arrested and under torture confesses that a white powder was given him by a stranger with instructions to put it into the Bishop's broth. He declares he was told it would but improve the flavour.'

Henry did not meet his Chancellor's eyes.

'Has he confessed on whose instructions he acted?'

'Not yet, Your Grace.'

Henry looked at his Chancellor helplessly. He was thinking of a pair of indignant black eyes, of a lady's outbursts of anger because of the dilatoriness which she sometimes accused the King of sharing; he thought of her ambitious family.

What if the cook, put to the torture, mentioned names which must not be mentioned?

Yet the Chancellor was looking at him expectantly. He could not take this man into his confidence as he had that other Chancellor.

Oh, Wolsey, he thought, my friend, my counsellor, why did I ever allow them to drive a wedge between us? Rogue you may have been to some extent, but you were my man, and we understood each other; a look, a gesture, and you knew my mind as these men of honour never can.

He said: 'Poisoning is the worst of crimes. If this fellow is guilty he must pay the full penalty of his misdeeds. Let him be put to the torture, and if he should disclose names, let those names be written down and shown to none other but me.'

Sir Thomas More bowed his head. There were times when Henry felt that this man understood every little twist and turn of his mind; and that made for great discomfort.

He glanced away. 'I will send my best physician to the Bishop,' he said. 'Let us hope that his frugal appetite means that he took but little of the poisoned broth.'

The Chancellor's expression was sorrowful. Fisher was a friend of his – they were two of a kind.

Death is in the air, he thought as he left the King's presence.

Crowds were gathered in Smithfield to watch the death of Richard Rouse. The name of the cook who had longed for fame and fortune was now on every tongue. He would be remembered for years to come because it was due to him that a new law had been made.

Several people who had sat at the Bishop's table had died; the Bishop himself remained very ill. Poisoning, said the King in great indignation, was one of the most heinous crimes a man could commit. And, perhaps because he would have been so relieved to know the Bishop was dead, he felt it his duty to show the people how much he regretted this attempt on the old man's life. The severest punishment man could conceive must be inflicted on the poisoner. After some deliberation the new law had come into being. The death penalty for poisoners from henceforth was that they should be hung in chains and lowered into a cauldron of boiling oil, withdrawn and lowered again; this to be continued until death.

And so the crowds assembled in the great square to see the new death penalty put into practice on the cook of the Bishop of Rochester.

Richard Rouse, who had to be carried out to the place of execution, looked very different from the jaunty man who had spoken to a stranger in a tavern such a short time before.

He was crippled from the rack, and his hands, mangled by the thumbscrews, hung limply at his sides.

With dull eyes he looked at the chains and the great cauldron under which the flames crackled.

There was silence as he was hung in the chains and lifted high before he was lowered into the pot of boiling oil. His screams would be remembered for ever by those who heard them. Up again his poor tortured body was lifted and plunged down into the bubbling oil. And suddenly . . . he was silent. Once again he was lowered into that cauldron, and still no sound came.

People shuddered and turned away. Voices were raised in the crowd. 'Richard Rouse put the powder into the broth, but who in truth poisoned those people who had sat at the Bishop's table?'

It was recalled that the Bishop had been one who had

worked zealously for the Queen. Now he was only alive because of his frugal appetite, although even he had come close to death. Who would wish to remove the Bishop? The King? He could send the Bishop to the Tower if he wished, merely by giving an order. But there were others.

A cry went up from Smithfield: 'We'll have no Nan Bullen for our Queen. God bless Katharine, Queen of England!'

✿ Chapter XIII ✿

KATHARINE IN EXILE

In the castle of Ampthill Katharine tried to retain the dignity of a Queen. Her routine was as it had always been. She spent a great deal of time at prayer and at her needlework, reading and conversing with the women she had brought with her and in particular with Maria, the only one in whom she had complete trust; only to Maria did she refer to her troubles, and to the fact that she was separated from the King.

Each day she waited for some news, for she knew that in the world outside Ampthill events were moving quickly towards a great climax.

She could not believe that Henry would dare disobey the Pope; and she was certain that when Clement gave the verdict in her favour, which he must surely do, Henry would be forced to take her back.

She had one desire to which she clung with all the fervour of her nature; only this thing mattered to her now. She had lost Henry's affection for ever; she was fully aware of that. But Mary was the King's legitimate daughter, and she was determined that she should not be ousted from the succession, no matter what it cost her mother.

'I will sign nothing,' she told Maria. 'I will not give way an inch. They can have me murdered in my bed if they will; but I will never admit that I am not truly married to Henry, for to do that would be to proclaim Mary a bastard.'

The great joy of her life was in the letters she received from Mary. What if the final cruelty were inflicted and that joy denied her! How would she endure her life then?

But so far they both had their letters.

Her faithful Thomas Abell had been taken from her when he had published his book, setting forth his views on the divorce. She had warned him that he risked his life, but he cared nothing for that; and when they had come to take him away, he had gone almost gleefully. It was well that he should, he told her, for many would know that he was in the Tower, and why.

News came to Ampthill. The Pope had at last decided to act, and he summoned Henry to Rome to answer Queen Katharine's appeal; he must, was the Holy Father's command, appear in person or send a proxy.

Henry's answer had been to snap his fingers at the Pope. Who was the Pope? he demanded. What had the Pope to do with England? The English Church had severed itself from Rome. There was one Supreme Head of the Church of England (under God) and that was His Majesty King Henry VIII.

This was momentous. This was telling the world that the rumour, that the Church of England was cutting itself free from Rome, was a fact.

But all this was paled by news of her daughter. Margaret Pole was with Mary still, and for that Katharine was grateful; Reginald had been sent to Italy, and Katharine knew that, much as Margaret loved her son, she was relieved that he was out of England, for it was growing increasingly unsafe to be in England and to disagree with the King.

Margaret wrote: 'Her Highness the Princess has been ailing since she parted from Your Grace. It has grieved me deeply to watch her. She has had so little interest in life and her appetite is so poor. Constantly she speaks of Your Grace, and I know that if you could be with her she would be well. She has had to take to her bed . . .'

The Queen could not bear to think of Mary, sick and lonely, longing for her as she herself longed for Mary.

'What harm can we do by being together?' she demanded of Maria. 'How dare he make us suffer so! He has his woman. Does our being together prevent that? Why should he be allowed to make us suffer so, merely that he may appease his conscience by telling himself – and others – that I plot against him with my daughter?'

But there was no comfort for Maria to offer her mistress, and at times Katharine came near to hating her husband.

Then she would throw herself on to her knees and pray.

'Forgive me, oh Lord. Holy Mother, intercede for me. He has been led into temptation. He does not understand how he tortures his wife and daughter. He is young . . . bent on pursuing pleasure, led away by bad counsellors . . .'

But was this true? Was he so young? Who was it who had determined that no one should stand in the way of divorce? Who but Henry himself? Once she had blamed Wolsey, but Wolsey was dead, and this persecution persisted and had indeed intensified.

She sat down to write to him, and wrote as only a mother could write who was crying for her child.

'Have pity on us. My daughter is pining for me, and I for

her. Do not continue in this cruelty. Let me go to her.'

She sent the letter to him without delay, and then began the weary waiting for his reply.

But the days passed, the weeks passed, and there was no answer from the King.

Stirring news came from Court. Sir Thomas More, unable to evade the great issue any longer, had resigned the Chancellorship rather than fall in with the King's wishes.

Katharine prayed long for Thomas More when she heard that news, prayed for that pleasant family of his who lived so happily in their Chelsea home.

William Warham died; some said that like Wolsey he was fortunate to finish his life in a bed when he was but a few short steps from the scaffold. He was eighty-two years old and in the last weeks of his life had been issued with a writ of *præmunire* – a small offence but one by which he had shown he had not accepted the King as Supreme Head. Perhaps the old man was forgetful; perhaps he had not understood that it was necessary now to receive the King's permission in all matters concerning the Church as well as the state. He had behaved according to procedure *before* the severance from Rome. These were dangerous times and the King was jealous of his new authority.

Fortunate Warham, who could take to his bed and die in peace.

Dr Cranmer became the new Archbishop of Canterbury. Henry need fear no opposition from him; he was the man who, with Thomas Cromwell, had worked more than any to extricate the King from the tyranny of Rome.

Lord Audley was now Chancellor in place of Sir Thomas More, and gradually the King was ridding himself of the men who might oppose him.

John Fisher had recovered from the poison and was still living, but he was very frail. Katharine prayed for him and often trembled for him.

She heard that the King had honoured Anne Boleyn by making her Marchioness of Pembroke and that he planned to take her to France with him as though she were his Queen.

This was humiliating in the extreme because it seemed that François and the French Court were now ready to accept Anne Boleyn as Queen of England.

But all these matters seemed insignificant when the news came from Margaret Pole that Mary had recovered and was almost well again.

'Still grieving for Your Grace, but, I thank God, growing stronger every day.'

'If I could but see her,' sighed the Queen. 'I would cease to fret on account of anything else which might happen to me.'

On a January day in the year 1533 the King rose early. There was a grim purpose about him, and those who lived close to him had noted that during the last months a change had crept over him. The strong sentimental streak in his nature had become subdued and in its place was a new cruelty. He had always flown into sudden rages but these had quickly passed; now they often left him sullen and brooding. All those men whose duty it was to be in contact with him knew they must tread warily.

The little mouth had a strong determination about it on that

374

morning. This was a day to which he had looked forward for six years, and now that it had come, the thought occurred to him that it was less desirable than it had seemed all those years ago. Waiting had not enhanced his emotions; perhaps they had grown stale; perhaps his main thought as he prepared himself for what was about to take place was one of triumph over great odds rather than the climax of years of devotion.

He was going to make his way to an attic in the west turret of White Hall, not so much as a doting bridegroom as a man who has made up his mind to some action; and, even though it seemed less desirable to him than it had previously, he was determined to carry it out simply because it had been denied him and he was eager to show that he was a man who would allow no one to say him nay.

When he was ready he said to one of his gentlemen: 'Go and seek my chaplain, Dr Rowland Lee, and tell him that I wish him to celebrate Mass without delay. Bring him to me here.'

Dr Rowland Lee, who had hastily dressed himself, came to the King in some surprise, wondering why he had been sent for at such an early hour of the morning.

'Ah,' said the King who had dismissed all but two of his grooms – Norris and Heneage. 'I wish you to celebrate Mass in one of the attics. Follow me.'

The little party made their way to the attic and very shortly were joined by two ladies, one of whom was Anne Boleyn, Marchioness of Pembroke, and the other her train bearer, Anne Savage.

Henry turned to Dr Lee. 'Now,' he said, 'marry us.'

The doctor was taken aback. 'Sire . . .' he stammered. 'I . . . could not do this.'

'You could not do it? Why not?'

'I . . . I dare not, Sire.'

The blue eyes were narrowed; the cruel lines appeared about the mouth. 'And if I command you?'

'Sire,' pleaded Dr Lee, 'I know that you went through a ceremony of marriage with Queen Katharine, and although I am aware of your Secret Matter I could not marry you unless there was a dispensation pronouncing your marriage null and void.'

For one second those assembled thought the King would strike his chaplain. Then suddenly his mood changed; he slipped his arm through that of the man, drew him away and whispered: 'Perform this ceremony and you shall be rewarded with the See of Lichfield.'

'Your Grace, Your Majesty . . . I dare not . . .'

It took a long time, thought the King, for these dunderheads to learn who was the Supreme Head of the Church. He was impatient, and he could see that this fellow was so immersed in the old laws of the Church that he could not cast them aside easily. Yet this ceremony must take place. Anne was with child. What if that were a *boy* she carried! There could be no more delay. It would be disastrous if Anne's boy should be declared illegitimate.

He made a decision. 'You need have no fear. The Pope has pronounced himself in favour of the divorce and the dispensation is in my keeping.'

Dr Lee drew a deep sigh of relief.

'I crave Your Grace's pardon. Your Grace will under-stand . . .'

'Enough,' interrupted Henry. 'Do your work.'

And in the lonely attic at White Hall, Henry VIII went through a ceremony of marriage with Anne Boleyn, while Norris, Heneage and Anne Savage stood by as witnesses.

❀ ❀ ❀

The King sent for the newly appointed Archbishop of Canterbury.

Thomas Cranmer, who had come so far since the Boleyns had brought him to the King's notice, was very eager that his royal benefactor should not regret having raised him so high.

When they were alone Henry explained to his Archbishop what he expected of him. There were many in England who clung to old ideas, and he was going to have every man who held any position of importance sign an oath which would declare his belief in the supremacy of the King. But that was for later. There was this tiresome matter of the divorce.

He knew himself never to have been married to Katharine, and he had been surrounded by rogues and vacillating fools – until now, he hoped.

The matter was urgent. He considered himself already married to Queen Anne, and he was certain that he had God's blessing because the marriage was already promising fruitfulness. He must have a speedy end to the old matter though, and it was the duty of the new Archbishop of Canterbury to see that this was so.

The Archbishop was nothing if not resourceful.

'The first step, Your Grace, is a new law to make it illegal for appeals in ecclesiastical causes to be carried out of the kingdom to Rome.'

The King nodded, smiling. 'I see where this will lead us,' he said.

'And when this becomes a law of the land, it would be meet for the Archbishop of Canterbury to ask Your Grace's leave to declare the nullity of the marriage with Katharine of Aragon.'

The King, continuing to smile, slipped his arm through that of his Archbishop. 'It is a marvellous thing,' he murmured, 'that all the wise and learned men who argued this matter did not think of this before.'

And when Cranmer had left him, he continued to think of Cranmer, whose ideas had been so useful to him. Cromwell and Cranmer, they were two men who had suddenly sprung into prominence and, because their ideas were fresh and bold, with a few sharp strokes they were cutting the bonds which for so many years had bound him.

He would not forget them.

It was a bright April day when Katharine heard the news. It came to her in a letter from Chapuys. Now that she was exiled she did receive letters more freely than she had when she had been at Court surrounded by Wolsey's spies, and so was in constant touch with the Spanish ambassador.

Often she thought that, had her nephew sent her a man with the energy of Eustache Chapuys some years ago, she might have had the advantage of very valuable advice. Chapuys was indefatigable. She had a great admiration for him; she knew that he was of humble origin and that he had come to England hoping to achieve fame and fortune; yet, when he had heard of the wrongs done to her, he had thrown himself so wholeheartedly into her cause that he had become the most ardent champion it had ever been her good fortune to have. Alas, she thought, luck was never with me, for he came too late.

Now she read his letter and the news it contained startled her.

The King, wrote Chapuys, had secretly gone through a form of marriage with the Concubine who was shortly to be proclaimed Queen. The fact was that she was with child by the King and Henry was taking no chances of the child's being branded illegitimate. Therefore, Katharine would shortly receive a summons to appear before a court which Cranmer was about to open at Dunstable. On no account must she answer that summons. Nevertheless they would conduct the court without her; but her absence would cause some discomfiture and delay; and owing to the recent law that ecclesiastical cases must be settled in England and not referred to Rome, they could be sure that Cranmer would pronounce the marriage null and void. She would see, of course, that there would then be no need of a dispensation from the Pope, because such a dispensation was unnecessary as the King would accept the ruling of Cranmer's court, which would be that Katharine and the King had never truly been married.

She sighed as she read these words.

She would obey Chapuys's instructions. He was one of the few people she could trust; and when the summons came for her to appear at Dunstable, following quickly on Chapuys's warning, she ignored it.

But her absence could not prevent the court's being opened and the case tried.

On the 23rd of May Cranmer declared that the marriage between King Henry VIII and Katharine of Aragon was invalid, and that the Queen of England was no longer Katharine but Anne.

The weary waiting was over. The matter had been settled simply by cutting the knot which bound England to the Church of Rome. There need no longer be talk of the divorce, for a divorce was not necessary between people who had never been married.

News came to Ampthill of the coronation of Queen Anne. Great pomp there had been in the streets of London; Katharine heard of how Anne had ridden in triumph under a canopy of state in purple velvet lined with ermine. A Queen at last! All the nobility had attended her coronation; they dared do no other; but the people in the streets had shown less enthusiasm than was usual on such occasions. Royal pageants were the highlights of living to them; they always welcomed them, especially when the King ordered that wine should flow in the conduits; but on this occasion there were few cheers.

Katharine's women tried to cheer her as they sat at their needlework.

'They say, Your Grace, that there was scarcely a cheer as she rode through the city.'

Katharine nodded, and Maria who sat beside her knew that the Queen was remembering her own coronation: coming to the Tower from Greenwich, dressed in white embroidered satin, a coronal set with many glittering stones on her head, her long hair hanging down her back: remembering the ardent looks of Henry, who had insisted on marrying her against the advice of his ministers. In those days she had believed that nothing could happen to spoil their happiness.

'I heard,' said one of her women, 'that my lord of Shrewsbury declared he was too old to shout for a new Queen. He also said that the new Queen was a goggle-eyed whore; and many people heard him cry "God save Queen Katharine who is our own righteous Queen!" '

Katharine shook her head. 'Do not repeat such things,' she warned.

'But, Your Grace, I had it on the best authority. It is true the people do not like Queen Anne. Many of them say they will not have her as their Queen.'

'You should pray for her,' answered Katharine.

Her women looked at her in astonishment.

'Pray for Nan Bullen!'

'Once,' said the Queen, 'I rode through the streets of London, the Queen, the King's chosen bride. He faced opposition, you know, to marry me.' She had dropped her needlework into her lap and her eyes were misty as she looked into the past. 'And look you, what I have come to. It may not be long before she is in like case.'

There was silence, and the Queen took up her work and began to sew.

It was clear to all that Katharine's thoughts were far away; and when the sewing was over, and rising from her chair she was about to go to her private chapel, she tripped and fell, driving a pin into her foot.

Maria and others of her ladies helped her to her bed, and in the morning her foot was swollen and it was necessary to call her physician.

During the next days she remained in her bed. She had developed a cough which would not leave her in spite of the warm summer weather. And as she lay she wondered what steps the new Queen would take to further her discomfiture, for she was sure this would come. She pictured Anne, riding through the streets filled with sullen people. Ambitious, haughty and bold, Anne would certainly take measures to show the people that she was their new mistress.

Katharine did not have to wait long.

She was still in bed on account of the accident to her foot, and her cough had not improved, when her women came to tell her that a party of men had come from the King, and at their head was Lord Mountjoy.

Lord Mountjoy! He had once been her chamberlain and a very good servant to her; she was pleased then to hear that he it was who had been chosen to convey the King's wishes to her.

But when he was brought into her presence she realised quickly that her one-time servant was now the King's man.

'Your Grace,' he told her, 'you will know that at the court at Dunstable your marriage to the King was declared null and void by the Archbishop of Canterbury, and leave was given both to you and the King to marry elsewhere.'

She bowed her head. 'I have been informed of this.'

'You will know also that the coronation of Queen Anne has also taken place.'

Katharine nodded once more in acquiescence.

'The King decrees that, as it is impossible for there to be two Queens of England, you will henceforth be known as Princess of Wales since you are the widow of his brother Arthur, Prince of Wales.'

Katharine raised herself on her elbow. 'I am the Queen of England,' she said, 'and that is my title.'

'But Your Grace knows that the Lords spiritual and temporal have declared the marriage invalid.'

'All the world knows by what authority it was done,' retorted Katharine. 'By power, not justice. This case is now pending in Rome and the matter depends not on judgment given in this realm, but in the Court of Rome, before the Pope, whom I believe to be God's vicar and judge on Earth.'

'Madam, you speak treason,' said Mountjoy.

'It is a sorry state,' answered the Queen mournfully, 'when truth becomes treason.'

Mountjoy handed her the documents he had brought with him from the King and, glancing at them, she saw that throughout she was referred to as the Princess Dowager.

She called Maria to bring her a pen and boldly struck out the words Princess Dowager wherever they occurred.

Mountjoy watched her in dismay, and as he did so he remembered the occasion of her coronation and how she had always been a just mistress to him.

'Madam,' he said, pleading, 'I beg of you to take care. It would be a grievous thing if you were charged with high treason.'

She smiled at him. 'If I agreed with your persuasions, my Lord Mountjoy, I should slander myself. Would you have me confess that I have been the King's harlot these twenty-four years?'

Mountjoy felt unnerved, and could not proceed as he had been instructed to do. Katharine sensed this and softened towards him.

'Do not distress yourself,' she said, 'I know full well that you do what you have been commanded to do.'

Mountjoy went on to his knees. 'Madam,' he said, 'should I be called upon to persecute you further, I should decline to do so . . . no matter what the consequences.'

'I, thank you, Lord Mountjoy, but I would not have you suffer for me. Take these papers back to the King. Tell him that I am his wife now as I was on the day he married me. Tell him also that I shall not accept the title of Princess Dowager because my title is Queen of England. That I shall remain until my death.'

Apprehensively Mountjoy went back to Court.

Disturbed by Mountjoy's account of what had happened, Henry decided that Katharine should be sent farther from London and commanded that she move her household from Ampthill to Buckden, there to take up residence in a palace which belonged to the Bishop of Lincoln. In the summer, when Katharine arrived, this place was charming, offering views over the fen country; Katharine had yet to discover how damp and bleak it could be in winter and what a disastrous effect it would have on her health.

She was extremely unhappy to move because, not only was she to change her place of residence, but she was also to lose certain members of her household. She had had too many friends at Ampthill, and they had upheld her in her sauciness, said the King. She could manage with a smaller household at Buckden; and one of the first to be dismissed should be Maria de Salinas who had always been her strong partisan from the days when she had first arrived in England. The edict had been that all those who refused to address her as the Princess of Wales should be dismissed. Katharine promptly forbade anyone to address her by any title but that of Queen.

She was desolate to lose Maria. This was the bitterest blow of the entire upheaval, and those who watched their farewell wept with them.

Katharine's stubborn determination was a source of great irritation to the King, but he was fully aware that the people who lived in the villages surrounding her were her fervent supporters, and he had heard that when she had travelled from Ampthill to Buckden the way along which she had passed had been crowded with people who shouted: 'Long live the Queen!'

She was an encumbrance and an embarrassment to him but he knew he must treat her with care. Therefore he finally allowed her a few servants – though he firmly refused to allow Maria to be one of them – whom he excused from taking an oath to address her as the Princess of Wales; and with this smaller household, Katharine lived at Buckden.

There was one fact for which she was thankful. Her chaplain, Dr Abell, who had written against the divorce, had been released from prison and allowed to come back to her. The man was too obscure, Henry decided, to be of much importance.

At Buckden Katharine endeavoured to return to the old routine. Her life was quiet, and she spent a great deal of time in her chamber which had a window looking into the chapel. She seemed to find great comfort in sitting alone in this window-seat.

She busied herself with the care of the poor people living close by who had never known any show such solicitude for their well-being before. There was food to be had at the palace for the hungry; the Queen and her ladies made garments for those who needed them; and although Katharine was far from rich she set aside a large part of her income for the comfort of the poor.

'A saint has come among us,' said the people; and they declared they would call no other Queen but Katharine.

Henry knew what was happening and it angered him, for it seemed to him that all those who admired the Queen were criticising him; he could not endure criticism. But there was one matter which occupied his thoughts day and night. Anne was about to give birth to their child.

A son, he told himself exultantly, will put an end to all

trouble. Once I have my son there will be such rejoicing that no one will give much thought to Katharine. It will be a sign that God is pleased with me for discarding one who was not in truth my wife, and taking another.

A son! Night and day he prayed for a lusty son; he dreamed of the boy who would look exactly like himself. He himself would teach him – make a man of him, make a King of him. Once he held that boy in his arms everything would be worth while, and his people would rejoice with him.

It was September of that fateful year 1533 when Anne was brought to bed.

Henry could scarcely contain his excitement, and had already invited François to be the boy's sponsor. His name? It should be Henry . . . or perhaps Edward. Henry was a good name for a King. Henry IX. But that was years away, of course. Henry VIII had many years before him, many more sons to father.

Queen Anne suffered much in her travail. She was as anxious as the King. Was there a certain apprehension in her anxiety? The King was still devoted to her – her passionate and possessive lover – but now that she had time for sober reflection she could not help remembering his indifference to the sufferings of his first wife. Once he had been devoted to Katharine; she had heard that he had ridden in pageants as Sir Loyal Heart; and his loyalty was then for Katharine of Aragon – short-lived loyalty. Was he a man whose passions faded quickly? He had been her devoted admirer for many years, but was that due to his faith-fulness or a stubborn determination to have his will which her cleverness in keeping him at bay had inflamed?

A son will make all the difference, the new Queen told herself. Holy Mother of God, give me a son.

The cry of a child in the royal apartments! The eager question, and the answer that put an end to hope.

'A girl, Your Majesty, a healthy girl.'

The bitterness of disappointment was hard to bear, but the child was healthy. The King tried to push aside his disappointment.

Anne looked strangely humble in her bed, and he was still in love with her.

'Our next will be a boy, sweetheart,' he told her.

And she smiled in agreement.

So they rejoiced in their daughter, and called her Elizabeth.

Margaret Pole was anxious concerning the Princess Mary who had never seemed to regain her full strength since her parting from her mother. Margaret knew that she brooded a great deal and was constantly wondering what would happen next.

Mary was no longer a child; being seventeen years of age, she was old enough to understand the political significance of what was happening about her. There was a strong streak of the Spaniard in her, which was natural as, before their separation, she had been so close to her mother.

Mary was restless, delicate, given to fits of melancholy. And what else could be expected? Margaret asked herself. What a tragedy that a child should be torn from her mother's side when the bond between them was so strong, and when her position was so uncertain with her father.

But for Queen Anne, Margaret often thought, Henry would not have been unkind to his daughter. She was his child and he was eager to have children, even girls. But those occasional bursts of fondness were perhaps the very reason why Anne would not allow Mary at Court. Could it be that the new Queen was afraid of the influence Mary might have on her father?

It was so very tragic, and Margaret, while she thought fearfully of her own son Reginald who had offended the King, continually asked herself how she could make Mary's life brighter.

Mary liked to play the lute or the virginals, for music was still her favourite occupation; but Margaret fancied as she listened to her that she played listlessly and there was a melancholy note in her music.

'Play something lively, something to make us feel gay,' Margaret suggested.

But Mary turned on her almost angrily: 'How can I feel gay when I am not allowed to see my mother, when I know she is not in good health and mayhap has no one to care for her?'

'If I could write to her and tell her that you are cheerful, that would do her much good, I am sure.'

'You could not deceive her. How could I be cheerful when I long to see her as I know she does me?' Mary rose from the virginals and came to stand by her companion. 'What will happen to us now that the Concubine has a child? They will say this Elizabeth comes before me, I'll swear.'

'How could they do that?'

'You know full well they could do it. They have said my mother's marriage was no marriage. That means one thing. The bastard Elizabeth will be declared heir to the throne until they get themselves a boy.' Mary's face grew hard and stern. 'I pray they never get a boy.'

'Your Highness . . . my dear Princess . . . forgive me, but . . .'

'I must not say such things! I must pray, I suppose, that the Concubine may be fruitful! I must pray that there is peace in this land, even though to bring this about I must declare my mother lived in sin with the King and I am therefore a bastard!'

'My dear . . . my dear . . .'

Mary walked away to the window. 'Reginald was brave,' she cried, clenching her hands. 'He was strong. He did not care if he offended my father. He would not have cared if they had cut off his head.'

'He would have died a martyr's death and we should have been left to suffer,' answered Margaret soberly. 'Let us thank God that he is out of the country at this time.'

'There is a party riding into the courtyard,' said Mary.

Margaret rose swiftly and came to her side.

'They come from the Court,' she said. 'I recognise those women as of *her* suite.'

'We want none of the Concubine's household here,' Mary cried.

'You must receive them, Your Highness, and hear their business.'

'I will not,' Mary said firmly and went out of the room.

It was not Mary however whom they had come to see, but the Countess. Two women were brought to her and they stated their business briefly.

The Lady Mary was no longer heir to the throne, for her mother was the Princess Dowager and had never been the King's true wife. Certain jewels were in her possession which were the property of the crown. It was necessary now that these jewels be handed to them, for they were messengers from the King and Queen and had papers to prove this. The Lady Mary's jewels now belonged to the Princess Elizabeth, and it was Margaret Pole's duty to give them up.

Margaret stood very still; she had grown pale.

'I know the jewels to which you refer,' she said. 'They are the property of the Princess Mary and I should be failing in my duty if I gave them up.'

'They are no longer the property of the Lady Mary. Here is an order from the Queen.'

Margaret studied the order. But I do not consider Anne to be the Queen, she said to herself. I shall certainly not give up the Princess Mary's jewels.

So she remained stubborn, and the next day when the party rode away from Beauleigh, Mary's jewels remained behind.

When Mary heard what had happened she praised her governess.

'Let them do what they will to us,' she said. 'We will stand out against them.'

'They will be back,' said Margaret apprehensively.

Mary held her head high as she declared: 'They know I am the true heir to the throne. They must. I shall never stand aside for this young Elizabeth.'

But how could they hold out against the King and Queen? They could show defiance for a while, but not for long.

Queen Anne, in her new power, would not allow Margaret Pole and Mary to flout her wishes. Shortly afterwards a command came from the King: The Countess of Salisbury was discharged from her duty as governess to the Lady Mary and the pension paid to her in that capacity would immediately cease.

When Mary heard the news she was stricken with grief.

'Not you too!' she cried. 'I have lost my mother and Reginald . . . you are all that is left to me.'

'I will stay with you,' answered Margaret. 'I shall have no pension but I have money of my own. We shall not allow a matter of my pension to part us.'

Then Mary threw herself into her governess's arms. 'You must never . . . *never* leave me,' she said solemnly.

But it was not to be expected that the Queen would allow Margaret to remain with Mary after she had dared refuse to obey a command. She would make the King see what a danger Mary could be. It was clear that she was truculent by her refusal to return what did not really belong to her. Queen Anne had a child to fight for now, and she was determined that her Elizabeth, not Katharine's Mary, should be regarded as heir to the throne.

Margaret saw that she had acted foolishly. What were a few jewels compared with real friendship, devotion and love? What would happen to Mary when she had no one to protect her? How would the news that Mary's governess had been dismissed affect Katharine, who had admitted often that she could feel some comfort knowing that Mary was with her very dear friend?

The edict came. Margaret Pole, Countess of Salisbury, was to leave the household of the Lady Mary, who herself was to be sent from Beauleigh to Hunsdon, where she would live under the same roof as her half-sister, the Princess Elizabeth. And to remind her that she was not the King's legitimate daughter, and therefore not entitled to be called Princess, she should live in humble state near the magnificence of Anne's baby daughter.

Bitterly they wept. They could not visualise parting, so long had they been together.

'One by one those whom I love are taken from me,' sobbed Mary. 'Now there is no one left. What new punishment will they inflict upon me?'

Eustache Cupuys had asked for a private interview with the King.

'Your Majesty,' said the Spanish ambassador, 'I come to you because I can speak with greater freedom than can any of your subjects. The measures you have taken against the Queen and her daughter, the Princess Mary, are very harsh.'

Henry glowered at him, but Chapuys smiled ingratiatingly.

'I speak thus, Your Majesty, because it is my great desire to see harmony between you and my master.'

'There would be harmony between us but for the fact that you are continually writing to him of his aunt's misfortunes. If his aunt and her daughter were no more . . . that would be an end of our troubles.'

Alarm shot into the ambassador's mind. Henry was not subtle. The idea had doubtless entered his head that life would be more comfortable if Mary and Katharine were out of his way. The Queen must be warned to watch what she ate; the Princess Mary must also take precautions. Chapuys's mind had been busy with plans for some time. He dreamed of smuggling the Princess Mary out of the country, getting her married to Reginald Pole, calling to all those who frowned on the break with Rome and the new marriage with Anne Boleyn to rise against the King. He visualised a dethroned Henry, Mary reigning with Reginald Pole as her consort, and the bonds with Rome tied firmly once more. Perhaps the King had been made aware of such a possibility. He was surrounded by astute ministers.

He must go carefully; but in the meantime he must try to make matters easier for the Queen and Princess.

'If they died suddenly Your Majesty's subjects would not be pleased.'

'What mean you?' Henry demanded through half closed eyes.

'That there might well be rebellion in England,' said the ambassador bluntly.

'You think my subjects would rebel against *me*?'

Eustache Chapuys lifted his shoulders. 'Oh, the people love Your Majesty, but they love Queen Katharine too. They may love their King, but not his new marriage.'

'You go too far.'

'Perhaps I am over-zealous in my desires to create harmony between you and my master.'

Henry was thinking: The man's a spy! I would to God we still had Mendoza here. This Chapuys is too sharp. We must be watchful of him.

He was uneasy. He did know that the people were grumbling against his marriage. They never shouted for Anne in the streets; and he was aware that when Katharine appeared they let her know that she had their sympathy.

'I come to ask Your Majesty,' went on Chapuys, 'to show a little kindness to Queen Katharine, if not for her sake for the sake of the people. There is one thing she yearns for above all others: To see her daughter. Would Your Grace now allow them to meet?'

'No,' said the King firmly.

'Then would Your Grace give me permission to visit the Queen?'

'No, no, no!' was the answer.

The Spanish ambassador bowed, and the King signified that the audience was over.

It was unfortunate that Katharine's request should come when Henry was pondering the insinuations of Chapuys. She was finding Buckden very damp and unhealthy. She suffered from rheumatism and gout, and she asked the King to allow her to move to a house which would offer her more comfort.

Henry read her request frowning, and sent for Suffolk.

He tapped the letter and said: 'The Queen complains again. Buckden is not to her liking. She asks permission to leave.'

'And Your Majesty has decided that she may leave?'

'I was turning over in my mind where she might go.'

'There is Fotheringay, Your Majesty. That could be put at her disposal.'

Henry thought of the castle on the north bank of the river Nen in Northamptonshire. Its situation was notoriously unhealthy, but it was far enough away not to give cause for concern.

'Let it be Fotheringay,' said Henry.

When Katharine heard that she was to go to Fotheringay she cried out in protest.

'It is even more unhealthy than Buckden!' she said. 'Is it true that the King wishes to see an end of me?'

She was weary of living and she was certain that if she went to Fotheringay she would not be long for this world. It was a comforting thought, but immediately she dismissed it. What of Mary? She visualised her daughter, shorn of her rank, forced to live under the same roof as Anne Boleyn's daughter, doubt-less expected to pay homage to the child. It was intolerable.

She must live to fight for Mary. Chapuys was full of ideas; he was constantly writing to her. He was ready to go to great lengths in her cause and that of the Princess Mary. And here she was, weakly welcoming death.

She would certainly not go to Fortheringay.

'I will not leave Buckden for Fotheringay,' she wrote to the King, 'unless you bind me with ropes and take me there.'

But Henry was now determined to move her and, since she would not accept Fotheringay, he declared that she should go to Somersham in the Isle of Ely.

'As this place is no more acceptable to me than the Castle of Fotheringay,' she wrote, 'I will remain where I am.'

But the King had decided that she should go to Somersham, for there she could live with a smaller household. Moreover he knew that she was far from well, and Somersham, like Fotheringay, was unhealthy. If Katharine were to die a natural death, and he could cease to think of her and the effect she was having on his popularity, he would enjoy greater peace of mind.

He sent Suffolk down to Buckden with instructions to move the Queen and certain members of her household to Somersham.

The Duke of Suffolk had arrived at Buckden and was asking audience of the Princess Dowager. Katharine, walking with difficulty, received him in the great hall.

'My lady,' said Suffolk, bowing, but not too low, making a difference in the homage he would give to a Queen and one who was of less importance than himself, 'I come on the King's orders to move you and your household to Somersham.'

'I thank you, my lord Duke,' answered Katharine coldly, 'but I have no intention of leaving Buckden for Somersham.'

Suffolk inclined his head. 'My lady, I fear you have no choice in this matter as it is the King's order that you should move.'

'I refuse this order,' retorted Katharine. 'Here I stay. You see the poor state of my health. Buckden does not serve it well, but Somersham is even more damp and unhealthy. I shall not leave this house until one which pleases me is found for me.'

'My lady, you leave me no alternative . . .'

She interrupted him: '. . . but to go back to the King and tell him that I refuse.'

'That is not what I intended, my lady. I have orders from the King to move you, and I at least must obey my master.'

'I'm afraid your task is impossible, my lord, if I refuse to go.'

'There are ways, Madam,' answered the Duke, 'and these must needs be adopted in the service of the King.'

Katharine turned and, leaving him, retired to her apartments.

She expected him to ride off to tell the King what had happened, but he did not do this; and sitting at her window waiting to see him leave, she waited in vain. Then suddenly from below she heard unusual noises, and before she could summon any of her women to ask what was happening, one came to her.

'Your Grace,' said the woman, 'they are moving the furniture. They are preparing to take it away. Already the hall is being stripped bare.'

'This is impossible!' said the Queen. 'They cannot turn me out of Buckden without my consent.'

But she was wrong, because this was exactly what Suffolk had made up his mind to do.

Secretly Suffolk was ashamed of this commission and wished that the King had chosen some other to carry it out; it was particularly distasteful to him, because he had, on the death of the King's sister Mary, recently married the daughter of Maria de Salinas who was such a close friend of the Queen. But his bucolic mind could suggest no other way of disguising his distaste than by truculence. Moreover he had orders to move the Queen from Buckden, and he did not care to contemplate what the King would say if he returned to Court and explained that he had been unable to carry out his task.

Katharine went to the hall and saw that what she had been told was correct. The tapestries had already been taken down from the walls, and the furniture was being prepared for removal.

Angrily she confronted Suffolk. 'How dare you move my furniture without my consent?' she demanded.

He bowed. 'The King's orders are that it and you should be removed.'

'I tell you I shall not go.'

She left him and went up to her bedchamber. Several of her faithful women were there, and she locked the door on herself and them.

Suffolk followed her and stood outside the door begging her to be reasonable.

She would not answer him and, realising that it was no use arguing with a locked door, Suffolk went back to the hall.

'Go into all the rooms save those of the Queen's private apartments, which are locked against us,' he commanded. 'Dismantle the beds and pack all that needs to be packed. We are moving this household to Somersham.'

The work went on while Katharine remained in her own

apartments; but Suffolk and his retinue had been seen arriving, and it was not long before news of what was happening within the manor house was spread throughout the villages. As the crowd outside grew, Suffolk, who had posted his guards about the house, was soon made aware that the Queen's neighbours were gathering to protect her. It was a silent crowd, watching from a distance; but it was noted that many of the men carried choppers and billhooks; and Suffolk, who had never been noted for his quick wits, was uneasy. Here was a humiliating situation: the Queen locked in her own apartments with a few of her faithful servants; he and his men dismantling the house, preparing to move; and outside, the Queen's neighbours gathering to protect her! Suffolk knew that if he attempted to remove the Queen by force there would be a battle. He could imagine Henry's fury when news of this reached his ears.

Yet something must be done; but the winter evening was near and he could do nothing that night, so he called a halt to his men. They should see about their night quarters and making a meal. They were prepared for this for they had not expected to complete their task in one day and night.

In the morning, Suffolk told himself, I shall work out a plan. He thought wistfully of the Christmas revelry which would be taking place at the Court. The new Queen and her admirers would certainly arrange a lively pageant. There would be fun for those at Court, while he had to spend his time in this gloomy mansion, trying to persuade an obstinate woman to do something which she had sworn not to do.

But in the morning the situation was the same. Katharine remained in her own apartments, waited on by her faithful servants who treated the invaders as though they did not exist.

Meanwhile by daylight the crowds waiting outside seemed

to be more formidable – young, strong countrymen with their ferocious-looking billhooks. If he attempted to force a way through them Suffolk knew there would assuredly be a clash.

More than ever he wished himself back at Court; but he could see only one possible course. He must write to the King and tell him the circumstances; he would be cursed for an incompetent fool, but that was better than being responsible for a fight between the King's soldiers and the Queen's protectors. Suffolk was shrewd enough to know that such an incident might be the spark to start a civil war.

Already the King was preoccupied with fears of a rebellion which might seek to set his daughter Mary on the throne.

Yet he was undecided. He put off writing to the King, telling himself that Katharine might relent. She was after all an ageing woman, a lonely woman who had suffered the greatest humiliation possible. Perhaps those yokels waiting outside to defend her would grow tired. So Suffolk decided to wait.

For five days he waited and still Katharine's door remained locked. She took her food in her own apartments and would not open her door to Suffolk.

His patience ended. He went to her door and hammered on it.

'If you do not come out, I shall take you by force,' he shouted.

'You would have to do that,' was Katharine's answer. 'Break down my door if you will. Bind me with ropes. Carry me to your litter. That is the only way you will get me to move from this house.'

Suffolk swore in his angry uncertainty. There were spies in this household. They were carrying tales to those waiting people so that everything that was happening in this house was known. He was sure that the Queen's neighbours were sending word to friends miles away, and that the ranks about the house were swelling.

He dared not take her by force. He and his men would be torn to pieces if he did.

He returned to the hall, looked gloomily at the dismantled room; then he wrote to the King, to Cromwell and to Norfolk, explaining the Queen's obstinacy and his fear of mob violence from the crowd which now seemed to be some thousands.

He despatched the letters and prepared to depart himself.

He saw Thomas Abell coming from the Queen's apartments and called to him.

'So, sir priest, you are still here with the Princess Dowager.'

'As you see, my lord Duke.'

'And upholding her in her obstinacy as you ever did,' snarled Suffolk.

'The Queen is a lady of stern ideals.'

'The Queen? There is but one Queen of England. That is Queen Anne.'

'There is but one Queen, my lord; and I say that Queen is Queen Katharine.'

'By God,' cried Suffolk, 'you speak high treason.' He shouted to his men. 'Take this priest. He will leave with us as our prisoner.'

He summoned all those servants, who were not with Katharine, to his presence and forthwith arrested several of them. At least he would not go back to London empty handed. Then he was ready to leave. He glanced round the castle which looked as though it had been sacked by invading soldiery – which in some measure it had – before he rode out into the courtyard and gave the order to depart.

The crowds parted for them to pass; no one spoke, but the looks were sullen.

Katharine came down from her private apartments and gazed in dismay at the havoc in her house. But when she heard that some of her servants had been taken prisoner, among them the faithful Abell, she ceased to care about the state of her dwelling. She thought of Abell going back to the discomfort of the Tower, where he might be submitted to torture as he had been before, and a feeling of utter desolation took possession of her.

Will there be no end to this persecution? she asked herself. Then she began to weep, for the strain of the last days had been greater than she had realised while they were happening; and although when confined to her room, unsure of whether she would be removed by force, she had not wept, now she could not prevent herself from doing so.

Two of her women came and stood with her.

'Your Majesty, pray return to your bed. There is more comfort there.'

She did not answer but held her kerchief to her streaming eyes.

'A curse on Anne Boleyn,' said one of the women.

Katharine lowered her kerchief and turned her stern gaze on the speaker. 'Nay,' she said. 'Hold your peace. Do not curse her. Rather pray for her. Even now the time is coming fast when you shall have reason to pity her and lament her case.'

She turned slowly and mounted the stairs to her apartment. Her women looked after her in wonderment. Then they shivered, for she spoke with the voice of a prophet.

Chapter XIV

IN THE CASTLE OF KIMBOLTON

Katharine continued to live in her private apartments, and the rest of the castle remained as Suffolk's men had left it: the tapestries unhung, the furniture dismantled.

Every day Katharine expected to receive a command from the King to leave Buckden for some place of his choice, but Henry was too occupied by affairs at Court to concern himself with her.

There was about this life an air of transience. She scarcely left her apartments, and heard Mass at the window of her bedroom which looked down on the chapel; her food was cooked by her bedroom fire, and those who served her, living closer to her, began to find love of her mingling with the respect she had always inspired.

The winter was bitter and she often felt, during those rigorous weeks when she lay shivering in her bed, that she could not live long in this condition. Her great concern was for her daughter who she knew, through Chapuys, was as much in danger as she was herself.

Chapuys wrote to her that she must take care what she ate,

and that her meals should be cooked only by her most trusted servants because he believed that in high quarters there was a plot to remove both her and the Princess Mary.

This threat did not diminish when in the March of that year Clement at last gave his verdict, declaring that the marriage of Henry VIII and Katharine of Aragon was valid in the eyes of God and the Church.

'Too late!' sighed Katharine. 'Five weary years too late!'

She knew that Clement's verdict could do her and Mary no good now, but could only increase the wrath of her enemies among whom she knew in her heart – but she tried hard not to admit this – was the King, her husband.

In May of that year the King ordered her to leave Buckden for Kimbolton Castle in Huntingdonshire; and this time she obeyed.

The reign of terror had begun. There were certain stubborn men who refused to take the Oath of Supremacy, and the King was no longer the carefree boy who was eager only for his pleasure.

His marriage with Anne was turning sour. Where was the boy for whom he had dared so much? Where was the tender passion he had once felt for Anne?

In Kimbolton Castle was the woman whom many still called his Queen. He was waiting impatiently for her death which surely could not be long delayed. The last years of anxiety and living in damp houses had ruined her health, he had heard; yet she clung as stubbornly to life as she had to her determination not to enter a nunnery.

A plague on obstinate women . . . and obstinate men.

He knew that Chapuys was dangerous, and he had refused again and again the ambassador's requests to see Katharine. How did he know what was being planned in secret? Was it true that plans were afoot to smuggle Mary from the country and marry her to Reginald Pole, that traitor who dared tell him . . . his King . . . that he disapproved of his conduct?

A plague on all men and women who risked their lives for a cause which was not the King's. They should see whither that road led.

Mary was as obstinate as her mother, refusing to travel with her baby sister, declaring that she was a Princess and would answer to no other title, continually pleading to see her mother; now she was most inconveniently ill, and it was being whispered that she had been poisoned.

Katharine wrote to him from Kimbolton: 'Our daughter is ill. You cannot keep her from me now. I beg of you, allow me to see her. Do you remember how long it is since I did so? What joy does this cruelty bring you?'

The King's eyes narrowed as he read that appeal. Let them meet! Let them plot together! Let them smuggle notes to sly Chapuys . . . plans to get Mary abroad, married to Pole – a signal doubtless for their friends in England to rise against him!

'Never!' he cried.

Those who did not obey the King should suffer the supreme penalty. In April of that bloodstained year five Carthusian monks were brought for trial and found to be guilty of high treason. Their crime: They refused to sign the Oath declaring the King to be Supreme Head of the Church.

'Let them understand,' growled Henry, 'what it means to disobey the King. Let all who plan like disobedience look on and see.'

In that May the tortured bodies of these five martyrs were brought out of their prison for execution. The degrading and horrible traitors' death was accorded them and they were dragged on hurdles to Tyburn, hanged, cut down alive, their bodies ripped open and their bowels and hearts impaled on spears and shown to the spectators, that all might understand what happened to those who disobeyed the King.

In June more monks of the Charterhouse were brought to Tyburn and similarly dealt with. And a few days later John Fisher, Bishop of Rochester, was brought from his prison to die the traitors' death. Fortunately for him, there were some for whom it was expedient to show leniency; so the King said he would be merciful. Not for the bishop, whom some of the King's misguided subjects loved, the barbarous death accorded to the Carthusians; Fisher was allowed to die by means of the executioner's axe.

In July Sir Thomas More was brought from the Tower of London, where he had been for fifteen months, and he too laid his head upon the block.

When Katharine heard of the death of these old friends she shut herself into her chamber and remained there alone.

She still could not believe that the gay young husband who had married her in the days of her humiliation was in truth the brutal murderer of good men. She still clung to the belief that it was those about him who urged him to these deeds. Now she feigned to believe it was Anne Boleyn, as once she had believed it was Wolsey.

Yet in her heart she knew that he was all-powerful; more so than ever now that he had cut himself off from the Pope.

John Fisher! she sighed. Thomas More! My dear friends . . . and the King's! How could he murder two such men?

But she knew. And she wondered: Who will be next?

She was very fearful for her daughter . . . and herself.

The winter had come again, and Katharine knew with certainty that she could not live through it. She was now so feeble that she must keep to her bed for days at a time; and some premonition told her that her end was near.

Once more she appealed to Henry.

'I do not think I have long to live. I pray you permit our daughter to come to me. You surely cannot prevent her from receiving my last blessing in person.'

She was hopeful when she had despatched that appeal because she persisted in believing that Henry was not so cruel as he seemed.

But this plea, like others, was unanswered, and she now understood that she would never see her beloved daughter again in this life.

Chapuys, hearing of the Queen's condition, was alarmed and went at once to the King. He was shocked to see the hopeful expression in the King's face. The man is a monster, he thought angrily.

'I ask Your Majesty's permission to visit the Queen at Kimbolton,' he said.

Henry ignored the request, and began to speak of affairs in Europe. François would not rest until Milan was his; and could he win Milan without the help of England?

Chapuys did not answer. Instead he said: 'I have heard from the Queen's physician that she is near death. She implores you to allow her to see her daughter.'

'It is a matter which I could not decide without consulting my council.' Henry took Chapuys by the shoulders and studied him intently. 'The Emperor ignores his interests when he meddles in matters which are outside his concern. If he refuses my friendship, why should I not make an alliance with an ally who is eager to be my friend?'

'Your Majesty cannot believe the Emperor would ever abandon Queen Katharine while she is alive.'

A smile of complacency crossed the King's face. 'Then perhaps it is not important. She will not live long.'

'It is for this reason that I ask your permission to visit her.'

Henry shrugged his shoulders. She was dying; she could not long be an encumbrance to him.

'Go to her if you wish,' he said. 'But there shall be no meeting between her and the Lady Mary.'

Ghapuys did not wait, for fear that the King might change his mind. He left Henry's presence and with all speed set out for Kimbolton.

Chapuys knelt by her bed and his heart was touched by the sight of her. The skin was tightly drawn across her bones; her hair, once so beautiful, hung limp and lustreless. Talking exhausted her. But she brightened at the sight of him; and when she saw his distress she told him not to weep, for, as he would see, death held no terrors for her, and since she was parted from her daughter life had little to offer.

Then she pushed aside her grievances and wished to hear

news of her daughter and to give instructions as to what was to happen after her death.

'I have so little to leave,' she said. 'A few furs, a few jewels . . . but they are hers; and she will love them, more because they were mine than because of their value. When you see her, tell her that I loved her dearly and that had it not been for my delight in her I doubt I could have borne my sorrows. Oh, my dear friend, I fear I have brought great suffering to this country. Worthy men have died and others have endangered their souls. Yet I am Henry's wife, and how could I deny that?'

Chapuys tried to soothe her, and it was gratifying to him to know that he brought her some comfort. He looked round the room, at the few candles, at the rushes on the floor. A humble room to provide the death chamber of Isabella's daughter.

But his visit so comforted her that she seemed to recover.

It was six o'clock on New Year's Day when a small party of weary travellers arrived at the gate of the Castle. At their head was a woman who declared that they were half dead with fatigue and implored to be given shelter.

The gate-keeper told her that none could be admitted to the Castle unless carrying a written permission from the King to do so; but the woman wept and begged him not to leave her without shelter in this bitter January night.

The gate-keeper was touched by the piteous spectacle the travellers presented, and consented to allow their leader to see Sir Edmund Bedingfeld whom the King had appointed steward to Katharine, but who was in fact her jailor.

When the woman was in his presence, her hooded cloak

wrapped tightly about her shivering body, she entreated him to allow her to warm herself at a fire, and she was taken into the hall of the Castle.

'Tell me,' she said as she stretched her white hands to the blaze, 'is the Princess Dowager still alive?'

'She is,' was the answer.

'I had heard that she was dead,' said the woman sombrely.

'I fear she soon may be.'

'I pray you let me see her.'

'Who are you?'

'I have letters to prove my identity.'

'Then show them to me.'

'This I will do in the morning. They are now in the possession of my women.'

'I should need to see them,' said Bedingfeld, 'before I could allow you to visit the Princess Dowager.'

The woman went to her two servants who were standing some distance away, but instead of speaking to them she suddenly ran to the staircase and began to mount it.

Bedingfeld was so astonished that he could only stare after her, and in those few seconds she took the opportunity to get well ahead.

'Who is your mistress?' he demanded of the women; but they shook their heads and would not answer; and by that time the woman was at the top of the first flight of stairs and had come upon one of the Queen's maids.

'Take me to the Queen. I am a friend whom she will wish to see.'

Bedingfeld cried: 'Halt, I say.'

The maid did not listen to him and turning began to run, while the visitor followed her.

The door of Katharine's bedchamber was thrown open and the maid cried: 'Your Majesty, Lady Willoughby has come to see you.'

Then the Queen tried to raise herself, and Maria de Salinas ran to the bedside, threw herself on her knees and embraced her.

When Bedingfeld entered the room he saw the two women in each other's arms. He saw the tears on the Queen's wasted cheeks; he heard her say: 'So Maria, you came to me; so I am not to die alone. I am not abandoned like some forgotten beast.'

The Queen's eyes met his over the head of her faithful Maria, and she said: 'Leave us. My dear friend has braved much to come to me. I command you to leave us together.'

And Bedingfeld turned quietly and shut the door.

There were not many days left; and Maria de Salinas did not leave the Queen's bedside. She told Katharine of how she had made the perilous journey unknown to anyone, because she had determined to be with her mistress.

'Oh. Maria, how happy you have made me,' sighed the Queen. 'The pity of it, there is little time left for us to be together.'

'Nay,' cried Maria, 'you will get well now that I am here to nurse you.'

'I am beyond nursing,' replied the Queen; 'yet not so far gone that I cannot rejoice in your dear presence.'

Maria refused to leave the Queen's bedchamber, and during the days that followed she it was who nursed her and sat by her bed talking to her.

There were times when Katharine forgot that she was in her bed in dreary Kimbolton, and believed that she was in the Alhambra at Granada, that she wandered through the Court of Myrtles, that she looked down from her window on to the Courtyard of Lions; and that beside her there was one, benign and loving, her mother Isabella. Maria sitting at her bedside could speak of those days and, with Maria's hand in hers, they spoke the language of their native Castile; and it seemed to Katharine that the pains of her body and the sorrows of her life in England slipped away from her. Here was sunshine and pleasure amid the rosy towers; she saw the sign of the pomegranate engraved on the walls – the symbol of fertility which she had taken as her own, she forgot with what irony, because the years had slipped away and she was young again.

Maria watched her with startled eyes, for she knew that Katharine's life was ebbing away.

She sent for the priests and Extreme Unction was given. And at two o'clock in the afternoon of the 7th of January 1536 Katharine died.

When the news was brought to Henry he was jubilant.

'Praise be to God,' he cried. 'We are delivered from the fear of war. Now I shall be able to treat with the French, for they will be fearful that I shall make an alliance with the Emperor.'

There was another reason for his pleasure. She had been a perpetual embarrassment to him while there were men to believe she was still his wife.

He dressed himself in yellow from head to foot and wore a waving white plume in his cap, declaring that the revelries were to continue because there should be no period of mourning for a woman who had never been his wife.

Queen Anne followed his example and dressed in yellow. Like the King she was relieved by the death of Katharine; but there was a shadow across her relief. She was aware – as were many at Court – how the King's eyes would light with speculation as they rested on a certain prim but sly maid of honour whose name was Jane Seymour.

Now there was a feverish gaiety about the King and his Queen. Death was waiting round the corner for so many. But through the Court strode the King, the little Elizabeth in his arms, demanding admiration for his daughter. Some wondered what the fate of that other daughter would be, remembering a time when he had walked among them with Mary in his arms.

'On with the dance!' cried the King; and the musicians played while the company danced with abandon.

Queen Katharine was dead; More was dead; Fisher was dead. They formed part of the procession of martyrs.

Dance today! was the order of the Court, for who could know what tomorrow would hold? Whose turn would come next?

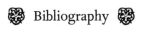 Bibliography

Aubrey, William Hickman Smith, *The National and Domestic History of England*

Cavendish, George, *Life of Wolsey*

Chamberlin, Frederick, *The Private Character of Henry VIII*

Hackett, Francis, *Henry the Eighth*

Herbert, Edward Lord, *History of England under Henry VIII*

Hume, Martin, *The Wives of Henry VIII*

Fisher, H. A. L., *The Political History of England (1485–1587)*

Froude, James Anthony, *History of England*

Froude, James Anthony, *The Divorce of Catherine of Aragon*

MacNalty, Sir Arthur S., *Henry VIII: A Difficult Patient*

Mattingly, Garrett, *Catherine of Aragon*

Pollard, A. E., *Henry VIII*

Salzman, L. F., *England in Tudor Times*

Sampson, Ashley, *Wolsey (Great Lives)*

Stephen, Sir Leslie, and Lee, Sir Sidney, *The Dictionary of National Biography*

Strickland, Agnes, *The Lives of the Queens of England*

Timbs, John, and Gunn, Alexander, *Abbeys, Castles and Ancient Halls of England and Wales*
Wade, John, *British History*

Uneasy Lies the Head

Jean Plaidy

In the aftermath of the bloody Wars of the Roses, Henry Tudor has
seized the English crown, finally uniting the warring Houses of York
and Lancaster through his marriage to Elizabeth of York.

But whilst Henry VII rules wisely and justly, he is haunted by
Elizabeth's missing brothers; the infamous two Princes, their fate in
the Tower for ever a shrouded secret. Then tragedy strikes at the
heart of Henry's family, and it is against his own son that the
widowed King must fight for a bride and his throne . . .

arrow books

ALSO AVAILABLE IN ARROW IN THE TUDOR SERIES

Katharine, the Virgin Widow

Jean Plaidy

The young Spanish widow, Katharine of Aragon, has become the pawn between two powerful monarchies. After less than a year as the wife of the frail Prince Arthur, the question of whether the marriage was ever consummated will decide both her fate and England's.

But whilst England and Spain dispute her dowry, in the wings awaits her unexpected escape from poverty: Henry, Arthur's younger, more handsome brother – the future King of England. He alone has the power to restore her position, but at what sacrifice?

arrow books

The Shadow of the Pomegranate

Jean Plaidy

Whilst the young King Henry VIII basks in the pageants and games of his glittering court, his doting queen's health and fortunes fade. Henry's affection for his older wife soon strays, and the neglected Katharine decides to use her power as queen to dangerous foreign advantage.

Overseas battles play on Henry's volatile temper, and his defeat in France has changed the good-natured boy Katharine loved into an infamously callous ruler. With no legitimate heir yet born, Katharine once again begins to fear for her future . . .

arrow books

Madame Serpent

Jean Plaidy

Sullen-eyed and broken-hearted, fourteen-year-old Catherine de' Medici arrives in Marseilles to marry Henry of Orleans, second son of the King of France. On the promise of a dowry fit for a king, Catherine has left her true love in Italy, forced into trading her future for a stake in the French crown.

Amid the glittering fêtes and banquets of the most immoral court in sixteenth-century Europe, the reluctant bride becomes a passionate but unwanted wife. Humiliated and unloved, Catherine spies on Henry and his lover, the infamous Diane de Poitiers. And, tortured by what she sees, Catherine becomes dangerously occupied by a ruthless ambition destined to make her the most despised woman in France: the dream that one day the French crown will be worn by a Medici heir . . .

arrow books

The Italian Woman

Jean Plaidy

When Catherine de' Medici was forced to marry Henry of Orleans, hers was not the only broken heart. Jeanne of Navarre once dreamed of marrying this same prince, but like Catherine her future must bend to the will of the King's political needs. And so, both Catherine and Jeanne's lives are set on unwanted paths destined to cross in affairs of state, love and faith, driving them to become deadly political rivals.

Years later Jeanne is happily married to the dashing but politically inept Antoine de Bourbon, whilst the widowed Catherine continues to be loved by few and feared by many – including her children. But she is now the powerful mother of kings, who will do anything to see her beloved second son, Henry, rule France. As civil war ravages the country and Jeanne fights for the Huguenot cause, Catherine advances along her unholy road, making enemies at every turn . . .

arrow books

ALSO AVAILABLE IN ARROW: THE MEDICI TRILOGY

Queen Jezebel

Jean Plaidy

The ageing Catherine de' Medici has arranged the marriage of her beautiful Catholic daughter Margot to the uncouth Huguenot King Henry of Navarre. Margot, still desperately in love with Henry de Guise, refuses to utter her vows. But even Catherine is unable to anticipate the carnage that this unholy union is to bring about . . .

In the midst of an August heatwave, tensions run high between the Catholic Parisians and the Huguenot wedding guests: Margot's marriage to Henry has not brought about the peace that King Francis longed for. Realising her weakening power over her sickly son, Catherine sets about persuading Francis of a Huguenot plot against his life. Overcome by fear, he agrees to a massacre that will rid France of its 'pestilential Huguenots for ever'. And so the carnival of butchery begins, marking years of terror and upheaval that will end in the demise of kings, and finally expose Catherine's lifetime of depraved scheming . . .

arrow books

A Blunt Instrument

Ernest Fletcher, a man liked and respected. So when he is found
bludgeoned to death, no one can imagine who would want him
dead. Enter Superintendent Hannasyde, who slowly uncovers the
real Fletcher, anything but a gentleman, and a man with many
enemies. But the case takes a gruesome twist when another
body is found . . .

Behold, Here's Poison

Gregory Matthews, patriarch of the Poplars is found dead. Imperious
Aunt Harriet blames it on the roast duck he ate, but a post-mortem
determines it's a case of murder by poison. Suspicion falls immediately on his quarrelsome family, and it is up to Hannasyde to sift
through their secrets and lies before the killer strikes again.

Death in the Stocks

When the body of Andrew Vereker is found locked in the stocks on
the village green, Hannasyde soon realises that this may be his
toughest case yet. Vereker was not a popular man, his corrupt
family are uncooperative, and the suspects are many.

They Found Him Dead

The morning after his sixtieth birthday party, Silas Kane is found
dead at the foot of a cliff. The coroner rules death by misadventure,
but when Kane's nephew and heir is found murdered, a new
and sinister case develops for Hannasyde to investigate.

arrow books

The Private World of Georgette Heyer

Jane Aitken Hodge

As an internationally bestselling phenomenon and queen of the Regency Romance, Georgette Heyer is one of the most beloved historical novelists of our time. She's written more than fifty novels – romances, detective stories and contemporary works of fiction – yet her private life was practically inaccessible to any but her closest friends and relatives.

With this classic biography we catch a glimpse into Georgette Heyer's world and that of her most memorable characters. With access to private papers and archives, Jane Aiken Hodge reveals a formidable, energetic woman, with an impeccable sense of style and, beyond everything, a love for all things Regency.

Lavishly illustrated from Georgette Heyer's own research files, her family archives and other Regency sources, complete with extracts from her correspondence and references to her work, *The Private World* is a delight and a must-read for every Georgette Heyer fan.

arrow books

Order further Arrow titles
from your local bookshop, or have them delivered
direct to your door by Bookpost

arrow books